September Snow

September Snow

▶▶▶▶

Robert Balmanno

A Caveat Lector Book

REGENT PRESS
Oakland, California

ISBN 13: 978-1-58790-093-8
ISBN 10: 1-58790-093-9

Library of Congress Control Number: 2006923679

First Edition

4 5 6 7 8 9 10

Cover design/photos by S. R. Hinrichs

Manufactured in the United States of America

REGENT PRESS
www.regentpress.net
regentpress@mindspring.com

To my mother and father,
Ginny and Bill Balmanno

Prologue

"Believe those who are seeking the truth.
Doubt those who find it."
　　　　　　— *Andre Gide*

SEPTEMBER 23RD, the first day in autumn, 2051 A.D., of the Christian calendar, or year 2051 C.E, Common Era, marked in archaeological time, became Day One of the New Gaia Era.

Along with the destruction of parts of the Earth's climate and a portion of the ozone layer, the Earth suffered equally devastating social change. All the religious hierarchies had been undercut and profoundly weakened. In the wake of this unprecedented event was the emergence and rapid spread of a brand-new religion, a religion capable of remarkable liberation, while, simultaneously, capable of equally profound repression. The religion was simply known as Gaia.

Gaia—signifying the name of the Greek goddess of nature—was not as in ancient times, a small patch of land, the deserted island of Delos in the Aegean Sea, a fertile valley in the Fertile Crescent, an oasis in the desert, or a fertile valley in Asia Minor—but signified the whole planet.

Society was divided into groups: the lowest section, four billion people, endured extreme poverty, the highest section, 2200 families, enjoyed extreme wealth. Between these groups were three groups" 'Suits,' 'Middle-middles,' and 'Upper-minds,' who in 2049 A.D., had been inaugurated by the magisters to administer the wealth of the world.

Out of the ashes of a decaying system, the Gaia system was erected. Its main feature were the Domes. The Domes consisted of isolated fortresses—akin to city-states, concentrated in selected cities rather than in nations as a whole. The Domes grew rich, mighty, bureaucratic and technologically advanced, forging links with each other through commerce. As the outside world fell into a cauldron of violence, anarchy and disintegration, the old international order disappeared. Year by year, the Domes grew increasingly powerful.

After the Dome system fully developed, practically everything that had once been localized became centralized—economically, politically, socially—and aside from primitive forms of oral conversation, practically all forms of communication had become centralized as well, with very tight control at the top.

In a span of forty-six Gaia years until 2097 A.D.—or according to the new calendar, YEAR GAIA FORTY-SIX—history and events of 2500 years were lost to the future inhabitants of the planet. At this point hidden truths were *rediscovered*, the "real" version of the events of the middle and the late twenty-first century existed only in the brain of a single man, Tom Novak.

This is his story: his take on the events of the Gaia revolution from between 2051 to 2097 A.D.

By the conclusion of that time, Tom Novak, the 103-year-old silver-haired man was the only person left alive who was relatively independent of the powers of the magisters because he could still remember how it had been before the revolutionary changes had occurred.

The special magister entered Tom's room. Without an exchange of salutations, he came straight to the point. "What happened to her? Tell me what happened to Iona?"

At first, Tom didn't reply. Then, at last, he said, "Why do you ask? Terrible things happened. So many people died. I couldn't see clearly then, but now I see it all too clearly."

"You didn't answer the question," the special magister said. "I repeat. What happened to the girl? To Iona. Stick to the question, please."

"Iona?" Tom murmured. "September's daughter?" He looked up. He lowered his voice. He addressed the special magister as if he were delivering a prepared speech. "People now who have never known another time, who have never seen another place, who were raised to see nothing, to question nothing, are not equipped to know. It takes an old man like me to compare the myths of the present with the hidden facts of the past."

Tom closed his eyes. He thought of Iona's mother, September Snow. He felt the past beating like a second heart in his chest. He felt the rush of blood pounding in his ears. He kept his eyes closed. For years, Tom could still hear her admonishing, whispering, her voice growing soft, then September's voice crying out to him. Time did not exist any more; it was all one. There was no such thing as time.

Tearfully, Tom opened his eyes.

Oh, Tom had loved her. He pined for her. Twenty-seven years before! He remembered the last time he saw her. Her image was on the vector screen he carried on his wrist. She was forty-seven-years-old. He was still a "youthful" seventy-six. It seemed so long ago when their world was ending.

Tom remembered how September saved the Earth. Destiny had given her the chance to keep the Earth protected in its original form, against the evil empire—the Gaia State—that wanted to change the Earth's climate permanently. September succeeded at preventing a change in the world's climate, a change that would have left the Earth permanently impaired. She poured sand into the weather-changing wind machines, no mean feat, after which thunder and lightning returned to certain places on the Earth. The planet was saved—for the time being. September was pilloried by the Gaia State. But she was revered by the rebels. Loved by them.

In the process of saving the Earth, the old rebellion was quelled, with all of its old adherents killed in battle, or after being taken as prisoners, quickly executed, (or nearly all—Tom, being secure in a special hiding place, was the exception—and Iona—if she had managed to survive her subsequent ordeals after her separation from Tom—being the only *other* exception).

Tom cursed himself beneath his breath. He thought to himself, 'Let History and the Muse be the judge, not you, you fool. Be silent. Do not speak. Do not reveal any of the so-called hidden truths that the special magister apparently seeks—especially regarding Iona.'

Tom looked at the special magister. But he did not say a word. His eyes became vacant. He seemed to fall into a trance.

Out of consideration for Tom's precarious health, the special magister decided it was not prudent to push him on the subject. So, for the time being, he decided to leave the old man alone. "All right, I'll let you be...," he hissed.

But before the special magister left, he shouted "Messenger!" over his shoulder.

The messenger responded by rushing into the room.

He saluted the special magister, snapping to attention.

"Watch him," the magister ordered. "If he says anything—*any-thing*—report it to me. Understand? If you wish, you may interrogate him. Please, don't apply torture. Not even of the mildest variety. He's too old and too frail. And watch it. We want to keep him alive. The shock to his system would undoubtedly be too much for him, if we push too hard or too fast. Go easy. You can talk to him, of course, you know. Understand?"

"Yes, your worship," the messenger murmured. "We've discussed this before. I understand perfectly."

▶▶▶▶

Two weeks passed. The messenger returned to the special magister's residence to give him an update.

Caused by genetic mutation from ozone-depletion sun poisoning, the messenger had wrinkles around his eyes and ears. Dark pigment stretch-marks creased his forehead. The disfigurement not only gave him a permanent frown, it also made him look ugly and fairly repugnant. The wrinkles and stretch-marks also made him look forty years older than his actual age. Because he was suffering from sun poisoning, he'd be lucky to reach the age of thirty-seven, in which case he'd look like an aged 90-year-old man. At age twenty-one, more than half of the messenger's life was over. He had come from the outside world, a world recoiling from war and devastation, but his parents died when he had been only three. At the age of six, three years an orphan, he had been picked up and brought into the Domes by the magisters.

The messenger knocked on the door.

"You may enter," the special magister said. He was seated at his desk. Contrary to the looks of the messenger, the magister had no stretch-marks on his forehead, nor wrinkles around his eyes and ears. He had spent his entire life under the protection of the Domes. He had lived a life in a state of opulence, coddled by caste privilege, safe inside the protective shell of the Dome-world. He had a body that was slightly overweight, running toward corpulence.

The special magister was also highly educated. He had received a different education even as measured by the standards of other magisters. This unusual background marked him as peculiarly indispensable, albeit potentially dangerous, to the Gaia government.

He was also special because unlike practically all the other magisters who were taught in a narrowly defined way to be technically proficient in their job, this special magister was trained in 'Hominid and Post-Hominid Studies.'

In the history of the Gaia regime, there had only been four

magisters who had been trained in that special way.

A quintessential mandarin, this special magister had all the confidences, though not necessarily the debilitating prejudices, of his caste. That's why he had acquired the sobriquet: *special* magister.

"Did Tom say anything to you?" the special magister asked. "Especially, did he say anything about the girl, Iona? That's the important thing. That's the one thing I most desperately want to know."

"Iona could have been an amalgamation," the messenger said, "of any number of girls, represented by her. A bunch of kids dead at the same time. Tom's always talking about people who have died—so many, I've lost count. Iona may lay claim to some historical truth, but in his mind, she's a fantasy. With all due respect sir, this is the stuff of myth. *Purely a legend.*"

"No," the special magister said. "She was not a legend. There's more to it than that."

"Review the facts carefully," the messenger said. "Iona, the actual girl, *did* live. But her life had a very short time-span. She disappeared thirty-five years ago, your excellency. According to confirmed reports, she died when she was five years old. It happened in Bolivia. Military personal, who came on the scene, saw her charred remains. They tagged her with a positive I.D. The reports in the files are incredibly old and dusty, but they're still in order."

"I'm not so certain," the special magister said, "No, I don't believe it! There's something fishy about the findings of the official report."

The special magister grew agitated. He tried to settle himself. To help calm himself, he lit an eight-inch-long cigarette. He inhaled. He filled his lungs with tobacco smoke. From the look of contentment seen in his eyes, the messenger could see that the art of smoking was one of the special magister's favorite pastimes. After forty-five years of the practice being outlawed, the higher authorities had allowed smoking again, at least among the elite.

"Iona and I were born one or two years apart—did you know

that?" The special magister said in a reflective tone. "If Iona is still
alive, she would be 40 or 41. Iona was born in the Year of the Seas. I
was born in the Year of the Forests. Funny names for a calendar, no?
Year of the Forests?—Year of the Seas—Year of the Polar Ice Caps? It was
a topsy-turvy time. There was a war—the Eleven-Years-War—which
engulfed the entire planet. Unspeakable horror occurred. It was a
devastating war. Over a billion and a half people worldwide died in
that war. What was the war fought for? For freedom? For profits? For
lost ideals? By the time the war was over, nobody knew what the war
had been fought over. For all the people who suffered during the
war, it was devastating, but for everyone else, it turned into a huge
virtual reality tape. But the war was real. It knocked out the pillars
of civilization, sending the old world reeling. By the end of the war,
further wild events were set in motion. The climate, which episodi-
cally had been going through strange, yet still minor—gyrations, for
several decades, went completely haywire. For nine weeks the ozone
layer completely disappeared—which caused more devastation to
the fragile membrane of the planet than the previous eleven years of
the Eleven-Years-War combined. Time and events became fluid. In
the breakdown of the social fabric, things got lost. The world was
put hopelessly out of joint. Revolution occurred in the climate. The
climate changed drastically. Then revolution occurred in the social
order."

　　"Oh," the messenger said, looking baffled. He was unaware of
any of this. "None of this exists in the official history."

　　"Oh that's right, you've lived mostly inside the Domes," the
special magister replied, understanding the messenger's predicament
and lack of comprehension. "But I remember. Up until the age of
six, you lived in the poisoned atmosphere of the Earth outside. The
devastation was at its peak—forty, fifty years ago. Before your time.
It was even worse outside."

　　"I never heard about September Snow," the messenger said.
"Or Regis Snow, September Snow's first husband. They were the
leaders of the rebellion that was waged ten years after the Eleven-

Years-War, right? Not until I interrogated Tom, that is, did I even come to know they existed. I could get Tom to talk about September. He'd talk about her. Occasionally, he mentions Regis Snow too, but he didn't much talk about him. But he refuses to talk about Iona. He doesn't mention the girl. *Except to reiterate—over and over—that Iona died at the age of five. He's vehement about that.* Excuse me sir...your excellency?"

"Yes?" the special magister said, sensing the messenger's unease.

The messenger began haltingly. "It's strange for me to have to listen to Tom talk about people who were not alive, that is to say, who were never mentioned in the official Gaia history as having been *born*. September Snow? Regis Snow? They are...*what?* Aside from them being leaders of a rebellion—*which, theologically speaking, was supposed to never have happened*—who were they? Were they figments of Tom's imagination? If they *actually* had existed, they must have been very special people. I do not wish to be seen in breach of the laws governing religious treachery, you see. As you know, I've always been a strict devotee of the official Gaia religion. My love for Gaia is absolute and thorough. I am devoted—I have always been devoted—to all of the sacred Gaia precepts...*always...*"

"Don't worry about that," the special magister said dismissively, curtly waving his hand. "Your loyalty is not in question. You're dismissed for now. I'll call on you later if I have need of you. In the meantime, watch him. Watch him like a hawk. Report to me anything he may say—*anything*. No matter what it is. But, especially, anything Tom may say about the girl Iona. September Snow's daughter, Iona. *That's so important*. Report that to me. Directly. Understand?"

The messenger nodded. "Agreed."

After the messenger withdrew, the special magister double-checked to make sure the doors were securely fastened and locked.

He didn't relax until he knew he was completely alone. He let out a sigh. He vented his feelings underneath his breath. He murmured fervently to himself, in a barely audible voice, "Oh Iona, oh dear God, oh Iona, are you still there—are you still out there—*somewhere?...*"

"After Regis' execution and death, Tom was the lover of September Snow," the special magister said, "that we know. We've established that. But after the death of September, did Tom look after Iona too? The protege of the old rebellion...the daughter of September...Iona. If only I can establish *that* link, between Iona and Tom, say between thirty-five years ago, to twenty-three years ago. Beginning with Iona, at age five, to around the time she became a young adult. Or at least, to the time she became a teenager. That crucial time...that would explain so much."

With the wave of his hand the special magister removed a heavy metal curtain grate and looked out through a large oblong-shaped window. What could he see? Nothing. There was nothing but thin air. He was one thousand feet high in a cylinder, in a tall, slender cylinder. He was at the top of a high control tower, like a space needle, high above New York City, looking at what had been left after all the destruction of what once was—a massive sea of humanity below.

The special magister rubbed his hands together. He repeated to himself the name of Iona. To him, the name of Iona was like a talisman. To him, she was like a goddess.

"Oh God. Oh, Iona. Oh God. Where are you?" The special magister asked. "Did you survive your ordeal in the desert, dear girl? Survived the march? In that roiling heat —140 degrees Fahrenheit. And if you did, were you later swallowed up by the wilderness to the south of the desert? Are you still *there?*"

The special magister whispered, "did it take a saint like September Snow to make us see what we had become? Will it take a goddess like Iona to make us see what we surely shall become? What our future holds for us? To see, as surely as the sun rises, the monstrous future we bear?"

Chapter One

"For of the wise man, as of the fool, there is no enduring remembrance, seeing that in the days to come, all will be forgotten."
— *Ecclesiastes, Hebrew Bible, 2nd century B.C.E.*

35 YEARS EARLIER...IN THE YEAR 2062 C.E...
OR IN THE YEAR GAIA ELEVEN.

TOM HAD JUST TURNED sixty-eight years old. He was a powerfully built man, handsome beyond his years.

The weather report was on. According to the all-points-bulletin international weather-service, snow was falling everywhere.

Tom Novak gazed intently out at the furrow of snow lying on the frozen ground.

From the vantage point of the Dome, in the foothills of the Rocky Mountains, the snow looked cold and inhospitable.

Tom caught himself drifting into a daze. He gazed out. He roused himself. Then he tried to make out a glimpse of the Rocky Mountains, but on that day it was difficult. On a clear day from the top of the grassy knoll in the high meadow where the Dome was situated, the mountains appeared nearby. Tom remembered seeing them above a deep swirling meadow of purple lupine and yellow flowers, beneath a stunningly blue sky: the long row of snowy jagged peaks, dazzlingly white, above the panoply of mountain flowers.

The mountains were beautiful. They looked like the bared fangs of a wolf. Snow was falling heavily, along the western rim of the North America continent of the Western Hemisphere. Snow had covered the Sierra Nevada, Cascade and Rocky Mountain ranges in the former coastal states of California, Oregon, Washington and British Columbia the night before, also draping the high plains of the Western Quadrant. Beautiful snow. It was also expected to snow over the Appalachian mountains in the east. In fact, a blanket of snow covered the entire region.

Tom could feel the strength of the storm, like a power in his blood, coursing through his veins. He had felt it before—this powerful feeling of the storm inside him. He had an uncanny feeling for all kinds of weather. Even as a small boy, his relatives knew he could sense any change in the weather. His great-grandfather, a full-blooded Seneca Chief (the Iroquois followed matrilineal descent, so it was only because his mother and his grandmother were full-blooded Iroquois Indians that he could claim to being a Seneca Indian), was famous for having the same ability regarding weather prediction.

It didn't matter that he was told that no one could predict weather more than a few days, or a week, in advance. Tom could do it. It was a unique and rare gift.

Tom stood on the apron of the studio, shifting his weight, moving from toe to toe, straining on the balls of the feet. What could he see? All he could see were like dots on Wallscreen—like old-fashioned radiation on an old-fashioned Telscreen television screen: nothing.

Snow was falling. Beautiful snow.

But he couldn't see. He sniffed the air, hoping to get that tingle in the nose such as after lightning struck, but there was nothing. It was impossible for him to detect anything inside the Dome.

He had been speaking on the country telecast circuit for nine years, yet he hadn't grown tired of the routine. He spoke with the aid of a teleprompter, which made his job childishly simple, he was agitated because at heart he still had hope that perhaps something he would say could make a difference.

Tom was a writer by trade, now an ex-writer, which in YEAR GAIA ELEVEN was like being an ex-heavyweight champion of the world after boxing had been declared illegal—he wasn't even useful for starring in the making of commercials. Tom was also a *born solitary*. The great-great-grandson of Seneca Chiefs, on his grandmother's matrilineal side, illustrious in the Iroquois underworld, the son of lowly born factory workers on both sides of his family, he was hardly a working journalist, much less a media mogul, but "country shows" were the last best card dealt to him in the passing of his years. He grabbed at it like a drowning man grasping at a straw.

For an ex-writer, he was a quiet man, both in his private life and in public. He liked keeping his affairs tidy.

At the age of sixty-eight, ten years after the end of the war, he knew that he had twenty-five years left to live, only if he combined old-fashioned rigorous exercise with a regimen of revolutionary biotics, both of which were *au courant*. Added to the first two programs were the truly revolutionary Vita-Man pills, reputed by all to guarantee the goal of extended longevity.

In the YEAR GAIA ELEVEN, the population of the world stood at close to four and one-half billion, down from the eight and one-half billion at the beginning of the Eleven-Years-War in 2040, when the Earth's population had reached its zenith.

Tom's country-wide telecast was about to begin when Leah, who was to read a poem, came in and shouted, "Happy birthday, Tom!" He looked up and gave a start. Leah was strikingly beautiful. She had deep-set blue eyes. She had waist-length blond hair, worn in a mammalian mane. Leah regarded Tom from across the stage. Her eyes were shining. Her breasts heaved gracefully.

Leah was lucky to have won a poetry prize in the annual Gaia apprentice-pregnancy training contest. She was very proud to have won the award.

The next day she was planning to return to Zone 6, the pre-birth and pregnancy institute, in Colorado Springs, but in the meantime, she was allowed to sit at the local TV station. She was lucky; they ordinarily would have sent her to level Zone 5—the pre-birth and pregnancy institute in Glenwood Springs (they still had mud-baths for pregnant girls there), where most of her friends were sent. Like Leah, her friends were the daughters of the `Middle-middles.' Accidentally, Leah had been sent to Zone 6, with the `Upper-minds.'

The pregnant daughters of the `Suits' were sent to Zone 7, the highest academy in Granby, nestled higher in the Rocky Mountains. At this location, they enjoyed better accommodations and the privileged treatment of personal trainers. The daughters of the `Suits' were looked upon, even by people in *proltown* (remnants of industrial slums left over from the old days), as the elite of the new Gaia society.

The government was encouraging women to become pregnant in droves, in order to replenish the population after the devastating Eleven-Years-War. Since females between the ages of fifteen and seventeen were considered by the government to be perfect baby-making machines, the government used all kinds of incentives to induce them. By YEAR GAIA ELEVEN (year 2062, according to old calendar), revolutionary biotics and Gaia-age genetics, for the future, had become "the rage."

Tom looked at Leah. Embarrassed, he sheepishly smiled at her. He blushed. He shot another glance at her. Averting his eyes, he blushed darkly. He was speechless.

Tom looked at her again, this time straight into her eyes. With barely controllable anger, he hissed: "Please! Don't flaunt it—your body—at me like that!"

Every time he shot a look at her, he felt a pang of desire. There were inklings of excitation and arousal, approaching tumescence.

Tears welled up in Tom's eyes.

Leah replied softly, slowly, "I'm sorry Tom. I didn't mean anything."

Tom knew his sexually over-agitated state had something to do with his Vita-Man treatment. Every time he took the pills, he felt like a young bull.

In Leah's social group, and others like it, the `Middle-middles' had converted to the new Gaia calendar. `Middle-middles,' and `Upper-minds,' who eagerly took to Gaia, received the best jobs, training, and a shot at the scarce "safe" housing. Some of the lucky ones even received housing in the all-weather-controlled Domes, or at least, were put on a waiting list. When Domes were constructed during the most dangerous period of exposure to sun poisoning, they were ordinarily assigned exclusively to the 'Suits.'

The sight of a young pregnant woman not only erotically aroused Tom, it made him feel alarmed and ashamed.

Leah was not indifferent to Tom, she rushed to hug him. "How are you?" she asked with glowing eyes. She clasped him to her bosom. She curtsied deeply, bowed her head respectfully, then made the Gaia religious sign of Earth, two hands held waist-high, to form an embryo bowl, her fingers extended out. Her supple breasts heaved heavily. To Tom, Leah looked like a fresh Italian fresco painting of a Madonna, a Godly face filled with sublimity and grace, two mounds of bosom displaying freshness, purity, whiteness.

"*Gawd!*" Tom said, but he squeaked the word quietly, suppressing the sound of the word like a sneeze. "I mean, Gaia!"

There was silence. "Gaia says the genetic material in the sperm and the egg which produced the present human population, could fit into a single Vita-Man pill," Leah said. "Isn't that true, Tom?"

Tom could tell Leah had been reciting her words by rote. It was something she had obviously learned at pregnancy school.

"Oh, I'm sure it's true," Tom replied. "It must be true. If they say so, it must be so." Tom knew he was lying, for he had no way of knowing if it was so or not.

Suddenly, Tom surprised himself. He looked at Leah's hands, still in the Gaia formation and he laughed out loud. It was the first time he had laughed so hard in years. He couldn't stop laughing.

Leah looked at him with a wondering expression on her face, as if she were asking, "What's the matter?" but Tom ignored her. Tom remembered how different things once were. It was like an insider's joke. In recent times, Tom still had trouble getting accustomed to the seemingly inexhaustible flood of religious signs demonstrated by young people in public. The Gaia State not only allowed the use of these seemingly endless Gaia religious signs; they openly encouraged it.

The signs, two generations earlier, had been highly clandestine and were suspect. Tom remembered that the Gaia faith had only a tiny underground following then. It was seen as being unacceptable to the financial, political and religious institutions of the time.

Prominent leaders of Gaia philosophy and practitioners of the Gaia religion were accused of being pagans. The witch-hunts in Europe in the Middle Ages and in the second half of the seventeenth century in New England briefly recurred again. Thirty-five years before, Gaia was a powerful religion, a powerful philosophy, but only for a short time, because, even in its heyday, it only attracted a small cult-like following.

Its followers consisted of outsiders—dissenters, heretics—in Europe and America. There were followers in isolated groups in Scotland, England, France, Germany and Russia. There were other groups in California, Oregon, Washington and British Columbia. There were also pockets of so-called Gaia people living in once vibrant, but decaying, cities: San Francisco, Glasgow, Hamburg, Liverpool, St. Petersburg, Marseilles, Sydney, Baltimore, Melbourne, Osaka, Nagoya.

Leah had reminded Tom that he was supposed to be celebrating his birthday. But he didn't feel like it. He had just turned sixty-eight, according to the new calendar (the use of the Gregorian calendar was forbidden inside the Domes.)

True, the Gregorian calendar was still used by many elderly people *outside* the Domes. Sometimes it was also used by young people who had become rebels. These rebels were disparagingly referred to as "anti-social," "anti-Earth," "anti-order," and most damaging of all, "eco-nihilists." They had permanently forfeited their chances of becoming `Suits,' `Middle-middles,' or `Upper-minds' in the new order, because they insisted on sticking to their subversive "grand-parent-like" ways.

Laws, dictated by the use of the new calendar for `Suits,' `Mid-dles-middles,' and `Upper-minds' had changed all groups beyond recognition. For the inhabitants of *proltown*, those who had sup-plied the economy with sinew, muscle and physical labor, for all the authorities cared, there was no longer any use for these inhabitants, (unless they agreed to expatriate themselves to do the dangerous work on the nuclear-powered wind machines in the Southern Hemi-sphere—otherwise, they were doomed to live out diminished lives in grossly deteriorating *proltowns*).

For the elderly, the penalties for not following the new calendar were lax, too. But the penalty for the infraction of using the Grego-rian calendar by `children above prol-level,' was harsh: first, loss of job status and residence, then loss of life.

In extreme cases, justice was swift. Only two weeks before, un-der the Emergency Powers Law, a young `Suit' had been publicly executed for an infraction, to set an example.

Tom turned his back on the snow outside the window of the Dome. Tom was technically sixty-eight years old, however, he could easily have passed for fifty-four. Vita-Man treatments were reputed to add twelve years to your life; well, after taking them, Tom be-lieved it, too. When the drug finally began to take effect, it took two years for it to take full effect. He felt younger. It changed his gray and whitish hair-locks to black. It sharply increased his sexual appe-tite. All of this was achieved at the real age of sixty-eight.

He tapped his foot nervously, resuming his vigil at the window, waiting for the TV technician to tell him it was time.

Why had he taken the job as a 'talk-show host'? *That* was one of the reasons, he remembered. He had told himself over and over—it was only now that he felt he had to remind himself. The Vita-Man treatment added more than a decade to his life, a life he feared could be shortened by illness, disease, old age. But old age, that was his biggest fear. He had seen his four brothers and more than three-quarters of his generation die in the wars. He had fought in the wars, too. He, too, was afraid. But that wasn't the only reason why, nor the only fear.

He had been told he had been selected by the government as one of twenty ex-writers to give lectures at hundreds of cities across the nation, along with giving "old-fashioned" radio-television talk-shows to the rural hamlets and villages for purposes of keeping the *past*—history, as they quaintly called it—alive.

For the time being, placating the elderly, with relics such as Tom, through old-fashioned TV and radio shows, was a priority of the Gaia State, albeit a lowly one. Placating the elderly with a *faux-sense* of comfort and a false sense of security which these programs in a small way provided, however, was seen by the Gaia State as having an important goal, particularly if the Domes decided in the future to unleash an ambitious program of mass incarceration, or even worse and more draconian in effect, mass euthanasia, directed against the elderly. The 'Suits' of the Gaia State had already been busy quashing speculations and rumors that the elderly—people over the age of 65—were being prepared with the future shock of their being killed off.

For the most part, Tom and his ex-writer cohorts had been recruited to, and co-opted by, the Gaia State—via the talk shows—primarily for the purpose of dampening down these rumors. Tom suppressed from his consciousness the possibility of the likelihood of this happening. But in rare and infrequent moments, he intuitively grasped that the Gaia State was capable of doing such a thing as a massive euthanasia, especially if push came to shove, under the pressure of extreme political expediencies.

Five times, Tom had even been asked to talk at Indian reservations. That was the reason for the talks—so the other ex-writers were told. That's why they had joined: for Posterity, for History, for keeping the old flames alive during the ensuing dark ages that were promised to come, in other words, for a just and noble cause.

But actually, the ex-writers had little choice in the matter, because the only alternative to accepting the job placement and doing the talk-shows was living a grim life in proltown, or being shipped out to the nuclear colonies, or living alone, under almost impossible living conditions, outside the Domes.

Only Gaia faith would keep everything going, or at least that's how the Gaia State advertised its mission, and how it established its claim to authority and leadership.

"God, it looks cold outside!" Tom shouted. He sniffed the air-for that tingle-in-the-nose feeling, but felt nothing.

Maybe that's why he felt depressed. He couldn't seem to predict the weather anymore.

Drawing Tom closer to her, Leah casually remarked: "They say that it will be eighty-three degrees Fahrenheit, outside the Domes."

"When?"

"Tomorrow. At twelve noon. At twelve noon sharp!"

As Leah spoke, her eyes were radiant. Her presence seemed to warm the room, although the room was air-controlled. Tom tried to ignore her but couldn't. He paled at the sight of her. He tried to shrink away. She inspired in him fear by virtue of her very physical proximity. There was probably no one else his age, he believed, who felt the way he did. He felt alone in the world.

"When?" Tom asked mutely. He was drawn to the window, more out of embarrassment than out of interest about what was outside.

"At twelve noon, like I said."

"Can they predict the weather like that?" Tom asked. "I mean, so accurately?"

"Yes," Leah replied. "Tomorrow. They said so. According to the all-points-bulletin international weather-service. And they're never wrong."

It was true, Tom thought. The all-points-bulletin international weather-service was never wrong. But he never believed in it. His ability to predict weather was the one, the only true power he had, and he secretly clung to it, even though he hadn't been able to test his true powers for eleven years.

The last time he had tested his weather-prediction powers, he sensed that the hole in the ozone layer had grown one thousand times larger than its original size. That occurred the year before the introduction of the new Gaia calendar.

For fear of being accused of anti-creationism, where at least you could throw yourself at the mercy of the civil courts, or far worse, being accused of anti-Gaia-heresy—a strictly religious offense—which meant immediate death, Tom wisely kept his weather prognostications to himself. He had seen others perish for speaking boldly. He had no intention of becoming a martyr. For the last eleven years, ever since he'd been enclosed in the Domes when he wasn't traveling, he couldn't sense anything weather-related.

During those eleven years, Tom traveled across the country from Maine to California, from Florida (*those parts yet not submerged below the new water line*) to the Pacific Northwest, noting that the international Wallscreen weather reports were always right, but his horse-sense, his "Indian-sense," told him they were not accurate. He still could not trust the "weather reporters" no matter what he was told.

"We're ready," the TV technician in the TV studio said to Tom, appearing out of nowhere. His eyes were quizzical. His jaw set. The TV technician was as thin as a pencil. He leered at Tom. As he turned to face him, a half-cynical smile adorned his face and a look

of pity came over him. Then the TV technician's eyes turned steely
and glinting. Perhaps the change was caused by a feeling of jealousy,
realizing Tom's special privileges, his freedom to travel.

From the TV technician's view, the inequity was unfair. He
needed a special pass from the government just to travel two miles
from work or from home, whereas Tom could travel anywhere he
liked, even when the Emergency Powers Law was enforced, as long
as he had his itinerary approved in advance. As part of Tom's job, it
was the greatest perk of all.

Seeing the TV technician approaching, Leah visibly withered.

"Get out of here!" the TV technician screamed at her. Leah
shrunk into the corner. "Go on!" the TV technician shouted. "Go
have your baby! Pea-brain! Clear off! I don't want to see your embryo sign, either!"

"What's that?" Tom murmured, glancing at the TV technician
absentmindedly. Tom was taken aback. Helplessly, he watched Leah
run away. "It's not that...," Tom began to stammer. "But what
about her recital? Her poem?" He didn't know whether to defend
Leah or not. Then he realized that the pecking order was ingrained
and despotic under the new regime of Gaia. A new command structure had been integrated into the Old Authoritarian War System,
OAWS.

The TV technician turned to Tom menacingly. "Absorbed in
your trance again, heh, chief?" he barked disapprovingly. "We don't
need Leah for a poetry-reading, do we? I've changed my mind, after
all. We won't be needing her for the show. That's final."

The TV technician enjoyed calling Tom `Chief,' because he
knew Tom detested being called `Chief.' The TV technician also
knew Tom was famous for his absentmindedness about things outside his realm of concentration. But Tom at that moment was not
in a trance, he was thinking about the TV technician's rudeness to
Leah.

"We'll get you through this charade," the TV technician barked
at Tom. Leah had left. Tom saw no point in protesting her treatment

or protecting her honor now. The TV technician turned to look at Tom. He looked as though he were laughing at Tom, which in fact he was.

"Farmers," the TV technician ejaculated, making a rude noise.

"Farmers?" Tom asked lamely. "What? I beg your pardon?"

"You heard me. That's right. Farmers. *Faaarrmmmmers!* Dirty farmers. They're going to be happier than pigs in shit. Storm's going to last all night, then like a miracle, storm will simply disappear. *Poof!*" The TV technician then snapped his fingers. "Like that. A miracle. Besides, they're watching!"

"They're watching?" Tom asked. "Watching what?"

"You know," the TV technician said. "It."

"It?" Tom asked. He fiddled with his coat. "What are you talking about?" He looked at the TV technician dimly. "What's *it?*"

"It."

"It?"

"The channel," the TV technician said. "You know?"

"Oh, the channel," Tom replied. "No, I don't know. What are you talking about? I'm sorry, I don't understand."

"Channel 80,000," the TV technician blasted in an impatient voice. "Where are you? Lights on? Anyone at home? Where are you? In deep space? Execution channel—international execution coverage tonight! Get it? Kill one, *ha, ha, ha,* terrorize a thousand."

The TV technician framed a picture. "Imagine. On Wallscreen! Picture this, Chief. See it on parade. With Emergency Powers Law, too. Gonna be a big hit. Gonna be a grandee! Jaws' going to be dropping when they see the condemned dying—slowly. Ha ha! Fifteen hundred men are going to drown, as they are tied to stakes, with their hands tied behind their backs, in water tanks, that will slowly—ever so slowly—be filled with water. Row upon row of the soon to be drowned, writhing in horrible pain. A first. Pan the crowd. Pan the to-be-executed. Then, fifteen hundred women are going to burn, as they are also tied to stakes, with their hands tied behind their backs—wood at their feet that will slowly be set ablaze;

row upon row of the soon to be burned, twisting in terrible agony. Great shoot. Lots of close-ups. I wish I was there." He anxiously licked his lips. "Most popular show on Wallscreen—first year running. Straighten your tie, Chief."

"Oh," Tom said, looking down. "Perhaps...." He looked down again. At other times, in other studios, he always felt the same. He felt useless, redundant, superfluous.

The TV technician looked at Tom as if he were looking at a person of complete insignificance. Tom gave the TV technician what he self-mockingly referred to as his "silent Cigar store Indian smile," a silent smile of apparent but not real servility—it always helped him in a jam, especially in his youth, especially when he was living with his parents in the proltown next to the plutonium plant, just outside the reservation. The TV technician could care less. The Golden Age of Wallscreen, an audience of one hundred and twenty-five million viewers, wall-to-wall, coast to coast, TV-headset-phone-Wallscreen system, was the future, not this.

"Yes," Tom said, nodding his head. "Yes. I'm ready."

"Right," the TV technician said, lighting a cigarette. He blew smoke into Tom's face. "Let's get on with the show. Action. Places. People, let's go. All right?" He clapped his hands together to get everyone's attention.

The TV technician turned his back on Tom, like a conductor turning to face his orchestra. "All right, everyone?" he said to his small army of TV technicians, sitting at their stations, in the innumerable control booths, arranged behind him. "Let's go!"

Lights were dimmed and the sound lowered. A message suddenly beamed:

GAIA

Heavy music crashing. The sounds of cymbals and drums raised to a high decibel.

GAIA IS ONE. UNIVERSAL SPIRIT. MOTHER EARTH. LIVING ORGANISM. LIVING PLANET. ALL IS GAIA. MOTHER EARTH. WE ARE ALL ONE IN YOU. GAIA

IS ONE. MOTHER EARTH.

"Year One: Year of the Prairies, Steppes, Farmlands and Crops.

"Year Two: Year of the Rivers, Streams and Swamps.

"Year Three: Year of the Polar Ice Caps.

"Year Four: Year of the Deserts.

"Year Five: Year of the Northern Forests and Vegetation.

"Year Six: Year of the Seas and Oceans.

"Year Seven: Year of the Mountains.

"Year Eight: Year of the Jungles.

"Year Nine: Year of the Animals.

"Year Ten: Year of the Minerals.

"Year Eleven: Year of the Fiery Core of the Inner Earth.

"Year Twelve: Year of the Atmosphere.

Years One through Twelve.

Earth—a paradise to save!

Earth—a paradise to save!"

The words were intoned magisterially, like a million voices singing shrilly to a haunting effect. Then repeated, the words were spoken with a disembodied, monotonous single voice: with God-like authority, like a wonder drug, like an old-fashioned twenty-first century advertisement.

Afterwards, Tom nervously began his speech. He cleared his throat. He repeated his opening lines, as he had done so many times before. He read the lines faithfully as they came across the teleprompter. He stared into the TV monitor. He cleared his throat. "I'm Tom Novak. Thirty-five years ago, I published a book entitled *Expressions Without Illusions*. Ladies and gentlemen, today, we have no need for books. In our post-industrial, post-cybernetic world, they are no longer necessary. I again come to speak to you. As you know, the signs of change are not to be found here on Earth, but in the stars..."

The old-fashioned talk-show began. From a synthesizer machine, there was ersatz cheering and electronically enhanced human applause.

Tom talked of the comedy of death and the tragedy of birth. He talked about the benightedness of nature. He talked about flesh-and-blood human beings; about their eroticism, pleasure, suffering. He talked about the greatest teacher of all—wisdom—whose name was pain. He talked about the tragedy of the human condition, the consolation that could be found against the tiny pains of everyday life, in child-like joy, in child-like wonder, in child-like trust. A world without envy. He talked about the things in life that made life worth-while. He talked about being strong, about being gentle. At the end, he stared deadpan into the TV monitor, and quoted from one of the essays of the famous dead writer, Theodore Dreiser:

"'Each according to his temperament...who plans the steps that lead lives on to splendid glories, or twist them into gnarled sacrifices, or make of them dark, disdainful, contentious tragedies? The soul within? Whence comes it? Of God?...In a mulch of darkness are bedded the roots of endless sorrows—and of endless joys. Canst thou fix thine eye on the morning? Be glad. And if in the ultimate it blind thee, be glad also!'"

Tom spoke in his usual way. He knew what he was saying was mainly pabulum (although he did not think that Dreiser's writing had been pabulum). He knew his purpose was to keep listeners reassured that there was a past, a continuity, while the Gaia State instituted reforms.

In a flash, Tom thought of the one and one-half billion dead—in the Eleven-Years-War.

In a flash, Tom thought of the fifty-six percent of the civilian population of the former United States of America that perished in the war as well.

In a flash, Tom thought of his four dead brothers. The last thought was the most poignant of all, because it was the easiest for Tom to focus on—the faces of his four dead brothers.

Thinking of the dead and the words Tom spoke—in his own ears—the words sounded tinny, as if they were echoes in an empty can. The dead had spoken with far more eloquence, simply by virtue of their silence, than the living could ever manage with their twisted, emasculated words.

Tom's hour was up. He wrapped it up. At the end, he repeated:

"The signs of change are not to be found here on Earth, but in the stars. This is Tom Novak...speaking to you again as anchor on the network...in Boulder."

The first and last sentences Tom spoke were always the same, but for the rest of the speech he could say whatever he pleased, as long as he stayed away from the subject of Gaia, for which he was not considered a proper spokesperson.

"That's a take," the TV technician said, quickly tearing his headset from his head. "Wrap it up," he shouted at his assistant.

Staring at Tom, with ill-concealed disdain, the TV technician added, "I wish we were done with this charade. Look at you. You're as irrelevant as a freak in a traveling carnival show. The only reason why I give you any consideration at all is because this is a State-mandated show. You disgust me."

Tom looked down, bowing discreetly. He buttoned his coat, placing his hat on his head. He tried to depart unnoticed. Except for the ever-watchful eye of the TV technician, he succeeded. Exiting through an infrequently-used side door, he shirked the limelight, skulking away with a mournful modesty, an almost anxiety-ridden humility. Tom felt low, humbled and humiliated.

Chapter Two

TOM WENT STRAIGHT to his room at the motel. He couldn't sleep. There was a beeping sound in his ear coming from a transmission of Wallscreen. Once you have the Wallscreen on, Tom discovered, you well-nigh couldn't turn Wallscreen off.

He turned on the inner-television line just by batting his eye. A hidden camera flashed on the wall, picked up by his signal. On the huge Wallscreen was his friend and trusty colleague, from their writing days, three decades before, Orsen Pipes. He had a cherubic grin on his face.

Tom was not expecting to see Orsen on Wallscreen. He was genuinely shocked and surprised to see him at all.

"What are you doing here?" Tom asked. He was delighted to see Orsen nonetheless.

"I thought you were in Arizona. You're not supposed to be here!" On Wallscreen, Orsen's face practically covered the wall.

"I know, I'm not supposed to be here," Orsen sniggered. His face was magnified hugely. "Oh, Arizona," he replied in a piqued voice. He was short of temper. "Oh, that."

Tom batted his eye twice. The camera receptor flashed twice. The screen went from a facial close up to Orsen's upper body, then the camera backed off to include Orsen's full body, at a correspondingly lesser magnification.

"I've been transferred," Orsen said, also looking at his screen. The view of Tom's body came in clearly. "That's better. I can see you, too. You know how to use this infernal new machine? For a second there, your head was as big as a pumpkin. I'm glad I found you here in the same motel. Indiscretion on the part of Central. Are you drinking again? What is that you have in your hand? A gin and tonic? Oh, lovely. What do you do with this new-fangled Wallscreen? I mean, say, you're naked. Say, you've just come out of the shower. You're dripping wet and so forth, and you're buck..."

"Nothing," Tom replied. "You do nothing."

"What?"

"Nothing. Put a towel around your waist, I guess." Orsen was homosexual, and proud of it, too.

"Nothing? But what if you're buck naked?"

"Nothing," Tom replied. He sipped his drink. "Bat your eye. Sensor screens read body motions. It's heat-and-motion sensitive. Works practically all of the time."

"I don't know what the hell you're talking about," Orsen replied impatiently. "Did you know I've been able to hide out here for three days...*three whole days*,...and nobody knows it?" He laughed gleefully in a high-pitched childish voice.

"What are you doing here?"

"What?"

"What are you doing here in Boulder?"

"Nothing! Like I said, there was an accident in my schedule. A mistake. May I come over and see you?"

"Of course, you may!" Tom replied with enthusiasm. He beamed a warm smile. He was thrilled to see Orsen's face and hear his voice. "I'm dying for company," Tom admitted. "This is wonderful. What a pleasant surprise. I'm in suite FXZZ. Come over. Oh, by the way, what about your handler?"

"Don't worry about him," Orsen replied.

Gleefully, Tom hung the TV-Headset-Phone-Wallscreen up by batting his eye.

Tom remembered the time when he first met Orsen twenty-five years before. Even then, Orsen's smile was forced and withered slightly, even when it was most affectionate. Before Orsen had turned sixty-three (he was now eighty-eight), he was a dry, owlish-looking man. Tom remembered that, twenty-five years earlier, Orsen taught for a short while at the Department of Pre-Visual Communication after it merged with the Department of Pre-Audio Communication—in other words, he taught *books.*

When Orsen arrived at the door, Tom offered him a drink. Under a thatch of white hair, a steely glint of bright blue eyes, a crow's nest of criss-crossing lines on a well-tanned face, the man appeared strikingly content with himself, at least at first glance. "The one thing Communicator-Eight gets is alcohol," Tom said. "Plenty of it. Copious amounts," Tom smiled. "What will you have, Orsen? A gin and tonic?"

"They give it to us to keep us quiet," Orsen replied in a preachy voice. "They've demoted me to level Communicator-Five. That's why they give it to *me.*" Orsen suddenly looked tired, like a man who had lost hope.

"Shush!" Tom said. He motioned to the Wallscreen, gesturing that the room might be in reception—that is, wiretapped. "As the saying goes, Wallscreen comes in and also goes out. Come in. Be quiet. Be still, Orsen, for Christ's sake." Tom looked at Orsen carefully. "What's the matter with you? You look like you've seen a ghost."

Orsen entered the room. "They won't tap us here," Orsen said. "They don't know we're in the same state. Did you know what this place used to be called before they turned it into a circus?" Orsen looked down. "That was during the middle part of the Oil Wars. We're talking about forty-eight years ago. Nothing's changed. They just put a make-shift Dome on top of it, that's the only change. Oh, I almost forgot. Also, the virtual reality tapes. And the Wallscreen."

Orsen refused to use the calendar. He had been threatened many times by his handlers and superiors, but he was an old man and set in his ways. Finally they threw their hands up and stopped trying to change him. He had said to Tom during a writers' conference, twenty-five years before, "The control of time—measured by the clock—was the product of the first industrial revolution, over two hundred years ago. It made mass production possible. It also organized and standardized chaotic human life. It dictated and controlled people's lives. Now they're at it again. This time they're messing with the calendar—you know, monkeying with the months, toying with the years...messing with our genes, messing with our whole genetic structure. You scoff, but wait and see. Then—bam! The future, you'll remember I warned you! For now, watch out!"

Tom smiled at Orsen with an air of genuine warmth. "Times change," Tom said. "Things change, too."

"Quite so, quite so. Times change. Things change. Ho hum, ho hum, it's true."

Tom could see Orsen already had had too much to drink. It had fortified Orsen's courage, or to put it more accurately, his irresponsible sense of recklessness.

It was dangerous to speak too openly, even in the privacy of a motel room. Tom offered Orsen a chair.

In the room there was Wallscreen, of course, and also a cheap collection of Virtual Reality tapes. There were tens of thousands of Virtual Reality tapes. There was a double-breasted cupboard full of them. The Virtual Reality tapes covered themes ranging from blood sporting, laser beam hunting, normal violence, abnormal violence, *ghoulish violence,* war, sex, to, of course, Gaia. Otherwise, the room was bare.

Orsen sat down. He said in a languorous voice: "These kids spend all their free time, all their recreational time, watching these Virtual Reality tapes. They surreally surround themselves in a Hieronymus Bosch-like, touchie-feelie debauch of images and representations—and for what purpose—*in order not to see!* What did we call it back in our time? What did we call it? Cheap thrills?"

"I liked my cheap thrills," Tom replied playfully. "But, I know what you're saying, Orsen, I do. They indulge in Virtual Reality tapes not to expand their reality's boundaries, but to evade it, to deny it, I know."

"These tapes were made for `Upper-mind' types," Orsen continued snippily. "In other words, complete fools. They're nothing more than cybernated idiots. Their children, too. They shouldn't have birthed their children—they should have *cloned* them. It wouldn't have made any difference! Trained monkeys! All of them! Interchangeable as tweedledum and tweedledee."

"Please, don't preach, so much," Tom replied. "'Upper-minds' are not complete idiots. Nerds, yes. But they're not complete fools. Just because 'Upper-Minds' use computers, doesn't make them idiots. They operate more than computers. And sometimes they run real things that matter, too."

"That's all that matters! That's all there is!" Orsen cursed in an exasperated voice. "Computers! Kids! Virtual Reality tapes are the only reality they know. They don't go outside. Of course, they don't. Sun poisoning! They watch everything on Wallscreen. They watch weird stuff. Sexual slavery, bodies as machines, commodity-fetishism, products as death. Not Aristophanes, Aeschylus or Euripides."

"The Greek tragedies?" Tom asked. "You expect them to *read* that?" Tom rubbed his eyes in disbelief. He rolled his eyes. "They're already living a Greek tragedy."

"Not Shakespeare, either," Orsen continued.

"An Elizabethan-age tragedian?" Tom asked. "You expect them to read *him*? You expect people to scratch their heads over the unintelligible mutterings of a Euripides or a Shakespeare? You expect that much from them? You expect too much."

Orsen lolled his head from side to side.

At that moment, Tom remembered something the Curmudgeon had once said. The Curmudgeon had been a guiding light and a mentor to Tom, but to Orsen, he had been a peer. Tom remembered the Curmudgeon saying about Orsen: "We all go through different socialization processes as children, Tom, but Orsen's—well—his might well have gone off the Richter scale."

Without skipping a beat, Tom said, smiling indulgently, "You're drunk, Orsen! Aren't you, now! You silly goat!" He looked at Orsen with affection. "Even when we were kids," Tom said, "nobody watched Shakespeare or Euripides, or read about them. Most of us read comic books. I had a normal childhood. Both my parents worked in a factory. Any reading I did was considered weird."

"Right," Orsen said. "Normal childhood." He laughed. "Kiss my ass. When you were a kid, there was no TV. You didn't know what it was like to be a child without TV."

"There was TV when you were a child, Orsen. Everybody had TV twenty years after the Second European War. Everybody."

"I didn't. Glad, too. I'm eighty-eight years old!"

Orsen waved his hand in the air. His finger was pointed magisterially. A disheveled forelock of hair tumbled over his brow. Drunkenly, he exclaimed, "The signs of change are not to be found on Earth, but in the stars! When I deliver my speeches, I am ordered to parrot that line." His voice trembled. He blew his nose. Having taken his handkerchief from his pocket, he wiped his face. He winced. "The signs of change are not to be found on Earth? Rather, in the stars? What do you make of this nonsense?"

"It's on the teleprompter," Tom said. "I say it. I don't make anything of it."

"Well then," Orsen insisted, "what do you *think* of it?"

"I don't think," Tom said, staring straight at Orsen.

"Come on," Orsen said. "You must have an opinion. What do you think?"

"I can only stab at a guess," Tom said. Then in an overblown voice, Tom recited, as if from rote: "When we are thinking of life, and its apparent frailty in the physical universe, we then find ourselves allied with our most remote ancestors, and all others in between, who looked to the stars in the night sky for the very coordinates of being, and by looking at those points of light, concluded that they were the boundaries of the physical universe."

"What does that mean?" Orsen asked.

"Mumbo jumbo," Tom whispered. "Hocus pocus." To prevent their conversation from being picked up on Wallscreen's auditory adapter, Tom whispered in a lowered voice: "They're throwing sand in our eyes." Then he added, speaking through clenched teeth, close to Orsen's ear, "I haven't the foggiest idea!!"

"Oh, I see," Orsen said absentmindedly. "No clue. You're Mister know-it-all, of course. But you still don't know the answer to that question."

"Oh, Arizona!" Orsen then exclaimed, his mind jumping from one topic to another. "I almost forgot. I've been assigned to the Oregon circuit. Oregon? Have you been to southeastern Oregon? Used to be a desert. It's a paradise now! Hadn't been allowed before. On the road, my handler said, `This is your last trip to Middle-middle. You're being demoted to a lower tier.' Lower tier? What next? Proltown? They never let me go to the cities. I was demoted once before—a year ago." Orsen rambled on. "`Cities have been quarantined for ten years,' they said. For our protection. I used to go to towns like Phoenix and Albuquerque, then they demoted me to places like Williams and Holbrook, and some Indian villages like Polacca and Moenkopi."

"You've been transferred, then?" Tom asked.

"Yes. I'll be speaking at small farmhouses next. Where's your next stop?"

"Cheyenne, Wyoming," Tom replied.

"Then where?" Orsen asked.

"Scottsbluff, Nebraska," Tom said. "Sidney. Ogallala. North Platte. Perhaps some smaller settlements in between, I don't know. The usual. Hicksville."

"Oh, Jesus!" Orsen said. "Nebraska! Hail Gaia!" Orsen shouted. He shouted the word `Gaia,' but not with the usual tone of reverence; rather he spoke in a tone of sarcasm and impudence.

"Shussh," Tom hissed. "Don't talk like that. You want to get yourself killed? Do you want some coffee? How 'bout some coffee?

The real stuff. I can get it. I still have pull. Did you know I once managed a roadside motel in the olden days?"

"What do you want, a wide-awake drunk?" Orsen bit his lip. "Have you been following the offerings on the 80,000 channels?" His eyes danced maniacally. He gestured with his fingers and eyebrows to make a mocking point. "The best 1,000 Heavy Metal hits? The Church of Rock Stars. St. Janis, St. Jim, St. Bob, St. John—Janis Joplin, Jim Morrison, Bob Dylan, John Lennon. Christian rock. St. Vitus Day Dance. Five hundred "feelie films"—Virtual Reality films, I'm talking about the good ones, where you feel you're not watching the movies, but where you're right in the movies. It is as if all that matters is having agreeable sensations. Virtual Reality tapes are like putting our brains in a vat of liquid and having them wired to nice sensations. The whole thing is to disconnect the mind from truth, engagement with the world, and freedom. Pleasant, yes, as far as it goes, but, all in all, a spurious form of freedom. The whole thing is the *ultima* of the mind-body split. A form of mind-body schizophrenia, if you ask me."

Tom said, "Okay. So what? So, what's the point?" This was not the first time that Tom had heard this kind of talk.

"Space travel to Venus, Mars, Jupiter and Saturn. Five new nature shows. *Fifty* new execution stations. They're building execution stations faster than Domes, for crying out loud. New gourmet cooking shows for the 'Suits,' 'Middle-middles,' 'Upper-minds.' You know what I call those clowns? I call them mucky-mucks, hoity-toities, woop-de-do's. *Cuckoo—Tom—cuckoo!* Two hundred new blood sport stations for the brain-dead peons in proltown. God help the miserable sods. Bitterest pill of all to swallow, those goddamn Virtual Reality tapes. And Wallscreen and Big Boy have caused our brains to atrophy, too. A splendidly pleasant way to go—yes—slowly yes—nimbly in the snow—it's still horrible. Even if you don't feel it...even if you have no sensation of dying...you're still dying."

"You want some coffee?" Tom persisted.

"No!" Orsen shouted. "No! No! No! There isn't time."

"Quit *shouting*," Tom said. "Quit talking to me like that! This isn't the way it should be, our meeting like this. The least you can do is try to be civil with me."

"How should I be?" Orsen asked. "There isn't time. There aren't twenty of us left, Tom. That's what I've been wanting to try to tell you."

"What?" Tom asked. "Slow down. What are you talking about?"

"The last time twenty of us authors got together was three years ago, remember? Right?"

"Yes," Tom replied. "I remember."

"Now the government won't allow us to stay in the same town at exactly the same time anymore. What are they afraid of? Fear of what? That we'll talk to each other? Share our experiences? It's out there, Tom. There's something going on *out there*—outside the protection of the Domes. I've heard about it. *I've heard all about it!*"

"Heard about *what?*" Tom asked.

Orsen frowned. Then he flashed an impish smile. "None of us has died from natural causes. They'll keep that from happening. The only way that we're likely to be killed by natural causes is to be eaten by wolves. They keep us older ones alive with a stepped up Vita-Man treatment. It causes us to be hornier than shit *and* lethargic at the same time." (Tom hadn't hear the term `horny' used as a sexual term in a long-long time, and he laughed to himself.)

"That's got to be the most pathetic state to be in," Orsen continued. "You suffer, in a milder form, don't be shamefaced, I bet you do. I've got a hunch they're killing all the elderly off in the country, slowly, something in the water, something in the food, it's impossible to prove, it's impossible for people to notice, they're doing it carefully, euthanasia, maybe they're saving us artists, writers, painters, sculptors, composers—for last of the last! So they can fool everybody."

"You're paranoid," Tom said. "Why would they do a thing like that?"

"Why not?" Orsen replied. "They're keeping us alive with the Vita-Man pills, right?"

"You're paranoid," Tom repeated. "Right then! I don't get it. What are you talking about? They're keeping us alive with the Vita-Man pills—*for purposes of extending our lives.* Why would they extend our lives, while at the same time, kill off the elderly? It doesn't make sense."

"Waiting for the elderly to die off first?" Orsen suggested in an uneven voice.

Tom just shook his head.

"What do you think?" Orsen asked. "They've executed five of us. Oh, you didn't know that, did you, *huh,* Mister-know-it-all? Three of us happened to have disappeared from their sight, Thank God." Orsen put his thumbs gleefully up in the air to form victory symbols.

"I hope the three who disappeared are safe," Orsen then added. "God knows..." His voice trailed off.

"Five executed?" Tom said. "Three disappeared? What are you talking about?"

Tears came to Orsen's eyes. "Ever since we entered this program, we've sold out. It's a fake program. Admit it, Tom, we're phonies. We started out as expatriates toward each other, now we've become permanent exiles toward each other! All we see, day after day, is an endless supply of buses, motel rooms and TV studios. We travel around in special wheeled vehicles to keep us protected from being exposed to the sun poisoning during the day. That's all we have, the Gaia State's Dome-to-Dome protection system. It's surrealistic. Do you meet people—I mean—*real* people—as if, on the street? I don't. Unless I sneak out at night, that's the only time I'm liable to see anything that isn't controlled. Those occasional times when my handler is away is the only time I experience freedom. Cracks in the bureaucracy? Oh sure, they're there. There are days when my handler is around, well, rarely. For example, I haven't seen my handler in twenty-four hours. He's pulling guard-duty, or he's

sleeping off a drunken week-end, or he's snuck off to see his wife."
Orsen prattled on, slurring his words. "I bet you haven't seen your
handler for a while, have you? You haven't, have you?"

"My handler trusts me," Tom declared. "Doesn't matter whether he sees me, or I see him, the trust is there. I don't worry about
that."

"Well then, you're the lucky one," Orsen said. "When they're
around, they help us. But their job is to keep an eye on us, too. They
keep us under surveillance. True, it's a weak system. It's a system
riddled with irregularities and inefficiencies. Gus disappeared. The
ninety-nine-year-old Curmudgeon disappeared."

"It's unclear what you're saying," Tom said. He grinned condescendingly. Then he couldn't hide his expression of joy. "Disappeared? You're kidding?"

"I am not!!" Orsen laughed. "Government's got their panties
twisted up over it, too. Gaia thugs, lording it up over us, are real
pissed off. *Jesus Christ!* The Curmudgeon is important to them, believe it or not! Slipped away right in the middle of the night! Not a
trace of him, neither hair nor hide. Disappeared into the ether, right
beneath his handler's nose."

"Into the night?" Tom breathed. *"Jesus!* Not a trace?"

Tom thought for a moment. He giggled out loud. "Tough old
bird. Hard as nails. One ornery amigo, the Curmudgeon. You know
the Curmudgeon once competed in a dog-sled race when he was
eighty-two? With artificial knee, crippled ankle and practically no
mountain-climbing experience, he climbed a mountain when he was
eighty-six. At the age of ninety-four, he had a hernia operation? Do
you want to know why? He apparently injured himself while trying
to sky-dive! *Crazy?* You bet. Escape? Sounds just like something
he'd do." Tom fixed himself another drink.

"Effervescent!" Tom continued, smiling to himself. "So many
years ago? Remember! Remember him! My mentor! My spiritual
guide! The Curmudgeon. Old Gus was. *For me.*"

Tom stared deeply into his gin and tonic. He became even more reflective. "More than a mentor and spiritual guide. The Curmud-geon—Gus—was the closest friend I ever had."

Orsen shifted. Tom brought down his drink. Tom shook his head and sobbed. Then he held his head in his hands. He started to remember. He looked up.

Seeing Orsen, thinking about the redoubtable Curmudgeon, memories chilled Tom. Tom thought back.

"I was poor then," Tom said, apropos of nothing. Orsen could see the change coming over Tom. He could see that Tom was suc-cumbing to a sentimental and nostalgic twist of mind.

"What?" Orsen asked. "Come again? What are you talking about?"

"Talking about my past now," Tom murmured. He saluted Orsen with his drink. "My past, that's what I'm thinking about. Can't stop thinking...you know. Every once in a while. Can't help it. Those thoughts continue to haunt me. I loved being alone—feared it too. I'm plagued... I was poor, then. You know. When I started out. Parents, both of them, worked in a factory. I was a latchkey kid. *Ragamuffin*. Almost a street child."

Orsen listened carefully.

"I was on my own," Tom continued, "when I turned seventeen. I was living in a small room, in a one-room shack. Had no car. No money. All alone on the frozen prairie. Nowhere. Just wrote. That's what I did. Wrote, wrote, wrote. *Oh, I'm pissing my life away,*" Tom added vaguely, moaning and putting his head in his hands.

"I remember," Tom then continued, "the fleeting moments of haunting memories that communicate to me vividly the solipsistic ecstasy I experienced. I am the grandson of American Indians on one side, and the grandson of—more shanty than lace-curtain—Irish on the other. What a mixture!"

Orsen gave Tom a studious air. "Go on! Continue!"

"'Expressions without illusions,'" Tom mumbled. "That was a title for a book, wasn't it?" Tom's eyes lit up when he noticed the pleasure showing on Orsen's face when he mentioned the title.

"Sixteen years all together in the making. Writing that last novel was the one monomaniacal mission I had in life. It took me eight years to complete the last one. That book was the one thing in my life, in my miserable existence, that gave me vitality, strength, the will to carry on, not to extinguish my life. After *Memories From Nowhere, Requiem to Illusion,* then the big one, *Expressions Without Illusions.*"

"You were lucky," Orsen replied approvingly. "You were allowed to keep the same fantasies, illusions and hallucinations all your life. The only difference is, the older you are, the more unrealistic those fantasies, illusions and hallucinations become."

"You've written over three dozen books, Orsen," Tom said. "You wrote even during the Eleven-Years-War. The Great Orsen Pipes. In fact, all of you elder writers were different from me. From 1995 to 2050 A.D., a thousand books between you. You geezers. I was different. I had only one important book. One *still* in print."

"It was a big one, though."

"Quite so," Tom said.

"Quite so. You had talent then. You still do," Orsen added sentimentally, emphasizing his words.

"It doesn't matter now," Tom said, shrugging his shoulders.

"Too true. They won't keep them. Not now," Orsen said. "Oh, you didn't know, did you?" Tom could see the pain registered on Orsen's face. What torment Orsen was going through, Tom could only guess.

"What?" Tom asked. "I heard rumors about materials being tossed."

"No," Orsen said, "not rumors." He drew a finger on the edge of his chair as though he were following a pattern. "They've purged sections of International Archives. They do it once every five years. There are only five of my books left in the International Archives now. But your one book is still safely there. Prominent. Some of the books have been safely hidden. Literary people saw it coming. They were prepared."

"They've destroyed the International Archives?"

"No," Orsen said. "Not destroyed. Only parts. Historical parts. Literary parts. They've purged. `Big Boy' does it. Only parts. They leave the religious and scientific stuff alone. They're very smart. They called it winnowing the chaff from the grain."

"You're kidding," Tom said. "They wouldn't do that."

"They wouldn't do what? They've already done it," Orsen said. "No, I'm not kidding, I'm serious."

"Paah!" Tom said, shaking his head. "I don't believe it! People are enjoying better weather now than ever before. You can't turn Wallscreen on without hearing about it. It's all over the place. Crop yields are breaking records. Farmers irrigate at night. Saves water. Less evaporation. Decreed by the government. Nobody's seen such incredibly good weather since the Eleven-Years-War. They've almost completely repaired the devastated ozone layer, at least that's what they say. They're no longer dependent on hydrocarbon energy. Looking to solar energy. People are happy. Look at the news. It's all over the place. You've become a prophet of doom. Nobody wants to hear that. Especially eleven years after the Eleven-Years-War."

"What's that got to do with the destruction of the books!" Orsen exclaimed. "You're naive. And you're always changing the subject. I don't want you mouthing government tripe...or official Gaia propaganda...not now. Not tonight! Of all nights! I don't want to hear it from you!"

Tom screwed up his eyes. He gave Orsen a scowl. "Be careful. What's so special about tonight?"

"But you're right," Orsen then added sadly. "Nobody wants to hear my complaints. I have become a prophet of doom."

"Writers were once a powerful force," Orsen continued in a sad voice. "We were once the ultimate repository of fine things, good fortune, the nobler aspects of civilization. Before our time...writers...story-tellers...we were bards. We were feared. We could bring ridicule and ignominy upon the powerful. Now what has happened? We are not only not feared, we are not even disdained. Why? We don't count. We are ignored. They don't have to kill us with malice, although I guess they've had to do that in five instances. I'm referring to the five executions of our writer colleagues. They must not have tortured them enough to have gotten confessions, because the executions were not televised. Someone has courage! They can kill us with indifference."

"Is there something out there you saw?" Tom asked. "Something you won't tell me about?"

Orsen perked up his ears as if he were listening for something, but there wasn't a sound in the room. "Time is short. You must look out for yourself, Tom. Don't be angry with me. I'm only talking to you. I'm only trying to tell you something."

Then Orsen broke down. He looked as if he could not get up. It was as if his face had fallen in. "You build up so many layers of rationalizations, so many tissues of lies, you don't know what to believe anymore."

"What's the matter?" Tom asked. "You look like you're dying."

Orsen bent over and whispered something into Tom's ear. "Climate modification."

"What?" Tom asked.

"*Shuush,*" Orsen said. "Climate modification. The answer is to be found in the stones."

"What?" Tom asked. "*What the...?*"

"Stones and rocks. They tell you everything. They can tell you about the past. They can tell you the future, too!" Orsen nodded.

"Never mind," Orsen then said. He sat bolt upright in his chair. "Do you know what month it is?" he asked.

"'Course I do," Tom replied cheeringly. "It's the month of Grasses and Vegetation. It's the month we celebrate Gaia..."

"No, not that Gaia crap!" Orsen snapped back. "*Real month.* Have you forgotten? Seen a real calendar? In how many years have you seen a calendar? I was going to say eleven years... But what is a year? It's the month of September."

Against Tom's protests, Orsen got up and pushed the chairs aside. Turning to the Wallscreen, he gave a strange gesture. Tom recognized it. It was a 130 year old "Hitler salute—hand thrust rigidly in a hailing gesture."

For good measure, Orsen then thumbed his nose rudely at the screen.

He showed himself out. Quietly, he shut the door behind him. On the landing, Tom thought he could barely hear Orsen laughing to himself, or maybe Tom was mistaken, maybe Orsen was coughing.

Tom heard the echoing sound of Orsen's footsteps padding softly, the fading sound of his feet walking slowly down the hallway, then there was no sound.

An hour later, Tom tuned Wallscreen to Orsen's suite in Boulder. The Wallscreen cast a wide-angled panorama that encompassed Orsen's living room.

With the flick of Tom's eye, the camera snaked into the kitchenette—nothing there.

With another flick of his eye, the camera snaked into the hallway. The camera then entered the bedroom. With a flick of Tom's eye, Wallscreen took in the total expanse of the bedroom. In the center, Tom saw Orsen.

A rope was attached to his neck. The rope was attached to an overhanging rafter.

By a few inches above the floor, Orsen was suspended. As if buffeted by a breeze, his body swayed. To the left, over to one side, tipped over on the floor, was a stool. Orsen had been asphyxiated. He had apparently hanged himself.

Chapter Three

"WELL, SO MUCH FOR GLOBAL WARMING," Tom said to himself skeptically as he rose early the morning after Orsen's suicide to see snow on the ground. Actually, the snowstorm was even more extraordinary because the previous year had been the world's hottest year on record—the Sahara desert had grown by two and a half million square miles and the Amazon, Central American, and Central African rainforests had shrunk by a half million square miles. Earth had become, in all its myriad ways, a hot spot.

These items were permissible topics for conversation. The polar ice caps had melted a bit. In some places, the oceans shoreline's had risen three feet (in other places more). Tom tried to remember what this month was by the old calendar. He thought—was it September? That's right! He remembered Orsen's words. *September.* On the ground was September snow!

Tom went down to the cafeteria and begrudgingly ate a light breakfast, pouting all the time. The special Gaia bus departed. Since it wasn't going to wait for him, he boarded it. The bus ran on solar power, again another forward march for science, he thought. A bus could travel 250 miles before it needed its storage batteries recharged. The country had already reached the point where it was dependent on imported oil for only ten percent of its energy needs. Even before it got to Fort Collins, traveling at ninety-nine miles an hour, the bus passed the largest nuclear fusion power plant in the state.

Electric cars, solar-powered buses, nuclear fusion power plants, air travel at Mach Three, great strides were being made by science. They were expecting to build two million new all-weather-controlled Domes by YEAR GAIA THIRTY. The country was expecting to be energy independent by YEAR GAIA FORTY. Such miracles! The future's prognosis was radiant. It was all in the news.

Tom sat. He felt sad about the passing of Orsen. But what could he do about it? Tom thought things could get bad, but not as bad as Orsen had made them out to be.

Orsen had been an old man. Was there anything tragic about an old man dying? You can't live forever. Orsen had lived a long and useful life. Looking at the new gleaming power plant, Tom couldn't help but beam with delight, although he felt sad, too. The plant, situated on 700 acres of rolling hills, was one of the biggest nuclear fusion power plants ever built, replacing the older and more dangerous nuclear fission power plants so that there could not be a repeat of the world-class nuclear disaster of Arahal and Hinganghat, fifty times worse than Chernobyl.

Unlike the nuclear fission reactors, a fusion reactor could not melt down; if anything went wrong, the fusion reaction, which was difficult to keep going, simply stopped. If there wasn't hope for the future, what hope was there? After the devastation of the Eleven-Years-War, simply to have been alive was to have hope.

The string of nuclear fusion power plants provided the power needs for most of the Western Quadrant.

And Tom recalled a trip his father and mother and he made across the country when he was ten years old. Why was he experiencing such nostalgia? So many years before his current thoughts? Why was he remembering his childhood trip *so vividly—at that moment*? Was it because of the untimely death of Orsen? Or was it because of a previously unnoticed side effect of the Vita-Man pills? Or maybe it was just because he was traveling the same stretch of motorway he traveled fifty-eight years before.

Tom remembered his family made a trip to New York City and Atlantic City.

Traveling across eastern Wyoming and western Nebraska, Tom remembered it had been a hot August day. The grasshoppers were flying about—after an infestation.

He remembered they were splattering hard against the windshield of Tom's dad's Ford Taurus.

The grasshoppers were zipping towards the car. But the car was traveling in the opposite direction at speeds up to eighty-five miles per hour. Like Kamikazes, the grasshoppers were hurtling themselves into the windshield—causing a smear to form on the glass. Splat!

Each time another critter bit the dust, Tom's father cleared his throat and pronounced in a voice filled with solemnity, "Takes guts to do that!"

Another large grasshopper slammed into the juggernaut. Tom's father repeated, "Takes guts to do that!"

This happened about once every four minutes for several hours! From time to time, Tom's father giggled hideously at the issuing of his own joke.

Did Tom's father believe the grasshopper had more guts than he had? Did he believe it was courageous—or virtuous—to fly hopelessly against fate?

Tom opened his eyes, and with a flick of his eyelids, turned on Wallscreen, (there was a minimized-version of Wallscreen located in each seating-compartment.) His favorite show was the nature show. Staring out at the audience was a narrator with a clean-shaven face, closely cropped "flat-top" hair and an out-of-fashion bowtie, reminding viewers of an old-time TV show.

The narrator said, "The weather has changed greatly over the last 100,000 years. Only during the last 20,000 years, the Sahara desert was once a green body of land—not a desert. It changed so fast! On the rocks were paintings of gazelles, giraffes and deer."

That was the nice thing about the nature channel, Tom thought. There was little talk about Gaia. The show was not preachy. It avoided sermons. At the end of the program were the ordinary obligatory shouts of 'Hail Gaia!,' but otherwise, the nature channel presented itself in an informational way.

The bus was stopped at a roadblock. Men wearing black leather outfits with blackened face-shields, so they couldn't be identified, carried high-powered laser rifles. The bus was waved through. The bus was stopped at a second roadblock. This time the driver was asked to step out and show his papers. Again, there was a phalanx of men wearing black outfits and blackened face-shields.

The bus was held up for ten minutes, then waved through. About ten miles down the road the bus broke down. The mechanic examined the engine. "It's the cellonoid. It's going to take a long time to fix. You best get out and stretch your legs. It's a doozy. I haven't seen anything like *this* in years."

Tom asked the mechanic why the roadblocks had been set up.

"The usual reason," the mechanic replied crisply. "They're on the lookout for smugglers."

Although Tom was not told that he was allowed to do so, he took a walk. He walked for a mile and then stopped beside an old denuded apple orchard whose ancient gnarled trees looked like skeletons. They had clearly died of old age before the end of the Eleven-Years-War. From the discoloring of the bark, Tom could tell that they had suffered from sun poisoning. Tom sat on a moss-covered stump.

For the longest time, he stared into space. A cat sauntered by.

It was a huge cat, weighing maybe twenty-five pounds, black and white, with colors woven so tightly together, and so beautiful, its coat looked like a cashmere sweater. Tom could tell it was a domesticated cat because it wore a bell collar. The cat stopped, sniffed, seated itself bolt upright. A hummingbird whizzed by. Three feet from the cat's head it hovered. Six feet from the cat, the humming-bird began to drink from the nectar of the purple lupine flower. The cat quizzically looked at the hummingbird.

Tom knew, of course, that cats and birds were natural enemies. He had seen birds dive-bomb cats from the safe haven of tree branches. He also knew cats were natural predators of birds. But the cat just gazed at the hummingbird with curiosity.

And neither was the hummingbird afraid of the cat. It even perched on a limb and stopped vibrating its wings for a while. In a state of vulnerability, it rested. When moving, a hummingbird's heart can beat ninety times a minute, its wings 900 times a minute.

Tom remembered Orsen telling him as they took long walks to-gether across the plains, once seeing a charm of hummingbirds whiz by their heads.

The cat did not move. Impassively, he sat. He was curious. In other words, he wasn't hungry. Then the hummingbird zoomed into the air, darted to and fro, and flew away.

The world was a great place to be!

"Well, they say in nature, when you sit perfectly still, you see interesting things," Tom chuckled to himself. He felt a pang of loss. The Curmudgeon had been famous for mouthing little phrases like that. The Curmudgeon had been accustomed to preaching it to younger writers fifty years his junior. He would sit like a yogi surrounded by a clique of neophyte writers, his long hair, streaked boldly in white and gray, framing the sides of his face, his pomade majestically swept back over his shoulders.

Tom got up, stretched a little, then walked some more. He wondered, was it true? Had the Curmudgeon escaped as Orsen said? If he had escaped, when and where did he escape to, Tom wondered as he continued walking.

Thirty minutes later, Tom came upon a stream. The stream ran through a lush valley. In the distance were beautiful mountains. Tom sat beside the stream. It must have been close to twelve noon. Already, he could feel the air warm on his face. All the snow on the ground had melted. Yes, it's true; it must have been close to eighty-three degrees Fahrenheit. How could it have warmed so quickly after the snow, Tom wondered.

Tom fell asleep. He was awakened by the sound of an army troop across the river, rounding up about forty people wearing civilian clothing. At first, Tom thought they were country people, farmers, then he realized that, judging by their colorful clothing, they were Gypsies, or some other type of itinerant people.

The group was elderly, with a smattering of middle-aged people. There were no children present. They were shot. The firing was so fast that they practically cut the people in half. Tom couldn't believe his eyes. The bodies collapsed, crumpling in slow motion. They collapsed only *seemingly* in slow motion, because there was hardly any sound. It looked like the guns weren't shooting bullets either, but rather laser beams.

One middle-aged man's headless, blood-spattered torso fell over the embankment into the stream, splashing, but other than that, everyone fell exactly where they were standing. The battle, or rather, the massacre, was over as quickly as it had begun.

Hidden from detection by a grove of trees and bush, Tom crouched beside the stream. A helioplane, a combination of helicopter and airplane, flew overhead. Tom had seen one before on Wallscreen, on Channel 26,000.

It moved quickly, dropping a jelly-like substance over the bodies. Tom watched.

The bodies burned for a few minutes and only left ashes—there was no odor of burning flesh, no funny chemical smell. No odor at all, nothing in the air, just the smell of ashes as if in a fireplace. The entire episode was over quickly.

The operation was accomplished with surgical precision. Even the one, lone torso, floating in the stream, was attacked, lit and incinerated. Five minutes later, the army left. The helioplane was gone.

'These boys know what they're doing,' Tom said to himself

grimly. It happened so fast, there was hardly anything left. It was like watching Wallscreen.

What had he seen, Tom wondered? He couldn't identify with these martyrs to an unknown cause, or was there a cause at all? Nor could he be touched by their bravery in a seemingly futile act. He had simply watched them. He had watched too many Virtual Reality tapes. He had watched too much Wallscreen. He was not involved in the action.

Maybe being the ex-writer, too, had taken the best out of Tom. He was unable to feel. He was only able to observe. He was disgusted with himself. It reminded him of the Eleven-Years-War—that is the watching of it on Virtual Reality tapes.

Tom wandered back to the bus, sick to his stomach.

He was afraid to let anyone on the bus in on what he had seen. He just sat in his seat stunned. Who would believe him, anyway?

Tom turned on the Wallscreen, using a flick of his eye.

Suddenly a voice on Wallscreen spoke, "In Moosejaw, Alberta, forty-five years ago, eight inches of rain fell in an hour and a half! Fickleness of nature! Fickleness of the weather! In a time before our time... Our time being the time of Gaia! Hail Gaia!"

Strongly irritated, Tom immediately switched off Wallscreen.

The bus arrived in Cheyenne. As Tom sauntered across the lane to his hotel room, he wondered, what would he talk about that evening? A further thought occurred to him, would it matter what the nature of the contents of his speech was?

After Tom's talk—*the usual cant and drivel*—he went to his room and completely broke down. He cried.

After crying his heart out, Tom went to the window and peered out. The moon appeared *strangely* blue. The moon also had strange silver ovals surrounding it.

Tom remembered that there was supposed to have been a natural explanation for this peculiar phenomenon. There were reports on the Weather station: the public had been told that the Gaia scientists were conducting atmospheric tests in the upper stratosphere.

Ever since YEAR GAIA FIVE, the Gaia scientists had been conducting tests. They were always conducting tests. How much of what they said was true? How much of it was false? Tom wondered as he thought about his great-grandfather, the bearer of the Bear spirit. Tom looked at the Bear constellation in the sky.

He wondered, why was he having trouble "smelling" the weather?

Tom decided to wander into "old town"—proltown.

After 6:00 p.m., even in calm Cheyenne, proltown was considered off-limits to `Suits,' `Middle-middles,' `Upper-Minds.' Like other ex-writers, even though Tom was half-breed, halfway between `Middle-middle' and `Upper-mind,' he knew he was breaking the law by entering proltown after curfew. He didn't care. He decided to go, anyway. The suicide of Orsen had unnerved him. The execution of the Gypsies unhinged him. Since he was at loose ends anyway, he decided he was ready for anything.

To get to proltown, Tom had to pass within close distance of massive Dome structures in Cheyenne. The largest Dome of them all—a central hemispherical one—served as a shell protecting three large villas and six smaller ones. Under the protection of its massive glass enclosure, these villas were an exemplification of the luxurious homes of the top, *the creme de la creme, the apex of the high elite* —situated even in a small outpost town like Cheyenne.

Along the way, Tom also passed a string of smaller Domes that protected the housing of the 'Suits,' 'Middle-middles,' and 'Upper-minds.' These four Domes were modest and unpretentious structures. They housed also two small green houses and some outlying administrative buildings.

In a small town like Cheyenne, the Domes were fairly small. But in the larger cities like St. Louis and Cincinnati, the Domes were larger. These Domes were grouped into complexes, sometimes as many as six and even twelve Domes clustered together. In cities like New York and Chicago, London, Paris, Berlin, Moscow, Beijing, Singapore, Tokyo, the Domes were larger still, sometimes grouped together into very large configurations.

In the largest cities of the world, the Domes were spread out over fairly substantial areas. These Domes were linked by underground walking tunnels, sky-link helioplane pads, highly efficient transportation bus-grid systems and underground communication links. Domes were a world—in and of their own.

At quick walking speed, it took only ten minutes for Tom to get to the edge of proltown.

After dark, proltown was a strange and mysterious place. Even from a distance, one could see the huge billboard ads, three or four stories high, with spotlights playing on them. They displayed moving pictures of naked women and men, showing them in a light where their genitalia were exaggerated and over-emphasized, not just to titillate, but to maximize sexual arousal.

These types of billboards represented a signatory emblem of proltowns everywhere.

Having slunk down the infrequently-used side streets, Tom entered the slum.

With his face partially concealed by a parka, Tom walked into a store on a street corner. He watched a child playing an unsophisticated computer "game-show," a primitive form of Wallscreen, specially designed for prol-children—horribly out of date for children in the Domes.

Standing next to the player was another child—*a friend perhaps?* The child standing next to the player at the controls observed the play, where he was killing Martians, using helioplane laser beams. The observer kept butting in with unwelcome advice whenever the player made what—the observer considered to have been—a wrong move. At first the player roughly pushed the other child aside, demonstrating his resentment at the intrusion. However, the third time the observer intervened with a simple suggestion, the other child playing the game gave up patience. Quietly and without warning, he took a gun from his pocket and shot the child dead.

The man working behind the counter did not move.

"I won," the child beamed, looking at his finished game of laser tag.

Tom regarded the four walls of the commercial outlet. He noticed that all of them were crammed with sexually-explicit movie advertisements. No Wallscreens, not even in their obsolete forms, were allowed in proltown, but these advertisements, which were more than just static pictures—in spite of their out-datedness—fielded depth and dimension.

These pictures did not arouse Tom, but on the other hand, they directed his mind toward a certain path of thinking.

Tom was aware of the existence of old-fashioned "strip" shows in proltown. He remembered his father referring to them in the olden days by different names: "peepshow," "bump-and-grind show," "joy ride," "sex show," "girlie show."

Tom remembered his father, like so many blue-collar workers of his generation, had been old-fashioned. Tom's father had been little inclined to see—much less take a curiosity in—the new-fangled virtual reality tapes when they had first emerged.

In the space of two decades, the new virtual reality tapes squeezed out most of the "old strip shows." The virtual reality tapes were state-of-the-art, so "new" and fantastic, they became wildly popular, except curiously in proltowns, where the older mode of entertainment never ceased to function, in fact, never ceased remaining popular.

On this trip into proltown Tom attended a 'thrill ride'. The stripper came on stage. She was young, over thirty-nine, almost below the forbidden age for strip shows.

As Tom remembered from his previous raids into proltown, there had been the same crazy lights, strange thumping music, drums, and lights dancing over her body. The stripper came out on the stage, looking like a temptress with a whip. She slowly began to peel off her clothing.

At her art, the stripper was not only adept—she was more than that, much more—she was masterful. Two minutes into her act,

Tom could see the positive reaction of the crowd.

Tom couldn't take it. Tears welled in his eyes. He felt disgusted with himself. He glanced at her, as she looked back at him, inches away from each other (Tom had taken a seat right up front), their eyes meeting, the lights pulsating on the dancer's body. Before he knew it, he burst into tears.

"It isn't that *bad*, is it?" the stripper asked, stopping her performance right in the middle of executing a difficult arabesque, thinking that maybe her 'acting' was sub-par, or even worse, incompetent.

"Hey, mister, my performance, huh? It isn't *that bad*, is it?" the stripper asked, feeling annoyed. "I work hard at this. For crying out loud, this is my business!" she exclaimed. She was half-offended by his tears, yet confused and motivated by them, too.

"You're sobbing so hard, they can hear you clear in the back row," the stripper added. *"Huh? What... gives? What's the matter with you? Are you sick?"*

The stripper was accustomed to customers showing no emotion at all, whether good or bad. She wasn't used to a grown man shedding huge, veritable tears! Tom's reaction was strangely incongruous. As he had done before, flinging his chair back, Tom fled the darkened cave for the outside nightlight.

Tom re-emerged into the dimly-lighted streets of proltown, swearing to himself that he would never return. His foray into proltown had been an abomination. Proltown was depressing, even for a man as pressed-down, against-his-will hardened, jaded, and world-wearied as Tom.

Then, as if such things were possible, things grew measurably worse.

As Tom walked with his head bent down low, he ran smack into a former child prostitute. With curly black hair and dimpled cheeks, she was still, what one might call, pretty. But the sixteen-year-old was painfully thin and gray-skinned from smoking the cheapest drug on a proltown street, a synthetic cocaine hybrid called Crystal.

Life on the street had prematurely aged her. She was seven

months pregnant, and still clearly working as a prostitute.

"Sometimes I can hardly breathe," she said to Tom. "Did your parents once live here?"

"A place like this. What are those rusty spots on your shirt?"

"When I cough, blood comes up. My mother worked as a maid washing clothes. My family lived in one room, and my step-father sexually abused my two older sisters until they ran away at the age of nine and ten. My mother threw me out because I was in competition for my step-father's affection. Do you like what you see? Do you want me?"

"No," Tom replied, feeling a wave of depression and repulsion overtake him.

The former child prostitute raised her shirt, exposing to Tom her pregnant belly. "Do you want me?" she asked. She laughed giddily. "Gaia! Gaia! Gaia!" she sang. She danced a jig, hopping from one leg to another, as she merrily sang. "Do you want me? Gaia! Gaia! Gaia! Do you want me, Gaia, Gaia, Gaia! Again an' again! Take me now!!!" She offered herself to Tom in the most uncompromising way.

Seeing that this ploy wasn't working at all, she lowered her shirt, in a state of extreme vexation and disappointment. Like a coquette, she placed her index finger to a dimple on her right cheek, trying, without any display of sincere affection, to attract Tom's amorous attention.

Tom could not get the impression out of his mind—that she was a child, trying desperately to act as if she were an adult.

This ploy on her part clearly was not working, either.

The former child prostitute gave out a throaty laugh, and spat out a wad of phlegm. She sniggered like a horse as she tipped her head.

Tom's hands covered his eyes as he fled from the scene.

Ever since that first evening long before, Tom knew that the Vita-Man pills were wreaking havoc on his hormones. It must have been the testosterone in the pills, he speculated. But then again, he thought, there was nothing he could do about it. Also, the Vita-Man pills gave him strength, day after day, he could feel that, too. It also kept him from aging. Vita-Man pills were the fountain of youth. If he stopped taking them, who knows what would happen to him, he wondered?

Proltown at night. He stumbled in the darkness. There were boxes of human feces in the gutter. There were boxes of corrugated paper products, filled with human feces, lying everywhere. Tom noticed them right away. They didn't sell flimsy paper boxes with products in them anymore. Not since the end of the Eleven-Years-War. But they still made and sold the boxes themselves. Cornflakes, refrigerators, toilet paper, none of these existed anymore. But their boxes did. And it was as if the boxes themselves were more a mark of distinction of modern civilization than the products they were manufactured to encase. The companies—Kellogg, Maytag, Apple—had ceased to exist three or four decades ago, but the Crown paper boxes were still plastered with brand-names. It was as if the names lent a sense of security, of changelessness, in a rapidly changing world, where people defined the immutability of their world according to the unchanging brand-names of their long-lost products. Tom, having lived as a recluse off and on for three decades, saw the falsely marked boxes as something that existed in a fantasy land, but he also saw that the falsely marked boxes also provided a sense of comfort to people, especially people living in proltown. Tom's parents, who had lived as functionally illiterate factory workers most of their lives, had explained this truth to him when he was a child.

Tom had taken the truth in, as he had absorbed so many other truths, as if it were present in his mother's milk. If there was any truth Tom understood well, he understood this, and for him, it was a truth that was in the blood.

Tom walked the streets. People he met on the street had a hollow-eyed look about them.

Proltown was populated by the displaced. It was made up mainly of unemployed and semi-unemployed industrial workers, laid off from the closed-down uranium mines, plutonium plants and strip-mines. Looking into their faces, walking through proltown, Tom couldn't help but see the faces of his parents—old, tired—faces of people who smoked too many cigarettes, drank too much alcohol. It stirred emotions such as he hadn't felt for a long time.

As Tom walked, suddenly shots rang out in the night. These were old-fashioned guns, guns from the old West—guns that made noise when they were fired, barking voices, like the sounds of Fourth of July firecrackers he remembered from his childhood. Two people who had been walking on the street, directly across from him, crumpled to the ground, writhing in agony. Then three more people, then four more, in front of him, crumpled and fell to the ground, wounded by gunshots.

A policeman wearing a full suit of khaki, came out from nowhere and, from behind, tackled Tom to the ground.

"What the!" Tom shouted in surprise, scratching his cheek on the pavement.

"Helioplanes," the policeman whispered. He gently held Tom down. "Stay down. Stay calm. Don't move."

"But I want to see!" Tom shouted. "I want to see what's going on!" Tom tried to protest but the policeman shut him up by hitting him on the side of the head. "I know you're breaking the law by being here after curfew, `Upper-mind,' but that doesn't matter. Stay calm. Nothing's going on. Another quiet evening in proltown. I am here to get you out of here. Are you an `Upper-mind?'"

"Well, sort of," Tom replied vaguely, trying to squirm away from the policeman's grip. Tom resisted. "Let go, will you? You're hurting me."

There was a minor explosion coming from the direction of the shots, then there was a scream, then silence.

"Thought so," the policeman laughed. "It was a terrorist. Most likely. Got him! Or perhaps, it was just another crazy man. It happens every time there's a blue moon. It's safe now. The wackos see those ovals going around the blue moon and it drives them crazy.

Maybe they ought to do a study about that—*what do you think about that?*"

The policeman helped Tom to his feet and to the edge of town. Along the way, he told Tom to never come back. "This is a bad place." He shook his head and admonished him. "This is a dangerous place, especially for 'Upper-minds' like you. There is no work for these people, you see. You computer nuts go crazy playing with your computers all day and night long. You go nutso. Need a change of pace. You don't just need it, you positively crave it. You need a change from looking at your computer screens all the time. I got you `Upper-minds' pegged to the nines. Any illicit contact with people who are different from you, who are not `Upper-minds,' becomes as tempting and as challenging to you as anything. It's like the allure of a forbidden fruit. One of you guys wanders in here about once a month. Purges are coming. Helioplane's coming. They're slaughtering people now. The civilians. In the long run, it won't make any difference. It will just make things easier for the army when they come to mop up. They're all being diverted into different tribes and into different urban gangs anyway."

"Helioplane's coming? The army? What does that mean?"

"Just that."

"Why are you doing this for me?" Tom asked.

"Doing what?"

"Protecting me?"

"That's my concern, isn't it?" the policeman replied. "That's my job. Directive 25. Emergency Powers Law."

"Directive 25? Emergency Powers Law? What about the others?"

"That's not my concern, is it?" the policeman said. He put his gun back in his holster. "They are nothing to me. I'm a PTPA first-class."

"PTPA first-class?"

"Proltown police auxiliary first-class. Cop, for short."

"Why not care about the others who were hurt?" Tom asked,

dusting himself off. "They are people, too, aren't they? I'm the one who's been breaking the law anyway. The curfew law, anyway."

"Oh," the policeman yawned.

The policeman took a stick of gum out of his pocket and popped it in his mouth. "Even below the `Upper-minds,' even among the `Middle-middles,' one of you fools wander in here from time to time, coming in here, looking to have a peek around. Every once in a while, even a `Suit' comes wandering in here. You're curious. You come in here out of curiosity. Or you come here looking for a child prostitute, or an old-fashioned `strip' show. I don't know why people are interested in a live `strip' show, the worst virtual reality tapes are better than the best live `strip' show. I expect they want the real thing, even if the real thing is inferior. Illusion is always better. They're almost all middle-age women. The youngest ones got to be over the age of thirty-nine. Anyone who is Gaia-power pregnancy age doesn't live here, they're given first-class treatment by the government—scholarships to a pre-birth and pregnancy institute."

"I saw a former child prostitute who was pregnant, and she wasn't more than sixteen years old. She was dying."

"Well, at least she wasn't starving, was she?" the policeman said chuckling. "She's an outcast."

"An outcast?"

"You know, red-lined."

"Red-lined?"

"You know. Come on. Where have you been? Written off. Child prostitutes can expect to live to the age of fifteen, but to survive to the age of twenty-two, that's a miracle. They live on the street. They don't expect to get Gaia care, even if they do manage to get knocked up, because few of them manage to survive. They're too badly diseased and too badly drugged! Nobody in here gets Vita-Man treatment, either. So the only people in here are young proles. Old people age and die naturally. If you want to call it that. Remember the sun poisoning at the end of the Eleven-Years-War? Either way, it amounts to nothing. Except that you might get yourself killed. Then

I have to bother filling out forms on Wallscreen. I can go camping any time I want. They give us special traveling and camping permits, for all of us on the police force first class. I can go camping in the mountains any time I want."

"What about the other people?" Tom asked.

Tom had at last surmised the policeman was probably talking to him to such a large extent because he was bored and saw Tom as a diversion.

"Those people?" the policeman asked, raising an eyebrow. "Those other people who killed each other?" The policeman laughed, then shook his head in disgust. "Those people—they can kill each other all they want. I don't have to fill out any forms. They are outcasts. We don't care what they do with each other."

"Outcasts?"

The policeman looked at Tom with surprise. "Haven't you heard a word I said? What's the matter with you? Where have you been? It's the law. They live lives of sloth. They've been declared outcasts. You know, they've been red-lined. Written off."

The policeman picked up a stick from the ground and pointed it at Tom. "You should watch the crime and police show more often. Educate yourself. I don't want to see you in here again, sir."

Tom walked back to the motel. Along the way, he saw liquid waste flowing openly in the gutter. "I know," the policeman said, watching Tom looking at the contents of the open sewer. "I know what you're thinking. It's getting worse. It means that sooner or later, they are going to shut the town down. You never see that kind of thing in the colonies, or in the all-weather-controlled Domes, no sir," the policeman gestured disapprovingly, "it means they're going to shut the place down."

This fragile bit of contact with the police officer lifted Tom's spirits, but only a little, and even then, ambiguously so.

Tom returned to the motel. For several hours, he paced the room. He retired to the bedchamber. But sleep did not come.

Tom thought about his parents. He thought of them because

his visit to proltown reminded him of a childhood memory: his parents working in a plutonium-enrichment plant. (The town they were living in at the time specifically reminded him of proltown.)

Tom remembered that both his mother and father thought the plutonium plant was a hell-hole, but it provided them with a livelihood—*that wasn't the right way of putting it*—it gave them *life*—that was the better way of putting it—until, alas, it took their lives.

Tom struggled through the night, drenched in sweat. He felt like an insomniac enduring a bad night. He felt such a strong sense of loneliness, a brooding emptiness; it was as if it was the first time he had experienced such a loss. His heart ached.

Tom did not feel alone. Rather he felt like he was on the edge of the abyss, the one-step-beyond-four-o'clock-in-the-morning despair, the enigmatic voice at 3:00 a.m., the phantasmagoria of the psychic split, a grim negation.

Tom retreated into a limbo of depression and desperation. He felt more and more isolated, confined in his mounting grief.

Tom rose from his bed. He wandered aimlessly to the kitchen. He grasped the edge of the back of the chair next to the kitchen sink, his fingers and thumbs drained of blood. His fingers were bloodless, white, clenching the back of the chair.

He felt overwhelmed by a feeling of being racked by fear, overtaken by a furious fury, consumed by a paroxysm of heat, subsumed by an emotional rising. He suffered a moment of unbearable choking and the taste of something terrible in the back of his throat.

He felt as if he was bordering on turning into a psychotic.

He felt as if he were abandoned—*marooned*.

He felt lost in space.

He felt as if he were a crewmember on a space mission to Alpha Centauri, cut off from all humanity.

He felt as if he were drifting in a vacuum of deep space, amongst the shining stars, millions of light years away from another planet, millions of years away from another human being, sole survivor of a clan of free-floating free-thinkers.

Tom thought about his desperate life. He thought: 'What would be the chances of a spaceship inadvertently—that is to say, by sheer luck—coming out to rescue him? What were the chances of being picked up?' One in a zillion? One in a billion zillion? No chance at all? All alone in the space of the universe. Away from his mother, as his Seneca Indian great-grandfather would have said. Away from his mother, the Earth, his great-grandfather would have said.

Being alone-in-reclusion had once served him for decades as a pillar of strength, as a divining rod of power, but now—drop by drop—moment by moment—the loneliness and the emptiness was having the opposite effect, it was draining him.

For Tom, for decades, to have been alone had been Olympian, exquisite, *splendid*.

He reveled in solitariness. He thrived on it.

He wrote for decades *that way*. Being alone had been good for him then. Once he even wrote what had been deemed a great book. But now—its polar opposite—not aloneness but loneliness, was the one thing that was slowly, imperceptibly, killing him. Vita-Man pills, to prevent aging, and the endless carousel of lonely motel rooms—these were the alpha and omega of his existence.

Tom got up and looked into the mirror. As he looked his image stared back at him. An old man with an excellent physique, an Indian, like other Indians, on and off the reservation, who had gone insane, just like he was going insane. They were all alone in a white man's world.

Funny...

The catapult of emotions subsided. Tom felt a pang of emptiness inside. He took the bottle of Vita-Man pills and poured them into the toilet bowl. He flushed them down. Acting out of anger—once and for all—acting out of iron will, he destroyed them.

But he had a spare bottle. He had kept it stashed in his baggage, just in case, always in reserve. He did not dare touch the spare bottle. As quickly as his unexpected strength had come to him, it slipped away. He lost his nerve. Maybe that was the despondency Orsen felt when he committed suicide, Tom thought. For a moment, Tom felt a sense of relief. He dropped on the bed into a coma, into a deep and profound sleep.

Sixteen hours later, when he awoke the next day, he felt emptiness and hollowness. He felt no sensation. He felt nothing. Life would go on. For his lack of emotion was simply that: an emotion by default, caged in passivity and resignation.

He rose early, ate breakfast, got on the special Gaia bus. The bus left early from Cheyenne that morning, twenty minutes ahead of schedule. He was used to the buses running early or late.

With a flick of his eye, Tom turned on Wallscreen: "...the coldest winter on record in the Midwest occurred during the winter of 2014, the temperature dropped to below minus 40 degrees. In Alaska, the coldest winter on record was in 1990, when the temperature averaged 70 degrees below zero. The driest summer on record in Great Britain occurred in 1975, when the country experienced a severe drought. On the other hand, the Thames river froze for the first time in many years—the last time during the winters of 1652 and 1653, respectively—then again, during the winters of 2025 and 2026." Tom turned off Wallscreen.

"Nonsense!" he sighed to himself. Extremes in weather were *not that* unusual: that was the obvious message that the government-controlled nature channel was trying to give. The exposure that led to sun poisoning wasn't unusual, either. Even a moron could understand the message the nature channel was trying to get across, Tom thought to himself. But then again, maybe it was true—maybe the climate was changing whereby the extremes were growing greater throughout the world, and not just by the century, or decade, or year, but by the month.

On the road to the Nebraska town, Ogallala, Tom's bus was intercepted. Tom's handler, whom he hadn't spoken with for over twenty-four hours, came to the back of the bus and sat down next to him. "You're going to New York City."

"What?" Tom asked. The handler anticipated Tom's next question.

"Don't ask," the handler said. "I know." He then smiled. "I've been reassigned. That's all. Don't be shocked. The conductor got a call. I'm shocked too, like you are. New York City. We've just received a Wallscreen call from New York. A helioplane is going to intercept us in fifteen minutes, right here on the Western Nebraska Carriageway. I got the call just a few minutes ago. Code Red."

"Why so abrupt am I going to New York?" Tom asked.

"I don't know."

"I haven't been there in over twenty years," Tom said.

"Oh, it's changed a bit I'm sure," the handler said.

Tom looked dumbfounded. He said uncertainly, "Why are they sending me there?"

"They're making a special report tonight on the state of the environment. On International Wallscreen. One of the `Suits' wants you to quote from your book. International environmentalism is going to be the subject of the show."

"You're kidding. Which book? They want me to talk?"

"I don't know which one. The show's the thing that's important, not your book."

"From *Memories from Nowhere?* From *Requiem to Illusion?*"

"No, not those. Not the obscure ones. The famous book. The `Suit' called it *Expression without Illusion*."

"*Expressions without Illusions,*" Tom corrected him.

"You don't seem very happy. You've always liked the nature shows. When it comes to nature, this is going to be a fireworks show."

"No, I'm happy," Tom said. "Thankful, too. I'm just shocked."

The handler smiled. "I would be, too. You have to be level Communicator-Twelve, or Communicator-Fourteen, or Communicator-Sixteen, to talk on International Wallscreen. Even for the short bits. This will be a great honor for you—Communicator-Eight."

"Will it? What line does the `Suit' want me to quote from?"

"The second passage. Page 139. It's in the archives. Pleiades Edition. That's what I've been told. That's what I've been briefed."

"I've got a copy of it somewhere. Oxbridge Edition, though, the original edition. My edition. I'll figure it out."

The handler got up from the seat. Before he did, he smiled at Tom. "This is your big chance. Don't blow it."

To find the passage, Tom got a copy of his book out of his baggage. It had been thirty-two years since he'd written it. He read. "Collingsworth said, `Never trust authority. The easiest lie to tell in the world is always the biggest one.'"

He laughed. He remembered it had been a throwaway line. It was a line he remembered he should have cut from the final text. Collingsworth would have never said that, Tom said to himself, it was out of character. Even after a hiatus of thirty-two years, Tom remembered clearly what he had written, and why this one passage had been wrong.

On Wallscreen, Tom thumbed through the Oxbridge Edition. It took him all of five seconds to find the quote on `Big Boy,' the centralized computer bank.

Tom turned on Wallscreen. He scanned the screen. "`The signs of change are not to be found on Earth, but in the stars...'"

What *the?* He couldn't believe his eyes. There must have been a mistake.

Tom looked at the screen. He read again. How could they make that stupid perennial statement part of *his* book.

He wasn't sure he had the right page. He checked again. It was right. He read it out loud. It was the same page. Compared to his own copy, the rest of the lines were correct and in proper sequence, only the second entry had been changed.

He read the pertinent lines again. Again, they were different from the ones on `Big Boy.'

"Good God," Tom said closing, reopening, then reshuffling the pages of his own copy, of his own worn, dog-eared book.

What happened? Now he remembered, he had read the Oxbridge edition only three years before, when they placed it in the
new archives. On the screen, this was the Pleiades edition. At that
time, all the lines had been correct. He was certain of it. Why the
change, he wondered.

Tom then looked up Orsen's books on `Big Boy.' Orsen had
been right. Orsen had written three dozen books, and only five of
them were in the memory bank. Then, to be thorough, Tom looked
up the Curmudgeon's books. To his chagrin, he discovered that
the Curmudgeon's books had been completely stricken from the
memory bank.

The Curmudgeon was the most famous *living* American writer,
following in the footsteps of James Fenimore Cooper and Mark
Twain. He checked again. All the Curmudgeon's manuscripts had
been purged from `Big Boy.'

"This is terrible," Tom whispered to himself. "This is unprecedented."

Suddenly, Tom realized, to his growing fear, something new
was happening.

His eyes stared at the screen of Wallscreen in terror. What was
happening? He forced down the desperation he felt growing in his
chest, rising in his throat. His mouth was bone-dry. He realized he
didn't have time to think about it. He didn't have time to think. He
would think about it later.

Chapter Four

ONCE THE HELIOPLANE got into "hyper-shuttle," it could fly at a top speed of 2400 miles per hour. Tom knew it would take him to New York City in no time—in less than two hours; or in an hour, if they chose to ramp up to fly at maximum speed.

The pilot was wearing sunglasses and had broad whiskers. He turned to Tom and said, "You can ride in the co-pilot seat. Co-pilot needs sleep." Licking his chops, he added, "This trip's gravy."

They took off from the freeway, rising straight up like an old-fashioned helicopter, from the Western Nebraska Carriageway. Tom looked down. Within thirty seconds, as far as his eyes could see, to the broad horizons, was a sea of dots of green, wheat and corn: a vast field of plenty. They had reached a height of five thousand feet.

"You must be a 'Suit,'" the pilot said, eyeing Tom carefully.

"No, I'm not. Not really. Hardly a 'Suit.'"

"Then you must be an 'Upper-mind.' Strangely dressed, I admit."

"Not exactly that either."

"What the hell are you, then?" the pilot asked chuckling. "What the hell are you doing in Nebraska? Are you a special scientist, or something?"

"No. I'm an ex-writer."

"A what?" the pilot asked. Looking incredulous, he shook his head. "Damnedest thing I've ever heard of. You're the first passenger I've ever brought from Nebraska to New York City, and I've been flying helioplanes for ten years. Hell, I've been flying helioplanes for ten *Gaia* years—ten whole *Gaia* years. What do you do?"

"You wouldn't believe me if I told you. So let's forget it, okay?"

"All right, all right," the pilot agreed. "Whatever you say, hang on. We've reached an altitude of five thousand feet. We're going to go into overdrive. Five minutes later, we're going to go through the first sound barrier, Mach One, 760 miles per hour. So watch your ears."

"I will," Tom replied, with a note of uncertainty.

"After that, it's gonna be like heaven. Have you ever traveled in a helioplane before?"

"I once went up in a helium balloon before," Tom replied jokingly.

The pilot laughed. "This is different. We won't have to go to Mach Two."

"Mach Two?" Tom asked.

"You want the answer in pilot terms or layman terms?" the pilot asked, laughing again.

"Layman terms, please."

"1300 miles per hour. At 36,500 feet. These are the newest helioplanes on the market."

"Oh?" Tom asked. "How fast did you say we shall be going?"

"Not nearly that fast. Just before the second sound barrier. Around 1200 miles an hour." Tom sat back and felt the air around his ears prick for a second. "Here we go," the pilot smiled. "Wow! Just like sitting in a dentist's chair, isn't it? Now sit back and enjoy. Take a nap if you like."

Tom turned on the nature channel. Watching the nature channel always helped him fall to sleep. There was a beautiful, graphic scene of rich and lush farmland. The voice-over said, "Beginning 12,000 years ago, what is now California baked in two mega-droughts, one lasting fifty-five years, the other thirty, the former five times more intense and the later three times more intense than the five-to-ten year cycle of droughts of more recent times. Recent findings suggest that relatively wet periods, as of late, have been the exception, rather than the rule, in California. But in the future, with inspired and new long-term planning, mega-droughts, or quite ordinary droughts, are not likely to recur."

The voice droned on.

Something occurred to Tom: "Why all this talk about past ecological disasters? Were they preparing people for similar disasters to happen in the future?"

With a blink of his eyes, Tom turned off Wallscreen.

He closed his eyes. He had slept deeply, but strangely, the night before.

Once they were above the clouds, he fell asleep.

Two hours later, he opened his eyes with a shock. What he saw was a thunderously magnificent view of New York City. There were Domes, looking like the massive sprouting of mushrooms, a few extremely large in size, some large in size, some medium in size, some small in size, dotting the cityscape, running all the way from the rebuilt World Trade Building to Battery Park.

Tom couldn't count all of the dome-like structures, there were too great in number. He guessed there were thousands of them. A few of the structures were different. They reached high into the sky. They resembled the skyscrapers of old, pinnacle-shape in design, however they had one major difference. At the top, they were covered with a roof, in the form of a Dome.

Tom looked down at the scene in a state of bewildering excitement. *"Good Gawd!"* he exclaimed. "I mean, Good Gaia. Will you look down there! How many people live there?"

"Three and a half million," the pilot said.

"That's not many."

"Eleven-Years-War practically knocked the city of New York off the face of the Earth, I can tell you that," the pilot laughed. "There have been other changes since then."

Tom pointed to the center of the islands of darkness. "What are those patches of darkness? Those places of darkness? Those. There are two others there."

"Others?" the helioplane pilot asked.

"Those holes of darkness in the surrounding shining light. There." Tom pointed his finger. "There must be three of them down there. There's another one!" Tom pointed with his finger. "Look down there. Look!"

"Oh that," the pilot said. "In the helioplane trade, those are what we call No-Go Zones. Fourth one doesn't count. That's Central Park. You fly over them, but you can't go into them at ground zero. Forget it. They are the forgotten zones."

"What?" Tom said. "No-Go Zones? Forgotten zones?"

"Right," the pilot said. "Like I said. They've been like that for a long time."

"People live down there in those places of darkness?"

The pilot chuckled loudly. "If you want to call it that. They live down there, all right. Like rats!"

Tom did not comment on the last statement. "Are they, what you call, `proltowns?'"

"If they were so lucky. Used to be proltowns. Long ago. They don't have proltowns anymore. Not in New York. Enjoy your stay in New York. You aren't going to be staying there. You're going to be staying in one of the Domes, I'm sure of that."

They landed on a fly-pad. "You'll be debriefed by a Querulous One for the show. This show's supposed to be a real blockbuster nature show, too, Tom, a fireworks show, as they call it. You know: `Earth! One planet! One interconnected planet!' One of the big yo-yos from the capital is going to be there, too. Enjoy."

Tom was taken to a Dome to refresh himself. He was placed in an elevator to take him to a geodesic dome on the one hundred and fortieth floor of a group of geodesic Domes piled on top of each other to form a crystal pyramid.

The operator opened the elevator door and beckoned Tom to enter. He said, "The patterns of geodesic Domes were designed by the great architect, Mortimer Stange. Our state of the art architecture is modeled after the science of geodesy—the branch of applied mathematics that determines the exact positions of points and the shape of areas of large portions of the Earth's surface, or the shape and size of the Earth, and the variations of terrestrial gravity. Each and every geodesic Dome, as a living unit, is, in this way, like a little model of the Earth." The elevator continued to rise.

The elevator operator went on with his prepared speech. "Since the first manned moon landing ninety-four years ago, we've looked on the Earth as a spaceship."

Ninety-four years, Tom wondered? He realized the elevator operator wasn't following *new calendar.* Wasn't that against the rules?

"We've tried to pattern everything after our concept of the Earth," the elevator operator continued. "Before Gaia, the great symbol of life was the circle. After Gaia, the great symbol of life is the sphere. We look at all dimensions of life as three-dimensional now. It's appropriate, don't you think, to look at the Earth as a planet?"

They stopped and Tom left the elevator. Tom smiled and asked, "Do you give this spiel to all of us country greenhorns when we come to New York?"

"That's my job," the operator replied humorously. "Though we rarely get country greenhorns like you, I can assure you. We get special functionaries from Washington, local Gaia dignitaries, and of course, the guests from abroad."

"'Suits' you mean?"

"Oh, usually people who are much higher than 'Suits,' I can assure you," the operator replied with a surly air of superiority, apparent snobbery and superciliousness.

"I didn't know there were people higher than 'Suits,'" Tom remarked.

The operator laughed. "The 'Suits' are for display. They are for Wallscreen. For the news. For the *visible* forms of government. The people who are above `Suits' are above ranking. They are rarely publicly displayed."

"If you need anything, ring the desk," the operator said.

"On Wallscreen?" Tom asked.

"On Wallscreen, of course. Or you can pick up the phone. This room is for people who are much higher up than the `Suits,' and they rarely use Wallscreen. They almost always use the phone."

The room assigned to him was a large, garish room. It looked huge. Tom felt misplaced. He felt as though a horrible mistake had been made, as though he had been mistaken for a potentate from a faraway kingdom.

There were fresh, fragile orchids in a glass case. There were multiples of Buddhist paintings from China, adorning the eight-sided geodesic walls.

Tom looked at the ancient Chinese Buddhist art on display. In the paintings, the eyes of the human figures bore such exquisite expressions of compassionate contemplativeness! The early works showed strong Indian artistic influence. The later works were Tibetan.

Tom recognized one of the works. It was the famous Lohan Cudapanthaka. At the bottom of the frame, it was dated "ca.1403-28." There were also paintings from the Japanese Kano school. Tom noticed that at least in art, magisters still used the old calendar; the old calendar had otherwise been erased from public records. *Strange.*

In one corner (actually there were no corners; it was more like a little alcove) was a single tenth century vase from Japan. In a well-lit glass case, at the center of the room, was a fifteen-foot-high statue, from Easter Island, a behemoth made of stone, weighing many tons. How did it get there, Tom wondered, on the one hundred and fortieth floor of a Dome-covered skyscraper in New York? There were peaches, grapes and nectarines arranged on tables, around the stone, as if they had been left there as little offerings.

Tom turned on the computer. It was a first-order, top-drawer maxi-computer. Death, not just to the violating individual, but to all members of his family, and also all members of his *extended* family, uncles, aunts, nieces, nephews—expiration of all remnants of name and family, seed and womb, to quote Gaia, sub-Leviticus—could be administered for possession of a maxi-computer or mini-computer. Personal computers had been outlawed under pain of death. The computer was clearly in violation of the law.

Tom saw numbers reeling on the computer screen: commodity indexes, stock prices, labor exchange indicators. The numbers changed by the second. Tom couldn't understand the whirling numbers, but he did understand enough to know they were a stockbroker's fantasy come true. Instantaneous information—prices, stocks, costs, profits—from every corner of the globe, at your fingertips.

Tom went to the next room, a large room, almost the size of a small ballroom. His curiosity was killing him. In glass cases were plants from all over the world—a hothouse, a greenhouse, lush green plants growing as if in nature.

He went into the next room, again a large room. There were glass cases containing stuffed animals, including a bear, a lion, an elephant. It was a taxidermist's dream.

He rushed into the last room. The room was dark and the ventilation had been turned off. He had to find the light switch. He turned it on. He froze. The sight he saw made him lose his breath. There were stuffed humans—aboriginals. Each case was clearly marked: New Guinea-Papua; Amazon basin; Himalayan mountains; Arctic region; Siberia—five specimens. They had been taken from the dark regions of the world, purported to have been left uninhabitable by the worst cases of sun poisoning, during the last nine weeks of the Eleven-Years-War. And the thought occurred to Tom: maybe that's why they changed the calendar—so we would *forget*.

Portraits of five human figures in the museum stared back at Tom. They were alternately clothed in feathers, leather loincloths, leather sandals, woven wool, seal skins. The Arctic Eskimo had an old-fashioned rusty wristwatch, which he wore not on his wrist, but hanging from a string of seashells around his neck. The Siberian aboriginal had a rusty Star Wars lunch pail strapped around his shoulder. The New Guinea tribesman had a calabash gourd, with aluminum wrappers of chewing gum attached. The Amazon warrior held a Zippo lighter in one hand and an old-fashioned bow and arrow in the other. Tom started to cry, then suppressed his tears. Portraits of the five were all true to life, all "anthropologically accurate"—in the sense they had been both recipients of ancient customs and recent relics. Long before Tom's birth, all aboriginal people had been touched by the modern world.

Tom felt a chill. He fled from the room. "Extinct!" he exclaimed as he ran.

He heard a knock. He turned and rushed through the rooms, shutting the doors behind him as he ran. He ran through the two adjacent rooms into the main room. At the last moment, he had enough presence of mind to turn off the computer before opening the door.

A `Suit' had knocked at his door. Tom could see him through the peephole. The `Suit' opened the door. He was a bruiser. He had a brutal face, and he was thick-set, especially around the neck and waist. "Let me introduce myself," the `Suit' said, speaking with a broad accent. "My name's Vertigo. I'm your handler for the evening. There's been a mistake. If we don't leave immediately, there's going to be a lot of trouble. I don't want any trouble. Understand?"

"Understood," Tom said. "Isn't it unusual for a `Suit' to be a handler?" he asked. His gaiety was forced. He knew he was failing to appear nonchalant, but the sight of the humans stuffed as if they were animals had not only shocked him, it had shaken him.

"Yes, it is unusual for a `Suit' to be a handler," the `Suit' replied grimly. He stared at Tom. "No trouble?"

"No trouble. I could have stayed in a simple motel room, you know."

"I bet you could have. You'll be gone on the early morning shuttle anyway. We've made a big mistake. How long have you been here?"

"All but a minute, no more, no more."

"I see," the `Suit' said. Suddenly the `Suit' standing in the doorway stared at Tom with a look of malice and contempt. "There's been a mistake. You're not supposed to be here. You were mistaken for someone else at the sky-pad. Get your coat. We are ready to take you to the studio. Have you taken anything? I hope not. Did you have a coat?"

"There are channels here you can't get on Wallscreen," Tom said dumbfounded.

"No shit. Now get your coat on. Right now! We're leaving. Christ almighty! I mean, *Heavens to Gaia!* In the right light, you do look like him. No wonder they mistook you for him. Turn to your side. Give us your profile." Tom did as he was told, presenting the `Suit' with his profile. "Christ, you do look like him. You're more muscular than him, true. Much better physical shape, too. But otherwise, you're his spitting image. You an actor?"

"No, I'm not an actor," Tom replied. "You said I looked like him? Who is he?"

"The magister, of course. He lives here. When he's in town. We must leave the premises. There's been a mistake. He was supposed to be flying in from Washington, at the exact moment you were flying in from Nebraska." There was a look of concern on his face. "Do you understand? If the security guards had caught you instead of me, you'd be dead. You're lucky I got to you first. Do you know terrorists are breaking into the Domes everywhere? Even outside the city? Murdering people in their beds? You could have been easily mistaken for one of them."

"I'm not going back to Nebraska? On a helioplane?" Tom asked, again unsuccessfully trying to appear nonchalant.

"Helioplane? Hell, no. Oh, that's right," the `Suit' replied apologetically, "I forgot. They told me you'd never been here before." He took his hat off, rubbed his face, then rubbed his shaved head. The `Suit' had been wearing an old-fashioned baseball cap. Tom hadn't seen one in years. The `Suit' put the hat back on, and sighed.

"We need to get you out of here quickly. Just as long as you make it on time, for the special report on Wallscreen. Once that's over, we don't care how long it takes you to get back. Come, we have little time left." He scanned the room nervously. "These upper-Dome types give me the willies. I hate these places. They're creepier than the trenches in the Eleven-Years-War."

"Do the magisters collect butterflies?"

"Some do, some don't," the `Suit' laughed. "Oh. So you noticed. The orchid in the glass. And the giant stone figurine from Easter Island. The giant glass cases. Peculiar, isn't it?"

"How could I miss them?"

"We got a magister on this floor who collects odd bits from garbage dumps in Egypt and Iraq. I guess the old rubbish makes him feel immortal. Some collect ancient relics from the outer world, others collect flora and fauna from the new one. Some don't collect anything. The ones who don't collect anything are the ones I dislike the least. They're always simple and business-like. Easy to handle. Like children."

"The outer world?"

"That's what they call it when they get together. They're joking around together. You know, areas of the world that have been permanently sun poisoned."

"How many magisters are there?"

"You mean in New York? Two hundred. *Three hundred*."

"How many magisters are there in the world?"

"I don't know. Forty times that. Fifty times that."

Tom stared at the `Suit,' in a state of fright. He did not move.

"You're shaking like a leaf," the `Suit' said. "What's the matter with you?"

"I always get this way just before a telecast. Nervous, I guess."

"Well, let's get a move on. Wallscreen can't wait all day."

"But why do you think they need me for the show?" Tom asked.

"How should I know? Why are you asking me? They once brought a poet from Greece to recite poetry. They called him the Oracle of Delphi. He wore a toga. He had a long, flowing beard. He was a guest of the magister from Oceania. He performed for the magistry community of the Pacific Rim and United Europe. Didn't you know, you're photogenic too," he smiled. "Like he was. It's all a show anyway. Barnum and Bailey. They like to use actors. That's why you're here."

"What's the name of the magister who lives here?" Tom asked.

"Didn't you know?" the `Suit' asked. "I guess you wouldn't. They don't have names. They don't go by names. They have code-numbers. None of them can be accessed on Wallscreen. Can't be traced by Wallscreen either. Or Big Boy either." He smiled. "They are numbers."

Chapter Five

TOM ARRIVED AT THE STUDIO just in time to watch the beginning of the show.

The show! History of the Universe! The cosmos as if on a movie reel!

Fifteen billion years of history according to Gaia, compressed into a ninety-minute presentation. The first five minutes were sheer Merlin. First there was the Big Bang. Then the universe was a milky filament—incandescent strands of light weaving and interweaving as if on a giant loom in space. A few minutes later, the action shifted to eight billion Gaia years before the present, birth of the solar system, then four and one-half billion Gaia years before the present, birth of the Earth—smoldering stone and rock.

Then the action shifted to three-quarters of a billion Gaia years before the present. The action depicted the genesis of molecules, aquatic life, terrestrial beings.

The action shifted to plant-life and animal-life. The age of the dinosaurs came and went. Mammals re-dominated. The age of Earth was three and one-half billion Gaia years, but hominids had been present on its surface during only the last four *million* Gaia years—relatively speaking, a flicker of the eyelid—a Johnny-come-lately in the pantheon of natural evolution. Anthropoids. Hominids. *Homo erectus.* Neanderthals. At last, *Homo sapiens sapiens.*

Humanity, in its present form, coming out of Africa, swarming across the surface of the world within a span of 60,000 to 100,000 years, bringing all other creatures into a state of extinction or subservience, the human species growing from a population of a few hundred thousand to a zenith of eight and one-half billion in the year 2040.

One man's life represented a microscopic speck of a tiny fraction, of a shaving at the end of a fingernail, at the end of an extended finger, at the end of an extended hand, at the end of an extended arm, of the whole body of biological time. One man's life represented a brief nanosecond—of a nanosecond—of a nanosecond—of an inexorable advance of time.

The scene moved to an ill-clad, emaciated family huddled around a stinking mud hole, then a wandering tribe of fully clothed nomads, then the first settlement: this to Tom was the best part of the show. Three minutes later was presented the first city of Mesopotamia in the Euphrates River valley—perhaps the oldest city of any significant size: Uruk! It looked so majestic, so fantastic, it was as if he were really there. Tom felt like the biblical Abraham, in the ancient Sumerian city of Ur, 4,000 years ago; Uruk was *one or two thousand* years older than Ur, built along a lake-side of pure and sweet water, surrounded by plains of rich soil, wheat growing on the land. Scene shifted. The remains of the city now stood as mounds of dust, blowing in the wind, a one hundred mile wide wasteland of pure, flat desert. That was all that was left of the city of Uruk, in the YEAR GAIA ELEVEN.

The contrast took Tom's breath away.

The voice-over said; "6000 Gaia years of primitive human *written* records—recorded from the beginning of Sumerian civilization to the time 'before Gaia,' B.G." The camera on Wallscreen captured it all.

Later civilizations appeared: Africa, Europe, Asia, Australia, the Americas.

Tom was wondering: Were they going to show a complete presentation of the history of the world? What a show!

Tom had never seen a studio like the one he found himself standing in. It was sophisticated beyond belief. The TV stations he had visited on the road were primitive, ancient way-stations in comparison. It was like arriving on another planet. He was missing the best section of the presentation, the next 1900 years: when humans were making a greater imprint on the Earth than the Earth was making on them.

The handlers rushed him in quickly, put on his makeup, then stuck him on the studio set beside the bright lights.

"You're in the nerve center of Wallscreen," his prompter said. "This is the closest thing in entertainment that's ever going to come close to being serious," she said with a throaty chuckle that turned into a shrill whistle of disgust. "I guess you're asking yourself why they keep me around? I don't know. I'm the last of our generation to work in this field. Right in the nerve center. I guess they keep me here because I'm good at my job. Somebody's got to know something about *real* history, and *real* science, even for a slapdash show like this."

The woman smiled wanly at Tom. "Creation *of the universe* indeed! Jesus Christ! Jeepers creepers! Why not wait for the director's cut?"

"Doesn't look slapdash to me," Tom said.

"First part, first part you saw—it's a plagiarism," the prompter said. "Borrowed from some tapes found in a Smithsonian archive dated 2033 A.D. Of course they had to alter the dates to make them into Gaia dates. This is for 'Suits' consumption."

She was at least as old as Tom. Tom realized by the telltale wrinkles on her face, the look of passion and fire in her eyes, framed by a face that was old and weary, that she hadn't been taking her Vita-Man pills.

Was it by choice that she refused to take them, Tom wondered. Tom carefully scrutinized her.

"They seem to want to legitimize—is that the right word—the present by demonstrating that it is part of the past," the prompter said with a cynical voice. "*History*—in other words. Why they think this is necessary, I don't know. That's why the Gaia celebration is so important to them. Its intent is to show the course of human history as part of the natural development of the Earth. It is precisely the combination of austerity and excess that makes the visual work unique. Otherwise, it's pure fantasy. Wallscreen-Virtual Reality-Film is the perfect medium, the only medium for the age of machines and computers and computer-trained people, because it is mechanically made, uses mechanically animated construction, montage, juxtaposition. It doesn't focus on the small inner life, but on the grand scale—on the History of Planet Earth."

"The history of planet Earth?" Tom asked.

"No," the prompter said. "I'm wrong. I mean rather, The *life* of planet Earth!" She nodded sadly. "That's why it's scary. I don't like to think about it."

"Scary?" Tom asked. "I don't get it."

"I mean," the prompter said, "that's why it's dangerous."

"Dangerous?"

"No," the prompter said. She repeated, "No." She shook her head. She looked perturbed. "That's not what I mean. I mean it's something that is false. I can't express myself well. I don't know what I mean."

"What's so scary about something that is false?" Tom asked.

"Because even though it's false, it looks profoundly true. That's what makes it scary. Wait till you get to the wars," she added with contempt and disgust. "It's all slaughter. They leave out all the parts about trying to control the climate."

"I see," Tom said. "But why me?"

"Why you what? You're the only ex-writer we have left of any stature—who isn't too old—to look good on Wallscreen. I hate to not flatter you, but that's the truth. Besides, most of your kind are dead. You look good on Wallscreen. You look like an actor. You have the most wonderful eyes. When you're given your cue, say your lines. We'll give you the lead-in by remote. Read the teleprompter.

You know how to do that?"

Tom nodded.

"Understand?"

Tom nodded again.

"Look. This show is grandiose. But the presentation is exclusively for the viewing pleasure of `Suits,'" the prompter added with a cynical voice. "We're not even including `Middle-middles' or `Upper-minds.' `Middle-middles' are too busy being scared senseless, like rats, which is all they are. `Upper-minds' are too busy playing with their computers, as if they are unable to see beyond *that* limitation. You could have had galley slaves shackled to their oars, and you wouldn't be able to tell the difference."

"I see."

"Tom Novak?" the prompter then asked. She looked at Tom.

"Yes? That's my name," Tom said. "How did you know my name?"

"You were once a writer, weren't you?" the prompter asked.

"Many years ago," Tom replied. He was embarrassed. "A long, long time ago."

"You are still a writer in my book," the prompter said. "I've read your book. In fact, I read all of your books. Even the obscure ones. Twenty years ago. *Gaia* years."

She turned to whisper to Tom, "I risk losing my life by saying this, but I must tell you. I risk blaspheming, but I don't care. You should be proud of yourself. I am."

"You are?"

"Yes," the prompter said, nodding her head. "I am very proud of you."

"When I first appeared on television shows, I always felt the technicians were a gloomy lot, so I got a kick out of getting them to laugh. But aren't they a bit like the secret police these days?"

"Change has been recent," the prompter replied. "Ever since they installed Wallscreen on every wall, nothing's been the same."

She drew her chair close to Tom's. "There is little time for us to talk," she whispered. Her voice was tremulous with emotion. "I must be brief. Remember the stones."

"Someone else told me that," Tom replied slowly. "What do you mean? The stones?"

"The stones," the prompter replied simply. "I don't have time to explain it to you now. Just remember!"

"I know, I know," Tom muttered.

"Yes?" the prompter asked with a ray of hope. Then she shook her head. "No." She threw her hands up, rolling her eyes. "You don't understand. You're quite hopeless, aren't you!" She cautiously looked around the room to make sure they were alone. "I'll talk quickly. The history of climatic disasters is found in the stones. The answer is in paleontology, you know, in the study of plant-life fossils and animal-life fossils found in ancient rocks. Don't you see, they discovered the truth. They won't tell us about it, but they've found it. Their attempt at controlling the climate has been tried before, but only with disastrous results. Up until now, it has been killing people south of the equator. Plentiful rain in North America, also parts of Europe—but drought in Africa and parts of Asia and South America. The Orion Project, when it starts, at the end of the Year of the Desert, is going to totally control the world climate. It would have taken a lot of experimentation to perfect that, but hey, they've had time. Total control on a massive, *planet-size* scale. A thousand times more powerful than the disastrous climatic change that occurred at the conclusion of the Eleven-Years-War."

Tom could not hide the shock he felt. He gasped. He could not believe his ears. He could not comprehend what was being said.

"Don't you see!" the prompter replied, sensing Tom's skepticism. "It's instantly going to kill millions of people when it's fully implemented," the prompter continued. "Don't you see! We're talking about perhaps as many as four billion people dying over a two hundred year period of time, slowly, unnoticed, undetected, as if it were a natural phenomenon. It will slowly change everything from the point of view of the ecosystem. Matters of geography and climate will reign supreme. It will also mean the final solution for world population control."

"How is this going to happen," Tom asked, "this climate control business? How did you come to know it?"

"I know."

"But how did you come to know it? How can I believe that you're not inventing it? How do I know that you're not fabricating it?"

"Someone has to know," the prompter replied. "Someone has to disseminate the information to the magisters, don't they?"

"But how should you know this?"

"Scientists cannot work without information, can they?" the prompter said. "At least they have to communicate with each other, more or less openly; that's the only way they can do their work. There are no secrets among scientists. I formerly worked at the Science bureau. But I was transferred here a year ago."

"There is nothing to believe in anymore, nothing," Tom said ruefully. "Everything is an illusion. Belief is an illusion. Hope is an illusion. Everything is an illusion. We are in a dead-end. There are those who know. There are those who don't."

"There are stones to believe in, the rocks," the prompter said with a wondrous and surprised expression on her face. "No, don't close your ears to me. Listen! There are rocks! We have learned something from them. Darwin was partially wrong. Do you remember your science classes as a child?"

"Sort of," Tom said. "What does that have to do with anything?"

"The order of life," the prompter said, "was not guaranteed by underlying laws of natural selection, as we were taught in school. In times of big change, in climate and geography, the number of animal types was greatly reduced—Darwin was *partially* right, but also partially wrong: it's in the rocks. The rule that determined who would survive and who wouldn't was not that of `the fittest,' but rather of those species that were best adapted to quirks of local environmental change. Local change! That's the key! In the past, relatively insignificant creatures, such as mammals, sixty-five million years ago, withstood drastic changes that eliminated other creatures, such as dinosaurs. The fact that we have survived, as mammals, while others have fallen, gives hope."

"I don't get it," Tom replied confused, shaking his head.

"You're looking 'too close,' you're not looking 'far enough away,'" the prompter replied. "The concept is, at the same time, *too basic and too radical.* The stones are bigger than that. The rocks mean more than that. You see, you're looking at it too close. You are not looking at it from far enough away. Distance yourself."

"How far away do I have to look at it?" Tom asked.

"At least, we have a chance to survive as a species," the prompter replied, "maybe not as a civilization, or as a nation, or as a tribe, but as a species! That is the message hidden deep in the rocks: in certain localized areas, we may survive. Here, there, in very isolated pockets."

A cyber-tech burst into the room. He shouted, "What are you waiting for? Get this man on stage! We're ready to go! Civilized man has arrived on Earth! We have no time to lose!"

The prompter warned Tom, placing her fingers to her lips. With a frightened reaction, she turned her face away. Tom could sense her fear. She grew silent, averting her eyes.

Accompanied on either side of him by two armed guards marching with full military precision, Tom was brought out to look at the screen.

Visual and audio extravaganzas commemorated the birth of Buddha, Christ and Mohammad. There was the music of Beethoven's Ninth symphony. Tom fell into a dreamy reverie. He closed his eyes. He refused to watch the huge Wallscreen display. It was 120 feet wide by 300 feet long. He kept his eyes shut. While being prepared by the prompter, he missed Greece and Rome, the Middle Ages, the Ages of Discovery. When he opened his eyes, the presentation was showing the American Civil War, the First and Second European Wars, the Oil Wars, then the Eleven-Years-War. Such unimaginable carnage filled the screen that Tom had to close his eyes and cover his ears. He thought he was going to be sick.

Then he heard a voice-over—sounding majestic and God-like—"All is going well now. Peace reigns. Prosperity is here. Gaia reigns."

Tom had been dressed in the fancy uniform of a Communicator-level Sixteen—the highest level communicator. He went on stage. He felt like a high ranking general. He felt ridiculous. With his muscles rippling and his excellent physique, he felt that he cut quite a figure in his otherwise ridiculous uniform. He looked like a six-star general. With fanfare blaring, he was introduced as a writer from the past—-a specimen from the period of the seventh cycle of man. That was something new—he did not know what the period of the seventh cycle of man meant, he hadn't heard that expression before, it must have been something new and `Gaian-esque.'

Tom did not understand the words that were spoken in the running monologue. He stood there, mutely listening. The thing about his entire experience at that point was that he loved Beethoven's Ninth, and he had blocked everything out of his mind just to listen to that sublime music.

On the screen, Tom saw the faces of twelve ex-writers, including his own. But no Curmudgeon, the executed or the disappeared. He saw the faces of twenty composers, Beethoven, Mozart, among others; twenty painters, Van Gogh, Michelangelo, among others; twenty famous scientists, Louis Pasteur, Leonardo da Vinci, Albert Einstein. He saw Abraham Lincoln and George Washington.

Montage.

It was obviously a trick from the virtual reality machines, a computer simulation revising historical documentation.

Tom wondered, how genuinely well-educated were the 'Suits?' Were they just monkeys in suits?

Suddenly he was given his cue. He began, clearing his throat. He read the teleprompter. "The signs of change are not to be found here on Earth, but in the stars," he intoned majestically. "I am quoting from my book, *Expressions without Illusions*. The Gaia Federation..." The teleprompter then went dead. Tom gasped. The screen turned off.

Exactly thirty seconds before that exact moment, in the anteroom of the studio, a sixteen-year-old girl, with braided hair—arranged in pregnant 'nouveau-Gaia' style—stepped forward from an elevator, broke into hysterics, making a huge fit, in the center of the room. Eventually, a phalanx of armed guards surrounded her. She resisted arrest. It was against the law, religious law, to shoot any pregnant girl. She broke free and ran from the troops. She ran so fast that only then did they realize that maybe she was only pretending to be pregnant. She ran into the security room where the largest number of security forces were quartered. This group was off-duty. She had taken them completely by surprise. There were more guards than usual because the girl had entered the room precisely at the moment of the changing of the guard, so that there were twice as many armed troops than usual: there were eighty-six armed guards in the room.

She looked at her watch. She counted to three. At the exact moment that Beethoven's Ninth reached its climatic conclusion, she reached beneath her tee-shirt. She detonated a bomb containing seventeen pounds of ball bearings. Instantly, she killed eighty-seven people, all that were present in the room, including herself. The bomb was primitive but from the point of view of effectiveness, it was sophisticated. The bomb was not meant to damage the building—it was low percussion in nature—it was meant to penetrate "meat." The sound of the explosion was not loud, it was not heard because it was timed precisely to coincide with the concluding moments of the mighty sound of Beethoven's Ninth. As a military operation, the maneuver was executed perfectly. No one in the Great Hall suspected anything.

Suddenly, thirty seconds later, the doors were flung open and the Great Hall was sprayed with a flash of killer laser beams. At first,

Tom thought it was part of the light show, so taken by surprise he
was, as everyone else was initially; but when everyone in the studio
began to scream and run amok, he sensed that this was not organized confusion, *it was* pandemonium.

The Great Hall had been attacked.

The people present had mistaken the explosion thirty seconds
before as part of the show. It had been mistaken as part of the music,
but they couldn't mistake this part of the maneuver.

A cyber-tech stationed at the control panel shouted, "Cut to
studio C, cut to studio C." Then he signaled by running a finger
across his throat, only just in time before a killer laser beam cut him
in half, severing the upper part of his body from his lower.

Tom saw five or six bodies lying on the floor in front of him.
Miraculously, one of them was still alive. He was making a howling
sound that trailed off into a whining gurgle, then the howling began
anew. Laser guns were so accurate, they almost always killed their
victims instantly, but when they didn't, they left a bloody mess.

Tom felt no immediate threat, in spite of everyone's running
around in flight and fear, and the growing number of dead around
him. It had nothing to do with courage—at first anyway. It was like
his experience at the stream, like the shootings at proltown; things
were happening too fast for him to react.

Perversely, his curiosity about the situation had gotten the better of him. It had overridden his impulse towards survival and self-
preservation. Besides, there were times when Tom was extremely
courageous: he had fought courageously in the Eleven-Years-War.

Then, from the foyers, on both sides of the stage, came troops
armed with guns. They weren't the regular police; they were members of the regular army—thirty-four of the original 120. Eighty-six
had been killed instantly, moments before, by the suicide-mission
of the sixteen-year-old girl who had successfully faked her pregnant
condition. The remaining regular troops were undermanned. Their
movements were uncoordinated. The attackers still had the advantage of surprise.

A young woman, of 'nouveau-Gaia pregnancy age,' pulled Tom away from the advancing troops and shouted into his ear, "Don't resist. You're coming with us." She was dressed in a guerrilla outfit. Tom realized that she couldn't have been more than sixteen or seventeen years old, about the age of Leah.

"There must be a mistake," Tom shouted at her as she took him by the hand and led him from the stage. "Where are you taking me?"

"Shut up," she whispered into his ear. "Shut up. Follow me, or you're dead. Haven't we killed enough already?" she added, in what Tom considered to be a surprisingly soft, sentimental voice.

Her confederates covered her escape with a burst of fire at the troops entering the main staging area from both the left and right, providing a cover for the woman with Tom in tow to exit down the main corridor. The guerrillas were all women, Tom realized. What were they, Tom thought—Amazons? Tom hadn't seen as many women fighters together at one time since Oceania.

When they emerged outside, Tom shouted, "There's got to be a mistake!"

The sixteen-year-old guerrilla fighter ignored his protestations.

They went down in the elevator, with her confederates guarding both the entrance and exit to the elevator. Tom knew that most of her comrades were not going to get out of the building alive. Most of them were going to be killed outright. Yet to Tom, taking it all in in an instant, they looked so firm and resolute. In a quiet, competent way, they looked so confident. The oldest couldn't have been more than twenty, and she was the commander of the group. It wasn't their dedication that impressed Tom—any fanatical or mindless person could have done that—it was their steely calm that was notable. Sacrificing one's life meant nothing to Tom; it was as cheap as life itself. He had seen plenty of that happen in the Eleven-Years-War. What impressed him was how their minds were working. He could see it in the hard-edged concentration of their faces, in the focused fierceness of their eyes. Reality wrenched him back from his reverie when he saw one raise her laser gun, as if she were about to swat a fly, and aim it at an approaching armed trooper. Then he thought, they had to be fanatics to do that.

Tom and his captor left the building through a side emergency exit and jumped into an awaiting van. She threw Tom into the back and placed a black bag over his head and pulled it down to his shoulders.

Tom heard the voice of one of his captors. It was a voice of vehement command, a voice of a strong mature woman, a voice that spoke with confidence. She spoke with ironclad certainty. "If he moves so much as an inch, don't hesitate. Shoot him dead. Do you understand?"

"Yes," the subordinate answered.

After traveling for thirty minutes, they removed his hood. Tom tried to struggle free, but he was handcuffed behind his back. He looked at the woman sitting across from him. He judged her to be over twice the age of the other women. Another of his captors, sitting beside him, tried to hold him down, but he shook her grip free with his shoulders. Adjusting his eyes to the light shining in his face, Tom carefully looked at the woman sitting across from him.

"So it is!" he shouted at the top of his lungs.

"Damn it!" the commander shouted. "This isn't the right guy! This isn't the magister! You've obviously got the wrong man."

The captor sitting next to Tom looked at Tom and then at the commander. "He fits the description. In all the commotion, we thought we had the right one. He's the magister. He fits the description. He's dressed like a six-star general."

"I've been trying to tell them this for some time, there's been a mistake," Tom pleaded in a quiet voice. "There's no such thing as a six-star general! It's only a costume, for Christ sakes!"

"Shut up!" the commander said in a low, embarrassed voice. "He fits the description all right. He looks like the magister. Except this is a goddamn sixty-eight-year-old Vita-Man junky actor pretending to be a fifty-four-year-old magister. Look at his eyes! You can tell." She composed herself. "There's been a mistake. We lose ten good people, and we got the wrong man."

Tom realized who the commander was. He had seen pictures of her before. They had been plastered on wanted posters across the country. They were seen by elderly people watching TV sets in rural settlements throughout the countryside. Two years earlier, they had also been featured almost daily on Wallscreen, calling her the worst criminal in the history of Gaia. Now hardly anybody heard anything about her. It was as if she had completely vanished. Tom thought she had been captured. And for the life of him, he couldn't remember her name.

"Damn it!" the commander shouted in a fit of rage and frustration.

"I understand, your grace," the captor said in a humble voice, as she sat next to Tom.

"Was there blood?" the commander asked.

"Was there blood? Even in the darkness you could see it and slip on it."

The commander looked down in disgust. "I'm sorry. God, I'm sorry."

"So am I. What else was I supposed to do, commander?"

"So. You measure things in blood?" Tom asked in an angry voice. "So! Madame Hitler!"

"I thought I told you to shut up," the commander shouted at Tom. "Shut your filthy mouth! Did anyone ask you to speak?"

With her laser gun, the guard sitting next to Tom hit him on the side of his head. With the impact of the blow Tom slouched over on his side.

Then he remembered her name. It came back to him in a flash, like a glorious dawn, like a bursting moment of insight. Her name was seared in his mind. Her reputation had preceded her. To the official Gaia movement, she was an ignominious person, a notoriously infamous figure, a world-class criminal. In all the official circles, on all the National and International networks of Wallscreen, she was portrayed as the number-one witch-demon, the principal corrupter of the morals of youth, the pre-eminent ringleader of the anti-Gaia movement.

She was even more dreaded, more hated, precisely because she was a renegade of the official Gaia philosophy and religion.

Only seven years before, she had been one of the highest-placed leaders of the government.

Only four years before that, she had been one of the most highly placed spokespersons for the official Gaia religion. Before she turned coat.

Her name was September Snow.

Chapter Six

TOM WAS THROWN into a place of confinement, a prison cell. *A thought occurred to him! His capture had been a mistake. Why was he being held prisoner, after they had realized they had gotten the wrong man? He wondered: realizing their mistake, why hadn't they released him? Maybe he was being held prisoner because he had recognized them? They feared, once released, he might reveal something about them. A further thought occurred to him...did they intend to recruit him?*

Before that happened, however, Tom saw his captors, when out of sight of each other, communicating by two-way walkie-talkies. At first glance, the contraptions looked crude. Like primitive toys, seventy times bulgier than teensy-weensy cell-phones, they were fashioned from plastic, durable metal and steel. After Tom became accustomed to them, however, they took on a theme of simplicity. By observing, he realized they were effectively doing the job.

In the YEAR GAIA ELEVEN, walkie-talkies were so awkward and out-of-date Tom wondered if the government knew they existed, much less knew how to cut into their transmissions.

Then Tom remembered he once saw a walkie-talkie in a museum display. He remembered they were a retro technology from the middle stages of the Second European War. Even by the end of the Oil Wars, walkie-talkies were considered as ancient and as behind-the-times as flintlocks, howitzers, and horse-drawn ammo-carts.

Why use them?

Perhaps conversation by walkie-talkie could not be intercepted or jammed by the government's listening devices, he speculated, being so antiquated. Maybe the walkie-talkies were all the rebels had at their disposal. Maybe it was combination of the two.

During his musings, Tom was transferred from one group to another. He was passed along as if he were some delicate object, descending through a labyrinth of cells, tunneling down darkened stairways, nine or ten stories underground, beneath what he believed to be a 170-year-old tenement building, without electricity or heat, inside the middle or lower section of the island of Manhattan.

Finally, he reached the bottom-level cell block: the "maximum-security" cell block.

Tom laughed. For him, the expression "maximum-security" had an archaic, strangely old-fashioned ring about it. He laughed teasingly when they directed him inside the cell. "Huh?" he exclaimed. "Sing-Sing! Alcatraz!"

"Huh?" his captor asked, staring at him dimly. His captor was no more than sixteen and one-half years old. She was small, slender, and beautiful. Tom noticed that all of his captors were attractive and remarkably beautiful. She did not have her hair arranged in a long, flowing "nouveau-Gaia" pregnancy style; instead, her hair was hacked off and arranged in a short, page-boy style. She held a laser gun to the back of Tom's head. She did not have a clue as to what Tom was talking about, nor did she care. She did not bother to tell him to shut up. "No one can hear you down here, so you can scream all you want," she muttered at last.

"What do you want after your revolution?" Tom said.

"You mean after we've won?" his captor asked. "Winning is all that counts. September insists that we don't bother calling it a *revolution*. She insists that historically, practically every revolution eventually turned into an anti-revolution, or a counter-revolution, within twenty-five to seventy years after its inception, as the aging revolutionaries, or the second or third-generation of so-called revolutionaries, continue to claim they are still acting in the name of the revolution, even as they are doing the exact opposite."

"How interesting," Tom smiled. "All right then. After you've won, what do you plan to do?"

"Be a custodian at one of the redistribution centers of placebos for the consolation of pains of everyday life," she replied sneeringly. "What do you plan to do, old man?"

Tom's face reddened with embarrassment. He realized he deserved the comeuppance he received for being patronizing to someone so young, yet of whose life he had so little knowledge. When he recalled his own youthful enthusiasms, he realized she had every right to react flippantly to his condescendingly arrogant attitude. But he wasn't about to let her off the hook entirely.

"Granted, you can call it a `revolution' if you want," Tom said, "or you can call it: `not a revolution,' that's your prerogative. But whatever you call it, you haven't changed it simply by changing it's name—it still is what it is."

She turned aside and switched on her walkie-talkie. She quickly spoke two words into the mouthpiece, then turned it off. "He's in," was her message.

For two days, they kept him locked in a bare brick, stone floor cell, with a black, iron door. During this time, Tom was given no food to eat. Each day, he was given a single candle which provided the only light in his cell. The candle cast long, dark shadows. In the room was a bed-board, a stool, a table, a bowl, a plastic cup, and endless time to think. Since the candle lasted only about ten hours, there were fourteen hours of darkness. By the second day he learned how to use the candle sparingly. The cell dripped water. Tom speculated that maybe the cell was close to, or beneath the river—but which river: the East River or the Hudson? Occasionally, there was a gentle rumbling sound, like the sound of a light, rolling earthquake. However, incarcerated as he was in the bowels of the Earth, he could not be sure. He knew that, deep inside, sound played tricks on you. Maybe it was the sound of an explosion, but an explosion that occurred a little distance away. He could only speculate about the nature and source of the percussion. Had there been a war going on? A low-level intensity war? A subway? An undeclared war? A war that he couldn't have been aware of, isolated as he was, on the traveling TV lecture tours?

Maybe September could answer these questions. But Tom didn't trust her, or his captors, a single inch. To him, September's group was a bunch of crazy and fanatical camp-followers, fifteen and sixteen-year-old girls, brainwashed beyond hope, controlled into following a deceitfully mystical cult.

On the other hand, Tom knew that Wallscreen, and Big Boy too, were pure propaganda machines. They served no other purpose. They were cynically used by a vengeful and merciless government.

In the end, Tom thought that all pro-Gaia co-religionists, and all anti-Gaia co-religionists, were equally demented. To live a simple life, like a monk, in absolute solitude, removed from the tumult of a crazy—and ever growing crazier—world, hopelessly spinning out of control, was to Tom the height of common sense. It was more than that: it was the pinnacle of wisdom and sanity.

At the end of the second day, he was given a large cup of coffee which somehow managed to take the edge off his intense, ravenous hunger. For the first time since his abduction, he felt his thoughts had congealed, had been made centered, had become whole.

The strangest thing of all occurred to him. With his senses stripped to a bare minimum, he thought it might intensify his powers at predicting the weather, a power inherited from his great-grandfather. He had nothing else to do. It had happened fifty years ago when he was living alone on the prairie, as well as dozens of times in between. He could "smell" the crackling of lightning an hour or two before it struck. He could predict rain five or six days before it fell. Farmers thought he was bewitched and had magical powers when he successfully made weather predictions, and he did so repeatedly, without error. He was a "genius" at predicting the weather.

Tom had nothing better to do, he had nothing to read, so he tried to "predict the weather." But in a cell, buried deep inside the earth, he realized it was useless to try to "smell" the weather, as it was futile to try to "smell" the weather in the all-weather-controlled Domes on the surface of the Earth. He couldn't detect anything. This is the way it had been for years.

So, from memory, he recited bits and pieces of Seneca Indian poetry, and later, longer stanzas came back to him. Idleness was driving him crazy. He realized he hadn't taken a Vita-Man pill for almost two days (he had some reserves but they had been confiscated right after his capture.) Twelve hours was the longest he had gone without taking a Vita-Man pill before. At forty-eight hours, he had set an all-time record.

There was a gentle knock on the door. September Snow entered. She walked in and came right to the point. "First, we're going to take you off the Vita-Man pills that you have been taking twice daily. Cold turkey. You will suffer from boredom. That boredom will be followed by pain, intense pain, beginning after the first seventy-two hours, but you'll eventually stop feeling like a marshmallow brain. You will be able to think a bit clearer. Then, within a couple of days, you will experience lassitude, loss of appetite, loss of libido. That's one of the many side effects of the pill. That's how they've kept you hooked. After ten days or so, you'll be fine, so long as you manage to keep off the pill. We've weaned others off the Vita-Man pills, so you won't be the first to go through it."

September smiled at Tom a frozen half-smile, a smile that was both cautious and yielding. "This addiction is similar to the addiction people experienced with tobacco, alcohol, phenobarbital substances and heroin, during the last century."

"Ten days?" Tom murmured. "That's how long you plan to keep me in this cell?"

"You're not going nowhere, Mr. Novak, so try to get used to it, all right?"

September was about ready to slam the door. She turned, as if she had forgotten something else.

"Oh, we know who you are. We've been informed of your identity. Did you know you weren't supposed to be in New York for the Gaia celebration? At the last minute the authorities changed their plans. That's what brought you in. We weren't informed about it until it was too late. So we got you mixed up with someone else, that's all. *Shit happens, doesn't it?*"

"That's a poor explanation for why I am being held as a prisoner, isn't it?" Tom said.

September turned and swiveled. It was as if she had forgotten something further. In a moderately peevish voice, she added: "By the way, I am an excellent scholar and a reputed historian, so don't call me Madame Hitler. I don't like it."

"So you won't answer me," Tom said in a quiet voice. "Okay. Fine. Be that way. But I've got a better question. When do I get fed? I haven't eaten in days."

"That's true," September replied, "we haven't fed you yet. Starting tomorrow, we'll begin feeding you two meals a day."

Tom began to get accustomed to the darkness. He liked the quiet. He was back in his element as a recluse. A war must have begun—or he surmised by the sound of the explosions. Most of the explosions were far away, but on occasion, they were near. On rare occasions, there were dangerously close. On those occasions, the walls shook. The explosions had become a mild annoyance to Tom once he grew accustomed to his cell. When intense, they kept him awake at night; otherwise he managed to get accustomed to them. Being nine or ten stories underground, Tom could only imagine the devastation that was occurring on the surface. Was there going to be anything left of the city? It was taking a pounding, he thought. In a sense, he knew he was lucky to be imprisoned: he was in a safe place.

His reaction to the withdrawal of the Vita-Man pills occurred just as September had predicted. First there was boredom. Then, for a short period, there was intense pain. Then, loss of appetite, loss of libido, lassitude. Thank God for small favors, Tom speculated; before he had been ravenously hungry all the time—a diet of beans, occasionally supplemented by rice, twice daily, always left him hungry; without the loss of appetite, his hunger pangs would have been more pronounced. After one week, he began to feel better. He noticed that he was thinking with greater clarity, his mind was sharper. After ten more days, he felt brisk and finely tuned. The cobwebs were clearing from his mind. He exercised daily.

September knocked on his door. She entered the cell.

"I think we can talk safely now. I think we're ready."

Tom smiled. "Ready for what? By the count of the candles, I think I've been here for at least thirteen days."

"Fourteen, to be exact. Are you all right?"

"Yes."

September was surprised. She expected her prisoner to be angry. She expected him to question her, even interrogate her. She expected him at least to wonder why he had been mistakenly apprehended in the first place—why he was being held against his will.

He was mild. He said nothing. He looked at his watch. Sitting in his chair at the center of the room, he actually looked contented! September thought. He was supposed to have been an ex-writer, September remembered, but she also recalled from his dossier that he had a reputation for being a recluse and a hermit, so his behavior made sense.

"We're going to have to keep you here for a little while longer," September said. Surprised at herself that she was actually pleased to see him, she struggled to keep a poker face.

"How much longer?"

"A week. Perhaps two. With the war going on, perhaps even longer. Actually, your release also depends on your behavior."

"Fine."

"You don't mind?" September asked. She was surprised at Tom's reaction, but also mildly pleased, because it fit the portrait she had of him, based on her knowledge of him as a writer; at least during his early years. Immediately after his incarceration, she began to study Tom's background and biography—that is, that of which they knew.

"No," Tom said. His laughter was soft and rich.

"You have come to trust us then?"

"Absolutely not!" Tom smiled. "Totally not! I think you people are crazy. You people are deluded. Make no mistake, I take no delight in your rebellion."

"Then why are you taking this so well?" September asked. "Why are you taking it, if you don't trust us?" September smiled. "I don't understand."

"I'm resigned to my fate," Tom said, "that's all. Actually, I must confess, I have another reason. As a child, I suffered from leukemia. I went through a regimen of chemotherapeutic treatments which lasted two years. Eventually I was cured—full remission. But that affliction helped me to cope with solitude and desperation."

"Is that all?" September asked. She was slightly embarrassed. This information was not in his dossier. None of the information from Tom's Indian period was in his dossier. September was a little skeptical of Tom's explanation, but she decided that it wasn't that important. "Well, I would have preferred that you had gotten up and punched me in the nose."

"Why?" Tom asked in an innocent voice. "You have a beautiful nose. In fact, you are not just pleasing; frankly, you are beautiful."

September was unnerved by Tom's placid reaction. In fact, she was beside herself for his lack of reaction at all.

Tom said, changing the subject, "Besides, there's a horrible war going on on the surface, that much I do *believe*. The bombs are exploding all the time. What is this place?"

"You are being held in the cavity of a vault."

"A vault?" Tom asked skeptically. He laughed incredulously. "What kind of vault?"

September gave Tom a smile. She relaxed a little. "It's a bank vault. There was a time, roughly between 1949 to 1991, Gregorian calendar, when two countries, the Soviet Union and the United States, built and amassed huge stockpiles of nuclear weapons and built delivery systems to launch them in order to threaten to destroy each other. Each of the Superpowers, as they were quaintly called then, had amassed enough explosive power to destroy the world at least one hundred times over. Just one nuclear submarine, out of a fleet of eighty, packed more thermonuclear wallop than one thousand Hiroshima-type atomic bombs. In 1946, there were nine nuclear weapons on the planet; by 1986, there were 60,000. New York City constructed special secret vaults to hold the important documents and archives of the city's banks in the event of an all-out nuclear war. We are in a bank vault *cum* bomb shelter of that era."

"Like in the catacombs of ancient Rome?" Tom asked. Over the years, the bank vault *cum* bomb shelter had been stripped of all its finery, all that was left were hollow underground cubes encased in bare concrete.

"Yes," September replied. "If you want to use your imagination. Yes, back then, the protesters were beats *cum* hippies *cum* cyberpunks, representing three different generations that feared a bomb-induced futurelessness from the nuclear age. Then the Cold War ended. By the time of the Oil Wars, the vaults were ineffective and useless. By the advent of the Eleven-Years-War, they were all but forgotten. All of this took place long before computers could simultaneously store information at widely separated locations, making the thought of `need-for-information' vaults pretty ridiculous. These long-forgotten vaults have become our makeshift command centers. We were forced to use them due to the likelihood of an all-out war with the government. Ten floors above us is the largest No-Go Zone in the city of New York. While you've been down here, half of the No-Go Zones have disappeared as a result of the war."

"Was that the explosions I was hearing then?"

"Yes, it was." September replied.

September paused for a moment, scrutinizing Tom. "You're off the Vita-Man pills; at least, we think you are. Studies conducted fifty years ago, suggested that pollutants, mimicking certain hormones, caused infertility in third and fourth generation offspring of grandparents and great-grandparents who had been exposed to high levels of pesticides and dioxins. As a result, there was a significant drop in the birthrate, and an increase of cancer, especially in the heavily industrialized countries. Research reported high enough concentrations of DDT alone, in some individuals, to completely inhibit reproduction.

"More research developed chemical agents to counter the fertility inhibiters, but there were no easy solutions for all of the problems," September continued. "However, as an indirect result, over a period of fifty years, the Vita-Man pill was developed..."

September's walkie-talkie suddenly buzzed. She listened, then said, "Yes," into the speaker. She turned it off. Addressing Tom, she said, "We'll talk later. A small problem has arisen in the air ducts."

"You talk like a scientist," Tom said.

"I'm only a dabbler," September replied smiling. "On the other hand, my late husband was a great scientist...well, never mind, we'll talk of that later."

"I don't see the point," Tom replied, folding his arms in militant defiance. He rocked back and forth, on the hind legs of his chair. Slowly he placed his hands behind his head. He regarded September with an impassive expression. It was as if he were saying, with a poignantly nonverbal gesture: `What are you going to do about it?'

"You don't see the point of what?" September asked in disgust. "We'd like to show you the reason why we are doing what we are doing."

"I don't see the point of that," Tom repeated in a strong, vehement voice. "There's nothing I can do to help you. Nothing."

"Don't be so hasty," September replied. "We'll be the final judge of that. We'll see."

"See what? I do have one more question though—at the moment anyway," Tom said.

"Shoot."

"Does this have something to do with the stones?"

"Stones?" September asked, initially baffled by the question. "What do you mean? The expression `stones' can carry many different meanings."

"You know...*stones?*" Tom asked. For an instant, he didn't look impassively at September. He had an honest and dignified expression suggesting genuine curiosity.

"Yes," September replied, "well, the war has begun. We don't talk in riddles anymore. We talk differently now. The code-words we were accustomed to using, even only a year ago, are no longer in use. The expression "rocks and stones" was used to describe a deeply historical approach, or more accurately, a *geological* approach, to the implications of the dangers of the Orion Project. A little emergency has arisen now, I have to leave. I'll be happy to explain it to you later, though. But, I warn you, it's very technical. It's a bit hard going, from a scientific point of view." She left Tom's space of confinement abruptly.

Later September had Tom's cell completely searched to see if he had any Vita-Man pills stashed away. She also had him strip-searched to see if he was hiding any Vita-Man pills on his person. When none were discovered (they had already confiscated his reserve pills), and the findings reported to her, she smiled and said, "His recovery has been so thorough, he doesn't even *know* he has recovered. This man has been out of his mind from taking Vita-Man pills for so long, he doesn't know which end is up. It's astonishing how many creative people there are who are kept in the dark, being subjected to a mild form of indirect sedation, either in their food or their Vita-Man pills—placed there by the government—without their ever knowing or suspecting it. We'll give him two weeks of privacy, so that he will have time to contemplate and recoup. Tom's inner character is, at base, somewhat iconoclastic, mildly skeptical, slightly sardonic, perhaps even agnostic or atheistic, but layered on top of that, are ten to fifteen years of degraded existence where he has had to suck up and kiss other people's asses in order to survive. Many years ago, he was once a recluse and a hermit, so an exercise in solitude will be a tonic for him."

September nodded her head.

"By the way, I want you to increase his rations by fifty percent," September said. "The man's still hungry. But he's strong and resilient. And he has spirit."

It was clear to all of her comrades September liked Tom; indeed, more than that, she was fond of him.

"He's a tough person," September said. "He will need all the strength he can muster—for the future struggle. Then we'll start to proselytize. In earnest!" September rubbed her hands together. "I can hardly wait to begin."

Chapter Seven

TOM WAS GIVEN THREE SQUARE MEALS a day. He began to exercise more rigorously. Three hours daily, he completed seventy-five sit-ups, one-hundred push-ups, capped off with a strenuous running-in-place exercise. He exercised in total darkness, saving his candles for his ever growing poetry self-recital. Gradually, he built himself up.

Tom urinated. The natural act was exquisite. By engaging in the act, he deeply and profoundly knew he was in perfect health. Such joy to be found in so simple an act!

He felt like a king, in spite of his incarceration.

Two weeks later, as September had promised, she visited him. "Now that we know you are completely off the Vita-Man pills, we can engage in serious interaction."

September led him from his cell and showed him Wallscreen video-tapes. The first tape ran for two hours. One of the subsequent tapes included Orsen's death.

"See?" September asked. "We captured these tapes in a guerrilla operation for information retrieval one month ago. They must have thought you guys were important to keep these tapes. Did you know the deceased writer?"

"Did I know him?" Tom replied. "'Course I did. His name is Orsen Pipes. Or rather, it was."

"So you say you knew him?" September asked.

"Yes," Tom replied. "They treated us as if we weren't important at all." Tom carefully looked at the screen. "As ex-writers, that is. We were nothing to them."

"Well, maybe you didn't know it," September said, "but maybe you *were* important to them, only you didn't know it. Look at these tapes. I ask you again, did you know the deceased writer? It's important. We haven't been able to identify him yet."

Tom asked September to run the tape again showing Orsen's death. She rewound the tape. It flickered on the wall. Well, that was one mystery solved, Tom thought. Apparently, Orsen did commit suicide. Tom watched the tape as Orsen threw the rope around the ceiling beam, stood up on a stool, tied the rope around his neck, and kicked the stool out from under him.

"I was with him before this happened," Tom said. "I remember. I saw him on Wallscreen."

"Did you say anything to him at that time that might have compromised you, or your standing, with the government? Think carefully now. Think before you give me your answer."

"No," Tom replied slowly, "I don't think so. I don't think I said anything that could have been held against me. I've always tried to be cautious in what I've said, especially in private. One can never be too careful. Although Orsen wasn't cautious. He was always shooting his mouth off."

"That's why you were ordered by the Gaia government to attend the Gaia presentation at the last minute, after the magister you were impersonating had apparently fallen ill," September smiled knowingly. "It's all becoming clear now. You said you knew this gentleman, this Orsen Pipes?"

"Yes," Tom replied, "I knew him. He was my friend." Tom paused for a moment. "I remember Orsen saying less than an hour before he died, or just before he killed himself, 'In any event, what better gift can we hope for than to be made insignificant?' At the time, I thought he was being philosophical...or I don't know, just being ornery. I now realize he was talking about his very existence.

The government keeps tapes like these?"

"Yes. We thought it would be too much of a burden for them to keep so many tapes on so many people but the incredible technology existing today makes it so easy for them to do so."

She looked at Tom, searching his eyes. Tom returned her stare. The look on September's face was not just one of sadness; it also included a look of anxiety and concern. Tom realized that if he asked September if she was feeling discomfort she would probably have replied in the affirmative. But he knew what she was feeling was not discomfort or unpleasantness, it was grief. He realized that September may have known more about the nature of the government's business than anyone else. September was subtle. She was accustomed to hiding her emotions. Tom understood that, although unexpressed, emotion ran deep in her. After all, maybe she wasn't such a crazed fanatic as he had at first presumed. But why all this expression of emotion? And why all this emotion over the death of a single person, someone she had never previously known?

"When he had decided to kill himself...?" she continued almost tearfully. "Perhaps that's what he was thinking? Maybe that? Maybe *just* that? 'What better gift can we hope for than to be made insignificant?' He thought he had nothing to live for. When an individual feels despair and pent-up rage and thinks there's no way out, he often commits suicide. When a community feels that it is offered the possibility for redemption through a heroic act, an act that may give hope to others, to the entire world, they may accept that choice."

"That choice?" Tom asked. "What choice?"

"What the Greeks called—*thanatos*," September replied in a solemn voice. "Death. So that in the future, others may live, of course. Otherwise, what's the point?"

"Orsen was once a famous man," Tom cried softly. "He was a story-teller. Once upon a time he was, anyway."

"Once upon a time," September nodded. "If the government has its way, he will not only be not famous; he will become a non-being. That's their specialty, suppression, then oblivion. Already, he doesn't exist on Wallscreen, Big Boy, or in the International Archives. He's fallen into a deep memory black hole. He's more than dead. He never existed. That's the tragedy. We have other tapes. We have many other tapes. We can watch them all, if you like. We can watch them all night, all the next evening, if you like." September gave Tom what amounted to almost a seductive smile.

Tom realized: September thought in terms of millions perishing, yet she was also capable of thinking in the context of one lonely person who dreaded the idea of just trying to carry on as a normal human being under current conditions—Orsen. "When Orsen died," Tom said thoughtfully, "his official age was eighty-eight. But he was notorious for lying about his age. His real age was ninety. Or ninety-one. I know. You mention millions dying, September, yet you also think of one person dying?" Tom asked carefully.

September shrugged. "You knew him, I didn't. Maybe it was his particular brand of personal vanity, this business of his age. The Curmudgeon knew. When they reached a certain age."

"Yes," Tom said. Tom gently hummed to himself a tune yet the title or the lyrics he could not remember.

September smiled. At first, she did not go on. She was wondering why Tom had given no comment when she mentioned the Curmudgeon by name.

"The Curmudgeon told me about you," September said at last, "although at the time, I didn't know who you were. You were an abstraction to me. Just something I might find in a dusty book. I don't know why they'd want to kill you off. None of you ex-writers write anymore anyway, do you?"

"We're not supposed to," Tom replied. "Not after the Eleven-Years-War. Not after the destruction of the Ozone layer. Too many important things were going on. There was no time for literature. At least, that was the judgment of the day."

"Oh."

"Do you have any tapes of the Curmudgeon?" Tom asked.

"The Curmudgeon?" September replied animatedly. "Why, of

course we do!" She beamed with delight. "I don't even have to look. Of course we do!"

Tom beamed with delight, too. "How did you know the Curmudgeon?"

"We don't refer to him as an ex-writer, he's always a writer to us," September replied happily. "A glorious and happy story-teller!" Her mood had changed. Instead of being withdrawn and somber, September had become joyful and vibrant.

"We have tapes of him. The Curmudgeon has been celebrated ever since he joined our little concern. I'm unhappy to report that he's no longer 'free from the fetters of false icons,' to quote the man himself. The fussy thing is going to be trapped into this *horrible age of self-discovery,* even if he is trapped, kicking and screaming," September smiled.

"He swears to us that he's going to turn 100 years old in three months time. We believe him too. Should we believe him?" September laughed. "Is he making it up? About his age?"

"He isn't making it up," Tom cried. He laughed. "You can believe him. He's a hoot! He will be 100 years old."

"You remember the old calendar, then?" September asked.

"Yes," Tom said. "Sometimes—strange—I used to forget the old calendar. Not the numbers of the years, of course, one remembers those, but I used to forget the names of the months though— when they were supposed to occur. Of course, I forgot the days of the week. The use of the new calendar made one forget the old calendar, naturally. We were all affected by the propaganda. Now it's coming back to me. In bits and pieces."

"Loss of memory is one of the contrived side-effects of Vita-Man pills," September said. "You're getting your memory back."

"Tapes of your own?" Tom asked absent-mindedly. "You mean you have tapes of the Curmudgeon! The Curmudgeon is alive, then!"

"Of course he's alive!" September shouted animatedly. "Of course he is! But then, how would you know that?" September realized that she was making progress with Tom. She had hit a strong point. She had touched a sensitive nerve. She could see that Tom was moved by the news of the existence of the Curmdgeon tapes.

"What are you talking about then?" Tom asked.

"The Curmudgeon escaped from the government's clutches a year ago. The government tried to keep it secret for as long as they could, but the truth finally got out. Orsen knew about it before he died, right? Truth travels fast. Even amongst the general population."

"Yes, you're right," Tom nodded.

"The Curmudgeon ran away one night. He knew they were going to impose euthanasia on him. He disappeared into proltown. Through the help of sympathizers he managed to escape, then he later arrived at a No-Go Zone in New York. He was passed around a beltway. Since then, he's been in our custody. He sought formal asylum with us, six months ago. He's a wily fellow. You knew him *then*? How long have you known him?"

"I've known him for fifty years," Tom smiled. "He was like a mentor to me. More than that. Like a father. As a writer, he was *everything*. Would it be possible for me to see him?"

"You mean, in person?" September asked.

"Yes."

"That'd be difficult. Next to impossible in fact," September replied. She seemed to be making a deep, impenetrable calculation. "Is this a matter of some importance to you?" September asked. She stared carefully at Tom.

"Yes, I adored him. As I said, he was more than a mentor to me, he was a father."

"Like a father?"

"No—not *like* a father," Tom replied irritably. "He *was* a father. He was the closest thing to being a father, especially after my real dad died." Tom mused.

"My father died in the middle of a rain-delay during the last game of the World Series in 2028 A.D.," Tom said. "He was found dead, slumped in a chair, in front of a Univision Screen. Ever since then, the Curmudgeon has served as a kind of surrogate father. Yes, it's important to me."

"Very well. I'll think about it. Is it *really* important to you?"

"Yes."

Suddenly, Tom gave September a skeptical nod. He grew leery. He did not wish to share his inner doubts and feelings with September; at least, not for the present. "Perhaps, perhaps not," he then replied in a diffident voice. His mood shifted sharply.

September was reading Tom's thoughts, and she looked at Tom carefully. "I know you don't believe me, but the Curmudgeon is truly in our custody. The Curmudgeon is alive. He is well." September gave Tom a reassuring nod and a warm smile.

Tom looked at September with discernment. He became abrupt and defensive. Then he erupted. "Prove it!" he shouted. The ferocity of his mood-change shocked and provoked him further. He didn't want to tell September that the Curmudgeon was, not only a father-figure, but probably the only friend he had. He wanted desperately to see him. Practically all of his friends from the beginning of his life to the age of fifty-five were now dead.

Tom did not want to go any further in sharing his loneliness and loss with September. He was aware that they were of two different generations, September and Tom. Thank God for that too, Tom thought. His generation had made a mess of things. Just as the Curmudgeon and Tom represented different generations. Tom remembered that the Curmudgeon was born on January 5, 1963, while Tom was born on November 12, 1994. Tom guessed that September was born somewhere around 2022-25, more or less.

Tom could not deny that he felt a powerful attraction to September, both as a woman and as an independent thinker, but considering her as an actor and shaper of events, he was skeptical of both her motives and her calculations, not to mention her conscience—in fact, he wasn't sure she had one.

Already, there was a yearning growing inside him, though. He

couldn't deny any longer the longing he felt for her. He sensed—
tragically, mysteriously—she was attracted to him, too.

Maybe that was why he felt angry with her. In spite of it—or
because of it—because of everything that had happened to him—he
still did not think he could completely trust September. Why should
he trust her at all, he wondered. For all he knew, in spite of her
clever polemics, September might have been a cynic, a person driven
by power, or a cold-blooded murderer. He had seen plenty of cold-
blooded murderers—especially in the war—cynics and people driven
by power, too.

But by mentioning the Curmudgeon, September had touched a
soft spot. His heart ached. He felt a little more trusting, a little more
inclined to believe her, and to believe in her.

Chapter Eight

THE NEXT DAY, Tom was removed from his cell by his prison guard. By this time, he had established that her name was Tamara, that she was sixteen, and that she was an emancipated ex-member of a sex-chattel circle run exclusively for the magisters' pleasure. She escorted him up a darkened stairway. "They destroyed half of our air ducts in a bombing raid yesterday," she volunteered. "The level of damage inflicted was bad."

"Have they gotten that close already?" Tom asked in a concerned voice.

"I'm afraid so," the prison guard replied. She seemed more beautiful with each word she uttered. Tom even had to admit to himself that he was a little captivated by her.

Tom asked his captor if she knew anything about September Snow. In thinking of a possible answer, Tamara grew thoughtful. "In spite of what you've seen of her, she is better known for her diplomatic skills than for her revolutionary fire; nonetheless, she's tough, professional, very much in control. Also, beautiful, don't you think?" Tamara smiled warmly.

Tom did not reply, although he agreed. He tried to imagine September as a diplomat. `What a hoot!' he thought as he tried to imagine her in the free-for-all exchange of diplomacy.

"How old is September?" Tom asked.

"Thirty-eight," Tamara replied slowly, "or thirty-nine. Maybe even forty, I don't know. I'm sixteen, Gaia generation, so it's hard for me to figure out the old calendar." She laughed, giggled a little, then finished with a snicker. "What's the matter?" Tamara asked. "You look a little confused as to why I have trouble using the old calendar."

"Why are you laughing?" Tom replied in retort. "You use the old calendar, don't you?"

"Of course," Tamara replied. "But only since I've joined the underground. That occurred less than a year ago." She grew somber.

"Unlike September or you, people like me haven't a clue what life was like before the Eleven-Years-War. The reason why I was laughing is because September is a human being, too. We're all afraid of her, but she's not untouchable as a human."

Tom realized Tamara was far more mature than her age suggested; far more mature that he initially had given her credit for, which left him vexed.

"Why do you talk to me so openly?" Tom finally asked, dropping his guard completely.

"What do you mean?" Tamara asked. She smiled demurely.

"I mean, you talk to me," Tom said. "I mean, you really talk to me. You confide in me. That's what I'm really trying to say."

Tamara smiled. "You're not the enemy. You're a writer. There are so few of you gifted ones left. You're *my* first. You're the only one I'm ever likely to meet in my lifetime. In fact, we are honored by your presence." She discreetly bowed to him.

"Then why, may I ask, am I kept locked in a cell?" Tom asked in a friendly tone.

"That's a fair question," Tamara nodded. "For the time being, it's necessary. Call it a precaution. Until you come to trust us a little more, at least a little more, it's a necessary precaution," she said as she motioned him into his new cell.

The cell was up five stories closer to the surface. The cell was located on a level that had both electric lighting and air conditioning, although intermittently both were shut on and off.

When he entered the cell, he discovered that he had a cellmate. The good thing about the cell was that it was three times larger than the previous one in which he spent the first five weeks of his incarceration. The cell was also brightly lit. It had a flush commode.

Tom's cellmate was dressed like a 'Suit.'

"Who are you?" Tom asked.

The 'Suit' smiled at him. The first thing Tom deduced from his too-readily given smile was that the man was an informer. He deduced that the informer had been placed in the cell to get information. But what information? Tom knew nothing—certainly nothing that could have been of interest to September and her band of guerrillas.

The 'Suit,' appropriately enough, was dressed in a suit. He was about thirty years of age; good-looking, as `Suits' usually were. His hair looked as though it had been recently trimmed. Tom's own hair had not seen a comb or scissors in three months. The man was clean-shaven. Tom could tell just by casual observation that before his imprisonment he must have enjoyed a healthy diet, even if his dull brain seemed to consist mostly of air. It occurred to Tom that his own mind was growing sharper every day—ever since he had been weaned off the Vita-Man pills. Miraculously, he found the ability to recite thousands of lines of poetry from memory, when only a month before he had to struggle to recall only a few dozen lines.

Tom found the change in the dexterity of his mental state odd and perplexing. He also deduced that this man was not really a 'Suit' after all. He was just a glorified 'Upper-mind.' In other words, a bean-counter, a number-cruncher, a low-level computer hacker.

The 'Suit' began to speak to Tom without introduction, or even an exchange of pleasantries or salutations. "The power goes off only when the surface is bombed," he said, staring at the ceiling, in a state of obvious boredom. "Except for the big one yesterday, there haven't been any bombings for three days. That's strange and *eerie*. Something creepy is going on. More than the bombing, that's made everybody jumpy. There's a tension in the air. Can you not feel it?"

"I can't feel anything," replied Tom. "Like I asked you, 'who are you?'" Tom directly questioned the inmate. "Please answer."

"I am, or was, second assistant to the chief of information retrieval."

"Information retrieval?   You worked for the Gaia government?"

"'Course I worked for the Gaia government," the 'Suit' replied indignantly, "you think I work for these nuts? We're right in the middle of a hornet's nest of extreme zealots. We're at wacko central. They'll do anything to get what they want. The only thing I can't figure out is whether they're fanatical militants or just militant fanatics." The last comment was supposed to have been funny.

Tom let the comment pass.

"Who was your chief in your job?" Tom asked.

"Oh, you didn't like my snide remark?" the 'Suit' replied, "oh well, very well. You want everything business-like. Fine. Fine by me. My chief was one of twenty, who ran an invisible pyramid. He ran a portion of a secret system of intelligence-gathering that ran all the way up to the 'Suits' and all the way down to the proltowns. Nobody knew his name. I knew my chief only by his code number. I was not given the code numbers of the other chiefs. Most people in the system don't even know that other chiefs exist. The Gaia government is big on compartmentalization and security. They like to keep things in separate boxes—particularly when it comes to intelligence and intelligence-gathering."

"What about the other 'Suits?'" Tom asked.

The 'Suit' laughed. "The other 'Suits' are public relations bunting," he sniggered jeeringly. "Apes. They don't have any real power. They live in fear—far greater fear—of the system than you or I. They have so much more to lose. They have their safe living quarters in the Domes, their salaries, their status, their chances for success for their children, their healthy food. But other than that, they have no power. They are very vulnerable. They are more vulnerable than

the dreaded people who live in proltown—for example." The 'Suit'
laughed again.

"The 'Suits' appear to have power," Tom replied.

"Sure," the 'Suit' said. "They appear to have power. But *only*
when it comes to media business—which is all smoke and mirrors.
They are like 'window dressing,' to quote my chief. 'They soften the
fears of the struggling souls, they allay the anxiety of the doubters,'
to quote my chief again. We're no fools. We know there are plenty
of doubters in the world. Not everyone believes in the official Gaia
religion, in spite of the fact they obviously pretend to believe. The
numbers are never lacking when it comes to finding victims, to engage in mass executions."

"What are you?" Tom asked.

"A secretary," the 'Suit' smiled. "That's all."

"Just a simple secretary?"

"That's right. A secretary. A secretary can have power. I am an
assistant—and only a second assistant at that."

"I thought you said 'Suits' have no power."

"Ordinary 'Suits.' Chiefs have to rely on their assistants. Even
second assistants. A second assistant can have a hundred times more
power than an ordinary 'Suit.'"

"Why do you talk to me so freely?" Tom asked. "I mean, why
do you talk to me so openly? Why should you trust me?"

"Who cares?" the 'Suit' shrugged. "Why not? If these extreme
militant fanatics lose, what difference does it make? If the government wins, what difference does it make? The point is, the fanatics
will lose."

"Man alive!" Tom exclaimed. "Such loyalty! You overwhelm
me! You make it sound so cynical."

"It is cynical," the 'Suit' replied breezily. "It has to be."

"What's the key to what they're doing?" Tom asked. "You're
into information retrieval...or so you say..."

"They're changing the weather. Or parts of it."

"What?" Tom asked. "The weather? Not this climate business

again!"

"The weather," the 'Suit' replied, nodding. "That's right. I don't know. There have been allusions to rainmaking. Opening the Heavens. Stuff like that. It's all pretty vague. That's all I know."

"It sounds almost like something straight out of the Bible," Tom quipped.

"Ironic, isn't it? Gaia is God. It's okay to worship God, right? But is it okay to try to be *like* God? Gaia is God, right? But what if Gaia is man-made? More importantly, what if Gaia is *only* man-made? This stuff can drive one crazy."

"I think you've inadvertently touched on something important," Tom replied. "So you don't believe in the Gaia religion?"

"The Gaia religion or the Gaia government?" the 'Suit' asked. "It's the same thing. There is no difference. Abase yourself before the idols of the state and you're considered a good Gaian. As the saying goes: illegitimate governments use religious beliefs to serve other divine purposes. And now, with the vast *technology* at their disposal..."

"Okay. So you don't believe in the government, either?"

"You'd have to be suffering from an advanced case of cretinism to believe in the government's truckload of malarkey. What a load of tripe! It's a hoax. It's all a scam."

"How is it you find yourself in this cell with me now?" Tom asked. He felt pleasantly amused to hear such ringing words of bravado being mouthed by a 'Suit,' especially as the 'Suit' was obviously enjoying the false courage of speaking while being in a safe place.

"I was captured by the underground at exactly the same time they captured an important magister," the 'Suit' replied. "You might say I was part of the baggage they picked up in their sweep. I was one of the 'Suits' they picked up with the magister."

"What's a sweep?"

"A sweep is when they're looking for somebody important."

"What happened to the magister?"

"I don't know. I was told he was returned to the government in exchange for a huge ransom, but, like I said, I don't know. I think the transaction might have involved some exchange of insurgent prisoners as well. These militant fanatics will stop at nothing to get what they want. They're *crazy*. This was not an ordinary magister they captured either. He was special."

"How long have you been here?"

"Seven or eight days."

"Seven or eight days?"

"I'm not worth anything to the government. So I don't expect to be exchanged for any ransom, large or small."

"What happened to the other 'Suits' who were captured with you?"

"I don't know. For all I know, they're dead."

The iron door creaked open and the prisoner was removed from the cell. One hour later, September entered. "This is your new cell. A cell for yourself. You have a wash basin and a commode. The plumbing is still working. Also, we will bring you books to read. Ovid, Thucydides, Shakespeare. Also Defoe. The *Adventures of Robinson Crusoe?* We thought that might be a nice touch." September smiled.

"What happened to the 'Suit'?" Tom asked.

"Wha...?" September hesitated, confused by Tom's question.

"You know. The 'Suit'. That was just in here."

"Oh, him. He's been taken care of. He's unimportant." September answered, dismissing Tom's question and the 'Suit' with that reply.

"Dante?" Tom replied, murmuring beneath his breath.

"What?"

"Dante. Could you bring me books by Dante?" Tom raised his voice.

"Dante?" September asked laughing. She clapped her hands together with delight. "I once had a cat named Dante. Right, then. Dante's *Commedia:* the *Inferno, Purgatorio, Paradiso*. All right. Ovid, Thucydides, Shakespeare, Defoe and Dante. Anything else?"

"Yes," Tom replied. He was suitably impressed by September's knowledge and awareness of writers. "*Istar's Descent into the Underworld*, the descent into Hell in Book Two of Homer's *Odyssey*, the *Tibetan Book of the Dead* and T. S. Eliot's *The Waste Land*."

"Anything else?" September replied sharply. "Such a tail-spinning descent from tragedy to pathos and finally to bathos. I'm impressed. I surely wouldn't accuse you of lack of morbidity—not by a long shot."

"Yes," Tom replied. "Something else. Something more. Comic books. *Spiderman. Batman. Superman.* Interesting to see an old comic book. To make by way of comparison, h'mmm?"

"Fine. But no comic books. I don't think we'll be able to find any, I'm afraid."

"All right," Tom replied laughing lightly, "all right. I'm in your custody."

Tom then said, "You said that the Curmudgeon is in your custody. Was that just a slip of the tongue or did you really mean it?"

"Come, let me show you tapes of the writers' executions."

"No," Tom said. He shook his head. He was adamant about receiving an answer.

"Come," September said, equally insistent. "Let me show you."

September took Tom to the screening room. She turned on the machine. Tom watched. The writers were executed one at a time. Individually, the hoods were placed over their heads, and their throats were cut.

"I remember," Tom said, "during the Eleven-Years-War, when they executed men for desertion or insubordination. They beheaded the guilty with an axe. This tape kind of reminds me of that."

"With an axe?" September asked.

"Yes."

"Why didn't they just zap them?" September asked.

"Discipline had become so bad the authorities wanted to do something dramatic to show the urgent need to save the situation.

They thought they had to do something drastic or the war would be lost. Hundreds of millions had already perished—and would the fallen victims, who had already died, would they have died in vain if the war was lost? Everything became crazy towards the end of the Eleven-Years-War. That's when we lost the last of our liberties under the old constitution."

"Anyway," September asked, "do you want to see these mass executions on Wallscreen? Five thousand people being hanged at the same time?"

"It's as Orsen told me," Tom said, dejected and absent-minded. "It's happening. I didn't believe him at the time. Have there been executions since then?"

"No," September replied. "The point of the executions was to discourage others. It failed. In fact, it not only failed, it was counterproductive. That's why you were never shown the tapes of the ex-writers' executions, you were only allowed to see the Wallscreen tapes of the mass executions, you know, the extermination of the so-called religious criminals. After seeing it, you writers would have been viewed as heroes, or as martyrs; at least, that's what the Curmudgeon surmised. You writers had a certain begrudging loyalty to each other, in spite of everything; at least, so the Curmudgeon thought."

"I don't believe you," Tom replied.

"If I showed you more evidence of the terror that the government has inflicted on us, would you believe?" September said. "If I showed you the testimony of live witnesses, people who have served the government, would you believe them?"

"No!" Tom replied. "No more lies."

"Agreed, they're *potential* liars," September replied. She stopped herself, realizing there was no point in continuing that line of discussion.

September thought of another tack. "Okay, Tom," she said coolly. "Remember when you were doing your traveling TV lecture tours? Your TV and radio talks? As an ex-writer? As a commentator?

Remember?"

"Yes."

"Remember when you used to make the statement," September said, "'The signs of the change are not to be found on Earth, but in the stars?' Not just you, but commentators all over Gaia-land have been making that statement—and others like it."

"Of course, I remember," Tom said. "I made that statement—and others like it—many times. The Gaia authorities ordered me to do it. That's how I always ended my program. I even made that statement in New York, when I was on Wallscreen... They even falsely put those lines in my book!! I don't know why they did that..."

"It's not a mystery," September said. "It's a code."

"What?" Tom asked. "A code?"

"A code," September said. "Inside the code is a countdown. We understand the code part, but the countdown? We know what's going to happen, but we don't know when. There's some sort of time-sequence involved. Eventually, what will commence is the destruction, the mass euthanasia, of the elderly. Naturally, they don't want the news to be bandied about as if it were public knowledge, stirring things up, before everything has been arranged, but they are communicating to certain people. *In code.* The Gaia State is going to kill off the elderly in the advanced parts of the world. Maybe they'll start here. Maybe somewhere else. We don't know where. But that's their plan. And it's secret. We're not sure when the program will begin. When the message is changed, we'll know more. But for now... I'll give you an example. *When the message is no longer in the stars...the code will then change...*"

"I don't believe you."

"Of course, you don't," September said, calm and unflappable. "Why should you? There's no way I can prove the existence of the code to you. Let's drop it, shall we? But it's the truth. It's the absolute truth. And the mass euthanasia of the elderly is going to happen. *In the advanced parts of the world.* Okay. I have a better idea. Let's try another tack. If I showed you the Curmudgeon, might you believe what he has to say? Would that make a difference?"

"It might," Tom said, blinking. He was unnerved. In Tom's mind, September's credibility had not been established at all. But in the case of the Curmudgeon—mentioning the Curmudgeon—September had hit a soft spot.

"I wish you would trust me," September said at last. "You're asking me to show you God, when all I can do is show you angels and devils—no more. I can't show you Lucifer. It's not like in Dante's book. And I'm getting a little annoyed at all this precious time you're wasting, too."

"You're talking about God!" Tom said. "I don't believe it. You believe in Gaia?" Tom asked September pointblank.

"What?"

"You know!" Tom said. "Gaia! The concept of the Earth being a living thing. The idea of the Earth being a divine manifestation of something sacred—itself being a manifestation of the spiritual, of the other-worldly. Do you believe in that?"

"Once," September replied calmly, "I did. *A long time ago.* I believed in Gaia. As a little girl, I believed in Gaia with all my heart. I was a secret admirer of the concept. I believed in it when it was practiced by those who lived in the underground, those outside acceptable society."

"What do you believe in now?" Tom asked.

"I don't know," September said.

"That's your religion, then?" Tom asked.

"Yes," September laughed. "How can a non-religion be a religion? If you insist on calling it that, I won't argue with you then, it's my religion. It doesn't matter. You can call it anything you wish. Over twenty-three years ago, I read your book, *Expressions Without Illusions.* I was sixteen at the time. It left a powerful impression on me. By the way, I read your other two books also. I waded through that thousand-page morass of material—*Memories From Nowhere* and *Requiem to Illusion.* I've read them during the last four weeks. All one thousand pages. Aren't you the least bit impressed?" September smiled warmly at Tom. "Tell me the truth." She smiled again. "Aren't you?"

"Yes, I am," Tom replied. "I feel humbled. What do you think of the books?"

September laughed. "Your books? They're obscurantist. I don't understand your philosophy, in fact, I don't think you have a philosophy."

Tom laughed. "What a marvelous critique! Admittedly, the first two were nothing more than compost heaps and fertilizer bins. The last one—*that* bloomed into a garden!"

Tom looked down. "I predict the weather. Or rather: *I used to be able to predict the weather.* That always has been the most important thing in my life. That's been more important to me—more important than writing."

"Yes," September replied slowly, "I can tell."

"You can?" Tom asked, incredulous.

"It's a talent you had. You talked about it in great detail. Especially in your second book, *Requiem to Illusion*. The character Samson..."

"Oh, yes," Tom replied, "Samson. The main character. He could predict the weather, too. He could predict it exactly like I could—in real life."

"What happened to your ability?"

"I can't do it anymore," Tom said, shrugging his shoulders, "that's all."

"It's been eleven years, right?" September asked. "Since you were able to predict the weather?"

"Yes," Tom said. "How did you know?" Tom looked startled and surprised. "How did you know how long it's been?"

"I do," September replied. Tom noticed that the expression on September's face had altered. She had a graceful look. "Am I right? Tell me the truth." September gave Tom a reassuring smile.

September no longer looked at Tom as a captive or as an enemy but as a potential friend. The books had caused September to admire

Tom. But was there more to it than that?

Tom could tell that she had genuinely enjoyed reading the books, but why? The books were boring and confused in many ways. And she was right: the books were obscurantist, especially the first two. September repeated the question.

"Yes," Tom replied quickly. "How did you know?" he asked, simultaneously excited and exasperated.

It wasn't useful for him to pretend he wasn't attracted to her anymore. Or vice versa. September was also attracted to him.

"There are reasons why," September replied circumspectly. She studied Tom's face. Watchfully, she looked for a note of credit, acknowledgment, recognition, a glimmer of hope; a nod of recognition. But Tom's face was expressionless.

"Those reasons have nothing to do with your ability to predict the weather, there hasn't been a thunder or lightning storm in this hemisphere for eleven years, Tom," September said at last. "A pre-Orion experiment was conducted. They artificially generated a hundred thousand lightning storms simultaneously worldwide to replenish the ozone layer in one quick effort. The whole experiment backfired. They haven't told anyone about it; naturally, they've kept it secret. They tried to improve the weather. They did succeed, in a sense, at least for us in North America, and parts of Northern Europe, but in the process they screwed up the rest of the world even worse than before. Hundreds of millions of people south of the Tropic of Cancer have perished over the last eleven years due to exposure to sun poisoning. There are plenty of lightning and thunder storms *elsewhere*. They changed the calendar, so when did it happen?"

"How did you know about all that?" Tom asked.

"Know about all what?" September replied sarcastically. "My husband had a hand in conducting the experiment, even though he had been against it from the start. He thought it was too risky. Tinkering with the climate was to him like opening Pandora's box. They forced him to conduct the project. He was largely responsible for the pre-Orion experiment. To his credit, he was also responsible for the creation of other things, fusion power plants, solar buses, the oil-coal-fossil fuel conversion project. Also, he was responsible for organizing the energy and power sharing program with Europe and Asia, before the program crashed at the outbreak of the Eleven-Years-War. He behaved more like a practical engineer than a theoretician. That was true all of his life. Well, he's dead."

"Your husband?" Tom asked.

"Yes," September said. "The late great scientist, Regis Snow."

"You were married to Regis Snow?" Tom asked. He was dumbstruck. "Regis Snow was the number one scientist. He was probably *the* premiere scientist in the world."

"Yes," September replied. "They killed him two years ago. Executed privately. There are no tapes of his death. What was his crime? He stopped cooperating. That's all. He couldn't stomach it anymore."

"You miss him?"

"'Course I do," September said.

"So your husband was executed?" Tom asked.

"Yes," September said. "The authorities learned quickly. I thought you had believed we were all crazed nut-cases. Militant fanatics, huh? Do you still think so?"

"When may we talk again?" Tom asked in an urgent, eager voice.

"Would you like to?" September asked. She was smiling at him. There was a look of genuine warmth and enthusiasm radiating from her face.

"Yes," Tom replied. "I wish we could speak again."

"I don't know exactly when that would be," September replied. "Perhaps we may speak again, when things are clearer—when things have settled down. I don't know when that will be, however."

Chapter Nine

A PROTON BOMB STRUCK overhead. A huge explosion came thundering through the cell-block. The aftermath of that explosion shattered the otherwise still, languid air of the cell-block.

The bomb had apparently scored a direct hit on the outer lip of the underground. It struck the exact spot that could cause irreparable damage. After the first explosion, there was a second explosion, the last one felt more conclusively than the first.

The second explosion apparently ignited with highly flammable material, causing a spiraling down chain reaction of charges that resonated through the various structures of the underground, burrowing deeper and deeper inside with each successive charge.

Tom awoke from a deep sleep. After the first explosion, Tom felt the impact of the second explosion.

In spite of the shock-waves traveling like currents of energy through the air, he was struggling to regain consciousness. He wasn't just groggy, his head ached powerfully. He felt as if his cranium had been struck by a hammer. With all the external mayhem, the struggle to raise his body and regain his feet were difficult. He felt literally pinned to his bed by an imaginary force.

Tom's body then instinctively recoiled into a ball-like figure. Tom tucked his chin in, drew his knees up to his chin, then, in so far as it was possible, covered his face, head and neck with his compressed arms and hands.

Viewed from the opposite side of the room, it would have seemed impossible for Tom to have made his body more compact— or tightly wound.

Tom exerted all effort to get his legs free—*to shoot his feet out.* He couldn't manage it. He struggled with the act of freeing himself. His eyes opened. His eyes were bulging with panic.

In the jangle of sensations, the cell was no longer dark. A glare of light shone through the doorway window casting a whirling kaleidoscope of dazzling light across the wall. Tom heard rumbling noises, popping sounds, like the sound of metal parts exploding under immense pressure.

Tom thought he could detect the smell of overheated generators. He looked out of his cell. People were running to and fro in a state of panic.

A young girl hurriedly discarded her walkie-talkie, throwing it on the floor. She retreated in a state of disarray. He heard her scream: "Acid, acid!"

Within minutes, there was an acrid smell seeping in through the crack underneath the door of Tom's cell.

Out of nowhere, September burst into the room. "We've got to get out. Come."

"What?"

"Come immediately!" September said, gesturing with her hand. "We have to get out of here!" September's face was wild, animated and heated. "Come! Now!"

Tom hesitated. He glared at September with a look of fear. His mind raced. He was startled and awakened from such a deep sleep, he was still groping with trying to comprehend the nature of the danger surrounding him. Added to that, he felt like he was suffering from the biggest headache he thought imaginable. His head felt like it had metamorphosed into a humongous pain-inflicting machine.

"Come quickly!" September gestured frantically. "Follow me. There's no time to lose. There is only one way out of this place. All of our underground organizations in the cities on the eastern sea-board have been destroyed. *We're the last ones left.* We're still strong in the American West and Europe, but we're weak in the center. The rebellion is going to retreat to its rural bases. Don't you see? It's all gone."

Tom hesitated.

"There's only one way out of this place," September continued in a frantic voice. "Are you going to sit and gape at me? I came back here for you, you bastard! Understand? I...came...back...*here. For you!*"

Slowly, dimly, reality was breaking through. Tom nodded his head hesitantly, then more resolutely. "Right, then," he muttered.

Tom took September's hand. They exited the cell. They burrowed their way out through the debris. In the darkness, they climbed a hidden stairway, a stairway that only September seemed to know existed.

"How can you see where you're going?" Tom asked. His throat was choking with fumes. The stairwell was engulfed in total darkness.

"I can't see, either," September confessed. "I've only been able to feel my way along...by touch. I've felt my way along this path forty, fifty, times with my eyes closed, just practicing. In my sleep, in my dreams, I've been expecting this to happen. I've been prepared. I even planted these oxygen masks and equipment along the way—just in case."

September handed Tom a scuba diving tank and mask. "Put it on. You'll need it until we get to the surface. There we'll find fresh air."

"Do you have one on?" Tom asked, placing the mask on, but waiting to place the air inhaler into his mouth. He could see nothing.

"Yes," September replied. "I just put my mask on. You can't see anything in this darkness."

"We're going to die," Tom said. As Tom spoke, he was neither upset nor even perturbed; he just said it as a normal statement of fact.

"We're not going to die," September replied calmly. "Three and half stories more, and we'll be out of here. I have a plan. I've been planning this escape *for weeks.*"

"Why are you doing this for me?" Tom asked. "You've only known me for a short time. All this time, you've referred to me as your captive. Why are you doing this?"

"I'll explain later," September replied. "Too difficult to talk now. Start breathing with your air inhaler. Put it on, Tom! Start breathing with it! Now!"

Tom did as he was told.

They climbed. They took each step with extreme care. They emerged from the broken and twisted wreckage of the collapsed stairway only minutes later. By the time they reached the top, the fires had spread throughout the lower vault and the lower floors were collapsing beneath them. They made it out just in the nick of time. Like the gaping hole of a super-bomb crater, the entire vault structure lay like a shallow bowl beside them. They sat on the pavement, staring down at the two-hundred-foot-wide crater, five stories deep; contemplating the mystery of their miraculous escape. If they had delayed a moment longer, they would have been crushed in the rubble.

When they emerged on the surface, the city around them was consumed in fire. The buildings had been torched by a raging fury. For an instant, September stared at the scene of destruction and carnage that surrounded them as if she herself were not present or in danger. She was captivated by the strangest of things: by the sheer horror of it all.

"A half-million people who once lived here, in this No-Go Zone, are now dead," September said with finality.

They were witnesses of a stupendous spectacle. A strip of New York, 450 yards wide and a mile-long, was burning. Towards the center of the island smoke and sparks from all of the fires were building up a wall of fire that was sweeping towards them and the river. There was a hiss and roar from the conflagration, a rushing, deafening noise in their ears. The roar they heard from behind and both sides was a cross between the sound of a tornado and a freight train rushing out of a tunnel at ninety miles per hour. They saw that previous fires had burned with a heat so intense that the bodies of their victims lay fused in clumps of ten or fifteen, their remains less like spores of burning charcoal, or even heaps of ashes, than like shadows cast against the burned buildings and paving stones. The fire was so intense, overwhelming, it incinerated everything in its path. Even then, Tom observed a completely preserved boot (everything else was destroyed), lying directly in his path. For the next ten years, whenever Tom saw a discarded boot lying in the roadside gutter, he would always wonder if there was a foot inside it.

They ran. They ran as fast as they could. Two huge fireballs raced down streets on either side, to left and right, fifty yards from them, singeing their hair. Again, it was a miracle of fate the fire did not consume them. A few yards to the left or right, and they would have been burnt to a crisp. If they hadn't had scuba diving masks and oxygen tanks on, they would have died of smoke inhalation as the smoke filled much of the breathable air around them. Overhead, they were surrounded by a swarm of helioplane lationships, firing with pinpoint accuracy. The laserships were aiming spotlights in all directions in the darkened sky.

Fortunately, they were only two and a half blocks from the East River. Thank God, Tom thought, for having engaged daily in his strenuous exercise routine. As a result, he was now in top form, in superb physical condition. He ran faster than he thought could have been possible.

Tom recognized the East River as it appeared in front of them. He recalled how the river looked from his childhood memories, or maybe it was a memory of the river from when he was a young man. When they came to the river, the two of them jumped in. Again, they were lucky because most of the river was in a sea of flames. They managed to jump into one small part of the river that, miraculously, was not coated with burning fuel and oil ignited by the firestorm.

Coming up for air, Tom tore off his mask. He looked around at the surrounding flames.

Once they cooled down, which didn't take long, the two got out of the river, climbing out on the shore—next to a pier. Already, the helioplane laserships had spotted them. They knew they had no time to lose before they were caught in the crosshairs of a laser gun.

Both of them knew they had been extremely lucky. Until now, in fact, they realized their luck had been nothing short of miraculous. Many times over—in his cell, in the vault, on the burning streets, in the river, they should have been killed, yet they had survived.

Tom was the first to see it. Although he instinctively perceived that September knew all along that it was there, probably deliberately, as she had planned, it appeared to him a veritable godsend. It was a helioplane. It was parked on a skypad, right next to the river, only a few hundred feet away.

Tom suddenly realized, then, too—from a long-lost childhood memory—they couldn't have been standing more than a few miles from the site of the old United Nations building, destroyed at the beginning of the Eleven-Years-War.

Soaking wet, the two of them, September and Tom, were indeed standing on one bank of the East River. Tom knew now, more or less, where he was, even if he had not been in the city for twenty years.

They ran. September didn't even have to explain. They climbed into the helioplane. It was empty. It was unlocked. They highjacked it. September overrided the control panel, then she started the engine. Tom was in the co-pilot's seat.

"I've been flying these helioplanes since I was eight years old," September said. "I'm good. I've got forty-eight blue-bonded ribbons to prove it."

"Well, you better be good," Tom said, "if we're going to get out of this mess. Especially the way these laserships are hovering ready to strike. It's going to take nothing less than an Amelia Earhart to get us out of here."

The helioplane took off. Immediately, September made a surprise move. She jockeyed the helioplane into horizontal mode. Immediately after takeoff, they had to pass through a thick wall of smoke of burning oil and rubber. Seconds after that, the helioplane accelerated to a fantastic speed of 300 miles per hour. September was proving herself a genius of a pilot.

They crossed not over, but *under*, the damaged Queensboro bridge, and flew the length of Roosevelt Island, just twelve feet above the surface. They flew under several more bridges.

Tom felt like he was at the Coney Island amusement park, fifty-five years before, riding on a roller coaster. "Wheee!" he shouted breathlessly.

"I don't think you're supposed to be able to do these maneuvers," Tom said, gasping for air. "At least, not at this speed. You must be doing one hundred and eighty miles per hour."

"I'm doing well over 300," September said nonchalantly. "I've fooled them for the moment. But they're going to catch on to what I'm doing, and when they do, we're going to be dead. We have to do something different. We have to do something extraordinary."

"Something extraordinary?" Tom sighed frightened. "What the hell is this anyway?"

Suddenly, after coming to a near stop, September touched a lever, and the helioplane shot up vertically, shooting straight up into the air. Tom's kidneys fell to his feet. Within twenty-nine seconds, the helioplane had climbed to an altitude of 6,000 feet. Below them, just eight hundred feet below, a lasership was gaining on them. "These short-range laserships can climb faster than we can," September said. "Can't help that."

They climbed higher. Slowly, the lasership started to close in on the helioplane. It was only a couple of hundred feet below them now. The lasership shot its laser, but missed the helioplane, although the shot was very close, crossing her beam. At 18,000 feet, the laser-ship started to lose its rudder.

"You're not supposed to do this," Tom said, turning to September. The helioplane started to shake. "Aren't you flying too high in vertical?"

"Maybe," September replied, "but if we don't do this, we're as good as dead. We're only supposed to go up to 12,000 feet in vertical. Most of the time, helioplanes never fly higher than 6,000 feet in vertical. This ship is specially equipped to go to 20,000 feet."

"20,000 feet!" Tom shouted. "Oh my God. We're going to die!"

At 20,000 feet, the jet-stream began to affect the short-range lasership, and its wings started to vibrate. The pilot engaged the lasership's stabilizers, but this had no effect, since the stabilizers had not been designed to function at a high altitude. Fortunately, the jet-stream did not cause problems with the flight of September's helioplane.

"It's like playing chicken," September said. "A short-range la-sership can go up to 12,000 feet, in vertical, without crashing, but what this lasership pilot is trying to figure out is why we didn't crash at 12,000 feet, or at 16,000 feet—which we should have. Now he's climbed to 20,000 feet. He's in trouble."

"Why *haven't* we crashed yet?"

"Luck," September said.

Suddenly, the attacking short-range lasership started to floun-der. It spun out of control. Within seconds, it plunged into the darkened waters.

"We're not out of this yet," September said, "not by a long shot. The long-range helioplanes will track us where we are now. There's only one way we're going to be able to get them off our tail."

"How's that?"

"Flying into a Class Omega hurricane."

"A what?"

"You heard me."

"A Class Omega hurricane?" Tom asked. "*Jesus H. Christ.* Will it work? What's a Class Omega hurricane? And how far do we have to travel to find one?"

"That's what I like about you, Tom. You're thinking fast. Nobody's going to follow us through a hurricane," September said, checking her viewfinder. "Looks like one is forming east of Cape Hatteras right now. Coming this way. A Class Omega hurricane? Boy, you don't know anything, do you? Remember when I told you that they've been messing with the weather? Well, these Omega 'canes form about once a week, hundreds of miles off the coast. A hurricane is just a heat engine, running on the temperature difference between the warm tropical ocean and the cold stratosphere. Given a large enough area of overheated ocean, the simple application of standard meteorological equations leads to the prediction of a hurricane. They occur all the time now on the high seas."

"But I've never heard of a Class Omega hurricane before," Tom said.

"They're brand new," September said. "Before the twenty-first century, there'd never even been a Class Alpha hurricane."

"Why do they occur now?"

"Before, in nature, even a Class Alpha hurricane would have been next to impossible. The only force that could have spawned one would be the impact of a large meteor, half a mile across, crashing into the ocean, or by a huge volcanic eruption, under a shallow sea, warming the ocean surface to 120 degrees Fahrenheit. A Class Omega hurricane's winds can flow at up to 500 miles per hour. Wind speeds can even reach supersonic. Updrafts roar at 150 miles per hour to altitudes of 150,000 feet, three times that of a normal hurricane."

"Won't it kill us?"

"The good news is this. A Class Omega hurricane never touches land. Although the storm is extremely powerful, it is concentrated and can be only fifteen miles wide or so, smaller than a regular hur-

ricane. It's just our luck that one's forming right now. If we fly at
Mach Two, we'll penetrate it in sixteen minutes, which, by my calculations, if we're lucky, will give us just enough time before they can
intercept. They don't know where to look for us right now—we're
too high—but when we descend to 12,000 feet, they'll be waiting
for us."

"Why can't we fly away from them at this altitude?" Tom asked.
"Since we're already up here, anyway?"

"Are you crazy?" September shouted. "We can't go to horizontal at this altitude! We'll crash for certain! Every second we stay up
here is dangerous. There's not enough dense air resistance up here,
we'll lose our rudder. It's a miracle we haven't already lost it. You
know, after all these years, the scientists still can't explain how air
resistance works on helioplanes and laserships when in vertical. The
only chance left us is to drop to 12,000 feet, go into horizontal, and
pray. Going into horizontal at 12,000 feet is taking an enormous
risk, and we've already taken a lot of them. Going into horizontal
shouldn't ordinarily be attempted above 8,000 feet; most of the time
it's not tried above 6,000. We have no choice. All we can do is hope.
We'll have to start out slowly, but if we're lucky, we'll still have time
to beat them to the hurricane."

"Then what?"

"We'll fly right through it. Like greased lightning. Hope it
hasn't formed to killer stage before we get there. Fly through the
eye, as it were. Once we're through to the other side, we're free.
Sort of."

"Sort of?" Tom asked. He was about ready to faint.

"Then we'll have to fly twelve feet above the surface of the ocean
so we won't get picked up by satellite detectors. They wouldn't believe us crazy enough, or desperate enough, to do that."

"That's how it's supposed to work?" Tom asked.

"I don't know," September laughed gleefully. "But I know
that's how it's supposed to work in theory. Cheer up. What are you
worried about? We shouldn't have accomplished what we've already

accomplished anyway. You worry too much. I should have left you back in the bank-vault cell."

They penetrated the Class Omega hurricane and flew right through it. Tom felt as though he was surrounded by sheets of white light and translucent glass that enveloped the helioplane. The sound was so shrill for the precious seconds they flew through the high density winds near the concave of the storm, just before and after the dead center of the storm, (dead center was indescribably calm—`the eye of the 'cane'); that Tom thought it was going to destroy his hearing.

Tom felt as though there was a strange sense of propulsion and, ironically, an eerie sense of restraint, that was pulling and tugging at the plane, at the same time, through the inner workings of the 'cane.

It happened so quickly. The experience was indescribable.

At a speed of 1200 miles per hour, it took less than twenty-five seconds to pass through the 'cane.

"Was that a mystery?" Tom asked. Their survival was due to fabulous luck.

"Have you ever done this before?" Tom then asked breathlessly, when they emerged on the other side, miraculously unscathed. "God, we passed through it so quickly!"

"I don't think anyone has ever done this before *in history,*" September replied, equally breathless. "Our timing was perfect. The Class Omega hurricane was in stage one. My husband used to study this phenomenon. Just one minute later, give or take, and we would have been dead. Thank God the `cane was only fourteen-and -a-half-miles across in circumference."

September screamed: "Hoo-wie! Yes-sir-ee! We made it!"

Tom could tell that after all the pressure, September was relieved, too.

"They can't follow us now," September said. "It's too late. The Class Omega hurricane has already gone into stage two, that is, killer stage. We're safe."

They hovered in place—at a stand-still—for forty minutes.

"We'll sit perfectly still," September said. "Absolutely still. They won't bother us. They don't know where we are!"

"Are we safe now?" Tom asked.

"Sort of," September said. "Well what we must do next will be *absolutely*, extremely dangerous."

"Oh great," Tom smirked. "Then again, why break precedence!"

"If we don't hit a normal storm, a water snag, a Class Omega hurricane, or a weather spike, we'll make it," September said. "We're going to have to fly so low they could harpoon us, but they won't be able to find us! They won't be able to see us on old-fashioned sonar or radar, but more importantly, they won't be able to detect us on satellite surveillance. Also, they'll expect us to be racing at top speed. We'll just mosey along at 120 miles per hour—they won't be able to distinguish us from primitive cargo planes or lost pirate frigates junking out from the Caribbean. In any event, they won't know where to look for us. We also have something else going for us. As far as I know, it's never been done before. For a while, we will be the last emissaries coming from the New World Anti-Gaia rebellion to visit the Old World Anti-Gaia rebellion. Isn't that exciting?"

"Thrilling," Tom said.

The rest of the trip across the Atlantic was somewhat routine, albeit dangerous. They looked down at the waves and swells flowing across the mid-Atlantic ocean, the sea-waves undulating below them. There was an occasional whitecap, glinting in the bright air. The sea was just twelve feet below. The pull and shift of the water was mesmerizing. When the helioplane slowly accelerated from ten miles per hour to sixty miles per hour, the water below seemed so close they could almost touch it, a huge swell occasionally coming within six feet of the bottom of the helioplane. It had a hypnotic effect on them. Then when they reached 120 miles per hour, everything moved fast forward. They flew twelve feet above the surface, just skimming the surface, avoiding the Azores and the Cape Verde

Islands, landing safely in Northern France, not far from Flanders, thirty-two hours later.

"You know it took Charles Lindbergh about the same length of time to cover the same distance, 135 years ago," September said.

They landed the helioplane and stepped on French soil. September surveyed the open field where they landed. The ground had been plowed, but the furrows lay bare.

"Hush," September said.

Tom regarded September. September closed her eyes. "What?" Tom asked.

As if in a trance, September intoned: "We are forty miles from the site of the battle of Agincourt, 1415; eighty miles from that of the battle of Waterloo, 1815; one hundred miles from that of the battle of Verdun, 1916; 500 miles from that of the battle of Wallensia, 2028. Agincourt, Waterloo, Verdun, Wallensia—those were the four coordinates I was given. The nineteenth century did not begin with the year 1800; it began with the end of the Napoleonic Wars in 1815. The twentieth century did not begin with the year 1900; it began at the beginning of the First European War in 1914. The twenty-first century did not begin with the year 2000, it began in 2040 when all the selfish vanities of man were replaced by the logic of the environment."

Tom was mystified by September. He marveled at her epiphany: her grandparents had taught her the 'old' history, and they had taught her well.

Silence surrounded them.

"I mention it," September said, "precisely *because* nobody cares. The First European War was the first war in which a whole generation of men on one continent were decimated—slaughtered—when one in three between the ages of eighteen and twenty-seven did not survive. The same happened in the Eleven-Years-War."

For a moment, September found herself sounding strangely like an over-earnest, over-intense schoolgirl. Why was she arguing with this widely known old man, she wondered to herself.

"Maybe the human race is dying out." Tom looked at September with a mellow expression.

"The Curmudgeon told me about it," September said as an afterthought.

"Told you about what?"

"Told me about your history. He told me about your four brothers perishing in the war. He told me about how you were the only one who managed to survive."

"Yes," Tom said. "The guns would roar. We would regroup and re-deploy. We would get mowed down. Like blades of grass. They'd use laser guns. Then it was our turn. They'd regroup and re-deploy. They'd get mowed down. The weapons technology was far too sophisticated and advanced for what we could do with it, with what we were capable of, in our primitive hands. The weapons technology dominated everything. We slaughtered each other. Both sides lost. We trounced ourselves into a permanent stalemate. It was an eleven-year-long meat-grinder. By the way, why are we here?" Tom said, suddenly looking up, trying to examine his immediate surroundings.

"What?" September asked.

"I mean," Tom said, laughing, "why are we at this exact location? Here in Europe? Back to Earth? Let's get back to reality."

"In the last radio message I received on the helioplane before our desperate escape, I was given coordinates determined by the exact distance in miles from the four battlefields I mentioned—in code, to find the intersecting point at which we were supposed to rendezvous. Central control of the Anti-Gaia rebellion doesn't like to waste time, it was a quick-snap decision. We've been called upon to perform a secret mission. That's why we weren't directly given the exact spot. It's very secret. We're here to pick up a prisoner."

September began to hum to herself.

"Maybe this terrible world," September said, "will make room—accommodate you—maybe make space for you." She looked endearingly at Tom. *"H'mmm?"*

Tom looked at September with a sense of unease and uncertainty, but also with expectation.

September continued, "For someone such as you—so measly—so stark and skeptical, so knowing and loving, such a trusting and caring soul, so endearingly small...such as you are...my love?" September threw Tom a darting stare. "A recalcitrant, but with the look in his eyes, combining irony and cynicism with human compassion."

Tom shuttered. He sucked on his teeth.

"You call me...*love?*" Tom gasped. "Love? You refer to me by using an appellation of affection. Am I not a dry stick to you? Am I not a bag of bones?"

"No," September replied, "you're not. You mean more than that to me. A lot more."

"More than that? How much more?" Tom asked. "Let us be serious about this for a moment."

"Just more," September replied. "More than a dry stick. More than a bag of bones. *Why do you say that?* I am serious."

"Just more?" Tom smiled. *"I am* a dry stick. I am a bag of bones. Worse than that. You're toying with me, aren't you? Oh please, madam. For everything I've seen in this world, it has made my eyes grow weary and it has caused my heart to shrivel like a pomegranate exposed under the merciless rays of an undying sun."

"Yes, I am toying with you," September replied after a pause. "And you're toying with *me*. Enough said. Everything I said though—I've meant—*everything*. You can trust me. But consider this and consider it well. For others to love you, you must first love yourself."

Chapter Ten

THEY WAITED TWENTY-FOUR HOURS before their contacts arrived. This was a benefit to both because they had an opportunity to obtain a bit of shuteye—which they both achingly desired. Having not slept in over twenty hours, they were not just exhausted, they were bone tired.

Tom realized September was much accustomed to the art of waiting. In a strange way, he took this as a promising sign. Whether in a state of danger—or in a crisis—or in a throng of calm and order, September always had a strength and confidence about her. Tom took great solace in September's steadfastness.

Not far from where September lay down to rest, Tom lay himself on the ground.

He put his hands behind his neck to form a pillow. Having taken a relaxed position beneath the shade of an apple tree, he fell into a deep, long sleep. Oh how much Tom loved sleep. Blissful slumber was the greatest tonic of all for him.

Twelve hours later they both awoke, rested and refreshed. They spent the remainder of time putting a few things in order, but otherwise, they lolled around a hastily constructed camp, enjoying themselves.

Ten hours later, the prisoner was brought in with his hands tied between his back. The partisans were disguised as farmers, wearing rough country clothing. The magister was also disguised as a farmer, but Tom could see that he was anything but.

The captured magister was wearing a broad loose farmer's straw hat, and his face carried a broad smile of connivance. He was a big, old man with a swarthy complexion and a large face that could have belonged to a rural constable. Impressive from his sharp nose up, his beady eyes blazed back. But he appeared corrupt from the mouth down, with his double chin folding over an oversized bull neck.

"You know what to do with him," the leader of the partisans said in a hardened voice. The partisan leader had a rough look, a look Tom had seen before. His tired, grimy, grizzled face had an expression that was brimming with sour, austere determination. The look said: *Nothing was going to go wrong on my watch.*

"Yes," September replied. "We're planning to take him to field headquarters in the Pyrenees."

As they handed the prisoner over to September, they simply looked at her with a quick nod of recognition. The leader of the group, speaking on behalf of the others, shook his fist mightily in the prisoner's face. "We want to kill you. But we follow orders." He turned to the September and said, "That's the only thing that saved his measly, worthless ass."

Having delivered the 'goods,' the band of partisans left as quickly as they came.

September began to interrogate the prisoner immediately.

The magister cracked a smile. He was almost smirking as he gave his readied answers. They talked for about twenty-five minutes. September asked him about the Gaia forces military strength, about basic economics, and about the trade situation. Finally, September came to the point.

"We want to know why you are so willing to talk to us," September said.

"The gig is up, that's why," the magister replied laughing. He was in a stoic, philosophical mood. "The reason why I'm willing to talk to you should be very obvious to you."

"What do you mean?" September said.

"No exchange of prisoners."

"Oh," September replied. "That does make everything different, doesn't it?" September smiled without smirking.

"Look," the magister said in a quiet voice, "I'll tell you everything you want to know." Suddenly, for the first time, it looked like he was pleading for his life—as if suddenly, he realized what was in store for him if he didn't cooperate. "During the Eleven-Years-War, the `Suits' tried to control everything at the top with *fake* nationalism. At least, they tried to do *that* in Europe," he said in a hurried, nervous tone. "Divide and conquer. It worked in the last century, here and there, on occasion, but it didn't work this time—the destruction was too widespread, the breakdown of order was too profound. The `Suits' then tried to set up a secret government. In China, they revived an old communist ideology as a form of quasi-nationalist ideology, as a sort of national religion, and that worked for a while *there*. But in Europe, the `Suits' tried to set up a `new world order.' It didn't work. The Europeans were too cynical for that. Even before the Third European War—*ahem, before they called it the Eleven-Years-War,* less than half of the population of Northern Europe actually believed in God, at least in a nominal sense. Did the `Suits' expect them to believe in a hoax called `the new world order?' In America, the `Suits' then tried to set up a Christian theocracy, with the Old Testament as a constitution, building on the old fundamentalist Christian coalition, which had a hundred times better chance of succeeding than a `new world order' in Europe ever did." The magister burst out laughing here, but more from nervousness than natural spontaneity.

"It could have worked. In fact, it should have. Ninety percent of the population of America fervently believed in some sort of notion of God, especially after the Ozone Layer eco-catastrophe was couched in terms of a wrathful God pointing his angry finger at his ever-erring people, but even a religious cover for blind naked power wasn't enough to hide all the materialism and greed. The magisters enjoyed the lavish tastes of a cocooned world. They lived narcissistically in air-conditioned Domes. They traveled in air-conditioned helioplanes. They were protected by their own goon squads, death squads, assassination squads. You name it, they had it. They were surrounded by a mountain of mobile phones and parabolic antennae. They were catered to by armies of secretaries and chauffeurs. They lived in a different country. What difference did *that* make? These changes had been going on silently for almost three generations already, largely unnoticed, undetected. They had their own schools—back when schools still existed—their own beach resorts, their own mountain resorts, their own banks, their own information networks, their own police force, their own security system. They were a secret nation, within a nation, long before they even started to build their goddamn Domes."

"Doesn't this sound familiar to you?" Tom asked September, smiling a retching saccharine smile.

"A Civilization built on Mammon," the magister continued, "couldn't justify itself in terms of an old-time religion that reminded too many people of the old antiquated ways that had been lost, gone forever. But they tried. Oh, they tried! It almost succeeded. But a brand-new religion, based on Gaia—the idea of the whole planet being a living organism—now that was the key to putting old wine into new bottles. We had old men dressed in long flowing robes, representing the seasons—sort of a cross between Catholic priests and the ancient Celtic druid cults, celebrating religious festivals based on nature's cycles of death and rebirth. It was so successful that the `Suits' tried the same thing in Europe, but the idea didn't catch on. What do you want from me?!" the magister screamed. He was literally burping with nervousness, he was pleading: `Don't kill me.' He knew he was in deep trouble; his life imperiled.

"But the Gaia religion was never good enough," September protested, ignoring his nervous display. "It was not sufficient."

"Right," the magister continued. "Right. It needed something more. I'll explain."

"More than just smoke and mirrors and men dressed up like a

cross between Catholic priests and the ancient Celtic cult of the druids, that's for sure," September said. "Something more. Something that was material."

"Right again," the magister replied, nodding with approval. "Something material." The magister nodded his head with eager excitement. "Don't kill me," the magister said in a low, matter-of-fact voice. "Please don't."

September turned her back. She continued speaking, "But if the fusion plants and solar panels and the rest, if the great efficiency and restoration recycling plants weren't enough, what else was required?" September asked. "The Earth was renewable. When the population crashed, we were already on the road to recovery—even if it takes seven or eight generations to do it. Even if it takes 500 years to do it."

The magister laughed. "The destruction of the ozone layer was the one thing—the only thing—that scared everyone to death. Scared them more than the war. Scared them more than the warming trends of the greenhouse effect. Scared them more than the huge virus epidemics. The people screamed: `Give us good weather! Protect us from the sun's poisonous rays! Do these things and then you can do anything you want with us!' When four people die, how easy it is to accept the death of twelve. When fourteen million die, how easy it is to accept the death of one hundred and fourteen million. It's one easy slide downhill. See? After the first person dies, how easy it is to accept the death of the next four billion. Or how about just one billion? Or just two billion? That's the price you pay, for the cause of maintaining social hygiene. What difference does it make? The numbers of dead are abstractions anyway, especially if they occur out of sight—especially if they take place with smoke and mirrors, on Wallscreen. Quantify things beyond a certain level of tribal understanding, and for the ordinary person, it doesn't compute, it doesn't make sense any more. Everything is easy to manipulate. Especially after you've crossed a certain level of abstraction. It's mathematical. Have you had the experience of seeing the phenomenon of a `Suit' watching a mass execution on Wallscreen while he is at the same time carefully eating his dinner?"

"So what was the one thing" September asked, "that was needed to make the Gaia religion work? Not smoke and mirrors. Not crosses between druid lords and Catholic priests. How about crosses? That would have been a novel idea. Alas, not even a change in the calendar, either." She could not hide her contempt and disdain for the man and his office.

"Climate," the magister said. "The key!" He nodded his head, trying hard to please. "Give people good weather, a healthy climate, plentiful water, so that their crops grow, and you've given them everything. People just want to eat. They don't want to admit it, but that's the truth. Give them that, and they don't care if you take all else away from them. Give them the illusion of freedom—Wallscreen—and they'll accept the reality of freedom's destruction. Provided you do it off-camera, of course. And you don't go too far. Provided you give them what they want in their bellies—by that, I mean all of their sense organs. In other words, *what they really want.* Take away the `Suit' government's power to regulate the environment, control the weather, computerize the climate, and you take away the power of the official Gaia religion itself."

"But why are you telling me this?" September asked.

"I don't have anything more to lose now, do I?" the magister asked. "Am I right?"

"Right," September said.

The magister displayed a wide smile. "The propaganda machine of the Gaia religion is simple and direct." The magister knew that this was his last chance. Like a drowning man grasping at a straw, the magister tried a new approach. He launched into a new spiel, without really thinking. "The government is not interested in providing information and facts. It is only interested in providing emotion and entertainment."

"We know that," September interrupted impatiently. "We've known *that* all along. Are you going to tell us something we don't know?"

"We use Wallscreen to keep people off the streets. It's cheap. It's inexpensive. It's a shoddy form of entertainment to get people to stop thinking about their problems, stop thinking about the problems of their families, stop thinking about the problems of their homes. The government viciously opposes any display of politics or philosophy on Wallscreen because it has learned its lesson well. Using all the wonders of technology, at first, it tried to produce new propaganda films to deify the new state, but that was bad for business. Worse than that, it was boring. Even when done by the best talent, by the best pros that money could buy, it was lousy, it stunk; regardless of the intended effect, it either put people to sleep or it made them think. That was bad. After the government learned its lessons, the only politics allowed on Wallscreen were executions—massively colorful and richly portrayed executions, a glutton's feast of executions. The government doesn't want people to think. And so the only channels that allowed politics on Wallscreen were the so-called nature channels, which became the only true and legitimate form of modern religion today. For most people, it's a terribly boring affair, except for the precious few, the dwindling few, who are still looking for answers, who are at least looking for explanations. Emotionalism isn't just the important key; it's the only thing. Philosophically and intellectually, Gaia is a *discombobulated* contradiction. It can mean anything to anyone—it means nothing. The reason why you can't understand the official Gaia religion or the official Gaia philosophy is because there is nothing to understand."

"So the nature channel," September said, "was the perfect combination of pseudo-science and pseudo-religion—talking in gobbledygook, about the rapid changes taking place in the world."

"Exactly," the magister said. "Precisely. There is no such thing as sophisticated propaganda. Sophistication and propaganda are contradictory. They are mutually exclusive. All propaganda is diversionary. Bread has always been important. But now circuses are more important. That is, on Wallscreen, at least!"

"I see," September said, laughing.

The magister laughed, too. "The government is corrupt beyond belief. There has been a total breakdown of money, a total breakdown of the official economy, a total breakdown of, well, everything."

"You understand," September said, "you have no future with us."

"Of course," the magister said. "I understand."

"But you continue to talk to us?" September asked. "Why?"

"The nearest city," the magister said, "or, should I say, the nearest former city, had roughly 2,500 masonry structures in this city of 250,000 people. Now only three or four dozen of the buildings still have roofs. The house-to-house combat took over 65,000 lives. A Dome replaced the city. The government of the Gaia religion in Europe knows it cannot win unless it comes up with a total solution. Whenever the magisters at the top (I'm talking about the grandmagisters now), start feeling distrust towards each other, somehow subordinates are quickly eliminated. That's why, after being captured, I sang like a bird. A directive is to be issued in less than one year, to kill off all people over the age of sixty, with the exception of `Middle-middles,' `Upper-minds,' and `Suits.'"

"We know that," September said.

"But there's something more perhaps you don't know. A secret directive is going to be issued later: the clandestine killing of all `Middle-middles,' `Upper-minds,' and `Suits,' over the age of sixty, too. Them, too! The grandmagisters chose the age of sixty as a cut-off so we could start afresh. Once the war started, the implementation of the first directive was to be accelerated. It's only a matter of time before the second shoe drops as well."

"But why?" September asked. "With the collapse of the weather systems in the Southern Hemispheres, and the creation of Forbidden Zones where the sun's rays destroyed all life forms, the world population will decrease even more. Why kill more people? It isn't necessary. And why turn on your own people?"

"Once several billion have been killed," the magister replied, "what difference does it make? Once you've crossed the river of no return, what difference is there? Why not kill two billion more? Why not kill six billion altogether? None of them will be around to talk afterwards, right? The dead can't talk. Then we can begin with a clean slate. With the exception of the magisters, there will be no one left who will be able to remember what it was like before the changes. Thirty years from now—forty years from now—we can take the minds of the young and fill them with whatever we want. A new Gaia man. A new Gaia woman. Simple plan."

"But that's total war," September replied in confusion. "That's total control based on total war."

The magister nodded and then turned to Tom. "You're an ex-writer, right?"

"Right," Tom replied. "How did you know?"

"I just do. All of the ex-writers have been executed," the magister said in a flat voice.

"What?" Tom gasped. "It's not possible."

"Every single one of them," the magister nodded. "Except for the four of you who escaped. The Curmudgeon, Guinevere, Martin and you. Of course, even *I* know who *you are*," the magister added, with a note of wounded pride. "You travel in extraordinary company."

"I didn't escape," Tom said. "I was abducted at gunpoint."

"Same difference," the magister replied, shrugging his shoulders. "Once the war started, they were all taken out and shot."

"Did they get tape?" September asked.

"What?"

"Did they tape the executions?" September asked.

"I don't know," the magister replied. He looked befuddled and confused. He looked at both of them carefully. "You know about me, then?"

"I do," September replied. "He doesn't," she added, pointing at Tom. "You gave orders for the massacres in Maastricht and northern Alsace-Lorraine, didn't you?"

"I was only following orders," the magister replied nervously. "There's no way that you could have known about that. No way. No sir. No, it's not possible. You couldn't have known."

"I do know about it," September replied. "We captured your data banks after Naples fell to the Anti-Gaia forces after the flooding."

"But Naples did not fall to the Anti-Gaia forces," the magister said. "Our reconnaissance is impeccably accurate on that."

"Wrong!" September screamed. "Every once in a while, we beat you! The Gaia government did collapse, but only in the Mediterranean. Your reconnaissance is *not* impeccable, don't flatter yourself. Your government makes its biggest mistake when it believes its own Wallscreen! There is no effective government in most of the Mediterranean basin now. But that's beside the point. You were responsible for the deaths of 80,000 people."

"A few here, a few there, what difference does it make."

"We now have irrefutable evidence," September said. "Total war has been declared. There are no prisoner exchanges anymore—you know that. Your own people have forsaken you. Now I am going to execute you, just as you would have executed me if our roles were reversed. Make no mistake. If we had returned you to your own people, they would have executed you anyway. Like those three advisors you mentioned. You know that."

"But, but," the magister protested softly, "I've cooperated with you."

"There's no point in pleading," September said, "it won't save you."

"Okay, okay, one last thing," the magister said nervously. "Give me one more chance. 'The signs of change are not to be found on Earth, but in the stars...'" He looked at Tom with an expression of exasperation. "You remember, don't you? You remember! From your traveling TV lecture tours? As a commentator? As an ex-writer? They're going to change it. The code is not going to be in the stars anymore. The code is changing. For all future script readers, it's changing."

"Meaning?" September asked. "Be quick about it. I'm running out of patience."

"They are going to begin the mass euthanasia of the elderly," the magister said. "On Day Ten of the month of conifers and deciduous trees, Year Gaia Eleven, senior officials met to work out the modalities of the 'Solution of the Elderly Problem.' Up until now, the killing has been haphazard. That's going to change. The killing will become ruthless, scientific, thorough. That's the message in the new code."

"Everywhere in the world?" September asked. "Or only here? Where? When? Tell me!"

"Not here," the magister insisted. "Only certain places. They're not worried about those savages in the dead zones. Why should they worry about them? They pose no danger to the Gaia State. *In the advanced parts of the world.* In America. In one year's time. That's where the program will begin. Then, depending on it's progress, it'll be extended elsewhere, of course."

September appeared unimpressed.

"Don't you see?" the magister pleaded, "scarce resources and valuable organizational talent will be diverted to murdering innocent people—just when the rebellion is struggling. Don't you see? The rebellion will have an opportunity to gain momentum!"

Tom was flabbergasted. A thought occurred to him, 'Maybe September had been telling the truth. Maybe she had been telling the truth, ever since the beginning, ever since we met.'

"No point in pleading with me," September said to the magister in a fierce voice. "It won't save you now. We've already had that information. You've told us nothing that we didn't already know. Your sentence is irreversible. You're condemned—that's that."

"Don't do this," Tom whispered to September. "You knew this all along," Tom said to September, taking her aside. "You knew this would happen." He whispered to her, speaking quietly. "You knew that you were going to execute him from the start, before you even began talking to him. Don't do this."

"Yes," September said nonchalantly. "Of course, I knew. You shouldn't be surprised." September drew her gun and stared at the magister.

"But why?" Tom pleaded. "Why the charade? Don't do this."

"Once again, to try to convince you that our cause is right. Why you haven't figured that out yet is beyond me. We knew all about the killing of the elderly." As she spoke to Tom, she stared at the magister.

"But I believe in the truth!" Tom said. "I do!"

"*What* truth!" September replied scornfully. "*Which* truth! If you won't believe the highest ranking magister when he tells you they are committing genocide, not just in America, but here in Europe, too. Whom else would you believe?" September looked at Tom with disdain and contempt. "This is not even just a magister we've captured here. This is a special magister."

Against his growing shrieks and mounting protests, September took the special magister by the arm behind a clump of shrubbery and shot him. September was an expert shot. She fired only one round to finish the job.

Chapter Eleven

"IS EVERYTHING OKAY?" September asked.

"No," Tom replied dejectedly.

"What's the matter?"

"You killed him," Tom said.

"So what?" September said.

"Aren't there courts of law for that?" Tom asked. "What makes you any different from them? You summarily executed him."

"We don't have time. He was guilty of crimes, wasn't he? The war has changed everything. No more time. Just watch from now on."

"But how could you...?" Tom began.

September interrupted him. "Yes, it was hard, Tom. But I'd be a liar if I said it was the hardest thing I've ever had to do."

They flew across the breadth of France, which was about the same distance as the width of Texas, but the landscape was significantly different. Tom was alarmed by the devastation he saw along the way, he was practically stupefied by how run down everything had become. It was as if a proto-chemical process on a massive scale had transformed Europe. It suddenly dawned on him: the change was permanent. On the roads, commerce, little that existed, was transported by horse-drawn carriages and oxen-drawn carts. Some of the carts were even drawn by humans. In one instance, Tom even witnessed an old woman in a cart being pulled by a harnessed dog. Electricity and indoor plumbing had all but ceased to exist. It dawned on him: the Dark Ages had been recreated.

As September piloted the helioplane, she whispered to Tom, "I do what I have to do. I can't afford to let my feelings get in the way. Don't you know how much *I* know this dehumanizes *me?*"

Tom put his arms around her in a warm embrace. "You are something else," he said lovingly, at once understanding the loathsome choices she had to make.

September closed her eyes and let Tom kiss her.

"Have you any idea how long I've waited for you to kiss me?" September asked.

"I don't know," Tom replied.

"So you believe in me?" September asked, opening her eyes and returning his kiss.

"Loving you," Tom said, still holding her in a warm embrace, "and believing in you are two different things."

"Is that all you have to say to me?" September asked.

"Before I was sixty," Tom replied reflectively, "I never would have said this, but now I can. Perhaps it is better to believe in something, anything, even if it is the wrong thing, than to believe in nothing at all. My great-granduncles used to tell me that during the Second European War, Baptists always fared better than Unitarians when surviving in the trenches. In the race between believers and nihilists, believers always seem to win over nihilists. Besides," Tom chuckled, "nihilists always end up killing each other. When nihilists run out of nihilists to kill, they kill themselves. Yes, I'm starting to believe in you."

"That's assuming that believers still have a chance to stay alive," September said, "let's not forget."

Perhaps September and Tom were in love with each other, even if they weren't aware of it. Strange things happen to people when they're thrown together by events outside their control. Heartbreak brings people together simply because they're able to share the same dreaded understanding of the unbearable adversity they face together—while—at the same time, it is only during such deplorable circumstances they are able to prove that their love can endure.

When they arrived at the foot of the Pyrenees Mountains, they were routed to a divisional headquarters. The divisional headquarters was located on a former Basque farm. The farm's gardens were overgrown and the orchards ruined. Tom noticed that sun poisoning had damaged the bark on the trees. The rooms of the Basque farmhouse had been expanded and had also been converted into a combined makeshift hospital, rest-area, and officers' mess.

For the first time, Tom was impressed with the show of Anti-Gaia forces. They actually had a sizable army stationed there, and he could tell by the size of that army there was considerably more to the rest of the army than he could see.

September went to talk to the corps commander of the Army of the Pyrenees. She introduced Tom to the commander. He had cropped hair and a ceaseless practicality of a soldier. At first, the commander appeared amicable but distant. Obviously a veteran of many campaigns, he was old, pale, and leaned on a crutch; he had lost a leg. In the old days, Tom knew, you could lose a leg in battle, due to infection, gangrene, or a terrible shrapnel or mortar wound; but now, you could lose a leg—clean and neat—to a laser gun.

Tom could tell that, clearly, was how the commander had lost his leg—and the loss had been recent, perhaps only a month ago. He was old enough to have remembered the Oil Wars.

September said, "Tom is a writer."

The commander thought for a moment, and squinted. "I think there can be no greater life than one devoted to solitude." That was the extent of his curt reply, and with steely eyes he went back to his duties.

They recharged and refitted the helioplane, then picked up two scientists to fly to a stone bastion in the Himalayas in Nepal. September told Tom to be patient. She promised that she would explain to him the necessity of why they were making the voyage—later.

One scientist was French and the other German. For six years, they lived together with a small coterie of other soil, water, and air scientists. Each group occupied its own cave, but they all met together in one large cave. The scientists came from everywhere.

The large, newly discovered cave with its ancient cave drawings was similar to the caves of Lascaux, Altamira and Avignon. Like the others, this cave contained Paleolithic Age animal paintings made by man's early ancestors. Maybe man had not progressed in 20,000 years—that was the bad joke they shared. They frequently teased each other over that witticism. Time would not let that particular ill-flavored joke wither.

"They were living in caves?" Tom asked, marveling in disbelief at what he had heard.

"Yes," September replied. "That is a consequence of the loss of the ozone layer. All over the world, people have begun in earnest to live in caves. Apart from the Domes, in the long run, that will be the only safe place to be."

"These scientists actually live in caves?" Tom asked again. "I can't believe it."

"I show you the times," September said, shaking her head. "If the scientists had wanted to live in the Domes, they would have had to accept government rule. They would have had all the money they wanted for their scientific work, but they would have had to accept the fact that they would be working for evil."

The two scientists, one redheaded, the other wearing a pince-nez, were seated in the back of the helioplane. During the trip, they stayed still. They stared vacuously into space.

Tom returned from the back of the helioplane and asked September, "Why are they so quiet?"

"They lost the lottery," September said. "Or perhaps—I should say—they won it."

"Won what? Lost what? The lottery?"

"They drew shorts."

"Shorts?" Tom asked. "What do you mean?"

"They've been selected for the `Post-Literate Oral Preservation

Society of Brothers and Sisters,'" September replied. She changed her position in the pilot seat, glancing at Tom.

"The Post-Literate Oral Preservation Society of *what?*" Tom asked astounded.

"The `Post-Literate Oral Preservation Society of Brothers and Sisters,' or PLOP-SOBAS, for short," September repeated. "Even as far back as the end of the Eleven-Years-War, our leaders thought it might become necessary, in the event of the destruction of our civilization, for all past knowledge to be preserved through a method employed in dwindling parts of the so-called `primitive' world up until very recently, but that, in most parts of the West, had not been used for centuries. They firmly believed that the greatest possible conceit would be technology becoming more and more sophisticated while the human content of that technology simultaneously became more and more primitive: the outcome being a devolution of the enrichment of human life coupled with the illusion that progress is made exclusively through technology. When the ozone layer disappeared for ten weeks, we engaged in a ten-year-binge to find a life-sustaining, isolated place, completely protected from the threat of intrusion, where a community of scholars, scientists, and poets could themselves become recorders of the past if all other forms of record creation were lost. The quest took us to potential locations in the outback of Australia, the Kalahari Desert in Africa, the southern Andes of South America, along Great Bear Lake in Canada, the Himalayas in Nepal; looking for the best place we could find. Actually, we found a place even better than any of those, but it proved to be impractical. We discovered a valley in the high northern Tibetan plateau above the source of the Yangtze River. We entered the valley after traversing three passes above elevations of 17,500 feet, 19,500 feet, and 21,500 feet, respectively. A primitive three-foot tall ancestor of the horse, never before seen by outsiders, lives there, but this valley was too inhospitable to support a colony of five hundred. The people of the Nyinba tribe of north-west Nepal helped us find a suitable alternative. A story had passed down a prophecy, for untold generations, that there was a hidden valley at the foot of a sacred mountain. According to the prophecy, when chaos ruled the world, a *lama* would lead the people to the hidden valley. One hundred years ago, people searched—but never found the valley. A *lama* taught that the valley could only be found when one was truly prepared to find it. If one was ready, it would not be very far away. Five years ago, by accident, we discovered the valley. We moved an abandoned Buddhist monastery, stone by stone, into this valley, to form the world's first Post-Literate Oral Preservation Society. The Society thus created a place where people can dedicate their lives to memorizing certain documents of human thought so it can be passed down orally to the next generation. This fund of knowledge will be orally passed down to the next generation forever. PLOP-SOBAS, for short."

"So, why have these guys drawn 'shorts'?" Tom asked. "This place doesn't sound so bad."

"Their assignment is to set to memory pre-Pythagorean theory, post-Neo-Platonic cosmology, pre-Newtonian, post-Newtonian and Einsteinian physics, super-string theory, theories of thermodynamics, relativity, quantum mechanics, so on and so forth," September said. "They must then be able to recite when called upon. When they are too old, and are approaching death, they will pass on their teachings to a younger person. The information will pass from one generation to the next, by word of mouth. Get it? They will never be able to leave, of course."

"But why?" Tom asked.

"Our fear is so great after the climate change," September replied, "we don't know what may happen next. We can no longer rely on written records—or, at least not exclusively. What if something worse than the ozone layer loss should occur?"

"Do you think that conditions are going to become that bad?" Tom asked.

"I hope not," September replied, "but what if they do? In light of what has already happened, would it not be prudent to assume the best will not necessarily occur, especially when you consider what is at stake, if something major does go wrong? And look at how much we've lost already by relying on computer data and on the central banks of information? By that measure alone, it is prudent. For example, 'Big Boy,' set up under the aegis of the Gaia State, is THE CENTRAL COMPUTER BANK. It's supposed to store all the information in the world. But it doesn't. It does nothing of the sort. There are gatekeepers who decide what goes in 'Big Boy,' and what does not. Even if you set aside the malicious aspects of 'Big Boy,' any centralized computer bank—hypothetical or otherwise—would have, by definition, a selective aspect."

"Still, I don't know," Tom replied skeptically. "Passing information through an oral tradition, by word of mouth...it's...so...radical. It's desperate. It's...pretty..."

"*Primitive?*" September suggested. "Huh? Is that what you're thinking? And why is the idea of an Oral Institute so unsophisticated? My grandparents read to me. That was the alternative to watching centrally programmed virtual reality tapes. True, my education was exceptional by the standards of the time, but my grandparents did this. It made me what I largely am today."

"But back then, and more importantly, before the time your grandparents taught you, they also wrote things down," Tom interjected. "People read what was written down—thousands of miles apart from each other, in different countries, between different generations, spanning centuries, even millennia. That was how culture spread. Everything was kept *not* in one bag—it was dispersed. That was done through one means, September: through writing. Through keeping written records. That's the only way it could be done!"

"But practically nobody reads any more!" September screamed. "Not any more! Not for decades! They watch Wallscreen! Before that, they watched virtual reality tapes! Before that, they watched, I don't know—other stuff, strange stuff. I was born in 2023. That was ten years before the last old fashioned TV show was ever aired."

Tom laughed. Only now he realized that September must have been thirty-nine-years-old. Everything had changed so much in the last twenty years. What was recently new had been replaced by something even more new, over and over, at an alarming rate. September obviously had little memory of television, for example, Tom realized. Not like he had remembered it as a child, anyway.

The flight was beautiful. They followed the land route along the Mediterranean coast, traveling over the European ports of Marseilles and Genoa. At Ostia, the port of Rome, they turned east across the southern spine of Italy, across the Adriatic Sea, across the Ionian Sea, to Piraeus. They flew south across Greece, across a stretch of the eastern Mediterranean, to the ancient Egyptian seaport of Alexandria.

During Alexander of Macedonia's military campaigns to conquer the world 2400 years earlier, the city of Alexandria was founded as a namesake for Alexander the Great.

Alexandria had once flourished as one of the richest and largest city of the Mediterranean. It was a crossroads, that, in its day, would have rivaled New York, a shining center of mainly Hellenistic—but also Egyptian, Assyrian, Babylonian, Roman and Jewish—art and living, home to the world's largest library and greatest university.

Over Pharos island, with its new Pharos lighthouse, September and Tom looked down at Eunostos harbor.

Taking this route was September's special treat for Tom. "Remember this—what you see—hold it in your mind," September said to Tom as she wore an enigmatic smile.

"The reason why? You'll discover later. Alexandria! The jewel of Egypt. The crown jewel of ancient learning. Remember!"

They crossed the desert to the south and headed east, crossing the high plains of Mesopotamia to the Zagros mountains. That's where they encountered trouble.

Five enemy patrolling helio-warplanes suddenly loomed over a nearby peak just overhead.

September reacted with lightning speed. She accelerated the helioplane up to 1100 miles per hour, and then took a barrel-roll into a gorge that led to a long, deep, narrow valley.

But she was too late: their helioplane had been detected. All five of the patrollers barrel-rolled and followed in pursuit. Flying through a narrow sub-canyon of the valley, one of the pursuing helioplanes crashed, hitting a bit of outcropping on the side of a canyon wall. It burst into flames.

As the pursuit continued, one of the enemy helioplane's engines started emitting smoke, and the pilot had no choice but to pull out and return to base. That left three remaining helioplanes for September to contend with.

September suddenly executed an extremely difficult and perilous maneuver, called "a duck-tail," which involved diving, flying upside down beneath the pursuers, then shooting up right behind the three enemy helioplanes.

What made the maneuver extremely hazardous was that, to complete it, September had to come to within fifty feet of the valley floor, flying upside down—practically suicidal at any speed, but more importantly, next to impossible at the speed she was traveling.

For a ghastly moment, Tom watched the floor of the valley sweep in a rush above his head. Then, blue sky once again appearing above, September closed in on her erst-while pursuers. With pinpoint accuracy she hit one of the enemy aircraft with a proton bomb, destroying the helioplane instantly.

One of the helio-warplanes suddenly broke from its flight path, suggesting it was conceding the field. He had apparently had enough and was ready to return to base. But the last remaining helioplane decided to try one last chance at bringing September's helioplane down.

He pulled up sharply; but unlike his colleague, (who had genuinely quit the field,) the second helioplane's maneuver was only a feigned retreat. Instead, as September's attention was drawn to the other retreating helioplane, which deliberately and slowly veered away, the pilot of the second helioplane did a quick lateral move, and suddenly came up at ninety degrees to her, closing fast.

September quickly realized the mistake she had made, but not quickly enough. And now the valley was narrowing even more, suddenly leaving her much less room to maneuver.

The pretended retreat had worked: September was in a defensive position. The pilot took his best shot, a laser blast that was intended to rip into the side of September's helioplane. Somehow, with great luck, the blow miraculously glanced off, causing the helioplane to shake and lose velocity, frightening Tom, startling September.

Once the ship had stopped shaking and the stabilizers kicked in, September didn't hesitate a fraction of a second. Tom noticed she had her `kill or be killed' expression on her face—that incredible look of invincible focus and white-hot intensity.

September executed another "duck-tail." With the valley narrowing into an acute V-shape, this maneuver was even more dangerous than the first and was a complete surprise to the other pilot, who had thought, for excellent reasons, she would never try such a dangerous maneuver *a second time.*

She came up on the enemy helioplane from behind and, before the pilot had time to pull up, hit him with two laser blasts, one harmlessly clipping the right wing, the other slicing through the main body of the ship. Moments later, the ship exploded into flames.

September pulled up from the V of the narrowly disappearing valley, and quickly figured the adjustments needed to re-route to their destination. She then continued on the newly set course, acting nonchalant, as if nothing had happened.

To make sure that their passengers had not suffered any harm during the ordeal, Tom unhooked his seat belt, rose from his seat, and stepped to the aft. After making the inquiry, Tom noted that both the Frenchman and the German had been shaken up a bit —knocked around—but otherwise, neither of them had suffered any permanent injury. Tom was relieved to learn of their condition.

Returning to the cockpit, he reported to September.

Tom said, "Who were those people in those helioplanes?"

Trying to sound as routine as possible, almost casually, September said: "That was a skeletal defense force operating under the Persian Gulf Petroleum Trust-fund. It's a subsidiary functioning by contract under the auspices of the greater Gaia-Dome World Federation. They're not official Dome helioplanes, true, but they're free to attack us at any time. They can attack us—any time, any place—just by finding us and coming after us. We can never know when they'll come. We'll never know: we can only guess. No matter how skillful and experienced we are, we can never know. When we least expect it, they'll hit us, coming as if out of thin air. I've seen it happen before. That's what happens when you insist on flying solo. When you think there's no danger, that might be the time when there's the greatest danger of all."

Tom swallowed hard and nodded his head in agreement.

"But those guys weren't looking for us, Tom. Our meeting was strictly chance," September continued. "They were almost *too* surprised to discover us. They *just* abruptly ran into us. But from now on," September added, nodding her head, "they might be looking. We must be careful, never let our guard down, be on constant alert. Otherwise," she concluded, after a yawn, "relax and enjoy the rest of your trip, okay, Tom?" She put her hand on Tom's thigh reassuringly.

"Okay," Tom said, trying to sound relaxed, breezy and nonchalant.

After crossing the high mountain plateau of Persia, the mountains of Hindu Kush, and the high mountain valleys of Kashmir, they flew along a route that followed the high Himalayas at 25,000 feet. They finally reached the remote northwest region of Nepal, bordering ancient Tibet. They were literally flying at the top of the world.

They arrived at the monastery.

The valley that sheltered the PLOP-SOBAS colony was about five miles wide, with three small rivers winding through it. The high Himalayas dominated the northern horizon, even from a distance of twenty miles away. There were birds, giant crows—called *goraks*

—which raided the newly inhabited valley, stealing from the newly planted crops. Winds always blew briskly through the valley.

The four of them emerged from the helioplane. The German, redheaded, broke the silence. He turned to his French colleague and said, "Think of what happened in that cave a thousand generations ago, Patrisse, the cave we inhabited, where a proud and powerful hunter, after painting images of hunted animals, ran his calloused fingers over a piece of bone on which he had long been making notches, and began to recognize a pattern—time, measured: days, weeks, linear time; perhaps, who knows, months? Seasons? It was the rudimentary beginnings of a calendar. Only the first steps, mind you, the first, incomplete beginnings; but still, the rudiments of a primitive calendar."

"Yes," the French scientist said, removing his pince-nez. He nodded. "That could have been how it started 20,000 years ago, Curt. But then, maybe not. Who knows?"

Gleefully, the German scientist pulled a long, modern bone from the inner garments of his robe. On the bone were notches he himself had carved into the bone over the years he had been occupying the cave. The two scientists laughed as they ran fingers over the grooves in the bone. The German scientist placed the bone back in his robe.

Tom was introduced to the provost in charge of the monastery. The provost, a short man, was reclining in a small chair. "We can survive because of three rivers," the provost said. "The three rivers are fed by five ten-thousand-year-old glaciers. No rain falls directly into this valley. Never has. We live in the rain-shadow of the mountains. If the glaciers should ever dry up, the rivers would disappear. We would also disappear, obviously. This is good because it reminds us—daily—that our lives would end if we should ever forget that we are connected with the flow of water in the world. We pray for strong sunlight, because the sunlight melts the glaciers, and the glaciers send water to the valley. The more sunlight, the more sun radiation, and therefore more water for irrigation; so lots of sunlight means more cool, fresh water for our fertile fields. That's why no one has lived here before. The hotter the sun, the more water we get! You understand? The greenhouse effect has actually made this valley habitable, whereas in the past, this was clearly not the case."

"We'll stop the exaggeration of the greenhouse effect, if we can," September said.

"You've always been such an optimist," the provost retorted and laughed uproariously.

Chapter Twelve

THE MONASTERY AND THE VALLEY were beautiful. Life was simple. Everyone worked. All of the inhabitants contributed. Even the highest `monk' performed common chores each day. The provost himself spent several hours a day tending a garden, and every other day, tending yaks, the hairy, mountain creatures that provided the community with milk. No labor was considered beneath a human's dignity. In every part of the monastery tasks were rotated as part of a fixed monastic routine.

Tom watched the `scientific,' `artistic,' `historical' and `literary' monks gathering in the morning, making their rounds.

At last Tom found September alone. It was the first time since they had left France.

She had hiked seven miles north from the monastery to the very foot of the mountains. The treeless valley, with its high green grasses, skirting the banks of the three rivers, seemed such a wild, strange place. The place almost felt haunted, which may be the reason no one in history had ever lived there.

Tom stealthily followed her, lagging about a half mile behind, hiding behind rocks whenever she turned.

The scenery around them was thought-provoking; beautiful and awe-inspiring, but in an eerie, unsettling sort of way. The winds always blew through the long narrow valley, often whistling, increasing the sense that the place was haunted. When he caught up with her, they looked at each other for the longest time before either of them spoke. Then Tom spoke, breaking the silence: "Maybe only once, after you've extricated yourself from the belly of the monster, can you see the monster for what it really is. The Global Gaia government is evil."

"Have you yet seen the monster for what it really is?" September asked. "It is an imperium. Have you seen it for what it really is?" September repeated with calm, stoic, philosophical quietude.

"No," Tom replied, "I haven't. I haven't seen all of it. But I think I'm beginning to understand what it is. You're right. The global state functions as an imperium."

"When you've seen all of the monster," September said, "when you've taken in the monster in its entirety, then you'll understand." She nodded. "The Gaia government is not a government really at all, not in the way we traditionally understand a government. Global Gaia power is just a series of Domes, tied together, trying to control everything within reach, and in doing so, it exercises a power monopoly. The Earth has become a life-support system for that power. It's simple and elementary. If they also control all channels of the mass media, they radiate the appearance of controlling everything, and, in fact, they do."

"It's such a pity," Tom said. "To talk like this in a place like this. It kind of ruins things."

"How so?" September asked. She was intrigued by his comment. "What do you mean?"

"It kind of spoils the moment," Tom said, amplifying. "It's so beautiful here. There is something ethereal about this place."

"Yes," September replied, nodding her head. "You're right. The only thing we need to consider now is the environment. That's the important thing. That's the key. That's why I came here alone. To meditate. The thing we have to do now is thwart the Domes from permanently altering the climate of the Earth."

"Is that an easy thing to do?" Tom asked.

"No," September admitted. "It might even be impossible."

"When are you going to tell me why I am traveling with you?" Tom asked, point blank. "What's it all about? Tell me."

"What's it all about? I don't know why you're asking me all these questions now," September said. "You shouldn't."

"Oh yes, I should," Tom replied firmly. "Why am I here? The question is plain and simple. What is my purpose in your scheme?"

"I'll explain it all," September said. "Eventually. The important thing is that you have an important role to play. That's all you need to know for now. I can't tell you any more yet."

"An important role?" Tom asked. "What role? And this role I'm supposed to be playing? What's its purpose?"

"Too many questions," September exclaimed. "Suffice it to say that I knew this would happen—from the very first instant I laid eyes on you. Oh yes, I knew it from the start. From the first moment we captured you at the Great Hall in the Wallscreen studio in New York. It was as clear as a bell to me then—just as it is clear now." September nodded her head with finality. "That's all you need to know. This is a matter of pre-determined fate."

"Can't you give me a hint?" Tom asked. "Are we going to be together for a long time or for a short term?"

"You want a hint?" September asked. It suddenly occurred to September that Tom deserved more information than he had been receiving.

"Yes, please," Tom asked coyly. "Give me a hint."

"You came to us as an ex-writer, correct?" September replied.

"Correct," Tom answered. "As you remind me—over and over."

"That doesn't mean you can't also be a teacher?" September said. "No?"

"A teacher!" Tom laughed. "No, no, I couldn't make it as a teacher. No by thunder, not in heaven, not in hell! Certainly not here!"

"How do you know you can't teach?" September asked.

"I was never a good pupil," Tom sighed. "How do you think I

could make it as a good teacher? I'd never make it as a teacher," Tom mumbled shyly. "Never. When I was a boy, you should have seen me at school. I couldn't hack it. You would have been shocked. You wouldn't have recognized me in school. I was lousy, terrible."

"Lousy? Terrible? What do you mean?"

"The teachers on the Indian Reservation loathed me. I was a class cut-up, you know, a class clown, a misfit, a malcontent. I was punished for being a troublemaker. I would daydream all day long. I'd gaze out through the classroom's window all day long. I was the biggest goddamn daydreamer in the whole class—no, worse—in the whole school. I was pretty proud of my reputation, too!"

"That was then, this is now," September smiled. "You'd be a fine teacher. Oh yes, Tom! Yes! I believe it. With all your experiences... You'd make a fine teacher. You'd be a marvelous teacher."

"A teacher?" Tom replied, sniffing skeptically. "You think so? I don't plan to hang around these monk-scholar-reciters, you know; I really couldn't hack it as a memorizer." Like a cantankerous child, Tom leered at September. "When I was very young, and later, when I was twelve, I ran away from school. The first time, they caught me in a wind-hollow, beside a river..."

September gave Tom a reproachful look. "Please," she murmured.

"Alright, I'll quit talking about my childhood," Tom said. "When are we going to leave the Himalayas?"

"Tomorrow evening or the morning after," September replied. "I'm not sure. We haven't decided yet."

"So soon," Tom replied gaily. "I find it agreeable to be here."

"We have several more places to visit!" September said, unintentionally sounding like a nagging scold. "Until we are in a safe place, we have to keep a move on. There's a price on my head. It's more than the economic net worth of three impoverished Third World ex-countries, with one hundred and thirty million slaves to boot, and a 100 nuclear-powered wind machines!"

September was knowingly and deliberately exaggerating, but

why not, she thought, she liked this man dearly: in fact, she was thoroughly fond of him.

"Did you not know that I'm the most wanted enemy of the government," September said, "and it's been so for three years? I'm the champion-enemy of the world! It has at last been said—it's true, it's true—it has at last been said, stop laughing—from the American proltown square, to the international magisterial geodesic sphere, to the slave quarters of Saint Helena and Sao Paulo, I am the champion-enemy of the world!"

September put her fists up. Like a pugilist, she looked as if she wanted to strike Tom like a boxer. "They'd give you a princely sum for my head. I want you to meet my daughter."

"Your what?" Tom asked dumbstruck. "Your daughter? What?"

"My daughter," September replied with an air of stillness. She dropped her fists.

Tom grew strangely quiet. "What did you say?"

"It's not that serious," September said. "Don't look so awestruck. Don't look so surprised, either. I have a daughter. So why is that such a big deal? There are only two now who know of her hiding place. I've gone to great lengths to keep the place a great secret. I've already given you some extremely confidential information. More than I should have, in fact."

"How old is she?" Tom asked quietly.

"Five," September replied. "What does it matter? She'll be six, though, in ten weeks, if it's that important to you."

"When will I have an opportunity to meet her?" Tom asked.

"Soon."

"Where is she?"

"She's safe," September confided. "In a secure place. That's why I've been so secretive. I'll tell you this much. It's a remote place. It's a place that's wild, arid, almost inaccessible; a perfect hiding place for a fugitive. But there's more. Regis, just before his death, programmed the world-climate power grid so this place would be part of a tiny habitable Eden. No one would ever be able to find the program anomaly because he deliberately programmed it so it would simply appear as a glitch in the system. And he deliberately made it appear so inconsequential, and so expensive to correct, that they'd leave it alone. There are important reasons for this."

"All right," Tom said smiling. "Very well. I accept the need to be secretive. Is this my treat that you were talking about?"

"No," September said. "Something else."

"When I first came into this valley," September continued, "no helioplane had ever entered it. That was six years ago. I came in on foot with a party of three. We had to travel over a 20,000 foot pass. Then we had to climb over a second 22,000 foot pass before we entered this valley. There's no direct way here. You can't travel here by following rivers. The only way in is on foot. All three rivers converge at the end of the valley, forming one river that cascades down through a 7,000-foot deep gorge. Impassable. The elevation of the valley is 13,800 feet above sea level. I will introduce you to the PLOP-SOBAS scholar who memorized the works of my late husband, Regis Snow. You can talk to her freely."

"Here?" Tom asked.

"Yes, of course, here. You can ask her any questions you wish."

"What I know about Regis the scientist," Tom said, "is only what the public-at-large knows about him. What I know about him could be summed up in less than five seconds flat."

"What do you know about him?" September asked.

"That he was great," Tom replied. "And that he died."

"Oh, wonderful," September replied. She appeared chagrined. "You know less about him than can be found in a brief obituary. Eventually, if the government gets its way, his name will be expunged from memory. Everything is kept so secretive. When he began his career, my late husband was in a unique position compared to all other world scientists. Because of the immense practical power entrusted to him by the government early on, he enjoyed a free hand to conduct tests and experiments. The broad scope of his scientific mind, combined with his experiments, taught him everything about what really happened to the whole world's climate and environment. Included were changes to the ozone layer, the forests, and the plankton in the seas due to the greenhouse effect. He understood more about these phenomena than anyone else. He studied not only the contemporary record, but the last 150 years as well. He had a comprehensive understanding. He understood the interactions of the greenhouse effect with the ozone layer depletion. He was able to predict changes due to these interactions. That's why, over time, he was given more power by the government, until they became increasingly dependent on him. He was free to travel. He had great power. Money! Resources! They gave him everything. When he discovered what was happening to the environment, it haunted him night and day. He did everything he could to stop the chain reaction as he saw it occurring. But in the end, all of the government's tinkering made matters worse. He realized the scientific truth almost too late. Then they had to get rid of him."

"How?" Tom asked.

"Not now," September said. "We haven't a second to lose. Let's get going."

"No," Tom said, smiling. "Wait. It's a seven mile hike back to the monastery. It will be dark soon. Do you have any idea how cold it can get at this elevation?"

"We've stayed too long!" September said. "Oh my! I've all but forgotten the time."

"Never mind that. We can never get back before dark. There's always morning." And then Tom smiled. "Besides, I brought a small tent in my rucksack. We'll be all right."

September smiled and hastily agreed to make camp.

In less than an hour and thirty minutes, it was dark. Under a bright canopy of stars, so bright under a clear sky, the air seeming ready to explode with light—the sky so clear, they could clearly see the brilliant Milky Way with the naked eye; they also could see the Andromeda Galaxy from the foot of one of the world's highest mountains, a 27,000-foot peak! The pandemonium of lights that the night sky played for them seemed as if played for them alone. The night sky had become translucent. Tom and September gazed at the stars as they pitched a tent beneath them.

Having set up the tent, as they prepared to enter, September stretched out on the grass and pulled off her outer greatcoat, sweater and blouse. While Tom stared at her, she unzipped the top of her trousers and stepped out of them. She was wearing tight black lace panties and a bra. Tom took a step toward her and hesitated. She tossed the trousers over her arm, turned slowly and walked towards the flap on the tent.

"September?" Tom gasped.

She stopped and smiled at him before entering.

"I'm going to bed," she said. "If you wish to join me, you may."

September entered the tent first. Tom was in tow only a few steps behind her.

September tossed her head back. They said nothing to each other.

"Nothing to say?" September asked as she turned to him. There was no reply. She gratefully sighed. "At last." She stared at Tom with an expression of relief. Her laughter was soft and rich.

That night, for the first time, they slept together. They did not speak. With a full measure of fervor, September gave Tom a passionate kiss. Their naked arms and legs intertwined. The tent was made from a special fabric designed for arctic conditions at high altitudes. It provided almost total insulation from the cold. Tom asked September about her daughter, but September said no. She would speak about her, but only later. During the night, without speaking, they made love. There was nothing hurried or frantic about their lovemaking; they just took their time, following their instincts, yielding to their natural inclinations. Tom was a little embarrassed and anxious at first because he thought September might interpret his slowness as being due to his advanced age, but then he realized that he just had to be himself. It was as if they had known each other for a long time, as if they had become familiar to each other by virtue of their shared ordeals and travails. Perhaps, if they had enough time, they would come to know each other by virtue of shared joys and rewards in life, too. If life were so generous.

After making love, Tom felt like an animal. He felt like a tiger, like an eagle, like a bear. The feeling was elemental. He felt filled with love through and through. The thought of his being like an animal thrilled him. It had been so long since he had experienced that feeling—to have recaptured it again was such a joy.

'How old must you be to lose that feeling?' Tom wondered. 'How long does it take to lose it?'

Before they dozed off to sleep, September asked Tom, "Are you a romantic? Tell me." September touched her fingers to his lips.

Tom held September in his arms. "I don't know. Talking about it makes me uncomfortable," Tom admitted guiltily. Tom shrugged his shoulders.

"Is that your age talking?" September asked. She put her index finger to his lips. "Tell me."

"Perhaps," Tom replied, "perhaps not. I guess I'm too terribly shy, also. Other than that, I guess I'm a romantic." Tom mulled the question over for a minute. "I guess I am." Tom gave September a warm, thin smile.

"What a strange romantic you are!" September laughed. She playfully cuffed him on the side of the ear.

That night, the temperature plunged to minus four degrees Fahrenheit, but just two hours after the sun rose, it was 34 degrees, just above freezing. That morning, looking at frozen ground, Tom said, "I don't need a weatherman to tell me the environment is screwed up, I can *feel* it. I can feel it, September. In my bones."

"How can you know?" September asked, staring at him. Sitting up, her clothes dropped to her waist. She fondled his face lovingly. "Even at your age, you're such a beautiful man. You have such a beautiful face. You were a *looker* as a young man, I can tell. You still are a *looker.*" She held his face in her hands. She caressed him with her eyes, feasting on him. She then leaned over to one side and smiled at him from behind. "How do you know, dear? Tell me."

"I just do," Tom replied. He grunted with a nod of extreme satisfaction and self-contentment. He shot a meaningful glance at September. "There's something wrong out there, isn't there? Something wrong—something diabolical, evil, in the air, isn't there? Are the people in this monastery going to survive the changes?"

"What changes?" September asked lightly. "Survive what? My dear?" she added.

"You know. The changes that are to come."

"Ssssh!" September said. She grew rueful and suddenly impatient. She became upset. "What changes? I haven't told you anything about that. I haven't spoken a word to you about that. I haven't told you anything."

"That's right," Tom replied, "you haven't. You haven't spoken with words, but you have communicated with me without them. You don't need words. I just know what you're thinking—all the time."

"You mustn't speak about that." September covered his lips with her trembling fingers. "Ever again. Oh God, don't say that. To say that is tantamount to saying no one on the planet will survive. Do you understand how serious that statement is? Do you understand? How did you find enough information to ask that question?"

"Let's just say I know," Tom quietly answered. He looked at September carefully. "Because you are keeping your daughter in a safe place, elsewhere. Someplace so hidden no one knows of its existence. Nobody *here* knows about it—of that much I'm certain. You are frightened to death about her safety. Aren't you? Admit it. It would not be an admission of weakness for you to face the truth. You love her, that's all. I know it's true. You can't hide the truth from me. If you are unable to care about the welfare of the entire world, September, you are at least able to care about the welfare of your own daughter, right? Tell me I'm wrong. I know I'm not wrong. It's true, isn't it? I know I'm right."

September remained silent. Her silence was an admission of some sort of guilt—or perhaps, more accurately, that she possessed dangerous knowledge. Subdued, they left to return to the monastery.

When they had to ford a river on the way back, Tom carried September piggyback so her feet and legs would not be submerged in the icy water. Not a drop of water touched her. As they crossed the icy river, Tom, like an experienced hiker, carefully stepped on the slippery submerged rocks. Hunched over on Tom's back, September lovingly spoke into Tom's ear, "And they say that chivalry is dead. Well, it's not. *I love you, Tom.*"

"Do you know what I'm going to do?" Tom asked.

"What?"

"I'm going to read everything I can," Tom said, carefully making his steps in the icy stream. "From the books you gave me in the cell—from Istar's *Descent into the Underworld,* from the section on Hades in Homer's *Odyssey,* from the *Tibetan Book of the Dead,* from Dante's *Inferno*—everything. Do you want to know why?"

"Why?"

Tom paused for a moment before he spoke. He was still standing in the middle of the river, in midstream. The water rushed past them, causing a wake that spread from the sides of Tom's thighs. "Because I believe they describe the world we are going to enter. The netherworld. The underworld. We will not enter this world the natural way—through death. We will enter it by living in a changing world. The world is changing because the human race has made it change. The human race has made a human-created hell. The nether world. The underworld. Just after our arrival at the monastery, while you were busy recharging and refitting the helioplane, the provost took me aside. He took me outside the monastery, alone and unescorted, unobtrusively unobserved. At a certain holy place he ordered me to swear an oath of secrecy. He pointed to a stone lying beside the path and said, `All of the history of humankind, all of it, all of the history of humankind, all of it, past, present, future, reside therein. Swear to it. You will never forget. To abide by this message in, or of, the stones—whenever it will be revealed to you. Swear...' Which I did."

"That's all he said?" September asked in a hushed, surprised voice. "What did he mean by that?"

"I don't know exactly," Tom replied, shrugging his shoulders. With September on his back, he continued to ford the river. He took each step ploddingly, skillfully, as if his entire life had been spent crossing icy rivers carrying a person on his back.

"To that one simple common stone sitting by the path—swear an oath—never to forget?" September asked. "What did he mean by that, Tom?"

"I don't know," Tom said. "I think it means he knows something terrible is going to happen." Tom bent down in earnest, taking one stride where he should have taken two, and finished crossing the river.

"He does?"

"Yes," Tom replied, chivalrously depositing September on dry land. "Though, whatever he knows, he's keeping guardedly to himself."

Chapter Thirteen

THE NEXT MORNING everyone noticed an added bounce to Tom's step. His face looked defiant. There was a look of joy in his eyes. Unlike in the past, before his captivity, when generally he looked gloomy, he smiled. His skin had a healthy sheen, thanks to the benefit of plentiful sunlight. When he smiled, his eyes crinkled joyfully, surrounded by healthy-looking worry-lines and wrinkles. He looked strikingly handsome.

Before his captivity, for perfectly understandable reasons, Tom had been careful to avoid `too much sun,' for fear of receiving a serious dose of sun poisoning. He took precautions. Here, in a secret Himalayan valley, for reasons explicable only to a privileged few, he and the others were protected from any serious possibility of being sun poisoned. Thus he could be exposed to the sun as much as he liked, as long as he remained within the hidden valley. Maybe the valley was shielded by Regis's protective system after all.

Tom said to September, with gratitude, "You're much better than Vita-Man pills." He took a deep breath and held it, for a long time.

"What's better?" September asked, not at first grasping the meaning of his statement.

"Why—just you!" Tom exclaimed, hugging her. "I'm going to take care of the helioplane," September mumbled. She reluctantly broke free from his embrace. She scurried off in the direction of the helioport, but as she was walking, she turned to face him and said, "We're not done! The two of us! Are we!" She didn't wait for his answer because she knew she didn't have to. Then she skipped away, and as she did, she turned and smiled brightly at him.

The PLOP-SOBAS sister responsible for the recital of recent scientific history greeted Tom with reserved dignity and, just barely, the necessary familiarity. The sage scientist scholar was not only beautiful, she had vitality. Her youth also surprised him. She couldn't have been more than thirty-five, which was remarkably young by the standards of PLOP-SOBAS sisters and monks, the majority of whom were over fifty.

"Your reputation precedes you," the sister said, offering Tom a coquettish smile. "Yes, I'm practically the youngest sister in the group. I'm sure that's the one thing you realized when you first laid eyes on me. I'm glad you've come to ask me questions. Besides, I need the practice—in fact we all need it—if we are to be the repositories of lore and knowledge. We don't know what the future has in store for us, do we?"

"That's true," Tom replied. "Have you read my book?" Tom asked coyly. "I ask this question out of curiosity. As you said, 'my reputation precedes me.' You see, I wrote parts of it before you were born. I'm as old as the hills, as you can plainly see."

"No, it isn't that you're *that* old," she replied, laughing. "It's just that there aren't that many people like you left around. I haven't had the pleasure of reading your books. I was the last of my age-group to study what was then called 'irrelevant' reading. I put all of my concentration on the study of science. Except for the children of the 'Upper-minds,' the ecclesiastical authorities took science permanently out of the school curriculum when they declared the first year of Gaia, eleven years ago. My parents were leaders of a super-regional 'Upper-mind' group, so I was given all the education

I needed *clandestinely*. They tutored me. That's another story. Let me bring you up to date. I met the Curmudgeon. What a charming man! Fearless as a bull. He has a strength—an inner strength. Traveled here on his way to Heard Island. He talked to me—about you, of all people—during his brief stay here. What a remarkable man!"

Tom was embarrassed, intrigued and complimented at the same time. "What did the old man have to say about me?" Tom asked. "If it's not too vain of me to ask."

"Not much," the sister sighed. "But I could tell you he was fond of you. That was as plain as the nose on your face."

"Are you sure you're a scientist? Perhaps you're a poet, only pretending to be a scientist."

The sister laughed at the flattering joke. "Seriously, he said little to me, Mr. Novak. Actually, he asked some questions about the future, the Earth's future. As I presume you are going to ask me as well. You two are my first."

"First what?"

"First bookers."

"*Bookers?*" Tom asked. "What do you mean by that?"

"That's the slang expression used by some of the monks here for ex-writers. Did you know that the magisters after they obtained power, waged a campaign against pre-Gaia-age books? Confiscated them. Burned them. Employed an *auto de fe*. This campaign occurred after they destroyed the private electronic banking system so that people were denied access to their money accounts except through powers invested in them through the Dome system."

"So I have heard," Tom replied. On another tack, Tom then said, "How was the Curmudgeon's health when you last saw him?"

"His health's okay," the sister replied. "At ninety-nine, he's still as healthy as he was when he was seventy-five, by my guess. Strong as an ox. Stronger indeed! He's incredible."

"You mean it?" Tom laughed. "He's in good shape?"

"In-des-truct-i-ble," the sister replied, pursing her lips together as she enunciated each syllable carefully.

"What did he say exactly, about me?" Tom asked.

"Boy, you're insecure, aren't you," the sister replied, laughing. "He said that, with a stroke of luck, you might be passing this way, too. I'm sure he'd like to see you."

She changed the subject with a knowing smile. "Did you know that Shangra-La, not the mythical one, the real one—there once was a *real* Shangri-La—was located 400 miles from here, at least as the *gorak* flies. If you traveled from there to here by land, though, it would be a 850-mile journey. That's how high and inaccessible our mountains are, and how deep, narrow and meandering our mountain valleys are! This monastery, at the foot of the Shangri-La Himal mountains, was transported here from Bhutan, during an eighteen-month period, four years ago. It took a veritable air force of Anti-Gaia helioplanes to do it. It was a last-ditch effort to save the world's spiritual, literary, artistic, and scientific heritage, which would have been destroyed in the event of a catastrophic environmental interruption, which many have been predicting. My name is Hypatia." She gave Tom a curtsey and a smile.

"Hypatia?" Tom said. "I greet you, Hypatia. You'll forgive me if I don't greet you in the official Gaia manner." In mockery of the official Gaia religion, Tom ceremoniously bowed to her.

Hypatia clapped her hands together. Unable to contain herself, she let out a howl. Then, slightly embarrassed and contrite, as if she were reacting to an older tradition she had not shaken herself free from, Hypatia unconsciously placed her fingers over her eyes. "My parents used to do that, too, when they were in charge of the `Upper-mind' school. We were all under strict orders to follow suit. And you do it so well."

"I'm trying hard to forget," Tom replied. "We were all under such strict orders. What a strange name—Hy-pa-tia? Is that how you pronounce your name? I'm not sure I've heard it before. What kind of a name is it?"

Hypatia smiled. "Two thousand years ago, it was a fairly common Greek name. *My parents always admired the Greeks, you see!*

Wisely or wrongly, my parents thought the ancient Greeks were the cradle of civilization. But my parents named me after a specific Hypatia—Hypatia of Alexandria. She was a scientist and mathematician in her own right, one of the great thinkers of her time. My namesake, Hypatia, was also an astronomer and physicist. More importantly, she was a brilliant scholar and teacher."

"Is that so?" Tom asked. "By a strange coincidence, we flew over Alexandria on our flight out here."

"You flew over the city of Alexandria?" Hypatia gasped excitedly. "I mean, you had an opportunity to see it? How'd it look?"

"The city apparently was once beautiful," Tom replied. "But because of the melting polar ice caps, part of the old port was submerged."

"Oh, forgive me," Hypatia exclaimed. She was thinking about the city's past. "Forgive me, I am overwhelmed by the thought of that venerable *place*. Hypatia, my namesake, was born in Alexandria in A.D. 355. In A.D. 415, Bishop Cyril of Alexandria, had her murdered. She had been a thorn in his side. She had been technically murdered by a band of followers of a fanatical Christian sect who stalked her and cut her into little pieces, using the sharpened chards of abalone shells. After her death, many attempts were made to obliterate her name. Her works were forgotten. After his death, the bishop himself was rewarded by being canonized a saint by the official church. Is it not ironic that, as a PLOP-SOBAS sister and scholar, I bear the name Hypatia?"

"How is that ironic?" Tom asked.

"Hypatia was a pagan, you see. She was a leader in the pagan world; yet in the end they were fanatical Christians who murdered her. I'm a firm believer in the concept of Gaia. I don't worship Gaia, of course, but I believe in its worth. Yet in the eyes of the Gaia government, I'm seen as an instigator of anti-Gaian thought. *In their eyes, I'm a bad guy.*"

"Yes, I sort of see," Tom replied lamely.

"Ahhh!" Hypatia said, clapping her hands together. "Let's get down to business. You've come to be informed. September told me so. You're interested in learning about Regis Snow? You want the short version or the long?"

"Gee, I don't know. How short is the short, and how long is the long?"

"The short version takes about twenty-five minutes, the long one is about ten hours."

"The short one, I guess, then," Tom replied. "I have a better idea. Keep going—keep right on talking—until we've run out of time. Okay?"

"Very well," Hypatia said. "Regis Snow was the greatest scientist of the first half of the twenty-first century. Not because of the depth of his scientific understanding, or his theoretical capabilities, or the number of scientific papers he presented. No, there were many scientists who surpassed him in these capabilities. He was the greatest scientist of the first half of the twenty-first century because he had the greatest impact on the actual, physical world."

"Long before the outbreak of the Eleven-Years-War," Hypatia continued, "Regis Snow had already made a name for himself in the applied sciences, with the introduction of safe fusion nuclear plants and solar-paneled buses, which were notable accomplishments in themselves. As great as these accomplishments were, he did even more. He was also involved in wind- and sea-generated power. His main field of expertise was the study of the atmosphere; more specifically, the greenhouse effect. So, from the beginning, he was all over the environmental research map when the climate change meta-phenomenon began to take shape. Let me take a moment to explain the greenhouse effect so you can understand how important it is. This is tired old stuff, but I'm going to go over it, because it's important."

Hypatia paused. "It's a non-controversial theory now, accepted by all schools of thought, which was not the case fifty years ago. The greenhouse effect is what protects life. Billions of years ago, the Earth's atmosphere was lethal for present forms of life. The atmosphere was mostly carbon dioxide with little oxygen, hydrogen, or water. But life emerged in these hostile conditions, and the resulting mix of atmospheric gases and water allowed for just enough warming of the atmosphere as a whole to sustain life. Too little greenhouse warming and the Earth would become like Mars—a planet without a protective atmospheric covering. Too many atmospheric gases and the planet would overheat and become like Venus. This balance lasted for billions of years. Then it went out of balance. Well, from a strictly planetary point of view, not that out of balance—we're talking about only a five to 30 degree change in temperature—but from the point of view of the life-forms on the planet, sufficiently out to cause significant havoc and destruction."

"When the greenhouse effect exploded," Hypatia said with animation, "it permanently shifted the trade winds and ocean currents. Suddenly, the world power elite, even before the end of the Eleven-Years-War, went into a state of panic. They were worried less about the destruction of the tropical forests than about the destruction of plankton, krill, and algae in the seas. Plankton was the living tissue of the Earth. It generated most of the world's oxygen. But something else was more serious. It was discovered that plankton, krill, and the like lived on an extremely fragile basis. Just a small change in the sea environment could cause drastic changes. If the changes occurred on a large enough scale, the effect would reverberate throughout the food chain. Eventually, the net result would be a lowering of crop yields. All during the crisis, they allowed the media, and later Wallscreen, to talk about the destruction of the forests. They even allowed limited coverage about the melting of the polar ice caps. Certain aspects of the crisis were discussed openly, other aspects were not. But the plankton destruction was strictly off-limits to the media—and that was because it went to the very heart of the matter. Shifts in the ocean currents—or more accurately, the altering of the ocean currents—spelt the death-knell for the stable chemical composition of the atmosphere because it altered the chief producer of oxygen, the ocean's plankton. Who was the greatest expert on sea-surface temperatures, atmosphere, and the greenhouse effect, and so who did the government naturally turn to?"

"Regis Snow," Tom replied.

Hypatia nodded. "You must realize that this is just a thumbnail sketch, a whistle-stop tour, of a highly complex, far-from-completely-understood development. So Regis was employed to arrest the destruction of the ocean currents. That's it in a nutshell."

"Phew!" Tom said. "So Regis cooperated with this scheme?"

"Yes," Hypatia replied. "Completely. The object was not to *change* the climate, but to *preserve* it. It was a defensive action, employed to rectify imbalances that had been caused by humans."

"When did he do this?"

"Beginning in 2044 A.D. And it was all done in secret."

"Where?"

"At first, in the South Atlantic," Hypatia said. "Between the Horse Latitudes and the Doldrums, where lie the southeast trade winds. The trade winds drive the surface water obliquely toward the Equator from both the North and South Atlantic, creating the great Equatorial currents. In the middle latitudes, the westerlies take over as the current's driving force. This is where the worst damage to the plankton initially occurred. As winds and currents approach the edges of the continents, they are turned, due to the Coriolis effect caused by the earth's rotation, clockwise in the northern hemisphere and counter-clockwise in the southern."

"Yes, I see," Tom said. "So he went in to restore the natural flow of the ocean currents so that the plankton, krill, and algae would regenerate and support life higher on the food chain?"

"Precisely," Hypatia said. "Huge nuclear-powered wind machines, in some instances hundreds of them, were set up to force the air currents back into their old, natural patterns. Regis set up a huge base of operations on the island of Saint Helena. What a strange and wild place *that* is. They called it 'the place on Earth that is the farthest from any other place.' Located 700 miles away from the nearest island—Ascension—to the north, the nearest coast, 1,140 miles to the west, 1,800 miles to the east. It is a small pimple of land, surrounded by ocean, in the middle of the south Atlantic ocean."

"Regis set up his operations there?" Tom asked.

"Exactly," Hypatia said. "The place was perfect for his experiments because it was so remote. Right in the path of the trade winds. Eventually, it became the center for operations in the Pacific and Indian oceans as well. It became the center for controlling all of the international ocean currents."

"It sounds like a great success story," Tom said.

"It might have been," Hypatia said, "but things went awry."

"Things went wrong?" Tom asked.

Hypatia smiled. "Every time they tried to set the motions right, something else went amiss. Let me give you an example. The greenhouse effect warmed the environment, right?"

"Right," Tom said.

"But the destruction of the ozone layer in the upper stratosphere, which occurred in the last two years of the Eleven-Years-War, cooled the upper atmosphere."

"Cooled the atmosphere, or cooled the environment, as a whole?" Tom asked.

"Well, both, you see," Hypatia said. "I think you're beginning to understand what was going on, why things were going awry. There were two trends, one warming, one cooling, going on at the same time. Here is where things get sticky. The combination of the two resulted in unexpected seesawing and oscillation of climates, with extremes becoming more pronounced, especially in or near the tropic zones and polar regions. Eventually, the move to alter the climate no longer was a defensive measure, but rather a direct attempt at manipulation. They could not effectively *control* the climate on a whole; they *could* control the ocean currents; but *not* simultaneously control the adverse effects resulting from the loss of the ozone layer and other oscillations. In other words, they could change the weather patterns, but they could not return them to their former state. Too many unwieldy factors were involved. Eventually, the weather patterns were changed to serve the interests of the government. They simply streamlined their operations to attain their own goals. There was a matter of cost, too. Have you any idea how expensive this was? Eventually the government became more repressive and began to coerce Regis into changing the weather for its sole benefit at the expense of the rest of the whole planet. When the Domes—through their increasing control of the Gaia State—acquired total power, all was lost. Once Pandora's Box was opened, making it possible to alter the weather, what followed gradually became more intolerable, until it became unendurable. Everything started to unravel. Regis at last became aware of the fact that much of the surviving Third World had been enslaved to serve the nuclear-powered wind machines, and the food-generating machines, to provide favorable weather exclusively for the north at the expense of the south."

"How old was Regis then?" Tom asked.

"Why do you ask that?" Hypatia asked. "Details, details." She closed her eyes and thought for a moment. "Let's see. Fifty-nine years old. Thirty years older than September, his wife."

"Regis Snow was *that* much older than September?" Tom asked.

"Yes. Why do you ask? Why is it so important?"

"Never mind," Tom humbly replied. He looked down. "Doesn't matter. Christ, if he were alive today, he'd be approximately the same age as me," Tom muttered.

Hypatia frowned.

"Please continue," Tom then added apologetically. He renewed his attention. "I'm sorry, so sorry for the interruption." He glanced up guiltily. "This is fascinating. Please, continue. What does the answer in the rocks mean?" Tom asked. "What does the answer in the stones mean? I've heard that expression over and over. It has been spoken to me by persons somehow connected with the Anti-Gaia rebellion. Even my old writer friend Orsen used the expression. Once and for all, please tell me what it means."

"Oh that," Hypatia replied. "Everybody wants to know about that old riddle. You're interested in it, too?"

"Yes," Tom replied.

"The point of the riddle of the rocks is obvious," Hypatia said. "There were two major catastrophic events in geologic time that had a direct impact on all living things worldwide. These changes were written in the rocks; that is how we read the Earth's history. One occurred approximately sixty-five million years ago, the other approximately 250 million years ago. We are talking about changes that are much more profound than, say, the waxing and waning of your normal ice ages. Both resulted in changes far more extreme than anything ever likely to happen now. The first occurred when there were huge lava flows bursting from the center of the Earth, lava flows that covered thousands of square miles of land. It resulted in wild temperature swings, seesawing sea levels, possibly even a wobbling of the Earth's axis. It destroyed practically all life forms. The enormous die-off has been called the grand daddy of all extinctions. Some ninety-five percent of all ocean species and seventy-five percent of all land creatures and most plants disappeared, later replaced by new life. We are talking about erratic swings in the worldwide climate that might have continued for a million years. The second destroyed the dinosaurs, and was probably the result of a huge meteor or comet plunging into the earth."

"But I don't see the point?" Tom said. "Maybe I'm too dumb to figure it out. I don't see it. You're going to have to spell it out."

"Why study the past—to understand the present—if there will be no future," Hypatia answered, "you see? The good news from the riddle of the stones is this: no matter how bad things become, no matter how much the environment is destroyed, no matter how much future humanity is imperiled, the catastrophes will never be as devastating as those two natural disasters. Humans can't screw things up that bad—that's the good news of the riddle of the stones. That's the saving grace, the ultimate hope. And that's why it was chosen as our rallying cry. The answer is in the stones. It is the rallying cry of our faith. In other words: `We do not face extinction, or at least, we do not face total extinction as a species.' For the rocks record the truth—a truth that far worse things have happened—caused, as it were, by natural phenomena, not by man. Get it?"

"Incredible," Tom gasped.

"And it is our faith," Hypatia said, "or perhaps it is less than that, it is only our *hope*. And perhaps it is just a forlorn hope; a hope that the inhabitable Earth will be able to sustain itself. A hope that the Earth is able to heal itself. That is the message of Gaia. The answer in the stones means, `We will survive these cataclysmic events, come what may.'"

Tom sat motionless, stunned.

A light signal pulsated from Hypatia's wristwatch. "Time's up! In fact, with this unrelated question you've asked," Hypatia said, laughing, "you've gone over the limit."

"Please, let us continue," Tom asked. "There's so much more I wish to ask."

"No," Hypatia said. "We haven't time. I've just been notified by my watch that September is waiting for you. You must leave. See?" She showed Tom the vector screen on her watch.

"One more question, one more question," Tom said, "and then I'll leave. You promised me. How did Regis die?"

"He was executed by the government," Hypatia replied. "Of course you knew that."

"I knew that," Tom said. "September told me. But what I want to know is, exactly how he died. You know, the circumstances of his death."

"I'll answer this last question of yours," Hypatia said, "and then you must leave. You have precious little time left. I'll answer it."

"Very well," Tom replied. "I appreciate it."

"Either from the point of view of perverse and grim irony," Hypatia said, "or from the point of view of looking at it as a practical joke, the magisters allowed Regis to choose the means of his own execution. He could be launched into space, his frozen corpse left to float for eternity among the stars. For his second choice, he could be buried in a plutonium nuclear waste disposal unit, thus preventing the decomposition of his corpse for at least a thousand years. Why so extreme a measure?"

Hypatia paused. "You see, the magisters were really quite infuriated with him. They feared that prior to his trial, Regis might somehow had furnished September, and through her, the Anti-Gaia rebels, information that would have revealed the system's inner core, the parts most open to sabotage, thus revealing the system's critical points of vulnerability. Regis built the machinery from scratch. If anyone knew how to destroy it, he did. AND HE ACTUALLY MANAGED TO DO THAT...though they don't know it. He managed to smuggle the plans out on Iona's three-and-a-half-year-old body, the plans placed and pinned inside Iona's diapers, when the girl escaped a few months prior to his apprehension."

"Is that the only reason why they were angry?" Tom asked.

"That would have been sufficient reason in itself," Hypatia said. "They were angry with him for other reasons, of course. They were not going to operate the climate-altering machinery with the same degree of efficiency with him gone. Practically all the other scientists who worked on the nuclear-powered wind machines were replaceable, but not Regis: he was indispensable—or near indispensable."

"Why didn't he escape instead of getting caught?" Tom asked. "He might have been more effective teaming up with the Anit-Gaia rebels. Wouldn't it have been better if he had orchestrated the destruction of the nuclear-powered wind machines himself, rather than having it done by proxy, through the transmission of his plans? After all, as you said, Iona escaped."

"Was he too bereft over what his experiments had already cost in human life to consider doing that?" Hypatia asked. "Or, on the other hand, would it have been too much for him to be directly involved in the destruction of the result of his hard labor, work conducted over a period of almost two decades? Maybe one. Perhaps the other. Maybe both at the same time. But I think there was a different, more important reason. The most likely reason, he knew it would have been too risky getting his daughter Iona out, and himself out, at the same time. So he chose to let his daughter escape—while he stayed behind, thus enhancing his daughter's chances of being able to escape herself. Maybe staying conspicuously present in his job was the only way his daughter was going to be able to escape. Iona's escape bordered on the miraculous, anyway."

"And so, Iona did escape," Tom said.

"Yes," Hypatia said. "Regis stayed behind. And now we come to matter of his execution. The point is that the magisters were willing to create an incredibly elaborate scheme, no matter how expensive, to make him suffer after death. They not only wanted to set an example; they wanted to set an *historical* example. The latter form of burial was appropriate when you considered that more than twenty years before, Regis had been instrumental in outlawing nuclear plants in the northern hemisphere. And aside from his weather-changing technology, he was still a much beloved hero."

"Which did he choose?" Tom asked.

"Burial in the nuclear toxic waste canister, of course," Hypatia replied. "The choice was obvious. He preferred life after death in purgatory, no matter how long that purgatory lasted, to life after death in eternal hell—which is what the outer-space option would have meant to him. So he chose the second—to be buried in nuclear waste. And curiously, the authorities complied."

"When was he buried in the nuclear waste?" Tom asked.

"It was exactly two years, six months, ago." Hypatia replied.

"How interesting," Tom said thoughtfully.

"You must leave Shangri-La now," Hypatia said in a passionate voice. Hypatia closed her eyes and bowed her head. "Yes—an insider's joke. That's what we call this place: Shangri-La. And you are never to return, even to visit."

"Do you think you sisters and monks in PLOP-SOBAS will survive the changes?" Tom asked. "Speak candidly. Please answer. I need to know."

"Honestly, we don't know," Hypatia said, bowing her head. "That is for our warriors to decide. You are going to be one of the lucky ones, though, Tom. I know this. I don't know where you are going, but I know it is a special place. Now will you please leave before it is too late."

"Good bye to you, doyens of oral history!" Tom shouted as he looked up the hill towards the main branch of the monastery. "And good bye to you, too, fair Hypatia."

Hypatia looked down and murmured in a low, whispering voice, "Let the true and *bona fide* forces of Gaia go with you, Tom. Not the false and pernicious forces of Global Gaia, not the evil forces of the false Gaia State, but the true forces of Gaia. And remember, Tom, always remember: as Henry Adams said in his book, a book I'm sure the magisters tried desperately to destroy: chaos is the law of nature, order is the dream of man. Remember that, when we are gone; remember that, when we are but a memory. And remember that the ultimate truth of the message is in the stones, and that is the ultimate truth of the message in the rocks. We are nothing, ourselves, except when we choose Gaia. But understand. Only when we choose the *true* Gaia."

Chapter Fourteen

I N THE REFUELED and refurbished helioplane, they flew out before dawn. They shot away from the Himalaya mountains and headed south across south Asia. At 30,000 feet, they flew over the Ganges plain at a racing speed of Mach 3. September opened up the engines of the helioplane to see what they could do.

After they had crossed some of the central highlands of southern India, September abruptly throttled the helioplane down into a gradual descent. They leveled off at 5,000 feet, slowly; then looked down. In the distance, they could see a river. September said, "I want to show you something."

Seated in the copilot seat beside September, Tom said nothing. He just nodded.

"There are dozens of rivers like this in India," September said. "Dozens of rivers like this all over the world, in fact."

"So?" Tom said. "What of it?"

"I'll show you, then," September said. "You must see it with your own eyes."

September gradually lowered the helioplane. When they reached a few hundred feet above ground, September banked the helioplane to provide a better view. Tom saw what September had in mind.

There was a struggling column of people stretched out as far as the eye could see. The marching column, two or three people wide, stretched along the length of the river. The line stretched out for many miles—a seemingly endless line of people.

"What are they doing?" Tom asked.

"Walking," September replied.

"Walking?" Tom asked. "Why? To avoid sun poisoning?"

"No," September said. "Sun poisoning takes five or ten years to kill. The effects are still gradual. They've been dying from so many causes over the last decade that sun poisoning is just a small item in a much longer list of life-threatening problems. A person dying from a fire or a flood isn't particularly worked up about the fact that he may die of cancer in a decade's time. In light of their desperate situation, sun poisoning is the least of their concerns. Starvation is their chief problem."

"Why are they walking?"

"For food," September replied. "To find it."

"Does the government know about this?" Tom asked.

"'Course they do," September replied. "When you are referring to the government, what you really mean is the Global Gaia plan, right?"

"Right."

"If you are speaking of that, you are really referring to the Domes, right?" September asked.

"Right."

"Triage," September said.

"Triage?" Tom asked.

"This is a part of the Third World that has been written off. These people are living below the level required of slave recruits. They are not an enemy to be vanquished; they are seen as scum to be extinguished. They—these people—have been written off, left to die. They are no longer viewed as human beings."

"Let's leave this place," Tom said. "This is depressing."

"Yes, it is depressing."

September pointed the helioplane up. As they reached 20,000 feet, she accelerated to a flying speed of Mach 2.

"I want to show you something else. But it's dangerous."

"What's that?" Tom asked.

"If you don't see the nuclear-powered wind machines with your own eyes, you won't believe that they exist."

"They do exist? Where are they?"

"About 3000 miles from here. The largest number are concentrated in the South Atlantic, the second largest in the central Pacific. I wish to take you to see a sub-satellite group of the third-largest concentration."

"Where is that?"

"In the southern Indian Ocean. The main body is located east of Durban in South Africa. There's a smaller group, however, located between the Seychelles and the twin islands of Reunion and Mauritius, so that's where we are going. They are probably the only sub-group of nuclear-powered wind machines within 3000 miles of here, where security is lax. Like I said, seeing them will court danger. We'll take a peek. Okay?"

"All right," Tom said.

They flew south and southwest across the Maldive Islands and then southwest towards the Cargados Carajos shoals.

"The South Equatorial Current," September said, "of the mid-Indian Ocean, is relatively important to the weather patterns of the northern climes. The weather patterns important to the Domes require that this current's velocity be maintained or increased so other weather patterns will behave to benefit the Domes. They don't care what happens to anywhere else."

September goosed the helioplane's power cells to reach the maximum speed of Mach 3.2.

Tom said, "I thought the maximum speed of a helioplane was Mach 4, not Mach 3.2."

"It is," September said. "The most sophisticated helioplanes can go quite fast, but they can't do much else. This helioplane is rigged for versatility—which is more important for our purposes. How did you know that helioplanes can fly at a maximum of Mach 4?" September asked.

"Hell, I flew in a helioplane from Nebraska to New York before you captured me," Tom said. "Remember? What a trip that was."

"Oh," September said, nodding. "That's right."

One hour later, they could just make something out in the distance. At first, from a distance of twenty miles, Tom thought it was mirage, but then when they were a little closer, he saw what appeared to be a miniature set of giant, octopus-like, seaborne creatures set on top of gigantic oil rigs, located just inside the horizon—he could only make out three of them. Actually, he wasn't sure what he saw. Finally, he could make them out a little better as they drew closer. There were three groups. Now he could see! The nuclear-powered wind machines were located in three clusters of twelve, each cluster separated from the other by a distance of three miles in a vast equilateral triangle. The individual nuclear-powered wind machines in each cluster were separated from each other by a distance of maybe one-half mile each. Each one looked like an enormous oil rig, with great tentacles reaching upward.

Then, as September and Tom flew yet closer, they were able to focus on just one of the three clusters, and then Tom could not believe his eyes. He could see that they were not tentacles at all but rather they were indeed nuclear-powered wind machines, elevated maybe an eighth of a mile above the sea; and the machines were spinning around and around, on a scale so massive he could scarcely believe his eyes. He thought that somehow someone had painted a picture and placed it on the retina of his eyes. These wind machines were generating wind that was moving at a terrific speed, causing wind shears of unexpected force and direction, and for that reason, September had carefully positioned the helioplane so that it wasn't anywhere near the wind's path.

"No, it's no illusion," September said, reading Tom's mind. "Keep your eyes open. This is not virtual reality, either. It's the real thing."

Tom was awestruck. No; more than that: he was *thunder*awestruck.

"Didn't I tell you that you wouldn't believe me unless you saw it with your own eyes?" September said. "Well, take a look. Take a good look. It's in plain view. Go ahead." Then she handed him a pair of binoculars so he could view the scene better.

"I can't believe my eyes," Tom said, rubbing them. Then he placed the binoculars up to his eyes again. He could not tear his eyes away. As if it were the Great Medusa itself, he had been mesmerized by the colossal sight of the nuclear-powered wind machines.

"That's when the worst excesses of the past came to a shuddering halt," September said. "Even though the greatest amount of the destruction of the ozone layer on a global scale lasted only nine weeks, it jolted everyone into a permanent state of shock. Now the only thing that the Third World had that the rest of the world needed was a good climate. After the one and one-half billion decrease in population by 2051 A.D., by the end of the Eleven-Years-War, that also destroyed the ozone layer, and after the resulting nine-week-long near eco-catastrophe, the only remaining valuable commodity worldwide was a good climate and safe, fresh, drinking water."

"So that's how it happened?" Tom asked, handing the binoculars back to September.

"The Domes could not steal the planet's water in the name of greed, or in the name of adversity, or in the name of self-interest, or in the name of survival, but they could usurp it in the name of religion—the Gaia religion."

"I see," Tom said.

"To control the fresh water," September said, "they had to control rainmaking. To control rainmaking, they had to control the wind. To control the wind, they had to alter certain ocean currents. Get it?"

Tom nodded. "Swallow the hoax, hook, line and sinker, or else."

"We're talking about a shift in the entire world's climate!" September said.

Tom remained mute.

"We've got to get out of here!!" September screamed. "Like now. Pronto. If we don't, these nuclear-powered wind machines are going to be the last thing we *will* see. They'll be on us quickie-quickie."

September turned the helioplane in one tight arc, and headed in the opposite direction.

Within a minute, the nuclear-powered wind machines had receded from sight. Quickly, they disappeared over the horizon.

Half an hour later, the helioplane changed course once again. They headed due south toward a tiny, lonely, uninhabited island eight hundred and fifty miles north of Antarctica; an island seventy percent encased in ice, nine months of the year; an island in the middle of the ocean, midway between Antarctica and the latitude of the southern tip of Africa, in the middle of no man's land.

Heard Island.

When Tom asked where they were going, September said it was time.

"Time?" Tom asked. "What do you mean, `time'?"

"Time you met with the Curmudgeon."

Chapter Fifteen

THEY FLEW SOUTH across the Indian Ocean. Thirty minutes later, the skies grew thick and gray. Soon, there were more clouds on the horizon—big, fluffy ones; five thousand feet high, ten thousand feet high—mauve, pink, resembling a menagerie of `cloud-animals.'

Eighty minutes later, in a break in the cloud cover, an island appeared—surrounded by an immense infinity of a wide-berthed ocean, but only for a fleeting second did the island come into view, then it was swallowed up by low-lying clouds.

"There!" September said, pointing down. For a moment, the island appeared again. "There! You see it. There! You see it!"

"Yes," Tom exclaimed.

Looking down from an altitude of six thousand feet, September pronounced: "It cannot be mistaken. It must be it."

September adjusted navigational instruments, then pushing the throttle full forward, the helioplane made a beeline for the spot of lightness in the sea of green.

They touched down on the surface. The only place they could land was on a steeply inclined pebble beach. Tom and September opened the doors carefully because there was no helioport on the island and the helioplane was listing almost 40 degrees. They stepped out of the helioplane, trying not the disturb the standing—but sleeping-while-standing—Macaroni penguins, surrounding them on all sides.

The penguins were standing upright with eyes closed tightly. On their faces were long, yellow, plume-like "eyebrows"—a characteristic peculiar to them alone in the penguin world.

Tom and September listened to distant sounds of water moving farther out at sea, then to the immediate ebb and flow of water, rising and falling.

The water at their feet, just below the helioplane, was making a loud noise. It was a powerful groaning sound.

The beach consisted only of fairly good size pebbles, hence the sound of `barking'—coming with the rhythmically rising and falling water-line, following the crests of the in-coming swells, along the line of the sand-less, pebbled beach.

The surrounding sounds were all the more audible because visibility was difficult. The sensitivity of their ears was all the more sharp for that reason. The cold gray dark-light blended into one solid block, so it was useless to try to distinguish sky from water. Tom immediately noticed that the island was barren of trees. At the higher elevations, the island appeared to be encased in ice.

The penguins surrounding them suddenly awoke. Stunned by the presence of the helioplane, they hurriedly waddled—splashing—into the icy water, in order to escape from the imposing-looking `foreign object.' Others followed, creating a sort of panic. Then even more followed.

It took more than a three or four minutes, flippers waving frantically in the air, for the Macaroni penguin to pass around the helioplane to the water's edge. Once they dove into the water, the penguin's flippers looked like they were battering rams on the surface of the water. Within minutes, most of them were already several hundred yards out at sea, swimming gracefully.

"Aside from a brave mariner," September said, "a few brave whalers, a stray scientist, who've come from time to time, this island has been rarely visited. What a strange place for a 100-year-old man to try to live in, don't you think?" September asked.

"This place is cold," Tom said with a shudder. "Small wonder anyone rarely visits. It's like a meat locker—*strange cold*. It seems to go right through you, b'rrrrrrrrr. Oh God, September, it's freezing here."

"Yes," September replied. "But I'm afraid it's true, he does indeed live here."

The Curmudgeon came down to the beach to greet the helioplane. "I've been expecting you," he said.

Even in the light mist, Tom couldn't mistake the Curmudgeon's Roman, beak-like nose. In spite of his age, the Curmudgeon appeared in good form. His locks of flaxen hair cascaded around his neck. He was wearing a huge fur coat. His face was deeply lined and creased.

"I bet you have been expecting us, old dear," September said in a playful, jocular voice. "Yes, you poor dear old thing," September said. Her laughter was rich and infectious. "You bear up in the weather! On the stormy seas! You don't just like the cold, you're not only fond of it—by God—I think you welcome it! I bet you do! Don't you? You dear poor old thing."

"Yes, I do!" the Curmudgeon replied, in a chipper voice. "I do. Fighting the cold—because in fighting it—it makes you strong. Indeed! A fine day it is, too, isn't it?"

He filled his lungs with a draft of air. He held his breath for a long time, then, exhaling noisily, his breath appeared as a strong white vapor in the freezing air.

"A rock I am!" the Curmudgeon said. He beat his chest. "Steady! Strong as a stone! Feel my muscle!" he said to Tom. "Feel my biceps! I may be nearly one hundred years old, but I'm still fit. A fine day. It's the Antarctica convergence that does it, Tom. Feel it?"

"Feel *what?*" Tom asked, his eyes crinkling in the cold air. His heart was pounding. He was literally swelling with pride. So many fond memories were racing through his mind. He was thinking of the Curmudgeon when the Curmudgeon was younger, and he was younger too.

"Feel what, Gus—huh Gussy?" Tom asked in an unashamedly affectionate voice. "Feel what?"

Tom had dearly loved the old man all his life; for the nearly fifty years he had known him. He was so glad to see his old mentor. As if he were a father to him, Tom adored the Curmudgeon! After so many years, at last, to see him again in person.

As if he were posing as a serious classical dramatic actor, using all the pomp that his bearing could muster, "it gives you vitality and exuberance!" the Curmudgeon said. He beat his chest ferociously, more vigorously than before. As if he were a cross between an Abominable Snowman and an extremely aged Tarzan, he shouted: *"Ahhhhh-yaaah-yaaaah-yaaaaahaaaaohhh!"* *It was as if he were the celluloid, movie ape-man himself, beating his chest as if he were a man-like gorilla.*

"Christ!" September giggled. *"Key-rist!"* She was shocked. Not believing what she was hearing she shook. "What an actor! Ham! Could this man at least try to act his age for a change..." September murmured. Shaking her head vehemently, she then thought: `Is it asking too much? *Jeez!* What a ham—no. Worse! What an irrepressible *behemoth* of a ham. This crotchety old coot is something else...Tom?' She started to ask Tom something, absentmindedly, her voice trailing off.

Deliberately ignoring September, speaking in an unusually mild and skeptical voice, Tom asked the Curmudgeon, "The Antarctica convergence, h'mmm?"

The old friends hadn't formally greeted each other, but then again, they never did when meeting after a long absence. And this occasion was no different from any of the others.

The Curmudgeon let out a huge laugh. "The Antarctica convergence Tom, `h'mm' indeed. This is Heard Island. It's on it!"

They looked out to sea. Some of the fog had parted. Beyond the rocks, they could see the pounding breakers. Every once in a while, there was a resonance from the sound of *kaboom!*—the sound of a mighty breaker hitting the rocks.

"We're on the convergence, similar to being on an earthquake fault line," the Curmudgeon explained. "Along the Antarctica convergence, northward-moving sub-Antarctic waters meet Antarctic waters, and sink below them in a laminar flow. An abrupt change in ocean temperature occurs, and with it a disruption of marine and bird life. Naturally, the magisters don't expect a human being to be living here. That's why I've been left alone. There have been no climate changes during all the monkeying that's been going on —*not here anyway.* In other words, they leave this barren island alone. Hah! For the birds! For the Macaroni penguins!" He let out a gargantuan laugh. "For me! Ha ha!"

"What about the hole in the ozone layer?" Tom asked. "Aren't you worried about that? In Patagonia, in South America, a whole colony of 50,000 pilgrims, 200 miles north of Tierra del Fuego, died from sun poisoning. Aren't you living only a few hundred miles south of that latitude? Don't you worry about it?"

"Oh, the ozone layer?" the Curmudgeon asked, cupping his ear. "Ha!" he exclaimed again. "We're safe here. Regis, September's late husband, made a spot safe here before he was executed. Didn't you tell him about it, September?"

September nodded her head. "You see, Tom, Regis shielded this place with the power grid, thus creating a place of protection. Around the world, there are twelve spots—isolated key spots—protected from both the climate-change scheme and from the sun poisoning rays due to ozone depletion. The minuscule spots are no more than pinpricks on the map. These spots are havens where we could hide certain illustrious people, with no chance of them ever being discovered. The spots are so small they can support no more than three or four persons for any length of time."

"With all this heavy cloud cover and rainy, fog-like ice, how much direct sunlight do you expect us to get down here, anyway?" the Curmudgeon asked Tom, interrupting September.

"The magisters found four of these spots in the last few years, by accident, it seems; so the system isn't foolproof. We lost Regis's key scientific advisor, who was hiding in one of them. Therefore," September continued, "I'm afraid they may find this one. From our informers and spies inside the Domes, we've received more bad news. We have good reason to suspect that this spot, and several others like it, are not only seriously vulnerable, but are under immediate threat of being exposed. We need to get you out of here, and we need to get you out of here fast!"

"When are we leaving, then?" the Curmudgeon asked in a noncommittal voice.

"Now."

"Now?" the Curmudgeon said with incredulity. "What the? You mean...now?"

"Yes, now."

Instinctively, he placed his hand over his mouth, as if to hide his queasy feeling of uncertainty.

"Yes, now," September repeated in a mild voice. "As in, *right now*. As in, *immediately*. As in, *this very hour.*"

"Oh, Christ!" the Curmudgeon shouted. "I've become so acclimated to this place! I've grown to like this place. You see...I mean, what I mean to say is...I love it!"

September simply rolled her eyes. In the form of non-verbal communication, she wanted to turn to Tom and say, `See what I've been putting up with?'

But instead of remonstrating overtly, wearing a thin smile, September mouthed dryly, with a look of cheery merriment, "I'm beginning to see why you call him what you do, Tom. They don't call him the Curmudgeon for nothing, do they?"

"No, they don't," Tom replied thoughtfully, laughing lightly.

Tom was about to add more. But before he could speak, the Curmudgeon overwhelmed him. His voice burst forth. He literally thundered: "I'm a Zen Buddhist! I'm a—I—am! I am!—I am! A raging Zen Buddhist!"

September was about to roll her eyes a second time with the intrusion. `So proud, so self-contained, yet so mentally preoccupied with himself, almost to the point of being a victim of an arrested form of retardation, overtly-engrossed with himself,' she thought.

The Curmudgeon's eyes fixed solidly on the ground. His entire body was conspiring to say that, come whatever, he was going to be listened to. No one was going to stifle his freedom of expression. September didn't know what to make of his words, but Tom did.

With a mischievous, baiting glint in his eyes, Tom asked: "What kind of Zen Buddhist, Gus? Huh? What kind? Huh? Huh, Gus? What kind? You kidding? A *raging* Zen Buddhist?"

As Tom needled him, he knew exactly what sorts of calculations were going on in the Curmudgeon's mind. On many an occasion, Tom and the old one had engaged in this seemingly pointless blather.

Tom had heard legends, 'stories,' told many times before: told over and over, related so many times they'd become more than just legends, but legends of epic proportions: about how when the Curmudgeon had turned six, he began to write poetry. At that time, he was the son of a itinerant, city-to-city traveling jazz saxophonist. The Curmudgeon had been born within earshot of the soon to be boarded-up steel mills in the southern portion of Chicago, according to old calendar, January 5, 1963 A.D.

Tom remembered that that's how the Curmudgeon got started in the poet's trade.

Beginning at the age of six, the Curmudgeon was always changing his core beliefs, at least during the first fifty years of his life (approximately half of his lifetime), so it was not usual for him to take his time in answering. 'When would that have been? The Curmudgeon's first big philosophical permutation?' Tom asked himself as he waited for the Curmudgeon to respond to his question.

But beyond a group of avant-garde poets, beyond the intellectual coteries of *ficcionero* fictionalists, beyond the dilettantes on the fringe, the world-at-large hadn't yet 'discovered' the Curmudgeon, and they wouldn't discover him for another forty-five-odd years.

He didn't become the world-renowned poet that he was later

to become, until around the year 2020. Then—bam! All at once! To be the poet of the age! To be the siren song of the epoch! By year 2035, he was the most famous poet alive! By year 2045, he was celebrated and feted throughout the world.

But Tom remembered Gus's small beginnings. Gus started out as a youthful and impressionable Augustine.

Ten years later, after traveling under the flag of the Liberian Line ships, as a young seaman in the merchant marine, the Curmudgeon eventually settled back into America.

By the time he was thirty, he was beginning to enjoy a small but growing reputation as a minor poet.

It was twenty years later though, after spending ten years as a hermit in Alaska, then five years in a Zen monastery in Japan (eventually kicked out because of his lack of vigor and inner discipline), then five years traveling around the world, then he came into his own.

"A Zen Buddhist who's really a kind of atheist," the Curmudgeon replied after an incredibly lengthy pause.

This was a kind of *"wordsmith"* word-game. September saw through it all too readily. Then she realized even more dimly, though she eyed the two of them with a disdainful sidelong-glance—what were they *really* doing? she wondered. In this freezing cold? Stamping their feet? Eyeing each other? As if they were a pair of tigers in a Siberian forest? `What gives?' she thought. `Oh, that's it. They're crazy. Why ask?'

"What?" Tom asked. "How can that be? What kind of atheist?"

"A kind of atheist who started out youthful, arrogant, analytical and cutting—like you—and over the decades became humble and intuitive," the Curmudgeon replied with a Buddha-like grin beaming on his face. "The kind of atheist who doubts his lack of faith or his relative absence of faith more than he doubts his reasons for adopting *faith.*" The Curmudgeon didn't just speak the words; he spit them out like bullets. "You would have made a true atheist,

Tom, if it wasn't for that Iroquoian Indian part of you. That's the only thing that held you up."

"That's a strange kind of Zen Buddhist's remark," Tom wryly observed, "not to mention a funny kind of atheist thing to say, too."

The Curmudgeon let out a boisterous laugh. "I was first an atheistic freethinker, then flip-flopped into being a Christian free-thinker, then changed back again into being an eccentric free-thinking Zen Buddhist. *Hell, I don't know what I am now.*"

"You're such a welter of contradictions," Tom observed. "You're not a philosopher, just a poet. Alas, you're not always a particularly logical poet, either, I might add."

"You two have this conversation often?" September interrupted, unable to restrain herself, shaking her head, not believing what she was hearing.

"Listen to the pair of you!" she said. "After so many years of separation, you've only had this reunion! And now you're talking past each other with such apparent nonsense."

"All the time!" the Curmudgeon and Tom replied together, chiming together as a single voice. They were happy to face each other in a state of disagreement. They had thrown their arms around each other. They were hopping up and down robustly, hugging each other with joy.

September thought they looked like a pair of grown-up or-phans, boys separated from each other at an early age, who hadn't seen each other for a considerable number of years.

But the sight of them had a wondrous effect on her. *They looked adorable. They looked like a pair of paunchy, naughty, impish, mischie-vous kids. What was the childhood story her grandparents used to tell her to rock her to sleep with when she was three years old: Peter Pan and the lost boys?* The sight of them almost made September wish she were a kid again (since she had turned eighteen, that was something that nobody had ever made her feel before!)

Their unseemly playfulness was infectious. September was afraid that she was going to catch their bug. It was enough to make her want to bust her gut with joy.

"Come into my hut," the Curmudgeon said at last. With unnecessary ceremony, and with a panache for dramatic flair, he carefully wiped his joyful tears away. He motioned towards his hut. The hut appeared ridiculous. A hut? It looked like a chicken hutch. It was built of driftwood and mud—mixed with straw (where did they get the straw—much less the mud, September wondered?). Also there were small, plastic sacks filled with cement on the roof. The hut consisted of two rooms and a dirt floor. The floor was carved four and a half feet into the ground itself, apparently to help protect it from exposure to the fierce winter winds. It was literally an old vagabond's hut, buried more than halfway into the earth.

"Where's my manners!" the Curmudgeon exclaimed graciously. "I'll refresh you with tea. Watch the doorjamb, by the way. It's low. You have to step down, and stoop to step inside. Don't worry about your bags."

"We have no bags," September replied. "We're not staying."

"Well, if you're not staying," the Curmudgeon asked in an absentminded voice, "then exactly how long you planning on not staying then, huh?"

"Just an hour," September replied tersely, in a formal and court-ly manner. "Like I had already told you. If you had only bothered to listen to me the first time. We'll be taking you too, to another place. You're coming with us. That's it—final! You have one hour to pack your things. That's why we came." She was all business and no-nonsense now.

"One hour, well!" the Curmudgeon exclaimed. "Well, one hour! Can't be helped. I'm sure it simply can't be helped!" He let out a *banshee* cry. He whined like a wounded, whelped cur. He shrugged his shoulders mockingly, over-melodramatically, as if he were expressing futility, resignation, fatalism in one sweeping gesture of mockery.

"Still, we have enough time for tea," the Curmudgeon said.

"Come." He was incorrigible. "We have much to talk about!" The Curmudgeon slapped Tom so hard on the back, it hurt Tom a little, though Tom suppressed making a reply.

"How did you find your way into the Anti-Gaia underground?" the Curmudgeon asked.

"I was kidnapped," Tom replied.

"Kidnapped, you say?" the Curmudgeon exclaimed. "You were kidnapped by the underground? *Noooo!*" He grimaced. "Is this true?!" He feigned a looked of bafflement. His dagger eyes shifted from one place to another.

"Yes," Tom said. "At gunpoint. How did you come into the underground, Gus? Were you kidnapped, too?"

As Tom watched the Curmudgeon's display of peculiar antics, Tom couldn't stop himself from laughing.

"No," the Curmudgeon replied. "Nothing like that." He roared with laughter. "Who'd want to kidnap me? I'm death itself. They should have cut me up and used me for bait, or boiled me down for tallow to make soap. If I had been born with hooves, they'd have put me in a glue factory by now."

"You were seduced by them, then?" Tom asked. "They used persuasion?"

The Curmudgeon laughed. "I haven't been seduced by anyone in over thirty years. Even then, it was mistaken identity! She thought me much younger. *And she had an excuse, she was drunk.* No, I chose to join the underground by choice. It's a miracle of the twenty-first century."

"What's a miracle of the twenty-first century?" Tom asked.

"That I was accepted by them," the Curmudgeon replied. "Think of it! An old wind-bag like me. Think of it! You say you were kidnapped? How could that be?"

"Originally, it was a case of being a victim of mistaken identity," Tom said. "They mistook me for a special magister—no, it was someone even higher up than a special magister, a grandmagister—anyway—a very important person in the Gaia-Dome system. I was an unwilling captive at first, I mean, in the beginning; but, later on...well...that all changed, as you see."

Tom looked at September with a look of awkwardness. His feeling of awkwardness was the result of a guilt by association. After all, September's ragtag army may have been demented and crazy, but they had helped him all the same.

"In the end, I guess, I owe them my life," Tom said at last. He looked appropriately contrite. "They spared me. Helped me. In the end, saved me. These crazy people. I guess I shouldn't call them crazy people—even if they *are* sort of crazy."

"And how?"

"What?"

"What I mean is, how did it happen?" the Curmudgeon asked.

"You see, the Dome people had me disguised to look like a six-star general," Tom explained. "I had been sent for. I had been ordered to act as a kind of actor, in a magister's show. They planned to have me speak at this presentation. It was for `Suits.' Viewed on Wallscreen. But the rebel guerrillas burst in on the party, and...next thing I know...there was a lot of blood...I don't exactly remember what happened next..."

"We'll have time to talk about this in greater detail when we arrive at our final destination," September interrupted. "We don't have time for this now. Not before we takeoff. We really must be going."

"By the way, where are we going?" the Curmudgeon asked.

"What?"

"My destination."

"South," September replied.

"We're not going north?" the Curmudgeon asked. He was breathless with surprise. "What? We're going south? There isn't much left farther south, is there?"

"Queen Victorialand," September announced. "Taylor Valley, to be exact. That's right, we're going to Antarctica."

"Antarctica!" the Curmudgeon exclaimed. "Then it's going to

be the South Pole!" He let out a little shriek of amusement. "Antarctica! Where's Taylor Valley? I've never heard of it!"

"That's right, Taylor Valley," September replied. "The place
we're going to is a secret valley. It's called Taylor Valley. The place
hasn't seen rain or snow or sleet, or any kind of precipitation, in over
three thousand years."

"Another hidden secret place," the Curmudgeon said in a joyful
voice, a voice that made him sound as if he were as happy as a child.
"Like Heard Island! Of all places! In the desert! In Antarctica!" The
Curmudgeon stopped. "I didn't know there was a desert in Antarctica, Tom, listen to me!" He got up. He walked over to Tom. He
put his hands on Tom's shoulders. He appeared serious. Clutching
Tom's shoulders, the Curmudgeon stared deeply into his eyes. Tom
was held spellbound (and a little frightened).

"Listen," the Curmudgeon began. "We are like disappearing
aborigines in the hot desert, Tom. On the wild prairie, on the frozen
wastes of the northern tundra, leaving a precarious past to an equally
uncertain future, of the musings of man, of the old, of the disappearing tribes—all of us who are left, forgotten and easily forgettable.
Remember this." He rambled on.

Tom averted his eyes. He looked down. "I don't know what
you're talking about," Tom said. "Why are you lecturing me in this
manner?"

Instead of retreating or relenting, the Curmudgeon then force-
fully grabbed Tom by the lapels. "No, don't look down, Tom. Remember this. Look me in the eye, Tom! Remember this! Remember!
Don't look down. It's important. You have many more important
things yet to do with your life! Listen to me!"

"Actually, we have something very special in mind for you, Curmudgeon," September interrupted. "Something special. A special
mission. Nobody else is going on this mission but you, Curmudgeon. We're counting on you. Of course, you'll never be able to
leave Taylor Valley. That's the price you'll pay for this unique honor.
You'll die there. It will happen soon. I hope this will make you...shall

we say...happy?"

"Happy?" the Curmudgeon asked. "How soon will I die?" he asked, sniffing air. His face was flushed. "Answer me." He let go of Tom's lapels. "If I accept this *so-called* honor."

"In three and a half months," September said. "The length of an Antarctic summer."

"Fine by me," the Curmudgeon said good-naturedly. He nodded his head. "Just so long as I can make it to my one hundredth birthday. That's all. I turn 100 in six weeks." He laughed. "That's all that matters! We're going to have a talk before we leave. Oh, that's right! We don't have time to talk. But we're going to talk. I don't care what you say! It's final. You hear me? But if we must, we'll save it for our arrival at my new destination. Let me show you a piece of this island. No, we don't have time. Hee-hee! I am not dead yet!"

The Curmudgeon escorted them into the other room of his hut.

He showed them his hammock. What they saw in the corner on a rickety desk was a dusty manual typewriter. How old was the typewriter? Ninety years old? One hundred years old? There was a sheaf of freshly typed pages sitting next the typewriter.

"You're still typing?" Tom said.

"Yes, I'm still working," the Curmudgeon said.

"No electricity here," the Curmudgeon continued. "Without electricity, you have the glory of the dusk time and the dawn time; the time that begins the day, the time that ends... With electric lights and all those whirling contraptions indoors, you ignore the splendor of the twilight. That's the experience of people living in cities. Sunrise and sunset, these are the important aspects of the day. I step out to observe them without fail. I observe the rain, the heavy mists, the overcast skies, or the rarity here on Heard island—the clear skies. It's nice to see that electricity is not essential to human happiness. But do I miss my electric pencil sharpener?"

The Curmudgeon stared at his sheaf of freshly typed pages with a murmur of laughter. "There!" he said. "That reminds me...

I began writing when I was six—that's right—six years old. That was back when I was living on the south side of Chicago. In Illinois. Right! I was a childhood genius. I wrote my poems in free verse and in iambic meter. I wrote my poems anyway that they wanted them. What did they call me then—a child prodigy? Well, I was one. Certified by the Illinois Board of Education. Won more childhood poetry and writing contests than you can shake a stick at. I was accustomed to typing my poems on a manual typewriter. Hellfire, just like the one you see before you—*right there on the table.*"

"First, I was eleven," the Curmudgeon continued. "The memories run together—blend into each other—in my thoughts. Wait. I started out when I was six. Now I do remember. In the beginning, I used pencil and paper. Then I graduated to a typewriter, when I was eleven. That's right. *1974?* Typed my poems out on a manual Smith-Corona typewriter. My daddy gave me a manual typewriter as a present for my birthday. Much later, between dry dock stints in the merchant marine, for purposes of safekeeping, I would hide my poems in a double-wrapped plastic bag in my old—I think it was an ancient model, a 1950'ish model, a Philco refrigerator."

The Curmudgeon moaned.

"That Philco refrigerator icebox was decrepit. Even by the standards of those days, it was *ancient.* It had a permanent crust of ice formed on both the inside and the outside of the freezer. Because of the heavy ice build-up, the freezer compartment was barely large enough to hold even a small bottle of Vodka. The semi-broken, or I should more accurately say—*malfunctioning*—refrigerator, made a loud whirring noise. I can still hear it! Hear it in my head today! That strange whirring sound of the refrigerator. Whirl... Whirl... Whirl...

"Because I lived in a fire trap," the Curmudgeon continued, "with a broken-down fire-escape, if the place burned down—which could have happened easily—could always retrieve that bulky sheaf of poems from my fireproof refrigerator. *In the case of an emergency.* The copy of poems in the refrigerator was the only copy I had.

When was that? *Around 1980.* The early 1980's. Why did I keep the poems? I don't know. In the beginning, that old refrigerator was like a poor man's bank vault for me. When I started out writing my poems—*seriously.*"

The Curmudgeon looked strangely calm. "I used a manual typewriter, before we had personal computers. Outside of NASA, or the military, or an Engineering Department, or a Science Department, at a University, computers were rare. They were large in size —*humongous* in size. One single computer filled a basement. *In the 1960's... In the early 1970's... Even the elites didn't have them!* I never used a personal computer until many years later. I couldn't afford one until I was well past thirty years old. That was an old one, an obsolete one. By then, I could afford a cheap one, a good one, even if antiquated. That was around the year *1994.* If my memory serves me correct, that was the year you were born, Tom. It was good. Cheap. It'd last forever. It'd be indestructible. Now you can be executed for owning a computer."

The Curmudgeon rambled on. September cut him short. She told him it was absolutely time that they must depart. She told him they couldn't wait another five minutes. "We must leave. Now. Can't wait another minute."

September always talked in precise terms, using precise numbers, always making calculations in precise time. But it always seemed to work like a charm—it always had the desired affect. She was a natural-born leader.

"Time to leave," September said, after looking at her watch.

"She's right," Tom added, "time to leave."

So the three of them, the Curmudgeon, September and Tom, loaded up the helioplane and took off. They headed for their next destination, Antarctica.

Chapter Sixteen

THEY FLEW SOUTH across the stormy waters of the South Indian Ocean to Antarctica. An hour later, the scene changed with the appearance of ice floes and icebergs.

As they approached the great ice shelf of Antarctica, September lost her bearings. She looked down, and there was an island that wasn't supposed to be there. She realized it was not an island at all—it was an enormous iceberg. It was so huge, it was thirty times the size of Heard Island; twice as large as the state of Rhode Island. "It must have recently broken off the continental ice shelf," she murmured.

"What's the matter?" Tom asked.

"It's not supposed to be here," September replied confusedly.

"What's not supposed to be here?"

"This island, no, what I mean to say is, this iceberg."

They then encountered the huge 300-meter-high ice shelves, along the continent's edge itself. After crossing the coastline, they gained altitude to fly over the Transantarctic Mountain chain which bisected the Antarctic continent.

Flying the helioplane along the Transantarctic chain provided a view of the bottom of the world that seemed locked in permanent winter, although it was the beginning of early summer in the Southern Hemisphere. In one direction, the featureless icecap disappeared uninterrupted to the pole, while in another direction, there was just the flat expanse of sea ice. They flew over beautiful mountain peaks sharpened razor thin by frost and swallowed up by more ice. The warming of the atmosphere melted a great deal of the polar ice and increased precipitation on the ice fields, which in turn added to the total amount of water both in the world's oceans and in the caps themselves. Yet through all these changes, something remained the same. Hidden in the Transantarctics was the continent's largest single area of bare rock, the 3000-square kilometers of the Dry Valleys. That was where they were headed.

September put the helioplane in hyper-drive. She turned to Tom and the Curmudgeon and explained, "Antarctica plays an important role in the world's weather patterns. The South Pole, like the North, draws warmer air toward it. But cold high winds found near the poles drive that back. This process creates low-pressure systems, or storms. That is why the seas around Antarctica always remain stormy. The Dry Valleys were first discovered by Captain Scott's men in 1901. They were following a glacier that flowed down through a mountain pass and the glacier terminated in a valley completely free of ice. The valley that lay before them was one of three major Dry Valleys, none of which have been covered with snow for thousands of years. Any snow that falls there soon sublimates, going directly from ice to vapor without passing through the liquid state. The same happens to the ice in any of the glacial tongues that try to invade these valleys. As a result, glaciers come to an abrupt end without a melt-stream runoff. Initially, the valleys were dry because the mountains blocked the moving icecap. They were kept dry by katabatic winds. These high-velocity winds are cold and extremely dry. They suck away all moisture. They make the valleys one of the driest places on Earth."

"Surrounded by mountains of ice!" Tom exclaimed. "I'm certain that these facts have something to do with your reasons for bringing us here."

"Exactly."

As they flew the length of Wright and Victoria valleys and into Taylor Valley, September continued her travelogue: "Here in

Taylor valley, the dry winds and lack of streams mean that the bare rocks have suffered no water erosion for thousands of years. Some rocks, however, have been eroded by wind, producing extraordinary shapes. She brought the helioplane to a hovering stop and pointed to a huge rock below.

They looked down and, here and there, saw the corpses of seals mummified by the freeze-drying power of the wind. September said, "Some of these seals have been lying here for 3000 years."

Awed, the Curmudgeon said, "This is where I plan to die." He nodded his head. "I, too, want my carcass, my body, to become like one of those mummies lying here. It will be my last earthly signature."

On hearing the Curmudgeon's words, September smiled.

Tom asked, "There must be a reason why we are leaving the Curmudgeon here. This place looks like Mars. It gives me the creeps." Tom shivered.

September nodded. "And in the dead of winter, it's almost as cold and inhospitable as Mars."

"Christ!" Tom whistled.

September turned to the Curmudgeon and said, "You'll barely make it through the summer. You'll never make it through the winter, you know."

The Curmudgeon nodded.

"We're going to provision you for four months."

"What's the point of this mission?" Tom asked.

September hesitated to reply and carefully deliberated before she gave a response. "The Oral Preservation Society at the monastery in the Himalayas is doomed. That's the whole point of this mission. We've known this for almost a month now."

"Doomed?" the Curmudgeon asked. "No? Are you sure?"

"Yes," September said. "The Domes recently discovered their location. We learned that from intelligence we received from our agents in Europe. The military command of the Domes are aware of its long-term mission—to preserve records of human past because of the possibility that a new enlightened age may arise in the distant future. The records would help rebuild a new civilization since everything else in the interim will have been destroyed. But this they cannot allow. It is our presumption that there will be total destruction of our way of life outside the Domes. We must preserve our history!"

Tom asked, "Then why haven't they destroyed the monastery yet?"

Again September weighed thoughtfully in her mind and carefully deliberated before she responded. She set the helioplane on automatic pilot, then turned to face Tom. "They want to crush the Anti-Gaia rebellion first. After achieving this goal, they plan to destroy the Oral Preservation Society at the monastery in the Himalayas."

"Do the people in the monastery know?" Tom asked angrily.

"Only the provost knows," September replied. "Why tell everyone they're doomed if there's even the slightest possibility it won't happen? But I think many at the monastery have already guessed the truth."

"And when the monastery is gone, all of the records of the past will be destroyed?" Tom asked.

"Precisely," September replied. This time she didn't take long to phrase her answer. "The only records of the past will be the ones the magisters and the Dome people themselves control, which in effect means they'll rewrite history to suit their own purposes, which is what they are doing now. Then when the monastery is destroyed, there will be no proof—or records—anywhere. The only proof left would be in the minds of the elderly. All they have to do then is wait for the elderly to die and educate the young people in accordance with a *falsified* history. Or they can accelerate the process by killing off the elderly in the very near future. We know now that this plan of euthanasia is to be in the offing sometime during the next year."

"So everything," Tom said, "all of what we have been doing, is futile, right? Everything? All this blood-letting? All this pain? All this so-called *revolution*? You make it sound like the Dome-people with their false Gaia religion nonsense have already won!"

It was September's turn to smile, even if it was an ironic smile. "If you're going to look at everything in the context of the next 500 years, yes." She smiled ruefully. "That's how long it's going to take for the planet to heal itself. We don't know, maybe longer. If you look at everything in the context of the next 1000 years, perhaps not."

"Thousand years!" Tom exclaimed. "Who cares about that?"

"We had better," September replied. "We have no choice."

"You really believe in Gaia, then," Tom gasped. He could not believe his ears. "The concept, anyway. You really do, don't you, September?"

"Yes, I believe in Gaia. The concept, yes," September replied slowly.

"But only in its power of independent spirituality," September said. "In that it's a metaphor for looking at things interchangeably, not as an institution. And definitely not in its ideological or philo-sophical implications. As a religion or a philosophy, it leads directly to mega-fascism. It can justify anything in the name of Gaia. A million human deaths. A billion human deaths. Five billion human deaths. And for that reason alone, I have been duped, falsely charged, and falsely condemned, as the false prophetess of an Anti-Gaia world by the truly false Gaia establishment. And what, after all, is the Gaia establishment? It is the Dome people. In other words, the magisters, the special magisters, and all their supplicants and slaves."

"I've been chosen to bury the records, right?" the Curmudgeon asked. "For distant future generations to find, right?"

"Yes," September replied. "You are the one who has been cho-sen. But these records aren't for the next generation, or the genera-tion after that, or the generation after that. These are for a hundred generations into the future."

The Curmudgeon grew quiet. "These records are intended for two thousand years from now, then? Do I have it right?"

"Right."

"And that's why you're burying them here? Right smack in the middle of a dry valley in Antarctica?"

"Right. Where they'll be left untouched for at least two thousand years; maybe longer. We don't want anyone to come across them 'by accident.'"

"By accident?" Tom asked. "You mean by that, you mean making sure that the magisters don't get them? How are you going to keep the Dome people from finding and destroying the records in the near future—or in the far future, for that matter?"

"We thought of that possibility," September replied. "They'll be buried as the Dead Sea scrolls found near Qumran were buried in the Palestinian desert, two thousand years ago. Picture stories, hand-written scriptures, printed pages, computer disks, CD-ROMs, fully integrated data, five different codices of information, from the very crude to the very sophisticated, all placed in the same time capsule, for some future generation to find, open, and study at leisure. It took an international team of linguists, secular historians and religious scholars alike, ninety years to decipher all of the 130,000 words of the Dead Sea scrolls found near Qumran. Two thousand years in the future, who knows how long it will take?"

"Who knows?" Tom remarked. "But you make it sound so simple. What about the far future? What is going to keep the records from falling into the hands of the wrong people at that time?"

"That's what prayer and hope is all about," September replied. "No, look, it's relatively simple," she then added quickly. "The Curmudgeon will bury the capsule. The Curmudgeon will die—forgive me for expressing it so tactlessly—but not before he has buried the records with a homing device, the kind we developed for our space probes. If there is any intelligent life out there, in the greater universe, it may take tens—or hundreds—of thousands of years to find it, or vice versa; in other words, it's probably useless for us to try, but this homing device will be for a better and, quite frankly, far more practical and appropriate purpose."

"In order to communicate with humans—assuming any are still around—in the distant future?" Tom asked.

"Exactly," September replied. "What's so crazy about that? The homing device will be activated two thousand years from now and will continue to emit a signal at three-year intervals for another thousand years."

"And so, if any human species develops with a fair amount of technology," Tom replied, "say between two thousand and three thousand years from now, they'll be able to pick up the signal."

"That's it," September replied. "That's the plan. They'll finally learn about our human past from the records we had buried. Assuming they can decipher the records and assuming they enter the dry valley. Using probability theory, mathematicians worked out calculations. Alas, there's still guesswork involved."

Tom shook his head. "So long into the future? Sounds like a long shot to me."

"It's a ridiculous long shot," September admitted. "But it's worth trying, isn't it?"

September disengaged the automatic pilot and, returning the ship to her manual control, brought the helioplane down to the landing spot.

She turned to the Curmudgeon and asked, "Dear old man, are you firmly resolved to do this? Frankly, we all assumed you would. I know it's a hell of an assumption to make, though!" She smiled at him.

The Curmudgeon didn't hesitate to respond. "I'm resolved. More than that, I'm positively ecstatic about it!" He beamed with delight. "And to think my mummy will be preserved in this valley. Think of it! For thousands of years! Maybe they'll find my remains too, amongst the carcasses of seals, when they find the time capsule. When they find all the records about this troubled time in humankind's past. If we are to be so lucky. You have to admit it Tom: all of this is great grist for one's imagination!"

Tom shook his head. "That's assuming there's going to be any people left around to find your carcass, you old buzzard! And we thought the Pharaohs of Egypt were goofier than shit, Curmudgeon! You beat them all!"

Turning to September Tom continued. "I can almost buy this crazy old bastard wanting to die here. But September, why did you choose him? Why can't you just bury the stuff and be done with it. Why does *he* have to stay?"

Tom shook his head again.

September noisily cleared her throat.

The Curmudgeon looked lovingly at both Tom and September. "Isn't it obvious Tom, someone has to stay. Someone has to make sure the knowledge is safe. I'm old, I don't have much time left anyway. There is a certain symmetry to it, don't you think?"

"It's just a final precaution," September replied. "We want to make sure we weren't followed. If anybody shows up, the Curmudgeon will let us know."

"Shall we be able to have a `good-bye' meal, at least?" Tom asked.

September nodded. "I don't see why not. We can stay for up to twenty-four hours, but no longer. After that, it will be very dangerous. We can't expect a 100-year-old man to set everything up for himself anyway, can we? Some of this stuff will require some sophistication to set up, although it will be easy to bury the time capsule. The homing device, the timing device—some very delicate instruments are involved."

It took them only twenty-five minutes to set up the tent. They spread their sleeping bags and settled in to sleep for a while.

It would have been the next day, but since the sun does not set during Antarctica's summer months, December through February, they awoke to bright sunlight outside. The date was November 27, 2062.

Chapter Seventeen

THEY SPENT the first ten hours setting up a `permanent camp' for the Curmudgeon. They spent the next five hours placing the twenty-foot by three-foot time capsule four feet in the ground, where it was protected on either side by a series of overhanging rocks.

For purposes of irony, the old liberated scientists, Regis Snow's old co-workers, had deliberately selected a conical shell of a fifty-kilogram nuclear warhead to store the most important records of the "library-for-the-future." They had reasoned, what better statement could they make about how close they were to total annihilation, in the second half of the twentieth century and the early part of the twenty-first century.

When Tom jokingly asked September if the nuclear warhead was American, Russian, French, British, Chinese, Indian, Pakistani, Israeli, Iranian or Korean, September replied, "What difference does it make, it's a human one—that's what matters."

To make it easier, the conical shell had been delivered to the site a year earlier.

On the helioplane, September and Tom transported all of the records with them. The Curmudgeon's job would then be to place the records inside the shell, prior to the capsule's burial.

The most intricate equipment they had to install was the homing device, which was a part of the time capsule. September made sure it was properly programmed. After she finished, she turned to the Curmudgeon. "We've dug the hole. We've placed the capsule. After we've left, you place the materials inside the capsule. Then when you've filled in the hole, it will be finished."

"What is the homing device's range?" Tom asked.

"Seventy-five miles," September replied. "Depending on what sort of equipment picking up a frequency the receivers have, however. Maybe as far as 150 miles. Being explorers, or just adventurers, they're going to have to come pretty damn close to find this burial site. We've purposely arranged for this to be a requirement—so that not just anybody may stumble on it."

Tom was clearly impressed by September's carefully thought out plan.

"The dry valleys of Antarctica are some of the last places on Earth to have been discovered by explorers," September continued. "It is also the least likely place to undergo any type of climatic change in the next 2000 years. No matter how crazy the gyrations of climate and temperature change become in other parts of the globe, they'll never get any worse here than they already are. We don't want anyone discovering this site prematurely. How long will the Gaia State and the Dome system last? We don't know. We want the time capsule to be discovered by somebody who has gone far, far, far out of his way to find this place. We want this discovery to be a real find. We don't want it to be easy. We want it to be hard."

They left the time capsule as it was and returned to camp. All the while, the sun never set. The orb hung above the horizon, rising a few degrees, then falling a few, but never dipping below the horizon. By their reckoning, the twenty-four hour a day Antarctic summer was only a couple of weeks from officially beginning.

They sat around in their sleeping bags, sipping coffee and nibbling on snacks.

"I've been putting together some of my thoughts over the past few years," the Curmudgeon said. "Better to speak to an audience of two rather than to nobody. Better to speak to you than to a bunch of seal carcasses." He chuckled. "And understand: these are the last things I have to say to you, so I ask you, be patient with me a little longer. Please indulge the final request of an old friend."

He didn't begin until he had gotten both Tom and September's attention.

"At the time Lord Siddharta," the Curmudgeon began, "of the royal Gautama family, later known as the Buddha—the Enlightened One—was born in northern India near what is now the border with southern Nepal, and at the time Confucius was born, at approximately the same time, give or take 200 years, in central China, and, 500 hundred years later, at the time the Jewish son of a carpenter, Yoshua, later known as *Jesus the Christ,* was born in a small village of Galilee, the human population was extremely stable. There were approximately 250 million souls living on the surface of the planet. How do we know the number of people? All historians agree that there were *probably* no more than 300 million. The point is that old prophets and the teachers weren't thinking in terms of billions of people when they taught with their sermons, parables, and examples of how to live *the good life*—they were thinking in terms of clans, tribes, and perhaps, just maybe, nations, that's all.

"In the year 1950 A.D.," the Curmudgeon continued, "thirteen years before I was born, there were two and one-half billion people living on Earth. In the year 2040 A.D., when I was 78-years-old, that number had grown to eight and one-half billion! It took over 250,000 years for the Earth's population to get to one billion, 250 years to get from one billion to two and one half billion, ninety years to get from two and one-half billion to eight and one-half billion!

"I'm lucky," the Curmudgeon added with feigned pride. "I was born eighteen years after the end of what we now colloquially call the *Second European War,* although during my life, up until twenty-five years ago, we called *that* phenomenon World War Two. We were privileged. We were the last generation to have it of the easy kind...*the old way*. It didn't matter if we called ourselves modernists, postmodernists, post-postmodernists..."

The Curmudgeon paused.

"Look forward! Think about today! What a difference thirty years make! The ordeals of the Eleven-Years-War made the ordeal of the twentieth century look like nothing. Then the aftermath of the Eleven-Years-War! The loss of the ozone layer! The deterioration of the environment. We must think differently. We must..."

It was obvious to Tom and September that the views of the Curmudgeon represented the painful contradictions and the horrible mental splits of the last generation of the world.

September took a sip of her coffee.

"The survival of the species," the Curmudgeon continued, "we know, over the next millennium, will be shaped by the imperatives of survival on six time-scales. Until recently, we've managed to survive on only five time-scales. For the last 100,000 years, that's been more than enough. But now, we must add another one. *Or the outcome will be fatal.* Survival on each of the time-scales has been different, of course. On a time-scale of years, the unit has been the individual. On a time-scale of decades, the unit has been the immediate family, the extended family. On a time-scale of centuries, the unit has been the tribe. On a time-scale of millennia, the unit has been the culture. Are you following me?"

At first, it was hard for September to concentrate on what the Curmudgeon was saying, but she now listened more intently.

"Good," the Curmudgeon grunted. "Culture requires not just the development of oral skills, but of written abilities as well, because stories passed on by an oral tradition alone may not expect to last more than 500 years without becoming somewhat disfigured, particularly if there is a radical shift in the material conditions of life."

September interrupted. "Historically, that's what happened with previous religions, right?"

"Why yes," the Curmudgeon said. "I'm glad you mentioned that. Written records on the origins of historical religions were written decades, sometimes centuries, after events. In almost all cases, the living witnesses were dead even before THE WORD was written down. It was the followers of the disciples—*of the original disciples*—of Zoroaster, Lao-tse, Buddha, Confucius, Jesus the Christ, Socrates, Mohammed, who recorded the words of the so-called masters—after they were gone. In some instances, 40 to 90 years later —Socrates, Mohammed, Jesus the Christ. In other instances, 200 years later, Confucius and the Buddha. In certain instances, 400 or more years later, Zoroaster and Lao-tse. The Hebrew Bible was edited and redacted once every 500 years or so, adding and subtracting bits along the way."

The Curmudgeon paused. "Where was I? What was I talking about?"

"The oral tradition?" Tom asked. "The transmission of it?"

"Right. I'll continue then," the Curmudgeon said. "In a static society, ideas hypothetically could be passed on by an oral tradition forever, but oral tradition is not sufficient to do that in a constantly shifting geographical reality—which is exactly what is going to happen to mankind in the next millennia. Even then, oral records will probably be grossly misshaped in twenty to twenty-five generations, because nobody will remember what it was like—nature-wise, climate-wise—when the events occurred, because nature and climate will have shifted so much. Are you following me?"

Tom nodded. September didn't bother to respond.

"As I was saying, on a time-scale of a 100,000 years, the unit has been the species, see? Well now, until now, that has been our thinking. But we must add another time-scale, a sixth one. I call it our sixth sense, because it's so abstract, it's better to grasp it intuitively rather than conceptually. The sixth time-scale will include the whole web of life: man, animal, plant, plus air, water, mineral. Are you following what I'm saying? The final one, the sixth, although it's the final one, is the most important one, because it's the one that makes the others possible."

Tom and September nodded.

"Now, each human will be the product of adaptation to the demands of all six time-scales, you see," the Curmudgeon continued, *"simultaneously.* That's why conflicting loyalties are bound to run deep. As it has in the past, it will be so in the future. In order to survive, we will need to be loyal to ourselves, to our immediate families, to our extended families, to all our tribes, to our cultures, to our species, to our planet. If our psychological impulses are complicated, it is because they'll have been shaped by complicated and different, even conflicting, demands. The central conflict in our nature will be the conflict between the selfish individual and the planet."

September turned to her empty coffee cup. As she did, she was listening intently. Even then, she did not look up, nor did she make eye contact.

"Nature gave us greed," the Curmudgeon continued, "or, in other words, the will to survive, and without that, we could never survive, in the forests, in the deserts, in the mountains, on the high seas, in outer space. But Nature also gave us love. Love of life. Love of wife, husband, children, uncles, aunts, to help us survive at the family level; love of friends to help us survive on a tribal level; love of conversation to help us survive on a cultural level; love of people in general, to help us survive at a species level; love of nature to help us survive at the planetary level. Human beings cannot be human beings without a generous amount of both greed—the will to survive if you will—and love. Do you see the conflict? Do you understand?" the Curmudgeon asked.

Tom and September nodded. They understood what the Curmudgeon was saying.

The Curmudgeon was a master at the art of oral delivery. The first time Tom remembered hearing the Curmudgeon speak was fifty years earlier, when Tom was an adolescent. It was difficult for Tom to realize that, even then, the Curmudgeon was fifty years of age—back then. Few people knew about him. Tom had turned nineteen; he was just a young man starting out in life. He had been just starting out in writing, too. Even on the eve of his one hundredth birthday, the Curmudgeon, Tom realized, had not lost his touch.

He was grand. For a fleeting moment, Tom imagined himself in the Curmudgeon's shoes, living another thirty-two years, to the ripe old age of one hundred. He tried to imagine what it would be like, but he couldn't. Now he was sixty-eight. To be 100! In the year 2094! That seemed like a date so unimaginably far in the future.

"These are closing words," the Curmudgeon then said. "These are my final remarks. You see, what I've been thinking about in the last few hours with you is Matsuo Basho, the seventeenth century Japanese poet. That's who I've been thinking about. So many people mistakenly thought the poet Basho was a proponent of Buddhism, you know, as a religion. He liked the idea of Buddhism, no mistaking that. It was a good way—*the way*—when trying to figure out how to live a life in a troubled world. I'm sure he thought that. He was never a proponent of Buddhism as a religion, however."

The Curmudgeon laughed. He raised his eyes. "I think of the poet Matsuo Basho when I prepare myself for death. I'm thinking of him more so, of course, as that day is drawing close. His Haiku poem *The Records of a Weather-Exposed Skeleton*. Basho wrote it as he was traveling around Japan at a very old age. He faced bandits, bad weather, tricky ordeals. It was frightening adventure, a harrowing journey!"

The Curmudgeon quoted:

> *"On a journey, ailing—*
> *My dreams roam about*
> *Over a withered moor..."*

The Curmudgeon stopped. He smiled, raising his eyes. "What a place to die! In a dry valley surrounded, only a few hundred miles away, by thousands of feet of ice!" He extended his arms—raising them on high.

"That's what I want this time-capsule burial to be," the Curmudgeon then added in a vehement voice. "If I'm allowed. *The Records of a Weather-Exposed Skeleton—or carcass.*" The Curmudgeon chuckled. "I hope they'll find my skeleton among those seal carcasses, 3000 years from now. If not my carcass, then my exposed bones. That's my final hope."

The Curmudgeon rose and went over to Tom. Tom rose, too. They nodded and embraced each other. They were moved by such a charge of emotion that they fell into each other arms.

"Remember Basho." the Curmudgeon said.

"Yes," Tom said.

The Curmudgeon crushed Tom to his chest. "`Do not resemble me. Be yourself."

"Yes," Tom nodded. "I will not resemble you. How could I? They broke the mold when they made you. I haven't smelled a thunderbolt in years," Tom then mumbled in a nearly inaudible voice. He was on the verge of tears. "I can see everything clearly. But no rain or thunderbolt or lightning though."

"How many years has it been since you've smelled your thunder and seen your lightning?" the Curmudgeon asked. "That's the question you're supposed to ask yourself. How long has it been?"

"Eleven years," Tom replied. "It's been that long since I saw a bolt of lightning." He stood erect and ramrod straight. He wiped his face. Tears came to his eyes, but he looked defiant.

"The special gift has vanished," the Curmudgeon replied evenly, "but it has not died. When you've smelled a thunderbolt coming, Tom, when you've tasted the first drop of rain on your tongue before it hits—when you've seen the bolt of lightning strike before your eyes actually see it..." The Curmudgeon smiled. "You'll smell your thunderbolt, you will. You'll taste your first drop of real rain, even if it takes seven years in the desert, trust me, stick with September, do exactly as she says, remember, do exactly as she tells you to."

"You bet, Gus," Tom nodded. "I'll try, of course. I'll do my best, Augustine."

"Good," the Curmudgeon said. "Right. I haven't heard you call me Augustine for a long time. How affectionate it is to hear you address by my proper name, my formal appellation. That's what matters."

The Curmudgeon then said, "the poet Paul Valery said, *'God made everything out of nothing, but the nothing shows through.'* Tom? Can you not see it? So clearly in a dry valley of Antarctica? Can you not see it? So clearly in the lushness and greenness of other valleys? Can you not see it in the barest, driest desert? Can you not see it? If not in the desert, then where?"

"I can," Tom said in a faltering voice. "The nothing that is. I see. Now and then."

"Tom...Tom...Tom...," the Curmudgeon murmured. "Think! Clearly, think on this. The poet William Blake said, *'Apocalypse does not point to a fiery Armageddon, but to our ignorance and complacency coming to an end.'*"

"Yes," Tom nodded.

"This journey has been my end," the Curmudgeon said. "It has been more than that. It is my epiphany, my conversion, my enlightenment, my awakening."

"Yes," Tom nodded.

"Is everything a matter of sheer random chance," the Curmudgeon then asked, raising his voice on high, "or is it fated and determined? Does chaos result from the absence of law, or from the operation of a law that we cannot comprehend? Is God nowhere? Or is She not everywhere—right now? What do you say? Remember Basho? Remember his poem, composed before he died:

> *On a journey, ailing—*
> *My dreams roam about*
> *Over a withered moor...*
> And then,
> *Myriads of things past*
> *Are brought to my mind—*
> *These Cherry blossoms!"*

The Curmudgeon smiled wanly.

Tom knew that the Curmudgeon, either deliberately or inadvertently, had knitted together two completely separate Haiku poems of Basho's, to make them stand as if they were one, instead of two. But it made sense.

"In the eyes of the magisters," the Curmudgeon said, "I was nothing more than a crushing bore, a total deviant, a deadbeat. For a time, I was convenient for them. Then what? A minor irritant? Then what? An annoyance? If I hadn't escaped from them at the time that I did, they would have snuffed me out with the absentminded dispatch of swatting a fly, or with the irrelevance of taking the garbage out on a Saturday night. I would have had to have worked much harder than I did to have represented anything greater than that to them. If I'd worked harder at being a nuisance, I might even have been an outcast pariah. But no luck. I didn't rank. We don't rank. That's the final truth. Poet? Pah. Poets are a dime a dozen."

September Snow shifted her weight. She was nervous. She felt ill at ease, not out of anxiety, the feeling came from somewhere else, she felt that she was, for once, out of her depth. The Curmudgeon looked tired. That's all, he looked tired, September thought.

"Watch," the Curmudgeon then said to Tom, "and remember. That's important too." The Curmudgeon riveted Tom with his glaring eyes. "Don't forget." He winked. He smiled. "Go in peace."

"That's it? That's your last bit of advice?" Tom asked. "Watch? And remember all you've said!"

The Curmudgeon looked down. "Yes."

As they were starting to leave, a wind began to blow. At first it was just an intermittent wind, but by Tom and September's departure time, the wind was steady, blowing constantly. They knew that when the Antarctic "summer" was over—three and a half months hence—the wind would kick up, but stronger. Eventually, the wind would blow twice as fast, then three times as fast. The weather would turn colder, then very cold. By the end of winter, it would be a harsh, relentless chill; and the wind would reach a howling crescendo of 170 miles per hour. The temperature would then drop to minus eighty-five degrees Fahrenheit. Darkness. Bitter cold.

"You were a poet all your life," September said. "You'll die one too." She spoke with a feeling of profound sincerity. She rushed forward and hugged the Curmudgeon. She gave him a long, lingering kiss of goodbye. For her part, the gesture was utterly spontaneous. Being spontaneous, it took the Curmudgeon by surprise.

"Oh my," the Curmudgeon said. He looked more than shocked, he was embarrassed. "Oh, my," he said, thoroughly chagrined. "You'll make Tom jealous. Oh, guess I was a poet, then. Guess I still am." He laughed. "Time to say goodbye to all that. Time to say goodbye. Bye, bye."

Before the winter storms would blow, the Curmudgeon would lie in a hollow, September and Tom reasoned, where his carcass would be preserved, which was, after all, his final wish. Perhaps he would lie just a few feet from the buried time capsule itself, sometime in late March, or in April, some time after the grand finale of Antarctica's summer, just lie there in wait.

Chapter Eighteen

THEY TOOK OFF, Tom and September, leaving the Curmudgeon behind. They flew the helioplane, heading west, skirting south 250 miles around the Falkland Islands, to southern Patagonia, on the southern tip of the South American mainland. Abruptly they turned north, flying near maximum speed. In order to fly over a continent-size landmass and not be detected by the military forces of the Domes, they flew in the shadow of the Andes Mountains.

September hugged the crevices of the rocks along the 4,500 mile mountain chain. At times, they passed within seventy-five yards of the sheer rock faces. September flew the helioplane as if she were a trained pilot.

While they were on this leg of the trip, Tom broke the silence that had existed between them since they had departed from Taylor Valley in Antarctica. He said to her, "Any belief, even a lousy belief, is better than nihilism. Even a half-baked belief, even a seriously defective belief, is better than nothing."

"Is that what the Curmudgeon thought?" September asked. She guided the helioplane along the sheer cliffs of the otherwise slowly undulating mountains—moving with each and every curve of the chain of mountains—all the time piloting the helioplane with verve and poise.

"No, I don't think so," Tom said.

"What did he think, then?" September asked.

"Something," Tom replied, "even if it is an illusion, even if it is a falsity, is better than nothing. That's what he thought."

"Then he would have accepted the notion of Gaia?"

Tom nodded yes. Then he shook his head. He had reservations. "He would have accepted life—whatever that life was. I don't believe he would ever have accepted the notion of Gaia; just life. In other words—yes, but..."

"Yes...but?" September asked. "I don't understand. Please explain."

"Yes," Tom explained, "the Curmudgeon would have supported the concept of Gaia, but no, only in his highly idiosyncratic manner. Do you see? He would have kept it simple. Life over death. That's all. Anything to him—anything—was better than nihilism. But life was all he believed in."

"That's all," September asked. "Nothing more?"

"That's all," Tom replied. "That's all that would have mattered to him."

"When did you start calling him the Curmudgeon?" September asked. "It seems like that name has always been pinned to him."

"Not always," Tom replied. "It was the year A.D. 2040. He was seventy-seven. He was old and crotchety. Everybody started calling him the Curmudgeon. The name stuck. Come to think of it, looking back, who'd have thought he'd make it another twenty-three years?"

September suddenly reduced speed. For a moment, she steered the helioplane 400 yards away from the wall of the mountains. With the helioplane completely motionless, she turned to Tom and said, "In one hour, we are going to pick up my daughter. Now I'm going to tell you your mission. I've waited until now because no one is to know where you're going—not a living soul. Understand?"

"Not a living soul is to know?" Tom asked. "No one? And my mission? What is it?"

"The reason why you are here. Why you are here, and why you

are so precious, so valuable. Why you are so vital to the future. You are going to be the living link between the past and the future. Do you see?"

September talked and Tom listened.

"When we were in the Pyrenees mountains, after we crossed the Atlantic to France; two weeks prior to that time, an ultra, ultra secret decision had been made by the central rebel command. It was that all of our expenditures, all of our effort, would be concentrated on accomplishing one goal and one goal alone—the total destruction of the Domes' worldwide network of climate-changing machines, those same machines that were designed, constructed, and managed by my late husband, Regis Snow."

Tom nodded his head. "You will not try to defeat them in the field?" Tom asked.

"No," September replied. "They are more effective at waging conventional warfare than we are, or ever will be. We'd have to be like them in order to defeat them, and that would defeat our purpose, wouldn't it, even if we were successful. If we were to face them in a straight, conventional military encounter, they would slaughter us. If we tried to hold out with a program of low-intensity guerrilla warfare for another four or five years, it would be a miracle if we even survived. From a technological point of view, they can outmatch us and outgun us any day of the week. Our last and best hope, is to destroy their weather-changing machines. In the end, they control all the minerals. They control all the weapons technology and weapons research. They control the police, the media, and the sources of controlled information, allowing them to remake `history' to suit themselves. They control the fusion plants. They control all the trade, well, they already have a monopoly on the trade..."

Tom interrupted. "Excuse me, but that sounds like practically everything."

"Not everything," September replied, "if we concentrate all our resources on one thing, the one thing we can free from their control: the water and the air. In other words, the control of weather and climate. That's the one thing we can take away from them."

"How do you propose to do that?" Tom asked.

"By returning the weather to nature, to the Earth, to the planet."

"What good will that do if you don't control everything else?" Tom asked skeptically. "It'll be a victory gained at too great a cost. Furthermore, can it be done?"

"Maybe it can."

"How?"

"From my late husband's plans, but more importantly, from some other highly classified documents we have just obtained, we know every weak spot and possible point where the system is vulnerable. Yes, the weather-changing apparatus can be destroyed. There's one hitch, though."

"One hitch?" Tom asked. "What's that?"

"All of us," September said, "who will be involved in the destruction of the apparatus will perish. We will die in the act that destroys them."

"You're certain of that?" Tom asked.

"Absolutely," September replied. "We can destroy the nuclear reactors, but none of us will escape. There is not a shadow of doubt about that. We can damage, indeed inflict serious damage on the apparatus in many ways, but it'll require seventy-five totally trained and totally committed suicide squads, each consisting of thirty people. We must destroy it so that it can never be repaired or rebuilt."

"Are you sure about that?"

"Absolutely," September replied. "There is no one who knew the system better than its creator, my late husband, Regis."

"How many people would it take altogether?" Tom asked.

"Twenty-three hundred people," September said. "Twenty-five hundred tops."

"Kamikaze?" Tom asked. "Suicide soldiers? That's who you've been training all this time, isn't it? Everything else you've been doing has been a diversion, hasn't it?"

"Yes," September admitted. "The trip to the Himalayas. The trip to see the Curmudgeon. The trip to Antarctica. Everything. The suicide soldiers are the *creme de la creme.*"

Instead of looking boastful and proud, September appeared almost embarrassed. But in spite of that, still resolute and determined due to the belief in her mission.

"And your daughter?" Tom asked quietly. "What are your plans for her? Surely, not to become a member of a suicide squad. She's too young for that. Or how old do these kamikazes have to be? Fourteen? Fifteen? Sixteen? How about six?"

Tom was merciless and resentful. He didn't care if he hurt September's feelings. He had seen enough of the results of violence to be bitterly opposed to its prosecution, regardless of who was right or wrong; regardless of who apparently served their own so-called righteous cause—yet in the process, murdered and maimed others.

"Yes, that's the whole point, isn't it?" September replied softly. She was struggling with something immense and powerful, Tom could tell; something tugging deep inside her. He wanted to wait for her to speak first, but for the first time, Tom noticed, September was tongue-tied and speechless.

Tom gently probed. "I figured there had to be a point to your capturing me in the first place, and rescuing me from the firestorm in the underground bunker in New York? You taking me around the world with you? Right, September? Even if it was a diversion."

"Right," September said.

"And the point had to be related to the cause, right?"

"Right, again. Although it was an accident when we first kidnapped you in New York. That was unintended, a real mistake. We really were trying to capture the special magister from Washington. But after you inadvertently fell into our hands, and at first we didn't know what to do with you, and couldn't easily dispose of you, then we started working out a plan. By the time we had held you in captivity for two months, I had formulated most of it. The rest—well, we just winged it, didn't we? I knew it was a matter of providence, it was meant to happen, when I knew I had to go see the Curmudgeon in person anyway, to take him to Taylor valley of Antarctica. And I knew that by taking you along, and with you talking to him, you would be thoroughly and completely won over to our cause."

"I was never completely won over to your cause by believing in the righteousness of the rebel's plan," Tom replied. "I was won over simply because I saw the total bankruptcy of the Gaia-Dome system. That's not the same thing."

"Fair enough," September said. "That's close enough."

"And the point has to be related to your daughter, too?" Tom then asked.

September said, "Right, of course, again. I can't fool you. You've got it all figured out."

"Well, what is it?"

"What is what?"

"The point?" Tom asked at last.

September looked at her watch. "We have to pick up my daughter in fifty-seven minutes. The last twenty-five minutes of flying time are going to require some absolutely incredible flying aerobatics. We're talking about full-tilt stunts, barrel roles—everything. And we don't have much time. I'll be brief. It's better this way. I have no choice. When we reach our destination, I'll tell you all."

"Promise?" Tom asked.

"I promise," September replied. "Trust me."

They flew into Bolivia, not too far from the base of Guallatiri mountain, in the Andes Mountains, near the intersecting borders of Bolivia, Chile and Peru.

The valley there was comparatively small. It was a two-mile high valley (valleys in the Andes Mountains were high, but the surrounding mountains were of course higher)—which they were suddenly approaching at an incredibly fast speed. There was nothing more than a hamlet there, no, actually nothing more than a dozen structures of indeterminate size. They were protected by the nearby towering rock-wall of mountains to the west, and the flat high sprawling deserts to the east. September was flying the helioplane at an incredibly fast speed.

Another secure place at the end of the world, so Tom thought.

"Another hideaway tugged away inside the mountains?" Tom asked September.

"Yes," September replied. "This one will be discovered by the magisters and the military forces of the Dome people very soon."

"How do you know that?" Tom asked.

"It's all according to plan. Because we want them to," September added. "Hang on, we're going in."

September did everything the helioplane could do, and some things it wasn't suppose to be able to do: tailspins, four-point rolls, figure eights, snap rolls, hammerheads.

She flew one long loop, a wide arabesque, then at one end, flew a grandiose line high above the valley.

Within a couple of minutes, Tom was completely nauseated, suffering from a tormented, queasy stomach. "What the hell are you trying to do?" Tom asked. "Get us killed? If you insist on flying these gut-wrenching, spine-tingling aerobatics September, I'm going to puke on myself. Then I'm going to black out and lose consciousness."

"I'm trying to draw their attention," September replied.

"Whose attention?" Tom asked. "The attention of the troops on the ground?"

"No," September replied. "Not them. The attention of the bad guys."

"Why in God's name do you want to do that?" Tom shouted hysterically. "I thought we've been spending all this time trying to evade them—trying to keep away from them!"

"Till now, yes, that's true," September replied. "But that's no longer operative. Because if they don't think we're dead—you, me, my daughter, see—the mission will fail." September laughed. "It's all part of the plan. Just relax. Go with the flow. You worry too much."

"Worry too much!" Tom shouted in exasperation. "You're going to get us killed!"

"Sticking with uncertainty is how we relax in chaos, how we are cool ourselves when the ground beneath us disappears," September said. "Just relax."

Completely unable to orient himself during the course of the aerial gymnastics, Tom finally closed his eyes and fought off his tendency to black out. When he was on the verge of blacking out, September at last landed the helioplane.

He opened his eyes. He looked up in surprise. A little girl of five or six was running across the dusty dry desert floor, shouting her mother's name. The distance from the out-buildings to the landed helioplane was about one hundred and fifty yards, so she had quite a distance to run. She was alone. She was wearing a tattered dress that was dirty and faded. She carried a broken doll with a scarred, broken, and hairless head. Her shoes were scuffed.

The mud wall out-buildings were painted light-green. The corrugated iron roofs were held down with huge, eighty-pound boulders, presumably to keep the roofs from blowing away during the fierce winter desert storms. The buildings appeared deserted. There was no one else around; no one visible anyway. A small gate swung open and shut in the desert wind. In a moment, Tom realized that, except for the little girl, the place was completely deserted.

"A band of our guerrilla troops temporarily evacuated this place four days ago," September explained to Tom. "The only thing left in the buildings are a handful of dead, unburied bodies and a couple of the very sick and badly injured, who were too far gone to be moved, and had no chance of surviving a forced march. And Iona, who was left behind to care for the three or four sick as they lay dying. Right, Iona? How's my precious little girl!"

September did not otherwise greet her daughter or give her a hug as she ran up to the helioplane. "Are there any left?" September asked Iona.

"The last one succumbed this morning," Iona replied, almost out of breath from running. "The others died two days ago, mommy."

"She's so young, yet she knows how to pronounce the word— *'succumb'?*" Tom asked dumbfounded.

"She's bright," September interjected. "How much food did they leave with you, honey? How much stores? Enough?"

"Enough food for four days, but enough water for six," Iona replied good-naturedly to her mother. "I'm a little hungry, that's all. But I'm not thirsty, that's the important thing. I'm all right."

"She's not even six years old and they left her in a situation like this?" Tom asked dumbfounded.

"She's been through worse," September replied. There was a long pause. "If we hadn't arrived, our band of guerrillas would have come back to pick her up in a day or two. And you're safe now, aren't you, darling?"

"Yes," Iona replied, "I am. I missed you, mommy."

"I've missed you, too, sweet thing. Now get in."

September looked at the doll that Iona had clasped in her arm. "Aren't you getting too old for dolls?" September asked in a stern voice.

"Look, Tom. The doll must be seventy years old. How remarkable! *I think it must be older than you!*"

September didn't make the remark in a callous or mean-spirited way, but her daughter took it differently. Tom could see by the look on Iona's face that she was far too sensitive not to be unaffected by it. Iona was not certain that she had not been seriously rebuked by her mother's words, even if that had not been her mother's intent.

"I found it lying under some rags, mommy. I didn't mean anything by it. I didn't mean to do wrong." She sniffled again.

September said nothing. Already she was preoccupied with far more weighty problems than the status of a doll that was about to fall apart in her daughter's arms.

"What kind of a mother are you?" Tom asked in a surprised voice. "After all, Iona's just a kid. Comfort her."

"What would you know about being a mother?" September asked Tom. "For that matter, what do you know about being a *father?*"

September was beside herself with rage, but it was just a passing moment of anger, and it quickly dissipated. "You have no children of your own, do you, Tom?"

"No, I haven't had the pleasure," Tom replied.

"So, you're not a father," September said. "So, don't be so harsh in judging me. I must be concentrating carefully on some important things right now, don't you see? Iona might as well start getting accustomed to being tough—and she might as well start right now. Either that, or she won't survive. It's as simple as that."

Climbing into the helioplane, they took off. September checked her watch. "Remember when I put you through all those aerobatics and then deliberately pulled the helioplane half a mile away from the wall of the mountains, fifty-seven minutes ago?"

"Yes," Tom replied. "I was wondering why you did all that. Especially after you had taken such extraordinary precautions so we could travel here undetected."

"I did that deliberately so that we *would* be detected by the military air arm of the Domes," September replied. "But it was a matter of being picked up by their sensors at just the right time—not too early, not too late. So they'd arrive looking for us, but only after we had an opportunity to hide. Timing's everything."

"Why, in God's name, would you want to do a thing like that, for Christ's sake?" Tom asked.

"You'll see why. Wait and see."

Once the helioplane was safely hidden in a tiny box canyon in the mountainside, September handed Tom a pair of high powered binoculars. After they had all exited the helioplane and crouched on a hill overlooking the hamlet, September said, "Watch. See for yourself. It's an old trick we've used before."

Tom took the pair of binoculars. A buzzing sound came out of nowhere. Within minutes, a single enemy laser-jet swooped down from a high altitude to the lonely isolated hamlet. Then, after making a pass, it disappeared. Several minutes later, five laser-jets swooped down from an altitude of the same height to the lonely isolated hamlet and blew most of the buildings to smithereens. As Tom carefully watched, he realized there was a disabled helioplane, half covered with a flimsy camouflage net. It was parked behind one of the large outbuildings, a building that had just been destroyed. On the second pass, the laser-jets swooped down and destroyed the parked helioplane in one explosion. Then the five laser-jets took off, streaking across the sky, climbing to 20,000 feet. The remaining laser-jet landed several hundred feet from the hamlet. Tom gave the binoculars to Iona so she could watch as the reconnaissance team scoured over the damage on the ground, taking their time as they did.

"It's working," September pronounced with an air of satisfaction. "We'll hide here for a day, then sneak out in our helioplane under the cover of mountains and a moonless night. They'll report back to their headquarters we're dead. They'll file a report about the charred bodies. You can be sure they'll file a full report. It's not so much outright lying as allowing them to jiggle the figures to give the message that their bosses want to hear. More than that. They get hefty bonuses—based on number of bodies counted. Body count, that's the important thing. If September Snow, and her daughter Iona, where supposed to be among the dead here, then they'll count it. I know they will. That's the only thing that matters to them."

September smiled. "This always works. I'm certain they'll report us dead. Mission accomplished."

"Officially, Iona, you're now dead," September then said. She put her arms around her daughter's neck and kissed her on both cheeks. Iona put her arms around September's neck and they embraced. "My dear daughter. And being my only daughter, that's the only way you're going to live—see? Understand? That's how you'll survive. My fair Iona—meet Tom. Tom, meet Iona. My lovely daughter. Isn't she lovely, Tom?"

As the two were introduced, they shook hands, greeting each other with a friendly smile. Tom beamed down at Iona. He was already feeling an attachment to her, something like a love growing inside him, this small child who was expected to be so grown-up. "Tom will watch over you," September then said at last, "dear, when I'm not near, when I'm unable to be close by."

"Where are we going, mommy?" Iona asked.

"To a place where you will be safe," September said, hugging Iona.

"You're still such a show-off, mommy," Iona said.

"Why do you say that?" September asked.

"We know how much you enjoy flying helioplanes," Iona said laughing. "But you don't have to be such a show-off, do you?"

Iona thought she was the only person who could have witnessed September's aerial performance, and thus, it had been intended for her enjoyment. But it had been intended for the military as well.

"Sometimes you are excessive in your zeal, mommy," Iona announced with a grown-up air. "If I don't tell you the truth, mommy, who will?"

"You're dead, too, Tom," September said the next morning, after they awoke after a good night's sleep. "Officially, that is. Like I said, we are going to a place where they will never find us. At least, in this small way, we will finally win some sort of battle. But how much more secure shall we be if we know for certain they will never be looking for us? H'mm? That's our sweetest victory. There will be no reason for them to look for us, since we're already dead, right? According to their own confirmed reports, that is. And I will drop out of the war for three or four years. *That should prove to them I'm*

dead! Besides, my colleagues need more time to prepare for the final battle. If the Gaians think I'm dead, they'll be less likely to expect a buildup to destroy the nuclear-powered wind machines. They'll be expecting another push in other sectors. They don't care much about you, Tom, so on that score, what difference will it make? For all they know, you died in New York. They'll have no reason to believe otherwise, to them, we're all dead. I shall be a mother again for a while, Tom. You will become the key to everything—to the future, that is. You should feel proud. You *shall* be proud."

"Are you going to explain everything to me?" Tom asked, "I mean, everything! This time! No bullshit, this time!"

September nodded. "Yes. I will. No bullshit, this time."

Tom just shook his head with a feeling of foreboding. "Christ. Now I have to live with two women."

September laughed. "We will land in a rebel stronghold along the former United States-Mexican border. This is one of the last guerrilla strongholds left in the Western Quadrant. The only other two are in California and in a border area between southern Utah and northern Arizona. They are very likely to disappear eventually. We will have to walk from there the rest of the way to our destination, I'm afraid."

"Walk?" Tom asked. "Did you say, walk? Where to?" he asked.

"Southwest, across the sands of the great northern Chihuahuan desert. And then due south, into the heart of Mexico's Sierra Madre Mountains. Don't worry, the journey's only about three hundred miles. By my calculation, that's about fifteen miles a day. About twenty days and twenty nights. It'll be an interesting trip."

"Three hundred miles!" Tom exclaimed. "Walking? You call that an interesting trip?"

"Piece of cake," September snipped. "We can't fly. They would spot anything that moves in the air. Air traffic is strictly controlled—under heavy surveillance. They watch anything approaching the Forbidden Zone. Air travel must be ruled out. But traveling overland will be relatively safe. It will be difficult for them to detect us.

Especially as we will be a party of three. Where we are going, there is only dry, sparse mountains, overlooking even drier, sparser desert."

"The Forbidden Zone?" Tom asked. "What's that?"

"We are going to travel near it, fifty miles north of it," September slowly replied. "There are no roads to our destination, there are only forgotten foot-paths, and even older, chancier, forgotten burro-trails. The government forces would never dream of us traveling overland, not by burro. And believe me, to be really safe, we'll take a long, circuitous route. We won't take any chances."

"Can Iona walk that far?" Tom asked. "I mean, that's three hundred miles. I mean, she's only nearly six years old."

"Each of us will take a couple of burros," September replied. "So there will be six burros between us. Iona can ride on one. We can make fifteen miles a day. What are you worried about? This will be your salvation, your redemption. You will be free. You will be in paradise. You will be alive. Stop whining. Compared to what is going to happen to the rest of the world, you will be the lucky one. That's for certain!"

Chapter Nineteen

FROM THE BOX CANYON in the mountainside, they flew north, hugging the eastern ridges of the Andes Mountains, passing near Lake Titicaca.

Several hundred miles further north, they slipped through the northern mountain pass of the Andes, heading out over the calm open Pacific water, heading north to the west coast of Mexico.

Soon they entered the well-patrolled areas of the open central Pacific. September returned to her stealth practice of flying at twelve feet above the surface of the ocean, and flying at a speed of 120 miles per hour, so as to escape detection from radar and sonar, but also to escape satellite surveillance.

When they intersected with the peninsula of *Baja California* in northern Mexico, September raised the helioplane's altitude, then put the plane into hyper-drive.

She headed the helioplane in a north-east direction. They were getting close to an enemy stronghold. It was time for them to go for broke. They had to move quickly—for the element of surprise and speed were everything now.

Within minutes, September pushed the helioplane at a break-neck speed, breaking not only the sound barrier at Mach 2, but approaching the barrier at Mach 3, a dangerous speed for such a helioplane, which had been built for flexibility and maneuverability.

September knew she was pushing the helioplane too hard, but

felt she had no choice.

Less than three minutes after breaking the second barrier, there was a snap in the fuel line. *September knew what happened.*

September detected the exact place where the break occurred—simply by reading the fuel gauge and the controls on the instrument panel. She knew exactly how critical and dangerous the situation was. She called Tom over to the pilot seat, and in an even, casual voice, said: "The fuel line's broken. Don't panic! You are going to have to go back, find the break, tape it, then hold it together tightly with your bare hands. Understand?" It was as if September was asking Tom to repair a gas leak on a stove, not a fuel line on a sophisticated helioplane, flying at a speed of over 1700 miles per hour.

"How long do I have to hold the fuel line together?" Tom asked breathlessly.

"Until we land. Go now. Or we're dead ducks. Ninety seconds to death. Find that leak and stop it!"

Tom found the break in the fuel line. Fortunately, it was easy to find. He grabbed the place where the leak had occurred, taped it together, then held it. He tensed the forearm muscles of his arms as he clamped the palms of his hands over the break—to make sure it remained sealed.

"They spend over $350 million dollars," Tom complained aloud to himself, "to build one of these infernal contraptions—more technology involved than you can imagine. You got to hold a broken fuel line with your bare hands—just in order to prevent the goddamn thing from crashing. What a waste! And this helioplane was built less than three years ago. Planned obsolescence, if you ask me!"

After he held it for an hour, Iona came over to relieve him. "Your hands must be tired. Mom sent me back to help you. We're almost at our destination. Let me help you for a moment so you can relax your grip. It must be killing you."

Tom smiled. Gesturing gratefully with his nodding head, he said his hands were actually sore, and he was feeling a cramp coming on. "You've arrived at the right time."

Iona took hold of the fuel line. She held it for a short time, just long enough for Tom to relax the crimp in his hand. "My mother thinks she's perfect," Iona said to Tom. "And most of the time she is. But the rest of the time, she's not. Just near-perfect. It's that simple."

Tom took the fuel line, and thanked Iona again.

"Just one little thing, only a simple faulty fuel line—and we're dead," Iona said, shrugging her shoulders. "You figure it. Mom knows best."

On the southern side of what had once been the former U.S.-Mexican border, eighty-two miles west of Ciudad Juarez, they landed at the site of a partially destroyed tank and tire factory.

The first thought occurring to Tom as he closely examined the partially demolished plant was: `Why build a factory in the middle of the desert?'

The tank and tire factory was a former *maquiladora* factory. Sixty-five years earlier, cheap auto parts were shipped in from rust-belt American states and cheap local labor was employed. The maquiladora program was "a huge success," from a profit point of view, until the maquiladoras were underbid by the Chinese and other countries. Later, the semi-derelict buildings were converted to war production and completely militarized during the latter half of the Eleven-Years-War.

Many of the former *maquiladoras* were located in the Rio Grande river valley, stretching 500 miles from Juarez to Matamoros, or in the far west, located near the old border city of Tijuana. This isolated tank factory was one of the largest plants built between these two larger concentrations of factories. It was a lonely outpost.

The buildings once housed a huge factory that mainly produced retreaded tires and later assembled vinyl components for the American bus industry, which was, finally, during the Eleven-Years-War, converted into a permanent major tank and armaments manufacturing plant. The buildings were gutted and destroyed by Third World terrorists after they captured and blew them up in one desperate struggle two years prior to the end of the Eleven-Years-War. This happened during the period when most of the deaths caused by the war occurred. Even before the terrorists arrived, conditions were so abhorrent workers were known to say of the place: *"El diablo* himself is afraid to live here."

The terrorist efforts also proved to be hopelessly desperate. Ostensibly for purposes of fomenting world-wide revolution (which failed disastrously), the action, and many more like it, were nevertheless successful in other ways. It effectively ended the Eleven-Years-War, by sapping the strength of the war effort by sabotaging many essential war industries.

The terrorists' actions also carried a huge human price; practically all the people who worked in the bombed factories were killed.

The working conditions had been worse than slave labor, anyway. When the uprising was suppressed, all died—terrorists and workers alike: in one stupendous act of "mass suicide".

Within two years of the destruction of the factory, the area infrastructure was destroyed, the population decimated. An exodus took place. There was hardly a soul left—not even a dog—three years after the mayhem and destruction. The worst outbreaks of sun poisoning then occurred—which finished off the remaining survivors. The few who did remain took off to the hills, evolving into scavengers and cannibals.

Miraculously, six years later, the climate stabilized itself. To the great bafflement of scientists, it was noted that this phenomenon occurred in isolated pockets here and there; the planet seemed to be able to `heal itself,' but only in localized environmental pockets. These stabilized pockets were inexplicable to the scientists.

Six years after the local climate stabilization occurred, the factory site became temporary headquarters for the Western underground army. It was the perfect place for the army to be located. It was completely hidden, three hundred miles from the trade routes. That's when September, Tom, and Iona arrived. They outfitted burros for a long trek across the Sonora desert into the foothills of the Sierra Madre.

They spent little time with the leadership of the army. They drew their supplies and departed in a hurry.

First they headed south, then turned east—to the shores of Lake Guzman. They skirted the place where the water flowed neither into the Gulf of Mexico, nor into the Gulf of California, but sank directly into a sinkhole in a mile-high plateau located along the continental divide.

They passed a peculiar-looking dump adjacent to the foul-smelling sinkhole. At regular intervals, they saw emerging gases, looking like puffs of smoke belching from a hole.

A huge tire dump was located beside a factory next to the old company building. The 100 acre dump was enclosed by a fence that consisted of rows of empty oil drums. It contained millions of tires—going through barely noticeable decomposition—because the process of decomposition would take over 150 millennium to complete.

The tires had been buried barely underground—seventy-five years before. Since that time, the tires had gradually risen to the surface, little by little, through muck and filth, at a rate of about an inch a year. As far as the eye could see, there were little mounds, two to six inches high.

The upper parts of the mounds had risen above the viscous ooze and mud. The mucky mire was stagnant and nauseatingly foul-smelling; but very slowly, the deposit of discarded tires was rising, a little at a time. This mountain, 1000 years hence, would be a permanent monument above ground—a lasting legacy of the accumulated debris of the auto-industrial age.

Future generations, if there were any, would be able to view the monument in awe and wonder.

"If they had buried the tires *one hundred and fifty feet* deep, in 5000 years, the tires would still rise to the surface," September allowed. "It's inescapable. Tires always rise to the surface in wet garbage dumps—it's a matter of physics. Synthetic rubber will rise above whatever surrounds it, if the matter is wet, unless it's held down by a barrier, a layer of concrete, for example, or something equally durable.

"The old tires were made completely of synthetic rubber; they were shipped to this refuse dump from places like New York, Pennsylvania, Michigan. The only way to `permanently' bury them would have been to have added a six inch barrier of concrete beneath the land-fill, but in order to keep costs down, the contractors skimped. They didn't care that in seventy-five years time, the refuse would rise. They were only thinking of the `here and now.'

"But there's more. Then undiscovered, there has been a deep lava flow, flowing deep under the surface, providing heat, and there is an artesian source of underground water also, flowing from the Sierra Madres through a layer of rare mineral salts. The combination of heat, pressure, mineral salts, and water has been producing a mineral soup here, and over time, little by little, this soup will react more and more with the synthetic rubber, causing the mass to swell, thus increasing its buoyancy, and forming a vast Styrofoam-like raft, slowly pushing its way to the surface.

"If a six inch barrier of concrete had lined the dump, the rubber would have pushed its way through eventually, although it would have taken longer. If Dante were to have been alive 500 years hence, I think this would have inspired one of his visions of hell."

"How do you know all this?" Tom asked. "You talk like a walking encyclopedia!"

"I just know it," September said. "There are worse visions of hell on Earth: abandoned nuclear-test sites and plutonium dumps, open-pit sites containing wastes from nuclear fission power plants, worst of all: the huge dumps of nuclear waste from the enormous climate-controlling wind machines in the Third World parts of the

Southern Hemisphere. It will take more time, but eventually they will also be seen, and when they are, it will be a ghastly sight. How can they be cleaned up? They're gargantuan."

"How do you know?"

"I've seen them," September replied, shrugging her shoulders. "My husband showed them to me. Once, I had a peculiar interest in industrial garbage: coal cinders, iron ore slag. Regis told me that we were supposed to avoid this place. Look! It's on the map! Believe it or not."

September showed Tom the map. The site was designated by an emblem of the skull and crossbones.

"Regis at one point tried to map all these places, but just as he was beginning to do so, the government ordered him to stop."

After they traveled another five miles, the sunset was approaching. The sunset was spectacular and beautiful. There were huge clouds. Everything was beginning to look as though draped in red silk.

Tom stopped his burros. He turned to face September. With his other hand, he halted her burros. "Where are we going? Beyond the horizon all I see is desert. And if we keep traveling like this, unprotected, with no sun screening, we will surely come down with serious sun poisoning. Sun poisoning can catch you unawares. During the Eleven-Years-War, I saw a lot of it."

"We eventually are going to make it to the foothills of the Sierra Madre," September hastily replied, cutting Tom off.

"When?"

"Trust me!"

"Where are we going?" Tom asked. "I want to know."

"There! That's where we're going!" September pointed to the south-west. "Let go of my burros!" she shouted in earnest.

Tom released the reins of September's burros. September finally calmed down. "I understand your concern. Everything's going to be all right. Trust me."

"Hold it right there," Tom replied. He wasn't satisfied at all.

He started pacing back and forth. He also halted the burro that Iona was riding. All of the burros had come to a halt. "What about this business of the sun poisoning? I've seen what it can do to you. Nobody is going into the deserts. Over the last ten years, people have been retreating from the deserts in droves. We're walking into a certain death."

September took a moment to reply, repressing an upsurge of anger. She was on the verge of losing her temper. "All right, we'll travel by night," she agreed. "If you know so much about sun poisoning! If there's at least one-half a moon, it will provide enough light for us to see by, so we'll travel by night. Otherwise, when there's a little sliver of moon, or no moon at all, we'll take our chances by day. A few days of sun poisoning aren't going to kill us, Tom. And when we get there, we will be protected from the sun's death-rays, anyhow. That's the important thing! Who's in charge of this outfit?"

"I just want to make sure you know what you're doing," Tom demanded.

"I know what I'm doing. And if I told you once, I've told you twice, let go of my burros!"

September snatched the reins of Iona's burros from Tom, almost striking him with the loose ends. She hurried ahead, after pausing to say in passing: "We'll rest for a couple of hours at the end of the day. Then we'll continue until daybreak. By then, we'll have reached the hills—I know of an abandoned mineshaft located about eighteen miles from here. We'll hole up there during daylight hours until nightfall. There's going to be a half-moon—at least for several nights running—and after that, we'll have the cover of mountains too. When there is no moon, if necessary, we'll travel by the light of the stars! So do me a favor, Tom. Trust me. For a change. Huh? All right? Do you think you can manage that?"

"All right," Tom replied in a peevish, partially mollified voice. "And don't strike me with your reins. You mind your burros. I'll mind mine! Let's go!"

On the second to the last night of full moon, they saw two large elliptical blue rings around the moon.

"What are they?" Tom asked September. "I've heard the nature channel's explanation of those rings." Tom looked up into the night sky to observe them. "The last time I saw them was before I went to New York. The scientists have been conducting atmospheric tests, right? That's why there are blue rings."

"The magisters on the nature channels have been lying to you, Tom," September replied in a tired voice. "They have not been conducting tests. Are you surprised to hear that? I don't think you are! The reality is, they've been trying to find a cheaper way to dump nuclear waste—the most dangerous fissionable material—as well as nuclear waste from the old plutonium pits. They are trying to devise a program to send it into outer space—and destroy it by implosion. They haven't got it all figured out yet, but they're still working on it. Giving them this much credit, it is at least one serious project that they really are concerned about."

Day after day they traveled but not once during the entire trip did Iona complain. Even when they had to go a day and a night without stopping for food, she kept her mouth shut. She never complained. She was a real trooper. One night they had to travel nineteen miles, walking ten hours from twilight to dawn, and one of the burros collapsed and was left for dead. She had to walk half that distance in order to give her burro a rest, yet she never complained. Even when they had to cut their water ration down to a pint and a half a day for each of them (and none for the burros), she still refrained from making any complaints.

Towards the end of their trip, they had to eat cactus and berries to supplement their dwindling food supply. Iona ate the bitter fruit berries of the desert thorn plant, and the yucca root—all without a murmur of discontent.

As time went on, they supplemented their diet with more of

what the desert could provide. Much of their time was spent digging roots and seeking berries. They kept traveling over the ridges and spines of the mountains, sometimes climbing over 3,500 feet to the higher levels of the Sierra Madre and then descending to the valley floor again. The route they had chosen was deliberately difficult so they would avoid detection. They practically never traveled in a straight line for more than two miles. Sometimes, Tom thought they were traveling around in circles, so crazily and seemingly erratic was the zigzag route they took.

There was no other way for them to utilize the precious little water reserves hidden away at little springs here and there.

All Tom could figure out was that they were traveling more or less west, then more or less south; occasionally backtracking, but mainly moving in a southwesterly direction. Iona liked the desert. She liked night-traveling too. And when she had to travel in the daylight hours, even when the temperature soared above 110 degrees Fahrenheit, she endured it. For a five-year-old girl who was almost six, she was strangely in her element. The desert itself, and more importantly, the foothills above the desert, were rapidly becoming her home.

To Tom and September, this habitat was a place that was permanently alien. But because she was young and impressionable, to Iona, this place was home.

Practically all of the earlier inhabitants of the desert were gone after the Eleven-Years-War. The climate had changed. Sun poisoning combined with a shrinkage of the water supply caused the population to dwindle and almost disappear. War and disease had ravaged the population, but there were still a few survivors, living in isolation. (A cave and a tiny spring were sometimes enough to support a small body of people.)

On the eighth night out, they accidentally came across a party of these `people,' who had newly metamorphosed into night scavengers and cannibals.

The scavengers were busy scurrying around the wreckage of a

Dome army helioplane that had apparently crashed perhaps a week before, when the trio chanced upon them. They were gathering bits of food left behind by the jackals and vultures, and also taking the dead pilots' aluminum sun visors.

They looked like primitive hunters and gatherers; completely naked, though covered from head to toe with dried mud.

They looked as though they had emerged from a futuristic science-fiction movie, except for an occasional sun visor (worn specifically by the leaders) and rubber-soled sandals (vestiges of the tire factory.)

They were clearly not modern `Indians.' The Indians had withdrawn deeper into the Sierra Madre, during the early stages of the Eleven-Years-War. They never would have succumbed to cannibalism, preferring death to that sordid `way of life.'

More than anything else, this sight made September content because she wanted Iona to witness the spectacle of people being driven under duress to such a low level of uncivilized behavior. She wanted Iona to remember exactly what she saw.

It was good for Iona to take a good look at this party of stragglers, living at such a low level of existence. There was little harm in doing so. The party could have been easily frightened away. September knew that if the scavengers and cannibals became desperately hungry, they would have had no qualms about eating each another. In fact, they often did.

September nodded to Tom and said: "Periodically, they starve, that is, if they are separated from the group, or if they opt to stay with the group, in their weakened state, they are eaten by others; or they die from thirst, or they fry in the sun, every once in a while, they even freeze to death! It still freezes on very unusual occasions here in the desert."

Five miles after they left the wrecked helioplane, Tom turned to September and said, "I noticed the scavengers were eyeing our burros."

"Those who are not blind, those who *can* see, *they* were eyeing our burros," September corrected. "They're hungry. Most of them are half-dead from sun poisoning. They all suffer from serious malnutrition. That's why they were eyeing our burros. Those people have had practically all of their humanity stripped from them. There's almost nothing left."

This was not a harbinger of Tom's and September's world, Tom and September realized in an instant; they realized it was going to be a harbinger of Iona's *future* world—at least, after she had become an adult.

Tom and September shuddered at the thought of Iona's future: maybe it was just as well that they didn't know what the outcome was going to be. Under certain highly conditional circumstances, maybe *ignorance was bliss.*

Chapter Twenty

THEY FOUND 'HOME.' It took them exactly twenty-two days of wandering in the desert, exactly two days more than September predicted. They lost three of their burros along the way. They were attacked twice (but only half-heartedly) by cannibals (who were only scavenging for food). One burro was lost to a combination of rock-fall and exhaustion, the other two were captured by cannibals.

Except for wreckage, they never saw a trace of a Dome's helioplane air force, or made sightings of enemy troops. They were only fifty miles from the Forbidden Zone. No one was going to find them. They were far south, hundreds of miles south—even the scavengers and cannibals didn't go there; there was nothing even for the vultures to eat.

Their 'home' which Regis had painstakingly set up was tucked into a remote corner, like a tiny oasis: a little hidden box canyon above a large hidden valley, just above the lower foothills at the far lower end of the southern Sonora desert.

There wasn't supposed to be any water there: at most, there was a dry creek, an arroyo, running through the larger valley, and an even less promising rivulet, a completely dry river gulch, running down from the box canyon. But they discovered a hidden spring. There was just enough water for themselves and the remaining burros.

Left by Regis, they had two large cisterns to store water and a
diesel tractor with its wheels removed that could pump water from a
specially hidden well if the spring dried up.

They took over three caves located on a hillside. Two were
small, the third was large enough for living accommodations. One
cave stored enough cans of diesel fuel to last ten months, should the
spring dry up. They could rely on the 200 foot deep well. The other
cave stored food, dried corn, dried manioc roots, and beans, enough
to last three years; if they foraged and carefully rationed their food,
it could last longer.

Regis had shielded an area of three square miles with a protective barrier against sun poisoning, so they could move about during
daylight hours without fear.

One way or another, they were eventually going to have to
grow their own food, no matter how carefully they shepherded their
reserves. For the time being, they were set up. They had plenty of
time to experiment with crop rotation. They could afford to make
mistakes to have bad crops, poor harvests, for at least three years.

(The climate had been altered and tampered with so much over
the last eleven years—there had been no thunder or lightning in
that area in all that time—they didn't even know *what* to plant or
when.)

There were no longer regular growing seasons—the seasons
had been inexorably scrambled. Instead of one season following the
other, such as spring following winter, there was a crazy patchwork
of weather: a little bit of summer, a little bit of spring, a little bit of
winter, all mixed up, because they were located at the southern edge
of the 300-mile-wide gray area separating the controlled climate of
the north and the Forbidden Zone.

However, they needed more than just food. They had to grow
cotton in order to make fabric for their future clothing needs. They
would have to make their own shoes—sandals—from plant stems.
Their own clothing, which they had brought with them, would only
last for three years at the most before it deteriorated—the only extra

clothing they had brought with them had to be abandoned after they lost three burros. The only alternative was to hunt large animals for skins. There weren't enough large animals for that purpose (there wasn't enough water in either the desert or in the lower Sierra Madre) to support deer and pigs, and there was precious little small game, hardly any rodents, squirrels, or snakes. Good too! If there had been the smallest edible critters, sooner or later, the scavengers would have encroached on their territory.

Otherwise, without knowledge of the hidden spring, the secret well, and the secret of the sun poisoning protection (which could only be found by accident—it was not shown on maps or charts) why would anyone live in such a wilderness? Ten miles to the west lay the scalding heat of the Sonora desert. It was a forge, an oven, a relentless inferno.

Immediately above them, the Sierra Madre foothill range was barely less relentless. To the immediate south lay the great barrier of the Forbidden Zone.

Regis could not have found a more perfect location in which to hide them.

Regis had specifically set up the arrangement with three people in mind: Regis himself, September, and Iona. With Regis' death, Tom was the stand-in.

If you had the skills of an ancient *brujo,* a shaman, then you could survive the old way, but just barely. There were only two shamans left. One was ninety-five-years old, the other ninety-nine. One lived about fifty miles away, the other about the same distance in another direction.

Both lived in caves three thousand feet higher up in the Sierra Madre mountains. Both were blind. They were the last of their kind—one was from the Yaqui tribe, the other from the Tarahumara.

The rest of their people had left many years before. They had traveled to the distant south. Harvested food had been left for them in two sealed storage bins, one for each cave.

How exactly had they survived while blind and all alone? Iona needed to wait another three years before she'd be allowed to visit them. Then she'd be able to stay with them for several months, in order to learn from them; especially their survival skills.

The two old men were their only neighbors.

Two weeks after their arrival, Tom and September celebrated Iona's sixth birthday, January 13th, 2063 A.D.

All they had were corn and manioc roots, but they considered themselves lucky; so they ate the bland food with relish. And water—presto! Roots, corn, beans, manioc root, yucca plants would be their fare for years to come.

Ten weeks later, Tom made contact with one of the two old Indians by traveling along a footpath. At their first meeting, the old Tarahumara Indian taught Tom how to snare squirrels, rats, and mice. "You must learn how to do this if you want to eat what the whites call `protein,'" the old Indian explained in a laughing, bantering tone. "Jackrabbits and prairie dogs died after the first sun poisoning eleven years ago."

As the Indian had been blind for many years, out of habit he kept his eyes closed while talking. "Deer, wild pigs, coyotes, all gone too. Only fresh meat you will find here are squirrels, rats and mice. Good news. We thought squirrels were gone. But they came back! Who knows, maybe in a few years, squirrels, rats, and mice will return to the lower region. And then, maybe deer and pigs will return. And horses. And cows. And birds!" A smile broke out on the Indian's face. "I would do anything to hear the sound of a bird again."

Tom found the old man amicable but inscrutable. The old blind Indian gave Tom the nickname, "Big river that flows through the desert." Tom couldn't tell if the old man was humoring him or just being flippant. But it didn't matter. The old man was the only other human being, besides Iona, September and Tom, living *that* close to the edge of the Forbidden Zone.

September, Tom, and Iona settled down to live as a family.

September and Tom truly loved each other. Tom thought September's most endearing trait was that she did not require proof of his love at unreasonable intervals. Sometimes they fought—a real knockdown fracas. Still, they passionately loved each other. It was a thrilling three years. With all of the drudgery, hardship and the endurance of scarcity, they knew that they were the three happiest people on the planet.

After all, living just above the level of survival, did not preclude the possibility of the existence of love.

Iona grew wild and was loved—*revered*—by her parents. In no time, Tom had became more a father than an uncle to Iona.

One night, as they sat, September lightly touched Tom's hand. Looking down at the scorched Earth she said: "Iona will be a wanderer. She must become extremely resourceful at surviving in a landscape of scant vegetation and irregular climate. This test will either strengthen her or it will defeat her. The blind Indians must teach her to survive as well." September rolled over on her side and began to weep.

"I love you," Tom replied. He put his arms around her. He tried to comfort her. "And I love Iona as if she were my own. I'll do my best to teach her. But why me? Why did you select me? Of all the choices in the world, you could have found someone younger, stronger, healthier, a person who was facing life afresh, someone who had the world by the tail."

"No," September nodded. "I wanted you." She did not stop crying.

"But why me?" Tom adamantly insisted. "I'm too old. Well, almost too old. In little over a year, I'll be seventy. And more importantly, I don't believe in Gaia. I never have. I don't think I could. I don't believe in your rebellion. At least, I don't believe in your rebellion—in the sense of being able to solve the world's problems."

"After this horrible age of Gaia," September replied, between sobs, "what person is better suited to teach my daughter about the past than a non-religious man unsuccessfully searching for an apparently unreachable, indefinable faith—a man who wrote as the primary work and contribution of his younger life, about the great illusions of humankind? Who could be better suited? Who could be more ideal?"

"I guess that's me," Tom said, laughing softly, nodding his head. "I've searched. I've found nothing. In spite of everything that has happened, after all the horrors that have occurred, after all the grim reminders of nature's lessons, I believe in something. Orsen's books! Curmudgeon's books! They're my religion—my poetry! I'm a hopeless romantic. The Gaians were right, in a way. I am a hopeless early twenty-first century man. But why are you crying so? We've made it! We're home! You have no reason to shed tears."

September burst into tears again. "Because I have not been honest with you," September admitted at last. She blubbered the words out between sighs and sobs.

"You haven't been honest?" Tom asked surprised. "How so?"

"No, I haven't been honest," September repeated. "I have not told you that there are other reasons why I have brought you here."

"Other reasons?" Tom asked. "What?"

"Other reasons," September replied flatly. She grew still and quiet. "All of us in the Anti-Gaia rebellion are doomed. We're as good as dead."

"Well, it's true, you're up against terrible odds," Tom admitted. "And it's true, it would appear that the Dome people have the drop on you. Defeating the magisters does seem like a daunting task. Frankly, I don't see how you have a chance of destroying the nuclear-powered wind machines. Some of them...yes. Maybe some. But all? You must be jesting. It would be impossible. Even if you succeed at smashing the nuclear-powered wind machines, you'll never penetrate the magisters' Domes. Never! The Domes are indestructible! The magisters' armies are powerful and well equipped. It isn't just a cliche when they say that an army marches on its stomach. Their armies are well-fed. Just in terms of manpower, their armies outnumber your forces three to one in Europe, ten to one in America, twenty-five to one everywhere else. They have at least a twenty-to-one technological advantage. True, your people have extremely high morale, but can that alone make up the difference?"

"No, that's not it," September replied.

"What?" Tom asked, baffled. "You're not afraid of those odds?"

"No, you don't get it," September replied. "Of course, I'm afraid. But that's not why we're doomed."

"Why?" Tom asked. "I don't get it."

"It's simpler. More basic." September began to cry again. Tears cascaded down her face creating deep creases on her parched skin.

Tom had never seen her behave like this before.

"I have never seen you cry like this!" Tom cried out.

"I am crying, that is true, I have reason," September calmly replied.

"I've never seen you like this before. You're ordinarily cool as a cucumber. In a crisis, you're composed, detached, analytical. We're not in a crisis, are we?"

September gathered her thoughts together before she began to speak. "The Anti-Gaia rebellion has been doomed from the start because all it can do is fight. It can destroy some of the enemy, but it can't replace what it has destroyed with anything positive. It can't live for the future. It has no hope for the future, Tom. It can't grow crops. It can't be productive. It can't organize a civilized society. If it can't do that, it can't make a new world. It can't do any of those things. Unless fighting, killing and destroying are the alpha and omega of existence, and they're enough—but they're not! Do you remember when you were our captive beneath the streets of New York?"

"Yes," Tom said. "Getting me unhooked from the Vita-Man pills—that made it worth it. And your jailers used to tell me that your diplomatic skills were far greater than your fighting skills. I believed them, too. I still do."

"Our army has no other purpose than to kill and destroy," September cautioned. "We have no goals. We have no vision. We have no other reason to exist. We have become a mirror image of the forces we oppose."

"So?" Tom asked.

"So? Isn't it obvious? I don't want that future for Iona. It may be my future but I want her to grow up to be different. I don't want her to be corrupted by the stench of killing. I don't want her to grow up to be a warrior. I want her to learn to do something else—something productive. And even if that something else is merely surviving—then I prefer that, too."

"I think I understand," Tom said nodding. "I will cooperate in any way I can. I'll be honest with you. I won't patronize you."

"I know," September replied.

When they returned to their encampment, they decided to make Iona as self-reliant and as self-confident as possible. They lived a simple life. In a sense, September was on her last furlough from war, her last leave-taking before an inevitable return to battle. They loved each other, Tom and September. They both worked together to make Iona strong. Even when Iona was only seven, they sent her alone on foraging expeditions. She became the best late-evening wild berry picker and wild root scrounger of them all. By the age of eight, she had developed eyes as good as the night eyes of a coyote or an owl. Towards the end of their first three years in the encampment, her foraging kept them from starving on several occasions. She wasn't just practicing the art and craft of survival; she was doing the real thing. By the age of nine, she had become a master of survival.

In three years, they managed to grow feral corn and manioc roots. The climate was too unstable for the beans, and the corn was successful only some of the time. Corn harvests were irregular. The yields were meager. But the manioc did well most of the time, no matter what happened to the weather. Manioc, otherwise known as cassava in the English language, was like a hearty potato of the Third

World—if anything, it was the hope of the future!

Manioc was literally the toughest crop left on the face of the Earth. In could grow 10,000 feet up in the mountains, or in low-lying tropical swamps; it could grow, with a little water added, in the desert. So they came to rely heavily on it. But when manioc roots were all they had to eat, it was barely enough. (The manioc plant was high in starch, but very low in protein.)

All of their stores were used up, except enough for a bare six months supply, and even with the greatest planning in the world, they couldn't stretch their resources any further. On one extremely cold, dry night, when the temperature dipped to one degree Fahrenheit—*that crazy weather!*—two of the last three remaining burros died.

Tom and September cut up the two dead animals for food. Only then, without the water needs of the two dead burros, was there enough water to irrigate the extra patches of manioc, but still there wasn't enough for all of their needs. Except the one season it rained! Cotton! For one season only! Cotton grew! As did the corn. One completely successful crop of corn! Perhaps there was hope for the future! One season it rained more than the usual, and for a short while, they experienced plenty of food. (Realistically, however, the rain was probably coming from the controlled climate area and there had been an unexpected overflow into the gray zone.)

After harvesting and picking the cotton, after constructing a spinning wheel and spinning the strands, they wove cloth. And now they each had a new set of clothes. Just in time, too, because their old clothes were reduced to tattered rags, making them all look like Robinson Crusoe.

They had to face the truth in other ways, too. With all the reserves gone, there wasn't enough for the three of them. The old Indian had proven ridiculously premature: the squirrels, rats, and mice did not migrate down from the higher Sierra Madre as predicted. In fact the opposite occurred: the little varmints actually retreated higher up into the mountains, five hundred feet higher, all the way up to the level of the Indians' caves. To say the least, deer, pigs, coyotes and birds did not return at all. Tom had to climb 2,000 feet just to snare a few squirrels, each time having to climb a little higher, in order to find and trap the thinning game. Meat became so scarce, he came back with barely enough to make the trip worthwhile. Iona turned nine years and three months. It was long past time for September to leave. In three more months, there would not be enough food for the three of them. There was not enough water to produce food for three people.

It was time for the rebellion to heat up. September intuitively sensed it, she could feel it in her bones; without talk, without needless speculation, Tom could sense it, too. Then it became official. One evening, September received a special report beamed by satellite to her vector screen wristwatch. It had been so long since she had heard from them, she had nearly given up hope.

After receiving the full report, September gave Tom and Iona the news: "Every day, during the previous three years and three months we've been in hiding, the reins of repression have been tightening. Emergency Powers Laws are no longer temporary, they have become permanent. New decrees have been issued that make the enforcement of the special powers more effective. Any infraction of the rules, no matter how slight or petty, results in the death penalty. Civil courts have been completely disbanded. The only courts left are ecclesiastical and religious.

"Technically, you cannot break a law now, all you can do is sin against Gaia. From now on, every act you commit is solely judged by a strict, religious criterion. Loyalty to the official Gaia religion is universally mandatory. Dispensation for the elderly has been eliminated. Starting in YEAR GAIA ELEVEN and ending in YEAR GAIA FOURTEEN, all the elderly—in North America at least, with the exception of the magisters, have been physically eliminated. A huge euthanasia plan has been completed. Over the next few years, this process will proceed in other advanced areas of the world. Other than the magisters, Tom is one of the few left over the age of sixty.

"A new rival clique of hardliners has taken over in the Gaia-Domes, having staged a *coup d'etat* within the ruling circle itself. This new group is more determined, and far more extreme than all of their predecessors combined. Total global warfare has been declared. According to the report, a full-scale attack on the remnants of the rebellion is in the offing. If I am going to leave, I need to leave now."

September loaded the burro with the last of the stored dehydrated beans and as much water as she could carry. She knew that her rations would last at least three weeks. If she ate cactus and berries along the way, she could stretch her reserves farther.

She was going to have to travel 500 miles. Her destination was the Colorado plateau, north of the Grand Canyon, where the rebellion had a substantial army still present in the field. Leaving the desert was going to be harder than entering, but, on the other hand, after more than three years of living in the sun, she was tougher and more adept at basic survival skills. She was depending on her newly acquired skills to pull her through.

Immediately before her departure, she gave the vector screen wristwatch to Tom, with a kiss and a message: "I'll call you at least once every two years. If possible, I'll call you more often. But I doubt if I will be able to. I don't know how many relay satellites we'll have operating. Where I'm going to, no one will follow me."

She hugged her daughter goodbye. She gave Iona many kisses. The leave-taking was painful and awkward. She knew that this was her last personal goodbye, to her daughter, forever.

An hour later, from the vantage point of the highest ridge of the foothills, Tom and Iona watched September and the burro traveling slowly across the shimmering Sonora desert.

They waved to September, and although she was far off in the distance, it was hard to tell, but it appeared September turned and waved back. The two of them, Tom and Iona, were quite alone now.

Tom thought that it was high time Iona learned how to acquire survival skills from the blind Indians.

Tom knew that time was of the essence. The Indians were old. One was already passed the age of 102. They needed to impart their knowledge to Iona as quickly as possible.

Chapter Twenty-One

AS IT TURNED OUT, in one case, it was too late. The Yaqui Indian had apparently died. They found his body, still warm, exactly where it had fallen. Judging by the pallor of his skin, he must have died only a few hours earlier, so their timing was haunting and auspicious.

With a seemingly pleasant smile on his face, the old man lay with his arms and legs outstretched, as if beckoning to be transported somewhere. *But to where?*

Tom and Iona could have no idea what he was actually thinking at the point of death—he just had the appearance of gesturing that way—perhaps his last thoughts were anything but.

Without ceremony, Tom and Iona buried him. They took back with them some of the stored corn, as much as they could, about forty pounds. Tom made a mental note that there was some corn left in the storage crib, a good 200 pounds. He knew that it might come in handy later.

The cave of the Yaqui Indian was fifty miles north of their home. The other Indian's cave was in the opposite direction, about fifty-five miles to the south, so it was going to be a one hundred mile trip between the caves, Tom realized. "We must hurry," he said to Iona.

"Why?" Iona asked. "What's the rush?"

"Because the other Indian is four years older than this one and we have a long way to travel. For all we know, he may be dead, too."

Iona nodded. "Very well. We won't waste time." For a nine-year-old, Iona had acquired a formidable self-confidence.

They did not take a direct route. Instead, they traveled to the other cave, following a spur of a higher Sierra Madre ridge, walking due south for 105 miles. From the vantage point of the top of the ridge, they were able to see a vast landscape, even though they were traveling mainly during the night and twilight hours to avoid sun poisoning. The vegetation appeared normal, although a little more sparse than before the weather-changing program that was introduced fourteen years earlier. There was practically no animal or bird life to be seen, although, at one point, Iona imagined she saw a large bird, perhaps a hawk, in the distance.

On many occasions, Iona repeatedly said to Tom she sensed there were larger animals out there, even though she had not seen a single one with her eyes.

When they arrived at the cave in the far south, the old blind Tarahumara Indian greeted them.

"I've been expecting you," he said with a wave of his hand.

Tom explained the purpose of their visit. The old Indian interrupted him. "I already understand the reasons for your visit. I've been waiting for you. `Mister big river who runs through the desert.'" He laughed. "I've been dreaming about this for years. The old *brujo* is dead?"

"Yes," Tom replied, surprised. "He must have died just before we arrived. How did you know he was dead?"

"I've sensed it coming," the old Indian replied in a tired voice. "I knew I'd outlive the old one. He thought he was going to live longer than me because he was younger, but there was no chance of that happening. You are wearing clothes that you spun yourself?"

With his eyes closed, the blind man crimped the cloth on Tom's sleeve. "Soft! This is home-grown cotton. You grew the feral cotton and made the cloth? You spun and wove it yourself? That means you must have constructed a spinning wheel."

Not waiting for a reply, the old Indian answered for himself. "Of course you did."

"How could you know what I was wearing?" Tom asked. Tom and Iona's bulgy, quilt-like clothes had no zippers, buttons, or clasps, just coarse pieces of string that linked the patchwork pieces together. The fabric was crude and frayed. The garments were ill-fitting. In fact, the two of them looked as if they were wearing a pair of gunnysacks.

"But you're blind," Tom said. "How could you know the manner of our clothing?"

"It doesn't matter that I'm blind, I can still tell," the old Indian said. "Where's the little one? How old is she?"

"She's here," Tom replied. "And she's a little over nine. She has not spoken a word, not so much as a peep, since we've arrived. How did you know she was present?"

Iona stood back alone, in a far recession, standing perfectly still. She had hung back a good thirty paces, keeping silent. Except for her normal heartbeat and shallow breathing, she had not made a sound.

"I can hear her breathing," the old Indian replied, straining his ears. "You say she's almost ten years old?" He smiled. "I can smell her. I can smell her hair. Well then, bring her to me."

Tom placed the child in front of the old Indian. Iona was neither frightened nor anxious. The old man reached to touch her face. Delicately, he felt with his worn fingers every curve of her face. With his thumbs, probing gently, he studied the sockets of her eyes. He looked up suddenly, as if startled. "Well, get out," he said, addressing Tom abruptly. "You heard me!" He waved his arm in the air. "Now! Out! Don't be wasting any more of our time!"

He coughed dryly. He held Iona loosely in his grasp. "I'll take good care of her. She's in my hands now. I'll make her smarter than a prairie dog, my great-granddaughter." He crooned in Iona's ear with a warbling, cracked voice.

"When shall I pick her up?" Tom asked laconically. "In a month?

Two months? How much time do you need?"

"She'll find her own way back home—on her own," the old Indian replied, shooing Tom away. "She has no need for an escort. You...leave. You...go. In fact, just go."

"When shall she return home?" Tom insisted patiently. "I mean, when may I expect her?"

"When she's good'n'ready," the old Indian replied in a testy voice. "You're not going to be around forever, 'Mister big river that blooms in the desert,' heh? Well, are you?" He laughed. "No, by thunder, you're not! So do us a favor, will you? Start getting accustomed to it. Wasn't there a time when you liked being alone? After all this time, have you forgotten how? Weren't you once a recluse? Eh?"

"How did you know that?" Tom asked. "I never spoke about that."

"I can smell it on you. Birds of a feather know each other without exchanging words," the old Indian laughed.

"Yes, there once was a time," Tom admitted. "Once. I was a hermit. A recluse. But I have much to teach Iona. I promised her mother I'd teach her. I'm responsible for her. I'm responsible for her *formal* education, too."

"Oh, her formal education?" the old Indian said with a droll note. He shook his head with laughter. "Well, there's a time for teaching, and there's a time for the hermitage. Now's the time for being a hermit. Get out!" he shouted with mock anger. "Out a' here! Before I sic my dog on you."

"You don't have a dog!" Iona laughed gleefully. She shrieked with peals of laughter. She placed her hands over her mouth.

Iona had kept her eyes closed, as if she were pretending to be blind, as if *she* were the old man. Iona not only looked serene; she looked happy. She was not frightened by the old man's manner. She did not find the old man threatening or intimidating. She found his manner strangely tender and sentimental, but in a way that she was not accustomed to. "I know you don't have a dog," she reiterated, mocking him.

"I don't?" the old Indian asked surprised. "Yes, it's true, *I don't have a dog,*" he admitted. He turned to address Tom. "Did you raise your daughter without morals? Did you raise her to spite elders, to show disrespect? I think she just called me a liar!"

Incongruously the old Indian grinned, as if he was taking Iona's inappropriate behavior as a matter of humor rather than as a point of impertinence. Tom did not know what to make of the old man. Was he a clownish buffoon? Or was he a strict authoritarian of a sort? Or both? Was he a *trickster?* Was he slightly touched? Was he *out-and-out crazy?* No, he was just a shaman, and apparently a competent one.

"Maybe *she does show respect to some,*" Tom replied, finally getting his last dig in, "but obviously not to you. You going to be all right?" he asked Iona. Iona nodded back.

"You sure?" Tom asked, looking still a little uneasy.

Iona nodded again. She appeared calm and untroubled.

Her expression suggested she believed what she faced was going to be pleasurable and fun; hardly something to be feared. She radiated a sense of wonder.

As soon as Tom departed, the old man took Iona gently into his arms. He rocked her back and forth. With genuine warmth, he cradled her. He whispered into her ear: "There are two ways to keep a dog's loyalty. You can buy the dog's loyalty—or you can earn it. Which of the two methods is the more effective?"

"I don't know," Iona said.

"If you buy it, that is to say, if you maintain the animal—with food and shelter for example—you have to buy the loyalty of the animal over and over," the old man cautioned. "His loyalty lasts only as long as his next meal. It is a loyalty that has to be replenished repeatedly. But if you *earn* his loyalty, you have to earn it only once. And it lasts forever. That's why, in the end, the Domes will lose."

"Forever?" Iona asked with awestruck wonder. "How do you earn something that can last forever?" she asked.

"By loving it," the old man said. "By showering it with love. That's what I'm going to teach you. Love is the only thing that lasts forever. Love is the only thing that conquers all."

Chapter Twenty-Two

The old man let Iona rest for a couple of days. Then he asked her if she was ready.

"Yes," Iona said, "I am. I want to learn how to survive."

"Are you sure?" the old man asked. "This is going to be an extreme ordeal."

"Yes, I am certain," Iona replied. "I want to learn how to survive—under the worst conditions you can dish out."

"Very well," the old man grunted. "We shall begin."

He blindfolded her and had her walk around as if she were blind. This lesson lasted for four days. But during the first part, Iona remained inside the cave, not going out into the sunlight. Unaccustomed to blindness, Iona bumped into things and was naturally very hesitant and tentative. Then the old man took Iona out one night with her eyes bound. Finally, after about two weeks of this, he took her out during the daylight hours with her eyes still bound. Then he taught her to forage without the benefit of sight. With her eyes still bound, she was completely on her own. If she found food, she was okay. If she didn't, she'd starve. In spite of the handicap, she adapted quickly to her condition of blindness. In fact, she fared well. She took to it as if it were a high-stakes Easter egg hunt.

"I'll teach you to hunt and forage as if you were blind," the old man said. "You'll come to rely on your hearing—touch and smell—rather than sight. That's important. It will teach you to be a master of your environment. Not to be a slave of it."

"But what is the key to success?" Iona asked, as she groped around in the cave using her hands instead of her eyes. "After all, I'm not blind, like you."

"The key to success is the cave," the old man replied thoughtfully. "And understanding it. The cave is everything. The cave is life. It can give you comfort, relief from heat, safety from exposure to the sun's poisonous rays. In a word, it's home. When the rains return, and they *will*, the cave will protect you from them, too. The cave is Gaia's natural dome. Some day, you may have to learn to live in a cave without light, without any indirect sunlight, without any fire light, without light at all. This power to live in darkness, in total darkness, will make you strong. Blindness, even if it is experienced for just a few years, is a good thing."

"The cave is like a *dome?*" Iona asked. "I've heard about the magister's Domes. I only vaguely remember seeing one, though. That was seeing it from the outside. A big shiny thing it was. Silvery and shiny. A great, big, geodesic dome. How beautiful I thought it was! I don't remember seeing one from the inside, but mother says I spent the first three years of my life inside one." Iona continued to talk with her eyes bound and shut.

"Where was the Dome located?" the old Indian asked.

"On a tiny island, in the middle of the ocean—an island all alone," Iona said. "I was too young to remember anything clearly."

"What was the name of the island?" the old Indian asked. He had a bemused expression on his face. "Do you remember?"

"It was called—I don't know—Santa Helena—no—*Saint* Helena. My father was important there. He was very important. I think he ran the place. I think he was, how do you say, `in control'?"

"He was `in control'? You mean, like God?" the old man asked.

"No, 'course not. Like a magister," Iona replied.

"Oh. Emperor Napoleon Bonaparte was exiled there, did you know that?" the old man asked, laughing. He looked up with his unseeing eyes.

"Who was Emperor—*what*—Napoleon Bonaparte?" Iona asked.

The old Indian smiled. "Napoleon was a little man. From a slightly bigger island than Saint Helena, called Corsica. Once ruled France, then almost the world. Never mind. Not important now. Not anymore."

"Did my father know him?" Iona asked. "My father knew a great many people. He was important."

"I'm sure he knew many people!" the old man replied, bursting out laughing. "I'm sure he was important, too. But he didn't know Napoleon. The Domes you were thinking of were man-made Domes. They won't last forever. The cave is Gaia's natural dome. It will last forever. That's why you'll survive. See? That's why you'll win, too."

"Win?" Iona asked her eyes still bound. "Win what? I don't understand."

"The war that your mother's been conducting all these years."

Iona was mystified. She found the meaning of the old man's words elusive, vague; to all effect, meaningless.

"You'll learn what you're going to win when you're older," the old man then said, as if reading Iona's thoughts. "You'll learn what to win when you're on your own. No one will teach you. It will be your most painful lesson, not Tom's, not mine, not your mother's; it will be your lesson. Do you understand what I'm saying now?"

"How can you tell?" Iona asked. "How do you know?"

"I can tell. By looking into your eyes."

Iona didn't know how to react. She knew that the old man was blind, but she also knew he had meant what he said, that he was `literally' looking into her eyes. If not into her eyes, then what?

"But my eyes are covered," Iona replied in protest. "You can't see them."

"I know, I know," the old man said, with his own eyes shut. He touched Iona's blindfold with his fingers, just barely grazing them with his light, tender touch. "I can see you—here," he said. With his hand, he touched his heart. "I can feel you, here." He slowly placed her little hand on his breast—over his heart. She could feel his heart beat.

A month went by, and Iona asked when the blindfold would be removed so she could see again. She was growing bored. Instead of removing the blindfold, the old man closed her ears with beeswax so that she could neither see nor hear. She foraged and hunted like that for a month. Until then, she was given only water to drink—a pint and a half a day. Later, he plugged her nostrils so that she could not experience hearing, sight, or smell.

Her foraging for herself with the loss of these three senses continued without stop for five weeks. This was no longer a high-stakes Easter egg hunt; it was gradually becoming a life and death struggle. Her coping under these conditions was erratic. She had good days and bad days. And very bad days. Sometimes she was profoundly disoriented; at other times, she felt as if she were an angel, gliding over the air, with her feet hardly touching the ground.

Then, on the last days, the old Indian gave her the ultimate test. He stopped giving her water. Now she had to forage for both food *and* water. This was no longer a life and death struggle; this was sheer terror. She would have to find water on her own. Tiny drops in the intertwine of the roots of plants, in the hearts of plants, between rocks in the earth, a precious drop of moisture here, another drop there. It was the worst ordeal and the cruelest test of all. All of her energy was taken up in this pursuit.

The old man leaned over and took the beeswax from one of her ears. "This is important you hear this." He hesitated. "You'll have to find this on your own. The most precious thing. A sacred thing. It's as precious as life itself. *Water. And water is life.* When you survive on your own, by groping and feeling with your hands, you'll be able to survive anywhere. There is nothing more precious in this world—nothing, you see—than water. Understand?"

After Iona reluctantly nodded her head, the old Indian gently replaced the beeswax in her ear and gently kissed her on the cheek.

The stress and burden Iona experienced under these harsh conditions grew more onerous, until she was ready to snap. She cried. She bit her lips until they bled. She beat her feet against the ground. In protest, she beat her hands against the wall of the cave. More than once, she gave in to a temper-tantrum (after all, no matter how `mature' she otherwise may have seemed, she was still only a nine-and-one-half-year-old girl).

She began to revert back to her `childhood.' But she was still a brave warrior. She was under strict orders to stay away from the spring. (It would take not a small amount of will power for a child of nine and one half years old to abide by such harsh, draconian rule—especially as, literally, no one was watching her, but nature, Gaia—if one could presume that such an "unseeing watchfulness" existed.)

"This is the most horrible displeasure of them all," Iona complained bitterly. "Besides, I don't want to survive. I want to *play*. Just like other normal children play. You are not my friend. You are not even a suitable master. You are as mean and cruel as a snake. I want to go home. Tom may be boring at times, but he's still my friend. And he's not mean and vicious like you are, either."

But I'm your friend, too, the old Indian thought to himself but did not say aloud.

When the old man realized that Iona had lost a significant amount of weight, that her tongue was cracked and split, that sores had broken out in her mouth from eating cactus spines and `wet dirt,' and, when she was lucky, insects and edible leaves, spines, and the roots of desert plants, he ended the ordeal. Infection had set in the wounds on her face and hands. She looked more animal than human. Her fingers were cut and split; they looked like the hands of a wage-slave cotton-picker of the river valley or Niyarit State. Her hands were calloused beyond belief. Her hands looked like those of an elderly ranch hand. Her extremities, both hands and feet, were bruised and bleeding. There was a cut in her scalp where she had

banged her head; a bad laceration that would take at least a week to
heal. Although Iona was starving, she did manage to find enough
water. She was ravenously hungry; delirious, often hallucinating.
The old man knew she had had enough, knew she had gone beyond
the breaking point. Even the toughest of people can only handle so
much. And Iona was only a child.

Why was he doing this?

He removed the bands of cloth from her eyes, the wax from her
ears, the cotton swabs from her nostrils, and in the process, returned
her, unimpaired, the powers of sight, smell, hearing.

Iona was happy, at last, to be freed from her confines. She drank
two full quarts of water, but she had enough good sense, in spite of
her powerful thirst, to drink the water slowly, just letting it trickle
into her mouth, stretching the process out over several hours, so that
she would not make herself sick.

At this point, the old man realized Iona had a natural born in-
stinct for survival—really, she didn't have to be "taught."

Within several days, after several well-balanced meals and plenty
of sleep, she returned to being her irreverent self. As soon as her
bindings were lifted, she changed. First of all, with her sight regained, she ate plenty. She quickly (much more quickly than the old
man thought possible) regained much of her lost weight. After all,
Iona could have easily cheated and removed her bindings on her own
without the old man knowing, but she didn't. She was *too* honest.
In spite of her suffering, and in spite of her repeated protests *about*
her suffering, she had freely accepted the ordeal as a test of honor.
There was no limit to her astonishing pride, nor to her stupendous
self-confidence. It was a matter of yoking those two highly charged,
airy, celestial, fire-like characteristics of being, and anchoring them
solidly to the Earth. That was also the point of the ordeal, the old
man realized, but only after it was over did he realize it. He too was
learning. He also found this amusing.

"Sight," the old man said to Iona, after her wounds had healed,
"is the most important thing in the desert. Hearing and smell are

important, too. Without them, the brain is useless. You must remember that. Only a blind man can teach you that. I have not seen anything with my eyes for over forty years. Except in my dreams. In my dreams, I see brilliantly. Many times, I've dreamt of you. And Tom. And your mother. I've dreamt of all of you. Right now, September is fighting for you."

"Fighting for me?" Iona asked.

"Fighting for your future. I dreamt of your journey across the mountains, too. It was like the journey my mother, grandmother, and great-grand-uncle took many years ago. Most of all, I dreamt of your mother. September! And your father Regis. In the future—they will be looked upon as gods. Remember that."

"In your blindness, old man, do you see only blackness or whiteness?" Iona asked.

"What?" the old man asked, a little taken aback by her question. He raised his head. "Huh?"

"I mean, do you see only darkness?" Iona asked. "Cobwebs of the dim? Or do you see radiance? Perhaps a sheen of whiteness?"

"Ah," he murmured, nodding. "Now I understand your question. In my blindness, I see only a milky haze. No blackness, just whiteness. Only a dim whiteness."

"Ah," Iona replied. She was a little disappointed by his reply.

"Sometimes, I do see a bright sheen of whiteness, though!" the old man added. "Sometimes, that is."

"I see."

"Mainly, I see only milky white. In other words, I see you, Iona. I see the future as it is—uncertain."

He looked up good-naturedly, coyly. "Excuse me, I think I just made a joke at your expense," he laughed.

"When I was blindfolded, my experience was different," Iona said. "When my eyes were blindfolded, all I saw was darkness. Blackness. Then when my eyes were bound—and I gazed up at the sun—I saw blood. Blood red. It was all strange."

The old man just nodded.

"Never mind," Iona said. "Doesn't matter. But somehow I feel that some day that experience will be important."

"Perhaps it will be," the old man agreed.

Iona felt a little ashamed, but the feeling quickly passed. Then she felt awakened. Her spirits soared. Her senses rocketed. With her senses restored, she felt as if she had been restored to a beneficial place. That was the aesthetic side of the old man's teachings in the primitive art of survival, but there was nothing mystical about the fact that surviving such an ordeal gave Iona a fresh vision of the physical world and a heightened joy in her senses. She became philosophical and cool (which was exactly what the old man had hoped for).

Iona said, "I've agreed with almost everything you've told me so far."

"What have you *not* agreed with?" the old man asked.

"I think there was one time when I first came here you said something I now think is wrong."

"Oh?" the old man asked surprised. "What's that?"

Iona thought a little before she replied. "Agreed—it's hard to buy a dog's loyalty. That's true. That's the nature of being a master and that's the nature of being a dog. But if a dog's dying of thirst, not just thirsty, but *really* dying of thirst, like I was, I think you can buy its loyalty with water."

The old man nodded his head. He roared back with side-splitting laughter. He slapped his leg with gusto. Then he smiled, as if he had withdrawn back into shyness, as if he had become embarrassed by his own enthusiasm. "Do you think so?"

Iona didn't think she had said anything profound or even intelligent, she was just making conversation. "Yes."

"Now you understand," the old man said.

"Understand?" Iona asked. "Understand what?"

"You understand the world. You understand the role of water in the world. That's how they managed to turn free persons into slaves, into dogs, Iona. That's how the magisters have bought their loyalty. See?"

"Bought whose loyalty?"

"The people who your mother is trying to save."

Iona laughed. "Were you trying to teach me two completely different lessons at the same time, old man?"

The old man nodded. "First, the lesson to survive. That's the most important lesson. Second, the lesson of experience. As a metaphor—to explain how the world works."

"Oh, how *very*, very sneaky of you," Iona said, wagging her finger in a display of mock disapproval. "What exactly is a metaphor?" Iona asked. "Tom has explained the abstract concept to me, but he often used words that were too big for me. I don't understand."

"Ah," the old man sighed, "I see. Well. Let me see. Let's see." He looked up. "A metaphor is one of the many paths to arrive at the truth."

"For example?" Iona asked. "A metaphor is like knowing the terrain of the earth through the bottom of your feet while walking with your eyes shut. Is that an example?"

"Yes, that's a practical example," the old man replied. "But there's an even more complicated one. The more complicated one would be knowing the color of a cloud by `seeing' the cloud with your eyes shut, and knowing what the color of the cloud is because you know what `cloud-ness' means."

"But I can't do that," Iona replied stubbornly. "That's impossible."

"Why can't you do that?" the old man asked. "I do it all the time."

"But you can't do that. Forgive me, but you're as blind as a bat. Worse than that. You're actually *blinder* than a bat," Iona added teasingly.

The old man pointed to the side of his head. "I do it with *this*. I do it with my imagination. My thoughts. And my memory."

"Your thoughts?" Iona asked. "But imagination doesn't exist. It's not for real."

"Yes it is," the old man replied in a solemn voice. "It exists, even if you can't see it. That's how the mind works. When it is living in the cave of life. My cave, for example. We are all living in caves."

Expressed on Iona's face was a look of perplexity. For a nine-and-one-half-year-old girl who hadn't seen a written word since she was five, it sounded like the old man was talking about *magic*.

"But that doesn't really matter," the old man said, laughing, understanding Iona's discomfiture and embarrassment. "You were made for the real world. *You were made to do things in the real world.* Trust me. Don't worry."

"What am I going to do?" Iona asked, blurting out the words in a rush.

"What?" the old man asked. He was taken completely off guard by the question.

There was a long pause. Then silence. *"What is going to happen to me?"* Iona then asked emphatically.

"Oh, *that,*" the old man said. "I don't know. No one can tell you what is going to happen to you."

"Not even my mother?"

"Not even your mother. Not even your dreams can tell you. Compared to the past, what you will do will be *different.*"

It took a moment for Iona to absorb this. "Where am I going?" she then asked, without showing fear.

"I don't know exactly where, but you are going to go into the Forbidden Zone. You are going to go to the other side of it. I don't know what you are going to find there. I don't know what is going to happen to you in your life. But it is time you must leave. Go now, my sweet. When I am dead, tell Tom that the corn left in the storage bin will still be there for him. Don't forget."

"Will still be there?"

"Yes, when I'm no longer here."

"Okay. All right. I'll be sure to tell him."

"It's important that you *tell* him," the old man added with a nagging note of persistence. "Don't forget. I've dreamt of Tom's future. He will have a long life. He has an incredibly long future awaiting him. It will last at least another thirty years. But he will have to learn to cope with his own form of blindness, *his loneliness.* You tell him that, too. Understand?"

"I understand," Iona replied. "I'll tell him."

"Good."

"One more question," Iona asked. "Every time I hunt for squirrels or mice, I sense the presence of *other* animals."

"What kind of animals?" the old man asked.

"Larger animals. But I don't see them. I can't see them. What does it mean? I know they're there. Are they *there?*"

"Yes," the old man nodded affirmatively. "They are there."

"Really?" Iona asked.

"Really," the man confirmed. "It is so. You sense the presence of their ghosts. Their spirits are alive in you: it means their bodies will return. Their souls are already there. It's only a matter of time. Their bodies will return. You have—what is called—spirituality. It tends to make things happen. We don't know how this thing works: spirituality. Spirituality is a mystery. Spirituality is a mystery we can not fathom. We can not understand the arcane properties of any form of mystery. But spirituality does change things. In *very, very* rare instances, it does."

Shortly after this conversation, Iona left the old man's cave.

Tom glimpsed Iona coming over the ridge. He folded his hands, then he nervously unfolded them. For over a week, in anticipation, he had been nervously waiting for her return.

Upon seeing Tom, Iona ran to embrace him. "Oh, Tom," she said, catching her breath. "Thank you for my time with the old shaman. I know everything I need to know."

"Granted, you've become a genius at survival," Tom replied.
"I just want to make sure you don't become a savage monster or a
creature of brutality. Your mother would not approve if I allowed
either of those things to happen to you, would she?"

Iona smiled. "You don't have to worry about that."

Six months later on her tenth birthday, Iona knew—sensed—
that the old shaman was dead. She knew the very instant he died.
She suddenly awoke in the middle of the night, as if she had been in
a dream. She knew he was gone. With her eyes closed, *in her imagination,* she could see his dead body.

Two days later, Tom and Iona visited the cave. Iona had been
right. They found the old man's body lying on the floor. There was a
look of contentment in his eyes, a gentle smile gracing his lips. They
simply buried him.

Chapter Twenty-Three

IONA, AT TEN, had sprung up so fast she was only five inches shorter than Tom. By the age of eleven, she was only four inches shorter. By the age of twelve, she blossomed. She only had to stand on her tip-toes to stare him straight in the eye, and by the age of thirteen and one half, she had grown to within an inch of Tom's five feet, nine inch frame.

Tom realized that a lanky thirteen and one half year old Iona seemed to have gained a wingspan. She was better coordinated than he was when he was seventy-six—that was an obnoxious and ridiculous comparison—but she was even better coordinated than when he was eighteen, *when he was in exquisitely perfect shape.*

Physically, Iona was no longer a geek. She had turned into a lean machine—suave and graceful. She exuded from every pore of her skin a fluidity-in-motion.

But first, there was the learning. For four and one half years, Tom taught Iona what he called Pre-Gaia classics. The `Pre-Gaia classics' were a condensation of history, aesthetics, and philosophy prior to the Gaia-AntiGaia Global Wars. Because of the shortness of time, the instruction had to be condensed into a relatively small course.

Five weeks after she had returned from the shaman, Tom said, "Arms are short. Feet must be planted somewhere so my teachings will have a home. Like it or not, that home is going to be you."

Within the time constraints, Tom taught Iona everything that he could.

"All history is philosophy," Tom began, "and all philosophy is religion, all religion is literature, and all literature is art, all art is music, painting, dancing, and all music, painting, dancing are the heart, brain, hand of man and woman, through all of time."

On a small scrap of animal skin, this was the only thing that he wrote for her to keep.

It was when it came to dealing with the concept of Gaia that Tom had the greatest difficulty in teaching Iona, because he didn't believe in the concept himself. Gaia was too vague, and in some ways, too insipid. For example, Tom thought that the philosophy of pantheism was, on balance, more logical than the apparent logic of the co-dependency theorem of the *life-and-environment-and-matter* interaction construct of Gaia. But he had reservations about the old-fashioned models of pantheism, too.

In fact, Tom, in his younger years, the gloomy author of *disillusionment-and-skepticism* literature thought it best to say that the answers to the most ultimate questions of the world were provisional at best, and at worst, incomprehensible, even unknowable. He thought it would have been better off for everyone to have left it at that.

Finally, Tom put it this way: "Religion, whatever its form, is important, because they can take away everything from you, and you better have something they can't touch, *even if it doesn't exist*. Some people don't like to call it religion. Some prefer to call it spirituality—as if it has something to do with your soul—as if it is a dream lying inside a deeper, more mysterious dream."

Tom paused. "They can take away your *material*...you see. Your health. Your life. But they can't take away your spirituality. I know you understand what those last three mean. But the one thing they can't touch, whether it exists or not, is your soul. Your heart! That's why those things are so valuable. And that's why, when people fight back, in times of adversity, like now, all over the world, the heart and the soul, 'religion,' in a sense, is so valuable. And that's the real truth of the rocks. Not science. Not geology. Religion. The heart and the soul! Of humankind!"

"What should religion teach me then, Tom?" Iona asked in a cranky voice.

"Love your neighbors as you love yourself," Tom replied. "There's an example."

"Well, I don't have any neighbors," Iona replied.

"Well, when you do, love 'em to death."

"Why do you believe in Gaia, then, Tom?" Iona asked.

"Because," Tom replied, in a snit of hopeless desperation, "because, well, it's the religion of the world. That's enough reason to believe! So there! Just...*because!*"

"Where's my mother?" Iona asked.

"You miss her, don't you?" Tom inquired. "I miss her, too. She's fighting."

"Fighting?" Iona asked, wearing a look of wanderlust and a Mona Lisa smile.

"Fighting for the world," Tom then replied. He knew that his response must have sounded inane and inadequate. Iona deserved better than that. "Fighting for *your* world. Fighting for the future. You're probably too young to understand," Tom said, sighing.

"Why haven't we heard from her yet?" Iona asked. "You promised she'd call."

"We shall hear from her, sweetheart," Tom said with an upbeat turn in his voice. "You asked me what faith is about?" he asked.

"Right," Iona said.

"Well, we shall hear from her," Tom said. "Okay? That's what faith is about. *We'll hear from your mother.* Damn it! Questions, questions! No more questions. You're driving me crazy. We'll hear from her. Enough, already!"

"I've created a miracle, you know that?" Iona said with a look of satisfaction.

"You've created a miracle?" Tom asked. He appeared skeptical. Suspicion clouded his face. "What miracle?"

"Miracle to beat all miracles!" Iona exclaimed. "For once, I've gotten you to shut up!"

Iona laughed hysterically. Tom shook his head. "Maybe I'm getting too old," Tom said. But Tom was happy to have been made the brunt of Iona's totally on-the-beam joke.

Knowledge was a good thing, wisdom even better. But without humor, Iona was a dull girl. *Maybe,* Tom thought, *just maybe,* gaiety was more useful than wisdom.

Chapter Twenty-Four

TOM RECEIVED A MESSAGE from September. After almost four years of total silence, he had all but given up hope of ever hearing from her again—though he never told Iona that that was what he had been thinking. To Iona, he said he had never given up hope. He had purposely deceived her.

Tom received the message while he was taking a walk, an hour after the sun had gone down; as was his wont, to avoid sun poisoning.

The wristwatch that September had given him gave a little pip. The sound of the pip was so unexpected that he thought at first he was imagining it. It pipped—one pip—then pipped again.

Tom turned the vector watch on. He said, knowing full well to keep his words short: "September, why did you wait so long to call us?"

"At last," September said. He could see her in the tiny rectangular screen. "We couldn't get the program to work. We had enough people to attack, but we weren't sure we could destroy more than fifty percent of the nuclear-powered wind machines, even if we destroyed that many, the Dome scientists would probably have to shut them all down. If most aren't working, the rest can't work either. All of them have to work together, or they can't work at all. But we wanted to have a greater margin of certainty of success than that. Too much depended on it. So after almost four years of preparation, now we can guarantee fifty percent destruction in the first wave of the attack, a further fifteen percent in the second wave, and eight percent in the third."

Tom had a thousand questions to ask September, but he knew that the important thing for him to do was to be patient, to let September explain everything in her own way. Only she knew how long she was going to be able to talk, before they were going to be shut off forever.

This was going to be their last conversation and without mentioning it, they both knew it.

"How did you do that?" Tom asked amazed.

"By creating a second and third force of auxiliaries."

"How did you do *that?*"

"By enlisting practically all the pirates, the sea-thieves, in the known world, and more than half of the *secret* pirates in the `unknown' world, into our program."

"Why are you able to say this to me now?" Tom asked. "Isn't this top secret?"

"After almost four years of preparation," September replied, "we are now jamming the Dome's switchboard system with one hundred million messages a second. If we are successful at this act of full-scale communication sabotage, their system's going to be jammed for the next seven days, long enough for us to complete our attack."

"How will we know if you are successful?" Tom asked.

"Oh, you'll know."

"How will *we* know?"

"You just will. We are almost out of time. I don't have time to explain. Iona must immediately depart on her own for the Forbidden Zone. She must depart now. She is to travel south. The journey will be perilous—difficult—to complete. But she must make the journey." September paused. "You know how good I've always been when it came to timing." September laughed. "Listen to me. She must make it to the twenty-third latitude no later than ten days after the attack, understand?"

"Yes."

"She must travel *that fast* through the Forbidden Zone. The Forbidden Zone is going to be fiercely hot. Understand?"

"Yes," Tom said. "How will she know when she's arrived at her destination?"

"She just will. All she has to do is follow the directions I've given. Goodbye, Tom. I love you. You will not hear from me again. This is our last communication."

"Don't hang up," Tom shouted. "How will we know when you are successful?" Tom asked. "Can you give us a sign?"

"When's the last time you've heard thunder? When's the last time you've seen rain? You'll hear a lot of thunder. You'll see buckets of rain. The climate control system will break down approximately three days after most of the nuclear-powered wind machines have been disabled. The rain will fall south through the gray area, but skip the Forbidden Zone, and then pour down on the Southern Hemisphere. It will be as if a cloudburst passed over you, and then afterwards, your land will revert to a natural desert. Goodbye, Tom. Iona must leave now!! Remember! Within the next few hours. She must take off right now, or she will have no chance of survival. Timing is crucial." September paused. "Did you educate her well?" she asked with a warm, hushed, quivering sound in her voice.

"Yes," Tom replied.

"Good," September exclaimed with relief. "I knew you would. God, my heart aches to be with you both. Goodbye, Tom. I don't want to, but I have to go..."

"Bye then," Tom replied. "Of course, good luck. You know...*I miss you...*" Her smile and her face flickered off the vector screen on the wristwatch. She was gone.

There was the sound of a pip. They had been cut off. Tom blinked. He waited, just staring at the face of the wristwatch for an hour (actually the time lapsed was only seven and a half minutes, but it seemed like an eternity). He ran like the devil to break the news to

Iona.

"Take your water, your prepared cornmeal, your bow and arrows, your face and feet protection, your flint fire starter, your..."

"That's all," Iona interrupted, drawing herself up. "If I want to be sure not to get bogged down." She had been planning to make this trip for many months.

"What about the animal skin with the words about philosophy written on it?" Tom asked.

"The fetish shroud of the forgotten era?" Iona asked, smiling.

"Whatever you wish to call it," Tom replied, bemused.

"All right," Iona said, "but this is ridiculous. Nobody's going to see it for what it really is. You realize that?"

"Yes, I realize that," Tom admitted. "Just do it in order to humor a foolish old man."

"Why didn't September talk to me, personally?" Iona asked.

"I think she would have," Tom replied, "she just didn't have time. She had to go. In fact, I think the satellite transmission cut us off, literally in mid-sentence, almost in mid-word. She had no choice in the matter."

Iona stared at Tom, as if to say, without using words, `I must go, too.'

"I know," Tom nodded. He knew exactly what Iona was thinking. He nodded again.

They hugged each other. Tom smiled. "Your world here will recede—little by little—over time—until it becomes a far distant memory, nothing more than the receding echo of a dream. As you grow older, you'll lose the memory of your mother, you'll forget Regis, you'll even forget me. You have to remember to remember. You have to consciously remind yourself of what you remember, or little by little, you'll forget everything. I taught you those memory exercises. Do them faithfully. Don't forget. Don't forget to keep doing them long after you've left here. That's the only way there is going to be a guarantee that the past will be preserved."

Iona smiled. "I know what your religion is," she said with a knowing smile.

"What's that?" Tom asked. "All these years, I haven't been able to figure that one out." Tom was both curious and bemused by Iona's comment. She may not have been an adult yet, but she was no longer a child.

"Your religion is the notion that there is a future," Iona said. "I've been observing you for some time now," Iona added, "and so I know. You don't believe in a personal after-life, or an after-life for anyone else. You don't believe in God or in any form of theology. The Neo-Platonic's wings attached to the mystical body of the old Christianity has never allowed that legend to fly for you. You don't believe in the ancient Greeks' notion of the Logos of the psyche. You don't believe in a Hindu's notion of reincarnation. You don't believe in the *Way of Tao* of Lao-Tze. I don't think you even believed in the old shamanism of the old dead Indians who lived in the caves. Your last defense against nothingness, against complete annihilation, is nothing else than the future. *Any* future."

"Guess so," Tom shrugged. "The student doesn't need the teacher anymore when the student starts teaching the teacher."

"So then!" Iona laughed boisterously. "Don't put all your eggs in one basket. Don't invest everything in me. If I'm not the future, maybe someone else is! After all, it's a big world!"

"Yes, it is," Tom laughed.

"Maybe that's religion," Iona said.

"What do you mean?" Tom asked.

"A *laugh* is religion, or at least, a *laugh* is spirituality."

"Maybe the Japanese poet Basho would have agreed," Tom said. "I know that the Curmudgeon would have agreed."

"Basho? The Curmudgeon? Who are they?" Iona asked.

"Not enough time to explain them to you now. Just so. To the point." Tom smiled. "Not enough time. A pity. You would have liked them. Doesn't matter. None of it matters now. Seventy-five percent of what I taught you over the last seven and a half years may end up being useless baggage, useless knowledge—in the long run. Maybe a few of these exercises will be helpful to you later on, but then again, maybe not. I don't know. By doing this, I hope I've helped you rather than harmed you. I guess only the future will tell."

Tom paused. "You were born too late to know the old world, that is to say, *my world*. But it's all relative, isn't it? Compared to the people not yet born, compared to people who will be born, say, fifty years from now, the people who will come after you, you will have far more knowledge about the old world than they will ever know, and by virtue of that, you will be seen as someone who is the fount of special knowledge for them."

"Will people come after me?" Iona then asked. "Without you, I'm all alone, Tom."

"Yes," Tom said, "I know. But there will be people. *There will always be people.*"

"Why do you say that?"

"I don't know. But I *believe* it's true."

They hugged again. Then Iona left quietly.

Chapter Twenty-Five

WITH IONA GONE, Tom got along as best he could. The desert beneath the protective rim of the hills seemed a little hotter, a little drier, a little more desolate than before. But Tom welcomed his aloneness and solitariness, too.

He had chores to keep him occupied. He counted the measures of corn in his storage bins. He calculated the amount of corn left in the two deceased Indians' caves. He shrugged his shoulders. He had enough food to last for quite a while.

He didn't consume much food now that he was only six months from turning seventy-seven years old. In all of those seven and a half years, the three of them had never had to use the generator to pump water from the ground—the spring had never dried up—but Tom also knew that if the world-wide climate-changing apparatus ceased to function, he was also going to lose Regis's protective security arrangement and he would have to fend for himself. There would no longer be any protection from sun poisoning. If September was successful, he was going to be driven out of paradise, out of the Garden of Eden.

After the third day, he couldn't stop himself from wondering how the destruction of the nuclear-powered wind machines was progressing. He wondered how successful September's guerrilla army had been. He wondered if the pirates, the sea thieves, had been reliable? He surveyed the horizon for a wisp of change, a spur of cloud, *just a sign.* There was nothing. What season was it? They hadn't had a *real* season in over fourteen and a half years.

The fourth day went by without incident. Then on the fifth he felt *something*. There was a twinge in his nose—a slight "tingle" smell of ionization in the air—a slight, almost undetectable twinge of lightning, of thunder, of impending rain. He felt nauseous and dizzy for an instant. He panicked for a moment. But the sensation passed quickly. He then felt deliriously happy. After eighteen-and-one-half years, he felt his powers coming back.

Each day, for a longer period of time, with greater intensity, the sensation grew more powerful. By the ninth day, then the tenth, it was so powerful, it kept him from sleeping at night. He was not getting his proper rest. He tossed and turned in his bed.

By the eleventh day after September's wake-up call, he was wound up so tight, he couldn't think straight. He looked haggard. His face was streaked with worry lines of anxiety.

Before sunrise, on the morning of the thirteenth day, he climbed up one of the highest mountains in the vicinity, 7,000 feet high. Sitting idly and waiting for something to happen was driving him crazy. He didn't watch out for sun-poisoning protection on that particular morning; he was sick and tired of even caring about it. What was the point, he thought. How long was he going to last out there alone, anyway?

Then he saw it: a wisp of smoke, looking like a tiny twist of rope, fifty miles away. Off on the horizon, it looked like it was only two inches high. It was strange—because the rest of the sky was brilliant, sky-blue and clear.

The tiny cloud (or was it a swirling dust cloud, or a mirage?) was barely discernable to the naked eye.

This caused Tom to chuckle. He lay down under a single pinon tree. The tree was dead. It had no leaves, no foliage; like so many other trees, it had died from too many years of exposure to sun poisoning.

He used the shade from the tree trunk to shade his face, which meant that in relation to the sun, he had to position himself snug against the trunk, at the tree's very base.

He decided to take a nap. He enjoyed naps. They had been his wont, his 'constitutional,' as he called it, ever since he turned seventy-five. He calculated there was going to be a partial moon that night, so there would be plenty of moonlight to guide him on his way home. It was still mid-morning, too early to take his normal 'constitutional,' but he lay down to rest anyway: after all, he had not slept well the previous few nights, and was tired.

And strangely, instead of taking a nap, he fell into a deep sleep, into a trance; almost a coma.

When he awoke, it was bright morning, maybe two hours after sunrise. Intuitively, from his deep, groggy state, he knew that he had slept more than around the clock: he checked his wristwatch. He had slept almost exactly eighteen hours!

He yawned and stretched. Then he jumped up. Something he saw had aroused him from his state of lethargy. Stretched over the horizon was a wall of solid blackness. He felt a strange twinge in his nose. The storm had a huge depth, with a texture and viscosity that was profound.

Tom had calculated that the storm center was, at most, twenty miles away.

He had almost slept through it all!

A blasting hot desert wind was fiercely blowing in his face as he studied the approaching storm.

Tom was about to scramble off the mountain when he saw it from the corner of his eye. True, it was only twenty miles away, but it was unmistakable. It was so tiny he could scarcely see. It had been a lightning flash. Then another and another.

The tiny pinpoint pricks of lights were almost lost in the huge inkwell of blackness that seemed to rise up from the mesa toward the ceiling of the sky. The tiny flashes were located towards the back of the storm system. It was too far away for him to hear the claps of thunder, except as distant indecipherable moans, like the distant sound of drums. Maybe he only *thought* he heard it. The storm would have to be at least five miles closer, before he could distinctly hear a thunderclap.

Maybe the storm was going to change direction, veer off, but no, it was coming right at him.

Tom got excited. He almost peed in his pants from the anticipation of the show about to commence.

This was it!

He knew the rain was coming. Maybe he still had the prophetic power to predict the weather? He had the gift. At last—after all these years—*that* most precious thing returned.

He was relaxed from his sleep, refreshed, energized.

As fast as he could, he raced down the steep mountain's slope. He wanted to make sure the cistern's water ducts were open so they could store as much water as possible.

Two hours later, the rain fell. There was the splatter of drops in the dirt, then he felt drops hitting his bare arms and face. A moment later, the rain came down. Within minutes, huge sheets poured down. The rain fell so hard it was as if heaven's gates had exploded.

Tom stood out in the open, allowing his body to be saturated— achingly inviting—anxiously welcoming—the rain.

He became completely soaked. But he didn't move an inch. His arms outstretched, he stood still. There was an ecstatic expression on his face.

And the smell! There was the smell of ions. The sound of the rain drumming hard, the lightning sparkling, the thunderclaps thundering—louder, closer—made Tom joyful. Now he heard something. The lightning was striking less than two miles away. God, he was happy.

Not for a moment did the notion of fear cross his mind; he was too filled with happiness and joy.

This condition lasted for about thirty minutes.

Then, as if it were possible, the rain came down even *harder*. There was an hour of deluge, wherein at least another two inches of rain fell, and suddenly lightning flashed in Tom's face. Not for a moment had Tom moved from the spot where he was planted. Huge sheets of rain fell. He was standing in a small lake of water, that grew to being six inches deep, and thirty feet wide. He looked up. About a quarter of a mile away, on the side of a hill, a mighty bolt of lightning struck with powerful force. Quickly, he counted, "One,..." Before he could say "two," he heard a clap.

A minute later, there was another bolt of lightning nearby. This time, it was closer, a hundred yards away. Before he said, "One," the sound of thunder resounded almost simultaneously with the flash, nearly splitting his eardrums. He almost fell over. He waited. He pictured himself killed by a bolt of lightning. In a strange and perverse way, he identified with the storm so closely he almost fancied the idea of his death. About fifty feet away, a great, powerful bolt struck an oak tree, destroying the middle third of the tree with its initial impact. Pieces of bark and tree debris flew by him, as from an explosion. The sheer energy released by the strike, and Tom's close proximity, knocked him to the ground. If he had been any closer, he would have been injured, if not killed outright. As he lay trembling, he felt the shock wave pass through him. There was a strong smell, a heady brew of ionization, in the air around him.

He lay on his back in a large puddle of water. The light from the burning tree reflected in a pool of light that shimmered on Tom's mud-covered face.

Tom was filled with great composure and equanimity. Unmoving, he just lay there and watched the tree burn itself out.

In the course of the four-hour storm, more than six inches of rain fell. Tom was filled with joy. When the rains finally stopped, not a second before, he raised up on his haunches, then fell back into a sitting lotus position, in the pool of water. Sitting cross-legged, he placed his hands on his knees.

During this time, Tom hadn't thought about anything. He hadn't thought about the primitive or sophisticated notions of Gaia, or about the primitive or sophisticated notions of `God.'

In one brief moment, his mind had become clear, blank, empty of contents.

Only once did his mind stray from the unique experience of blissful emptying. For one brief moment, Tom thought of September. When all other thoughts were apparently gone, there still remained the thought of her. And it seemed to burn a permanent imprint on his brain.

In the storm's immediate aftermath, the six inches of rain brought a massive and severe flooding. The flood wiped out the little reservoir that Tom, September, and Iona had assiduously constructed seven years earlier, for purposes of storing small amounts of water for their garden. The unexpected rain was too devastating to be of any use (aside from filling the cisterns, which it did).

The floods washed all the dead trees and deadwood due to sun poisoning into the arroyos and then sent them crashing downhill in torrents of water with the rest of the debris—and, alas, also carrying away the good nutrient soil. That accomplished one good thing. The storm, the flooding aftermath, cleaned up the landscape of the dust that had been accumulating for more than a decade and a half.

For Tom, it emphasized the problem that had existed all along for humankind. There had always been an abundance of rain. The problem was that seventy percent of it fell directly into the oceans, and at least another fifteen percent fell on terrain that prevented it from being effectively utilized for agricultural purposes.

Regardless of losing the ozone layer, and perhaps even regardless of the five to six degree warming trend, if all of the Earth's water could have been used efficiently, the Earth could have supported twelve billion people indefinitely, using all the innovations of modern science harnessed for the purpose. *Except for one thing: within the limits of actual available water,* the Earth could have supported only six billion, perhaps for many decades, perhaps even for two hundred years; but not indefinitely, not for thousands of years. The Earth simply didn't have the long-term carrying capacity to accomplish that. It was only the incidence of the Eleven-Years-War that brought a relatively stable crisis to a premature boiling point. Without the enormities of that war, plus the dangerously rapid warming trend, plus the ozone-layer depletion (all three of the dice, so to speak, coming up on one spot simultaneously), the Earth could have limped along effectively for another two hundred years, perhaps longer, regardless of whether the world's population was six billion or nine billion or twelve billion.

In the year 2040 A.D., the Earth's population just happened to have drawn the worst of the lottery—yet in spite of this ongoing tragedy and mega-catastrophe, Tom knew, right in the middle of this fierce storm, *that no one would be able to see the worst for many years.* That was the greatest legacy of the tragedy—not being able to see it all until it was over. (And that was also something brand new.)

And then there was no one left to re-kindle the fire of hope.

Without history, there would be no future, and no extended human memory, and without extended human memory, there could be no future possibility of human freedom—or life itself.

That's what the Domes and the magisters were really up to. That was their master plan.

From the swirl of all these thoughts a reason emerged why the thought of Iona suddenly became so urgently important to Tom, Iona, the future.

That's how Tom figured it: If the nuclear-powered wind machines had been destroyed by September's rebel force (which must have happened, otherwise, there wouldn't have been the huge ex-

treme deluge of rain he had experienced) and if Iona survived her
ordeal through the Forbidden Zone and whatever she found on the
other side—AND ADMITTEDLY THAT WAS A BIG 'IF'— and if
the Gaia State discovered that Iona actually *hadn't* died at the age
of five, in Bolivia, then Iona's life in the future would be in grave
peril; because the evil empire would then want to destroy Iona, the
daughter of September, the leader of the old rebellion...because the
daughter...

As the old saying went: 'kill the offspring of your enemy when
they are still young, otherwise that offspring will rise up and smite
you. The tenacity of your opponent is one thing. But the un-
quenched revenge of the young is even more potentially dangerous,
to be revisited upon you, at a later date in time.'

Yes, Tom realized, there was reason to hope. But it was impera-
tive that if he should ever fall back into the clutches of the Gaia State,
he would have to remain absolutely silent on the subject of Iona.
To save her, for the future, she would have to remain deeply locked
inside him.

Chapter Twenty-Six

TOM LIMPED ALONG on his own for another four years. He could no longer move about in direct sunlight, or in a short period of time, he would have succumbed to sun poisoning. After all, Regis' protective shield was gone. He couldn't even try to hunt during the daylight hours. He was too old to try to hunt at night. He ate all the corn that was left in storage. Then he recovered all the corn from the Tarahumara Indian's cave, and ate that, too. It kept him in good stead for a year. The rains did not return. A permanent return to the natural weather patterns was not going to happen overnight, he realized. He suffered. Then, for a horrible three-year period, there was no rain at all.

The spring dried up and permanently disappeared. Fortunately, he was able to start up the kerosene-run generator to pump water from the well. The old tractor technology of the pump was a god-send. It kept him in drinking water, plus water to grow a little corn and a little manioc, during the critical three years when no rain fell.

Without the kerosene, tractor engine, pump, and the deep well, he would surely have died of thirst or starved to death. The old twentieth century technology kept him alive during that time. Then, after three years, the kerosene ran out, the pump no longer worked and the deep well went dry. He had reached bottom.

There simply wasn't enough for his sustenance. Finally, Tom realized that he had to leave, or starve to death. It was only a matter of time now. He took everything he could carry. Traveling light at night, he made it to the Yaqui Indian's cave fifty miles to the north. He managed to hang on for another year there, living on the stored corn and the tiny trickle of spring water; but even the spring water ran out.

Maybe, in the fullness of time, the environments of the Sonora desert and the Sierra Madre mountains would return to all their majestic splendors, in all their flora and fauna, but for the time being—for the immediate time anyway, for a man of eighty-one, Tom Novak, living alone in such a harsh environment—it was a certain death-trap.

First, he traveled north, traveling only at night, ten miles at a stretch, spending the day time hours either in caves, or under large rock overhangs, or in abandoned silver or copper mines. His survival depended on sheer willpower and good fortune, fortunately he was blessed with both.

Only on three occasions did he have to stay out in the open, exposed during day light hours, lying in the shade, with all his clothes wrapped tightly around him, taped as if he were a mummy, to protect him now from sun poisoning.

Tom knew, or rather *sensed intuitively,* that the sun poisoning was more virulent now, far more dangerous than the usual, perhaps even almost as bad as the nine weeks at the very end of the Eleven-Years-War, when it killed so many people and destroyed so much plant life. During those nine critical weeks, almost as much as one-sixth of all the trees in the entire world had been killed.

Now, more than ever before, Tom knew he had to carefully protect himself. The sun was his enemy. Every fiber in his body, every pore in his skin, screamed out this mortal truth.

He detected no signs of human life until he arrived near the old mining town of Cananea. Even then, he kept out of sight. He was enormously afraid to make any kind of contact with anyone, but he also knew that he had no choice in the matter; sooner or later, he was going to have to.

During the night, he passed by the old pueblo of Cuitaca (there was no one living there at the time, but there were recent signs of human habitation, just barely potable well water), and twenty-four hours later near midnight, he passed by the abandoned railroad town of San Lazaro, where, in a bizarre twist of fate, Tom happened to find a discarded pair of dark sunglasses lying alongside the long abandoned railroad tracks.

In the darkness, how did he see the sunglasses lying in the dirt? A glint reflected from the quarter moon, provided the tiny sliver of light that guided him. He picked them up. He tried them on. The sunglasses fit perfectly.

From then on, he was able to follow the old railroad tracks that ran twenty miles up a valley and continued to the old town of Nogales.

Only recently, Nogales had become the most remote military outpost of the by-then completely dominant Dome people.

Walking up the center of the main street, Tom walked into a dusty almost ghost-town. It was about high noon. He was wrapped up like a mummy.

In his white homespun cotton cloth, and wearing his sunglasses, Tom looked like the Invisible Man—or Saint Lazarus, having just risen from the dead, passing through the land of Canaan; looking like a hapless fool.

Just before he entered the town, he found a tree-branch lying on the ground. He cut away the side branches to make a rod. Holding it like a staff, across his chest, it enhanced the overall impression he gave of being a totally bizarre person, only recently arrived from the other side of the world.

To his great surprise, Tom was taken in by the town commander for exactly that reason. The commander was filled with ennui and an unbelievably profound weight of boredom. He felt that it was grossly unfair that he had been assigned to what he considered to be the post at the edge of the world.

Nogales was suffering from the worst aspects of sun poison-

ing—even in the military substructure, it was considered a very un-
healthy posting. If the commander had only the right connections
in the regional hierarchy, he could have been posted to Los Angeles,
Portland, Seattle, San Francisco, ALL FOUR GRAVY POSTINGS,
or at least, Albuquerque or Tucson, but not Nogales! Connections,
connections, as in all bureaucratic and administrative organizations,
it was always a matter of having the right connections.

Through a mixture of wit, intelligence, and charm, Tom managed to convince the commander that he was more likely to be a
source of entertainment for the commander—alive, although incarcerated in a makeshift jail—than he could have been hanging by his
neck from a makeshift gallows.

So the commander took Tom for what he really was: a gifted
conversationalist. The commander greatly enjoyed Tom's satirical
wit. Tom became what everyone else on the post referred to as 'the
house pet,' or more simply, a year later, 'the mascot.'

The commander should have executed Tom, simply for the
crime of being over the age of sixty, (which was now the law), but
the commander was tired of executing people.

Everyone who wasn't a magister—was to be executed if they
reached the age of sixty, that had been the standard order for the
last seven years running, but the commander was a bit of a maverick,
and he liked to flout the law whenever he could, so he deliberately
ignored it.

Four days earlier, the commander's troops were ordered to
sweep through the area where Tom had just passed to intercept and
round up all cannibal-scavengers they could lay their hands on. The
cannibal-scavengers' night raids against the recently arrived cattle
had been driving the commander to distraction.

In the troops' round-ups, over one hundred scavenger-canni-
bals were captured and summarily executed.

This event, unwittingly, unintentionally and ironically, made it
possible for Tom to survive. For if the commander hadn't given the
order to clean up the area, exactly four days before Tom's arrival,

traveling alone, Tom most certainly would have been set upon, robbed, killed, and inevitably eaten by the cannibals. That outcome would have been absolutely certain—no wonder Tom couldn't "find" any people during the last leg of his trek. Tom's timing could not have been more fortunate.

Fate had been smiling on Tom all along. If Tom had been a religious man, which he wasn't, but if he had been, he might have thought that Providence had a hand in it, but that wasn't the case, and he knew it. Instead, he thought that it was just fool's luck.

So, to stay alive, Tom knew that the role of fool was his best and final card to play. That's where his survival lay.

So in this capacity, he served as the commander's mascot for fourteen years. (Tom's ability to spin out long yarns kept him employed.) Then, very unexpectedly, the commander died from the result of a massive heart attack.

Within months of his death, a new commander was installed in his post. A week after that, an itinerant businessman, with a surprisingly unique entrepreneurial spirit, happened to pass by.

This confluence of events miraculously saved Tom's life again.

In the businessman's visit at the Nogales military base he was wined and dined by the newly installed commander. As part of the evening entertainment, on a stage, Tom was placed on display as a kind of exotica. Tom, in tattered clothing, his hair long, streaked with white, his beard also long, having turned flaxen white, was paraded in front of them.

The itinerant businessman gasped. "Good Gaia. Look at him! What a sight! What with his straggling hair, his long white beard, and his gloomy, detached eyes, he looks like a prophet of old. How old is he?"

"*That question...* It's a bit of a mystery," the new commander grunted. He turned to Tom. "How old are you?" he asked.

"Ninety-six," Tom said. "If my calculation is correct."

The itinerant businessman laughed. "Is that possible? All of the elderly were supposed to have been killed off not just years ago, but eons ago. How'd he escape the mass euthanasia of the elderly? Unless you were a magister, nobody escaped the big *kill-off*. Where'd he come from?"

"I don't know. All I know is he came from a hiding place."

"Where was this hiding place? I don't know of a single case of anyone who escaped the mass euthanasia of the elderly. It just didn't happen. Heavens to Gaia! I don't know a single case. Happened back in GAIA YEAR ELEVEN through FOURTEEN, right? Back then, he would have been twenty years passed the cut-off date, anyhow."

"His hiding place, you asked? I don't know. Deep in Mexico."

"What do you plan to do with him?"

"Kill him."

"Don't do that. I've a better idea. Sell him to me."

"What?"

"You heard me. Sell him to me."

"That would be in violation of the law. The general euthanasia of people over the age of sixty is still on the books. It's forbidden."

"Don't worry about that. I have a special sanction with the magisters. I will pay you well. I will take this burden off your hands."

"What do you plan to do with him?" the new commander asked.

"I've been given a small section of a prison in a former Chicago stockyard. Over the past year, I've been setting up a *curiosity show*. I've already got a number of exhibits in my presentation. I've put together quite a show. Among my exhibits are cases of people suffering from extreme sun poisoning and extreme cases of genetic collapse. I have some cases of extreme mental retardation, too. Man, do the fans really like that. Tom could be added to the menagerie. He would be a man who is thirty-six years older than he should be and is still alive. That *would* be a pretty amazing thing to look at today. He should be placed in a museum display, anyway. I will turn a nice, hefty profit..."

"And the law?" the new commander asked suspiciously. "How

do you get around that?"

"My main clients are magisters. Tom would be an exception. They'd give me a special license. What difference would one human being make, more or less. How often do you get a chance to look into the face of someone who's, say, fifty-five years—older than you are. For the magisters who are in their early 30's, even better—he would be sixty-five years—older than they are. You realize that most of the young people now don't know what happened back then. No, no, no, great material for my show."

They closed the deal. Tom was shipped off to Chicago.

Chapter Twenty-Seven

THE SPECIAL MAGISTER, a man we had introduced at the beginning of our story, was seated at his desk. He got up, walked over, and with the wave of his hand, removed a heavy metal curtain grate and looked out through a long, oblong-shaped window. What could he see? Nothing. There was practically nothing but thin air. He was one thousand feet high in a cylinder, in a tall, slender cylinder. He was at the top of a high control tower, like a space needle, high above New York City, looking at what had been left after all the destruction of what once was—a massive sea of humanity below.

Like his father before him,—and in the final fifty-one years of his life his grandfather before his father, the special magister had spent his life inside the Domes. From birth, for thirty-six years, he had spent his life in a state of opulence, nurtured in a state of caste privilege, safe inside the protective shell of the Dome-universe.

Only the previous year, at age thirty-five, this gentleman had acquired the sobriquet: *special* magister. With his special education in 'Hominid and Post-Hominid Studies,' there were only four like him in the entire Gaia-Dome system.

He returned to his desk. He read a bulletin. At the bottom of the bulletin was an item that caught his interest.

The first items in the contents of the bulletin were nothing special. There had been a couple of coups in the Domes in Europe (the rulers of the European Domes were a fussy, erratic lot, typically more volatile than the more stable rulers of the American Domes) and there was some growing evidence of some noticeable climate change in Greenland and North Africa. This was the boring and predictable news. It was followed by more of the usual: the rise in the business climate between America and Europe had occurred, while at the same time, business had gone slightly in decline between America and the Far Eastern Pacific Zone. Then at the bottom of the bulletin there was one bit of news that was different. In particular, it caught his eye. *"Group of rebels destroy garrison in Mexico. For one month, threatened Dome. When subsequent interception was attempted, unable to locate group. All scouting expeditions unsuccessful. Cannot be spotted. Origin of rebels: completely unknown. Route of retreat of rebels, also completely unknown. What to do?"*

The more the special magister thought about it, the more troubling this last bit of information became.

His intuition told him to make a special note of it.

Then he remembered what he was required to do the next day. His presence was required at a trade show in Chicago.

The special magister murmured to himself: "I hate going to these shows."

From New York he left for Chicago the next day.

In Chicago, after an all day attendance at what the special magister considered to be a boring trade show featuring the display of New Farming Implements and New Weapons Technology, he was wheedled by some magisters into attending an after-hours, 'illicit' event.

The special magister tried to beg off. "I'm tired. I beg you. It's been a long day. No thank you."

But his colleagues insisted. Many of those present were younger than him. Their insistence was adamant. The ringleader, a blond hair, blue-eyed fellow, who couldn't have been more than thirty years old, spoke on behalf of all. "You've got to see this show. I'm sure they don't have anything like it in New York. It's a must-see."

"Sickies, aboriginals and freaks, no thank you," the special magister said in a tired voice. "I've been to these dungeons and mental institution pits before."

"You're too set in your ways! Just like your old dead father. Ah, this show is different!"

That night, they picked him up at one of the central Domes.

Most of the displays at these kinds of shows nauseated the special magister. What disturbed him the most were the mental retardation cases. Men and women, with shaved heads, bound hand and foot, were forced to conduct themselves in multiple positions of humiliation and knavery. When their tongues—spouting forth gibberish bouts of nonsense, began to grow silent—they were doused with buckets of water, and their tongues wagged and the flow of gibberish nonsense started up again. Some of them engaged in the most frightful form of calisthenics. They all smelled badly. The repetition of these shows had always left the special magister demoralized. To his chagrin, upon viewing these proceedings, the other young magisters hooted and jeered, enjoying themselves, like tempestuous children.

When the special magister insisted he'd seen enough, his hosts said there was one more exhibit he had to see before closing time.

The last exhibit was a cell holding a single individual—a single individual only.

It was Tom.

He was seated in a chair. His hair and beard were long and flowing. He wore on top of his head a crown of green laurels. In his hand he held a staff, burnished the color of gold flake. Bunched around his shoulders he wore a robe. His naked thin knees stuck out in front of him.

In front of the cell there was a sign: "Ninety-seven-year-old man. Miraculously preserved! Miraculously still alive!"

The special magister looked carefully into Tom's eyes.

Tom looked back, staring straight back at him. The two of them stared at each other for a minute. Tom reminded the special magister of his grandfather who had died three years before, at the age of eighty-two. As the special magister stared into Tom's face carefully, he realized Tom and his deceased grandfather bore a certain resemblance. The special magister shivered. Very strikingly, he remembered something from his childhood.

The special magister insisted on seeing the owner of the show, without delay. When he found him, he insisted on seeing him privately. In a backroom, the owner took him to his office.

"How did you come to acquire this man?" the special magister asked the owner, referring to Tom.

The owner's eyes shined with a greed-filled allure caused by his smelling the potential for making a profitable transaction. His eyebrows shot up. "You have a professional interest in this piece of property?"

"I could have you put away for this, for trafficking in this serious contraband," the special magister shouted in an angry voice. "Just answer the question. Don't play games with me. I am in no mood to be humored."

"I bought my share of him from a certain businessman who had a partnership with me for a while back, a year ago. He had picked him up in the Western Quadrant, in Nogales, near Mexico."

"Mexico?"

"Yes. Near the old border."

"How did he get *there?*"

"I don't know," the owner said. "My understanding is he was from the south. How he eluded the euthanasia—so many years ago—now that's a mystery beyond my comprehension."

"He can talk?" the special magister asked.

"Oh, yes, he can talk, alright," the owner said. "He doesn't talk much, though. Very rarely, anyway."

"I noticed he has a cough. Is he sick?"

"Yes."

"If he dies between now and the coming of the morning, I'll have you killed, understand? Have him cleaned up, properly clothed and decently fed. Then have him brought to my hotel room tomorrow afternoon, 3 o'clock sharp, understand?"

"Yes."

"You're to mention nothing about this to anyone, understand? You'll be given a small token of reimbursement for your trouble. From now on, you are to act as if you have never known anything about this man, understood?"

The special magister confiscated the contraband from the owner and sent him packing with a warning.

He secretly transported Tom back with him to New York. He placed him in an unused room, in a retirement home, set up specifically for the use of old retired magisters.

He gave explicit written instructions to the caretakers that Tom was to be well taken care of and he was even allowed books to be read, if he asked for them.

When a caretaker asked him why he was keeping him alive, in spite of the rules, the special magister replied, "I have this strong suspicion that some day this man's memory will be of some value. I am banking on a hunch. Only a slight hunch. Time will tell. We shall see."

"A hunch?'

"This man once knew my grandfather. Actually, he didn't know my grandfather—rather he impersonated him, stood in for him, as an actor, in a 'History of the Cosmos Show,' or a 'History of the Universe Show.' It happened in New York City. If my memory serves me well, it occurred in YEAR GAIA ELEVEN. I was six-years-old at the time. I think he may know something about what is going on in Mexico today."

"How could you be sure it's him?" the caretaker asked. "After all, you're referring to something that happened thirty years ago. You were just a little boy. Would he look the same? How could you swear it's him?"

"I know, I know," the special magister said. "Odd, isn't it? Maybe I'm wrong. Maybe it's just something I want to believe. This is all speculative on my part. But I think there's something here. And if there isn't something here today, maybe, just maybe, there will be something here tomorrow. Or the day after tomorrow. After all I've seen in life, I'm a patient man."

Several years went by and the special magister visited Tom once a year to see that he was being maintained in a proper way. The special magister stepped into the room to examine Tom for just a minute or two. Most of the time, he would visit him at the time when Tom was asleep. In those instances, he would linger for up to fifteen minutes, just watching him sleep. (Tom really did remind him of his deceased grandfather.) Having ascertained that Tom was okay, without saying a word, and never bothering to identify himself, the special magister would then—without fail—retreat from the room. But he would return, a year later. The caretakers continued to act according to the magister's instructions, not having been given—in the intervening time—any subsequent counter-instructions. This went on for seven years.

In this regard, Tom had been lucky. He had been treated in the same way as if he had been a retired magister himself, and by virtue of that expert treatment, his health was resuscitated.

Then the special magister received a special bulletin that unduly alarmed him. The rebels were acting up again, this time with a success and a ferocity that had left some of the leadership of the Gaia state in a state of near-panic. He knew that it was time to set Tom up for some special interrogations.

He brought a messenger for the explicit purpose of conducting some interviews.

It was GAIA YEAR FORTY-SIX, or year 2097, according to the old calendar, and Tom now was 103-years-old.

And after the special magister's first visit with Tom, where he first quizzed him about Iona, he found documents in some hidden archives (accessible only to the highest level of magisters, of course), that provided information that placed Tom definitely closer to September, and hypothetically—in theory—closer to September's daughter, Iona (if she was still alive.) The information also included that Tom had been an ex-writer. It also included a few odd bits of other information.

Now the special magister realized that in finding Tom, he had stumbled on a potential gold mine. In fact, he had made the biggest discovery of them all. *And he knew it.* Maybe—just maybe—Tom might have further information hidden in his mind about the new rebels, and maybe he knew something more than he had previously disclosed—about Iona.

Then the special magister received a further bulletin which closed the circle. He received a new news bulletin. It read in part: "Dome Army of 50,000 dispatched to destroy new rebellion. Complete failure. Dome Army of 50,000 destroyed. Repeat, total failure. Leadership in Western Quadrant in a state of complete disarray. Rebellion has grown. Base in Nogales has been overrun. Domes in Tucson and Phoenix have been bypassed. Rebellion heading north. Gathering strength. Building momentum. Waiting for further instructions. Rebellion was larger than first anticipated. Recruits have been drawn from far away—from even across the seas. FOR THE FIRST TIME! FOR THE FIRST TIME! lower-level personnel have left the Domes to join the rebellion. Needlessly to say, this has never happened before. Or at least, this has not happened for over thirty years. We have captured a few of the rebels. By interrogating them, we have learned a few other things..."

The special magister was shocked. The most important thing to him was to find out who the leader of this rebellion was, and if this leader had any links to the past.

This was the fourth time he thought of September Snow, since he was a child of nine, when he vaguely remembered his father, breaking all the rules, showing him a secret communique with her name mentioned in it.

At that time, after her execution, the name of September Snow had then been removed from all official reports. Like her deceased husband, Regis Snow, September had become a complete non-person, *persona non grata,* erased from memory, a non-being. From the YEAR GAIA THIRTEEN to the YEAR GAIA FORTY-SIX, there had not been a mention of her in any history, in any report, or in any communique.

So, armed with his extra information about September, the special magister decided to visit Tom's room one last time. He would dispense with using the messenger as a go-between. In all the weeks leading up to that time, from the messenger the special magister had acquired a substantial amount of knowledge about September and Regis, but nothing about Iona.

The special magister knew it was high time that he change his style and methods.

There would be no more threats of intimidation, no more bullying, no more brow-beating.

The special magister decided to change his tactics completely. Since Tom had not much longer to live, there was no point in beating around the bush.

It was time to cut to the chase.

Chapter Twenty-Eight

THE SPECIAL MAGISTER was framed in the doorway of Tom's room. Due to Tom's failing eyesight, the bright light glaring from the hallway behind the door was diffused. Tom blinked repeatedly in the attempt to discern what he was looking at.

Tom stuck his tongue out at the special magister. His enfeebled movements confirmed his incredible age. Yet in spite of the inevitable aging process, Tom's face still showed defiance and determination.

Tom had the noble features—the striking and handsome eyebrows, the high noble cheekbones, of his Native American heritage. He still had all the attributes received from his Seneca-Iroquoian mother. His will-o'-the-wisp hair cascaded over his shoulders. His hair twisted and curled before the split-end tips rested on his flattened, nearly concave, stomach. Tom's beard had turned flaxen white. His hair shone with a silver-blue glow.

Tom's eyes, inherited from his Irish father's side, had once been strikingly blue, looking like ancient burnt-holes in his face, but from the recent glaucoma, they had turned milky blue. With difficulty Tom saw the special magister, through this milky haze of washed out blue. He shaded his eyes with one hand, a gesture that occasionally seemed to improve his vision.

With the fingers of his other hand, he delicately pulled a strand of stringy white hair down from his head. Pulling the strand, he stretched it taut, twenty inches in front of his eyes. He studied the strand of his hair carefully. He rocked back and forth.

Even before the special magister had opened the door, Tom knew in advance the identity of his visitor. He knew it was going to be the man who dressed himself in purple.

Tom let go of the strand and allowed it to fall gently across his face.

Tom's unfailing instincts told him that it was inevitable that the special magister would come to visit him for purposes of trying to extract information about Iona.

Tom knew that the special magister would have to be more forthcoming in telling him what he knew about September at the end of her life, if he hoped to obtain any 'real and useful' information about Iona.

The official Gaia record had stated that Iona had died at the age of five years, ten months, in Orturo province in Bolivia. But if Iona hadn't actually died, if her death had been faked—*perhaps:* Tom might had known something that would have indicated that she lived beyond the age of five. That was what the special magister wanted to investigate.

"I see you're still alive?" the special magister said to Tom in a slightly strained voice.

"Yes," Tom replied. "Just barely."

"In good health though, I pray?" he asked.

"Oh, this horse isn't quite ready for the glue factory yet."

But Tom was lying. He was dying. He knew it. He wouldn't see out three or four months, probably wouldn't even make it to the end of the year. For once, he figured, he held all the cards. They couldn't threaten him with his life since he was already on the threshold of losing it.

Even to torture him—even if there was the slightest chance it might work—was too late. Torture would kill the frail Tom outright. Tom's condition was too delicate for the special magister to even contemplate it, or to consider using less dangerous mind-altering drugs, for, alas, they had their uncontrollable side effects.

Really, this meeting was all that Tom was hoping for. Maybe the special magister could tell him exactly what happened to September. How she died. What she did before she died. How she looked. What she had been thinking. (Every single day Tom had thought about September over the previous twenty-seven years, ever since he had last communicated with her other over a wristwatch vector screen.) Maybe some information about what she felt. That was what Tom cared about *deeply and passionately.*

Framed by the light through the jail-cell door, dressed in an `after-dinner' suit, the figure of the special magister appeared stately, majestic; almost inspiring reverence. He had a paunch and a receding hair-line, yet his *clothes* seemed to negate these `frailties'; giving him a regal, august, exalted air.

The special magister's attire was entirely made of satin, light purple on dark purple.

Remembering, in his youth the Roman Catholic church services of his father, Tom indulged in the whimsical notion that maybe all the attire of the magisters and special magisters resembled *that* old church-clothes business: *ersatz* archbishops, red on white, in satin only, with miter and crowned hat; or ersatz cardinals, red on red, in satin and silk. But now these had, so to speak, evolved into the echelons of the Gaia hierarchy, so they were purple on white for the magisters, or light purple on dark purple for the special magisters, or purple on greenish-blue purple, with very tall white hats like bejeweled balloons, for the grandmagisters.

The grandmagisters, however, didn't show off in public, except on the rarest occasions. Rather, they avoided the limelight, especially during the last twenty-five years of their rule. (The more inaccessible they became, the more august and exalted they appeared.)

Maybe it was just a matter of how psychologically imposing they could appear. Then it occurred to Tom—the real reason. Only magisters, special magisters, and grandmagisters had not suffered the debilitating effects of premature aging due to sun poisoning. Only they had been completely spared, and this made them different.

They had been shielded by the Domes. They did not suffer any "premature wrinkle line syndrome," which was the fate of many of the others lucky to be living in the Domes. At the age of thirty, they actually *looked their age,* not sixty-five, as did the messenger and some of the others in the Dome population.

It was their special clothes, and special makeup, that made them appear august.

"Well, well," Tom said nodding. "Again you visit me. I know you're a special magister. Do you actually have a name? Or do you use code number?"

"Code number!" the special magister bellowed, then laughed. "You do go back a long way! That practice died out thirty-three years ago." He then chuckled lightly, wagging his finger. "I knew you had a strong memory. You must have an intensified awareness of the terrible fissures of this century." He smiled impishly. "You have a wild look about you, too, but kind. Yes. What a strange face you have."

"What's your name, then?" Tom asked.

"My name?" the special magister asked with a touchy air of self-importance.

"Your name." Tom growled. "Since you don't use code number. You've visited me to make certain I was alive—once a year—over these past seven years. I know. I was aware of what was going on. Even those times you thought I was asleep, I knew you had come. I'd ask the caretaker afterwards if it had been you: *the mysterious man dressed in regal purple.* And then you had the messenger conduct these interrogations of me about September more recently... Where's the messenger? Have you dismissed him?"

"Lloyd."

"Lloyd?" Tom skeptically asked in a mild voice. He then burst out laughing. "Is that what you call yourself?" Tom asked. "Lloyd?"

"Lloyd Thompson, *the fourth,* to be exact," the special magister replied with a note of embarrassment.

"I know my name sounds funny," Lloyd said. "Have you dined yet?"

Tom nodded. "Doesn't take much nourishment to keep me going these days," he said. With his slender, withered hand, he patted his exceedingly flat and tiny stomach gently.

The special magister folded his delicate hands and, from the waist, bowed ever so slightly. "This is my favorite scene in the Gaia-Domes," he said. "A `Suit' eating his dinner on a wheeled TV gurney as he watches mass executions on Wallscreen, his fork poised with food to be shoved into his mouth as he pauses to watch some unfortunate being suffocated to death... After this repast, anthem. He's singing his damn fool head off as he marches in place—*forward*—toward some shining abstraction... Here's his thinking. How else can I fight against the logic of the magisters? It's hypnotically compelling. This is how they think: `War is logical. The planet is small, though damaged. Produce is limited. Scarcity is the order of the day. So conflict is instinctive, visceral. Why don't we admit how much we hate each other? Control the water to control the world. Control all forms of religion to control the minds of all people. When you control the minds of people, you control their bodies and their actions.' That's the magister's *modus operandi* in a nutshell."

"You are a magister," Tom replied blankly, as if that were the most important point to note.

The special magister immediately walked over to Tom's desk and hurriedly riffled through the sheets of paper that lay across it. They were all blank. Then he quietly examined Tom's clean, dry quill-pen, picking it up and setting it down. He couldn't help but notice that the ink was still in the inkwell, not a drop, apparently, used. These, and the paper, were the only objects on Tom's desk. He then looked inside the desk. Nothing but more blank sheets of paper. He was disappointed. Contrary to his hopes, Tom had not written a single word.

Unsuccessfully hiding his disappointment, the special magister looked up. "So, you're still too proud to write anything, huh?" he asked in an airy voice. "Is that it? Ex-writer? You won't answer the questions that the messenger puts to you either. Is that it?"

"I won't play the fool for you," Tom curtly replied. "I won't act like an addled crazy man for you, either. I've grown weary of playing such tiresome roles. If you play them too often, you start believing them *yourself*. I haven't written anything in almost fifty years. After fourteen years of playing the role of conversationalist and storyteller, a year of playing the idiot, and seven years of being hidden away as a convalescent, the roles become stale."

Tom leveled his eyes at the special magister. "Wouldn't you agree?"

The special magister smiled. There was a short pause. Then they both smiled at each other. It was as if they had determined that, although they were adversaries, somehow they knew they could still act in a civil manner towards each other. Nonverbally, the ground rules had been set. Tom knew that he respected him according to some arcane definition of standards because his manner had changed from their last meeting. He had become *friendly and diplomatic*.

"I won't humor you," the special magister began. "As you well know, nobody reads your books anymore. Not even the precious few of us who still had access to them an odd thirty years ago. I haven't read any of your books."

"I presumed," Tom replied, "that you had no interest in them—even in the olden days." Tom had a wizened expression on his face. "And, of course, not anymore. I used to have a lot of vanity about that stuff, back then. But after you've become 100 years old, some of the vanity, thank God, begins to crumble. I've had three years, almost four, under my belt for my vanity to further recede. It's been eroding away. There's almost none left."

"Oh, I had no intention of appealing to your vanity," the special magister protested. "I'm only interested in the truth."

"Are we going to talk about something real, then?" Tom broke in cuttingly. "If not, you're wasting my time."

"Talk's cheap," Lloyd replied, as he laughed in a friendly way, almost with an air of friendly pomposity. "I knew you quit writing a long time ago, by the way," he said. "I should have known that nothing would induce you to change, certainly not at this stage of your life. You certainly weren't going to change on my account."

"Give me a reason why I should," Tom asked.

"What do you want?"

"You *know,*" Tom mouthed slowly, "what I want."

There was a pause. Then after an even longer pause, Tom broke the strained silence with a deep, melancholy sigh.

"Beneath the ancient streets of Rome, 2,000 years ago, the catacombs were reputed to hold the remains of more than six million Christians," Tom said. "I think that was written by a British historian a long time ago. Where are we now? Where are the remains of the Anti-Gaia rebels of 2058 to 2070?"

"Were there that many Christians buried beneath one city?" Lloyd asked. "I'd have sworn there were only one-sixth that number. Weren't most of those buried in the catacombs, ordinary Roman non-Christian pagans? *They falsified history, even back in the olden times, didn't they? Tsk, tsk!* By the way, the dates you're quoting, 2058 to 2070? What you mean to say is between YEAR GAIA SEVEN and YEAR GAIA NINETEEN, don't you. I'll have you know there will be no toleration for the practice of calendar treachery, inside of this cell, or outside of it."

Tom ignored the special magister's rebuke.

"But to answer your question, they weren't buried anywhere," Lloyd added, "those who were captured at the sites of the nuclear-powered wind machines were immediately executed and dumped into the sea. They were just thrown overboard. Food for the fish. But I do know a lot of history about the period when they were vanquished. And more importantly, I know the story you're seeking."

"What story is that?" Tom asked, pretending ineffectively to display a poker face.

"The story about September, of course. I have a proposal," Lloyd then added quickly, licking his lips in anticipation. "We exchange information."

"Exchange information?" Tom asked. "For what? What do you mean?"

"Yes, you know," Lloyd said. "Trade—one for one."

"No, I don't know," Tom replied.

"My information for your information. Piece for piece, part for part, fairness for fairness. I tell you what happened to September—and you tell me, in return, what happened to, say...for example...Iona. Isn't that simple and fair? What do you say?"

"Are you prepared to argue fair for foul and foul for fair?" Tom asked. "I thought it was understood that Iona died at the age of five. I repeat: 'Iona died at the age of five.' I have repeated it so often I thought it was going to make me go crazy. Ever since the messenger started interrogating me, he let it slip out once that the death of Iona had been recorded in some dusty official Gaia report... No?"

Lloyd didn't respond. He remained silent.

Tom glanced downward. He scowled menacingly. Suddenly, he closed his eyes, as if he were overwhelmed by a wave of resignation. He looked old and tired. Fatigue had set in.

"Will you tell me everything?" Tom asked, his eyes shut.

"Yes," Lloyd said. His eyes spoke of honesty, even if his words sounded more like those of a deceitful politician. "Everything. That is, everything I happen to know. I can't do any better than that, can I?"

"All right," Tom nodded. "But you tell me first. Then, after you've told me, I'll decide whether I'm going to tell you anything at all, depending on whether I like what I hear."

"But that's no deal," Lloyd protested. He shook his head. "That's not fair. You get everything. I get nothing."

"Are you going to lecture me about fairness now?" Tom asked with an exaggerated wide-eyed grin on his face. "Oh, please don't."

"No, I'm not," Lloyd replied shamefacedly. "I guess I can't."
He blushed. He looked genuinely chagrined. "You're right."

Now he looked positively embarrassed. Tom's glaucoma-rid-
den, milky-blue eyes followed Lloyd as he moved from one side of
the room to the other. Lloyd reached for the only spare chair in the
room. He drew it over, and sat down. Tom tried to focus on Lloyd.
Lloyd was now seated directly facing him, their chairs barely separated, their knees nearly touching.

"September waited until the end of the third wave of the attack
before going after the nerve center in North America. Earlier, she
had been coordinating all of the attacks from a secret rebel base.
Then, two days after the initial attack, she must have been coordinating all of the actions from the island of Saint Helena, after they
captured it. She must have known the island like the back of her
hand, since she had lived there for many years. The attack was so well
planned and so well orchestrated that it was far more successful than
they expected. Their one bold stroke was a brilliant success. September must have had the satisfaction of knowing this at least two days
before she was captured."

"They captured her?" Tom asked.

"Yes."

"Then what?"

"She was executed," Lloyd said in a flat voice. "They tried to
get her to talk. But it was useless." He shrugged. "They were professional. They knew what they were doing. I wish I could say more.
But that's all that happened. She died."

"No last minute speeches?" Tom asked.

"Why?" Lloyd asked, surprised. "Don't be daft, man! She'd
been successful. She destroyed the entire nuclear-powered wind
machine complex. Without Regis Snow, there was no way we could
rebuild the world-wide network. Why would she have reason to
indulge in last-minute speechmaking? She had accomplished everything she set out to do. But there was one last thing she was reported
to have said."

"What was that?" Tom asked anxiously.

"I can't verify it," Lloyd said, shaking his head. "It's only a rumor. It was something I heard from one of the old grandmagisters, told to me in the form of an anecdote. He said it to me in passing—when I was a young man."

"What was it?" Tom asked, gasping.

"I don't think I should even tell you." Lloyd shook his head again. "It's only a rumor. It could have been false. The grandmagister could have made it up, for all I know."

"You tell me all the same," Tom insisted.

"She was reported to have said: `You can hold a scorpion in the palm of your hand as long as you like, long enough until the scorpion suffocates. But you can't stop the scorpion from stinging you before it dies.'"

Lloyd paused. "The interrogator was reported to have rejoined: `Yes, but the Domes have an iron fist.' September is said to have answered back: `We were only a scorpion, true. And apparently, not a totally lethal one. But thirty years from now, you will face the fox. And that will be different. You will hold that fox to your belly, till it dies, but you won't be able to keep it from biting you.'"

Lloyd paused. "The interrogator is reported to have rejoined: `True, but the Domes have not only an iron fist, they have fortitude of iron in general.' September is said to have answered: `Yes, but the Domes began as flesh and blood and, like everything else, will end as flesh and blood. I predict it. On that day, the fox will feed on your heart.'"

"She said that?" Tom acclaimed approvingly. "That certainly sounds like her. Where did they end up burying her?"

"You think they were going to give her the decency of a burial?" Lloyd said, guffawing. "A potential shrine for people to visit so they could pay homage to her long-lost memory? Not likely! They cremated her, then scattered her ashes. They left not a trace. Eradicating her memory—now, that's a much taller order, isn't it? But all the events surrounding September Snow have been erased from the official documents. All of the past, all of the history—that you once held dear—have been erased by the intelligence organs of the Gaia State. Let me make it clear to you: all signs of memory of that time, when Regis and September were alive, have been systematically eradicated, *branch, trunk and limb.* Yes, yes, we have been nearly successful in that department, too. Very nearly."

"Nearly?" Tom asked.

"Almost one hundred percent."

"The messenger lied to me," Tom said. "Not only are there people independent of you living beyond the Forbidden Zone, they are people who know about September and Regis Snow. I know they do. Their memory is alive! I know it. I just know it."

Lloyd had the look of a shabby, duplicitous politician. "In a sense," he nodded, "the messenger did lie to you. But it was an honest lie. He doesn't know, *officially.* No one does. As you may have guessed, they were living beyond the former Forbidden Zone. But I know about them. I won't lie to you: there are a scattering of primitive groups—some groups small, some larger—living, here and there, outside the Domes."

Lloyd paused to almost exaggerated effect. "After decades of despair, after hopeless nights, it fills your heart with hope to hear it, doesn't it?" He gloated. He smiled an executioner's smile. "I can tell simply by looking at the hint of gleam in your glaucoma-induced milky-blue eyes—oh, YOU ARE POSITIVELY ECSTATIC! I'm sure you see them as the hope of the future of humanity. Let's talk about Iona, for the love of God. I'll tell you about these `other' people, if in return you'll tell me *something* about Iona. Throw me a bone, Tom."

"Nothing doing," Tom growled, smelling a trap. "You keep right on talking about those `other' people and leave the memory of Iona alone."

Lloyd shrugged, seemingly without a struggle, agreeing to Tom's request. "There are many tiny groups, but they don't amount to a great deal. They don't pose the smallest of threats. It's more of a bother to destroy them than to leave them alone, since they are so inconsequential. However, there are two larger groups. One has been around for quite a while. They are more religious than we are, a thousand times more so! They are always at their prayers. Totally other-worldly spiritualists they are! They are no harm to us. The other group was formed only recently, during the last seven years, in fact. They were formed as if...out of thin air. The latter group is far more dangerous. We call them the 'new rebels'."

Lloyd nodded. "Yes, this latter group is a problem. Every time we get a sighting of them, they simply disappear!"

"Into thin air?" Tom asked.

"Yes," Lloyd said, scratching his head. "We think it may have something to do with their leaders. They were troglodytes—once. They had inhabited caves. Until recently they did, this much we know. Only during the last few years have they come out into the full light of day. As far, that is, as we can tell. Cave-dwellers are dangerous. They are not subject to the destructive effects of exposure to ozone-depletion sun poisoning."

"What have they done?" Tom asked.

"Seven years ago, they destroyed a garrison, threatened a Dome, and then they completely disappeared. For four years, they were inactive. Back in their caves perhaps? Then in the past three years, they came out again and destroyed two Domes. They have also managed to defeat two fully armed and deployed garrisons, garrisons it took us two years to train. When they threatened the security of four Domes, we sent an army of 50,000 out to intercept them."

"And?" Tom asked.

"They defeated it."

"Are they a remnant of the old rebels?" Tom asked.

"No," Lloyd said, shaking his head. "That's what confuses us. Besides, the old rebels, if still alive, would be too old to fight. All the rebel strongholds from the old days were completely destroyed. The last group of rebels active were located on the mesas and in the mountains, north of the Grand Canyon, on the Colorado river

Plateau, in the Western Quadrant. That was the location of the last holdout of September's old rebel army. Ironically, they managed to hold out there for ten long years, longer than any other rebel group in the Western Hemisphere, after September was killed—before we destroyed them. They had a good location, a favorable location, north of the Grand Canyon and along the western slopes of the Rocky Mountains."

"And you destroyed them?" Tom asked.

"Yes, we wiped them out," Lloyd replied. "This new group has nothing to do with them. They are younger, much younger; indeed, most of them were not born until several years after September's rebels were defeated. Some are still children. Many of them are in their late teens; although the vast majority are in their early or late twenties—and there are also a couple of old birds... They fight like lions. They don't suffer from genetic sun poisoning. How they've been spared *that* when everyone else living outside the Domes had succumbed to it, I don't understand. Because of the caves? But this is why I mentioned the old rebels. The new rebels started out in southern Mexico (we think), then moved to central Mexico, then moved to northern Mexico. Some of them have moved even further north. Perhaps their goal is to occupy the region inhabited by the old rebels, north of the Grand Canyon and along the western slopes of the Rocky Mountains?"

"Are they really competent at conducting warfare?" Tom asked.

"Yes," Lloyd nodded. "They've defeated an army of 50,000, haven't they? They call themselves `The Unseeing Watchfulness of Gaia.'"

"The what?" Tom asked.

"Oh, I can't imagine that they made up the expression themselves," Lloyd continued with a sly nod. "Most of them were infants or not yet born when September blew up the nuclear-powered wind machines so many years ago. Someone who knew intimate truths about the old days must have taught them *that* expression." Lloyd looked at Tom carefully. "And whoever taught them must have learned it from someone else."

"Oh," Tom said, pretending to be baffled.

"Enough," Lloyd said, his eyes narrowing. "'The Unseeing Watchfulness,' was an expression in your novel, *Expressions Without Illusions*. It was an expression coined by you, Tom. It was the closest thing you could come up with—that could have implied the existence of a vague concept of a vague possibility of an existence of God. You coined the expression sixty-five years ago, remember?" Lloyd continued. "They just added, 'of Gaia' to the 'Unseeing Watchfulness,' I'm sure, as a sort of afterthought. To *politicize* it."

"You said you didn't read any of my books," Tom murmured.

"Yes, well, I lied about that one, too, didn't I?" Lloyd confessed with a sneaky, chameleon-like expression on his face. "'The answer is not to be found here on Earth...but in the stars?'" Lloyd asked, smiling devilishly. "Remember?"

"Yes, I remember," Tom said. "Any leaders older than in their late twenties?"

"Yes," Lloyd replied.

"How many?"

"Fifty—maybe more—" Lloyd murmured, "are in their early thirties. Perhaps they constituted the core group that the larger group grafted itself upon. They are so healthy, it's as if they were magisters themselves. Strong. Very strong."

"Anyone older?" Tom asked. "You make the group sound larger than they probably are."

"Yes, well, over time, the group has grown larger. Especially as of late. *Very large.*"

"I mean, are there any of them who would be in their forties?" Tom asked.

"Yes," Lloyd said, hesitating at first.

"Uh-huh," Tom said, nodding his head with confidence. "How many are there who are over the age of forty?"

"A couple, we think."

"That's all?"

"Maybe three or four, altogether. We are not quite sure."

"I see," Tom said. He had no intention of revealing his secret. Wild horses could not have dragged the truth out of him. He wasn't about to talk.

Tom realized that that was the reason why the special magister Lloyd was so concerned with finding out if Iona was the leader of this group of new rebels. That's why Lloyd was so fearful, so obsessed, *and so upset*. The past was coming back to haunt him.

Such joy! The thought of Iona's success filled Tom with hope.

This thought, even more than the thought about September's last words, provided him with a sense of peace. He smiled. He asked in a deliberately confused voice, "Is she alive?"

Lloyd replied: *"Is* she alive! Or...was she *killed!* That's the question!" He was frustrated. "That's the question. If Iona lived beyond the age of five...had not died...as I have suspected, she could be alive today...*perhaps*. She could be a leader of this new group. She would be a prime candidate, wouldn't she? It's important that we find this out. *We don't know what we're dealing with!"*

"It is not the environment that does you in," Tom said, "it's your failure to rise to the challenges the environment poses that does you in. The environment outside was terrible fifty years ago, forty years ago, thirty years ago, twenty years ago, perhaps even five years ago. But is it so bad now? How do you know? You trust the Gaia State to tell you the truth? How bad will the environment be twenty years from now? Thirty years from now?"

Then Tom changed his tack.

Mustering his energy, he looked at Lloyd with an expression of determination and defiance. "I have nothing more to say to you. I won't answer *that* riddle for you—the one about Iona."

He kept his promise. He refused to speak. *Silence...*

No matter what Lloyd tried to do, he could not induce Tom to talk. He quoted lines from Tom's book, and then presented documentation from captured rebels; documentation that repeated the

lines over and over again, using the exact same text, saying precisely
the same things, as if the captured rebels were quoting from a prayer
book, or, more likely, an `oral' prayer book they had memorized.

(Already, Lloyd realized, that for the rebels, historical facts had
been overlaid with mythical elements which expressed hidden, arcane, and hopelessly non-transmutable meanings. To this brand-new
generation of rebels, Regis Snow and September Snow were in the
process of already no longer becoming historical figures, but were
becoming part-mythical, part-legendary entities. And by the same
token, the quotes from Tom's book were no longer the literature of
simple `words,' which Tom would have fought to the death to make
sure that they stayed—after all, his literature was about debunking
human illusion, not encouraging it,) had become, of all things,
prayers.

But Tom, day after day, would not confirm or dismiss the sig-
nificance of his words and the coincidence of the `prayers' of the
captured rebels. He remained absolutely silent. He gave Lloyd no
satisfaction. He stayed resolutely quiet. He spoke not a word.

Tom finally died. But just before he did, he spoke one last time.
He snarled and said to Lloyd, whispering into his ear, grasping his
shoulder, raising himself up from his litter: "There's a storm coming.
It's coming. I can smell it. I can smell the ions forming. There's a
twinge in my nose. Can you smell it?"

"No, I can't," Lloyd said. "When is this so-called storm coming?" Lloyd asked.

"The storm's going to come in nine and one half days," Tom
said. "I predict! There will be rain, thunder, lightning. Lots. Rain
falling from the sky. Lightning striking. The roaring sound of
thunder. It will catch everyone, including you—and your so-called,
worthless, asinine `weathermen,' unawares. The storm will appear
out of nowhere. There will be no advance warning. You won't know
that it's coming, not even thirty minutes in advance. The sky will
suddenly darken...as if the angel of darkness had descended...as if
there was darkness at noon...as if time had stopped for you. And,

Lloyd, time will stop for you."

Tom laughed victoriously. "He hee! Yes!" he said. "You'll see."

"Lloyd! See!" Tom whispered again, as if he were speaking with his last breath. He let go of Lloyd's shoulder. "There's a powerful storm coming," he said.

He paused. "I'm dying. I have one last request. Give me eight hours on my own—so I can make peace with myself. Will you allow that?"

Lloyd nodded in agreement.

Tom lay on his bed. He was all alone in his room. He thought hard, using all his powers of concentration. In his mind, with his eyes shut, he made a number of calculations. He remembered all the numbers and dates from different calculations because each year, during the previous twenty-seven years, he calibrated these numbers and dates in his mind, updating them each year, as if performing an exacting science, as if performing an exercise in mental dexterity and agility—in order to keep his mind sharp—in order to prevent encroaching dementia from setting in. He had always had a love for numbers and calendars. When Tom was all alone, he made use of this love of numbers to make these calculations. He realized that it was the Year 5858 according to the Hebrew calendar. That was it! He nodded his head with satisfaction. He remembered. He made the right calculation. He realized it was the Year 5286 according to the Mayan People list. Right again. These calculations were easy. The ancient calendars had original touchstone-points for the making of the calculations.

Tom realized it was the YEAR GAIA FORTY-SIX according to the Gaia calendar.

Keeping his mind focused, Tom thought again. He made his calculations. He realized it was the Year 2657 according to the Buddhists, Year 2155 according to the Hindus, Year 2097 to the Christians, and to the Islamic way of marking time, the Year 1520 after Mohammed's hegira.

Where was the reign of time, Tom wondered? Where had it

gone to?

Then Tom switched gears...

During his lifetime, Tom thought about all of the people he had known who had perished, their deaths not witnessed by survivors. They had been erased from memory.

First, the Seneca People. His native tribe. One of the great nations of the Iroquois Confederation. The heritage of Tom's Iroquois mother. For all intents and purposes, they had been lost two centuries before. The Seneca People were practically obliterated by European man around 1830 A.D. All that survived had been a remnant, in the nineteenth and twentieth centuries, and an even smaller remnant, huddled along the banks of the Genesee river, when Tom was born. Also in Oklahoma. Indian territory. A few intermarried with other Indian tribes, or whites, or both. Second. Tom thought of the nuclear-power workers in proltown. That's where Tom's parents lived and worked during a part of Tom's childhood. The plants were all but destroyed when nuclear power generation was uprooted and moved permanently to the Southern Hemisphere, in the year 2035 A.D. Third. The suffering and loss of a billion and one half people who perished in the Eleven-Years-War of 2040 to 2051. Also, the loss of Tom's four brothers in that war. Now that must have been a horrifying and terrifying loss—surely! The loss of his four brothers in the war. Fourth. His gifted colleagues—the writers, who ten years after the end of the Eleven-Years-War, became known as the "ex-writers" of the early 2060's. They were destroyed. Fifth. The huge mass euthanasia of all the elderly in mid-2060's. Sixth. The mopping up and destruction of the Anti-Gaia rebellion. The destruction of the entire old rebellion—root, branch, limb. Done with extreme thoroughness. Seventh. The two blind old Indians in the Sierra Madre mountains above the Sonora desert in Mexico. One had lived to the age of 99. The other had managed to live to the age of 102. And while he was thinking about it, Tom had almost forgotten his old mentor, the Curmudgeon, who presumably, in Taylor Valley in Antarctica, had made it to the ripe old age of 100, just barely, satisfy-

ing his own long last dream. Tom had been able to live longer than
all three of them, he admitted to himself with a chuckle. Given four
more weeks, Tom would have made it to 104!

Tom tried to remember the faces of all of those who had perished.

Why had he managed to keep on keeping on, for so long? What
had given him the will to endure, through all the many trials, contrary to any apparent reasons for continuing to have hope?

At first, Tom thought it had been the memory of September
Snow. The memory of September Snow had been something that
had kept him going.

Although that had been true, Tom realized that there had been
something else.

It had been the hope that Iona had somehow survived. That was
it. Iona's success in continuing—leading a new rebellion. That had
been Tom's secret, *deep, deep secret* wish. Tom had managed to stay
alive after all these years, in such an abysmal state of fear, dejection
and defeat, because if Iona survived—*and by virtue of that, the future
survived too*—and thus he had the will to carry on.

The future had not only survived, it had made a damn good
struggle of it, apparently. After all, the new rebels had defeated an
army of 50,000! They had destroyed two Domes and threatened
four others. Their advanced guards had entered and secured their
presence in the Western Quadrant!

Tom realized that unconsciously he could not simply allow himself to die in a state of despair. He realized that he had willed himself
to live, even up to the age of 103—even on the verge of turning
104—because he could not stand the notion of perishing in a state
of despair.

During all the years, that's what had kept him alive, Tom realized.

Tom had hope. Now that he had hope, he could successfully
and completely shake away the horrible veil of despair, once and
for all. Tom realized he could now allow himself to die. He could

give up the ghost. It was that simple. Why? Because he knew that Iona had lived! The ideals of those who had perished would live on through *"The Unseeing Watchfulness of Gaia"* (the title which the new rebels used to describe themselves and their mission.)

What—in the final analysis—did Tom believe in? He realized the answer. It was this: Tom believed in man.

When the magister returned eight hours later, he found that Tom, in the meantime, had died. On his deathbed, Tom had a blissful and seemingly devotional expression on his face.

Lloyd would not have the body buried. Tom had to be cremated. His ashes were scattered in the air, above the ocean. That was common practice by the authorities in disposing of the remains of `un-Gaia' people. Pauper's grave, unmarked grave, no grave—that was the final resting place for the `un-Gaia' people. In the YEAR GAIA FORTY-SIX, either you were a full-fledged member of the official Gaia religion, or you were nothing at all; you were a nonperson, a total nonentity.

Lloyd wanted to remember and record the life of Tom, but the system of which he was a part would not let him.

But in spite of this he did so secretly. Before Lloyd died, forty-five years later, living to the ripe old age of eighty-eight, he buried a record—*his own secret history*—of his times.

There were so many other things that Lloyd wanted to save for posterity, so just before he died, he placed these records in clay jars and buried them in his back yard. He knew that if he had left the records to the devises of the Gaia State, they would be destroyed. He did not trust the new rebels to leave behind a reliable narrative account of their own. Although the new rebels were free, they were illiterate (and still barbaric). In their struggle to survive, what sort of records would they have been able to leave behind on their own, *if any?*

The special magister was unaware of the 'time travel—nuclear warhead' capsule that had been buried in Taylor Valley in Antarctica—therefore he could not speculate on what would happen if both his own documents, and those documents left by the Curmudgeon at the bottom of the world—were to be found—more or less at the same time—in the distant future. Especially if the primitive rebels lived in a state of illiteracy and darkness for many, many generations, say 1000 years, what a mighty combination that would make! What if both sets of buried documents were to be discovered or at some other fantastical time in the future! Say 2000 years in the future? Or amazingly, 2500 years in the future?

Publicly, Lloyd was a proud and obedient servant of the Gaia State, and he was a benefactor of the Domes system, but privately he held heretical beliefs. He also harbored independent ideas about certain historical events, especially the explosive and revolutionary events that had occurred during the time of Tom and September, *and also the equally strange times of Iona...*

Lloyd's views and version of events were not the same as Tom's views and version of events, not by a long shot; but his views were not the same as those of the official Gaia State either. So, if eventually found, his documents would have amounted to something important.

In the late afternoon, on the day Tom died, four weeks before he was to celebrate his 104th birthday, taking his secrets with him (Lloyd realized in the context of his grandfather's life, Tom being fourteen or fifteen years older than Lloyd's grandfather had he survived; Tom's death was as if all the great and major libraries in the world had been burned down), Lloyd looked out the window of his executive suite in the high cylinder, and wondered: Was Iona one of the important leaders of the new rebellion?

The special magister felt in his bones that Iona Snow had to have been a great leader of the new rebellion. It could have been no one else. He knew it had to be she. Even if he couldn't get Tom Novak to confirm it—and even if, without that confirmation, he couldn't prove it—he knew it was she. *He knew it.*

There were too many lines from Tom's book that the captured rebel members quoted, as if they were reciting the lines from a written document. Too many lines for them to have quoted—for it to have been a coincidence.

Lloyd remembered the lines one of the captured rebels was quoted as saying, *"History philosophy, philosophy religion, religion licrator (literature?), licrator (literature?) art, art song, paintin' and dancin'; and song, paintin' and dancin' are the heart, brain and hand of man and woman, throughout all of time. I know... It's on the skin."*

Lloyd doubted the lines could have been taken from Tom's book. But Lloyd felt the quote was something Tom might have said, then subsequently related—passed on—orally. The quote had the ring of Tom's voice, though spoken by the young rebel, the original text may have been garbled and thereby rendered with some degree of inaccuracy.

After all, the young rebel quoting the lines was a complete illiterate. He could not read nor write. He could not sign his name. So ignorant he was, when attempting to quote the lines, it was as if he was unable to understand a huge part of what he was supposedly quoting!

The young rebel had no grasp of the meaning of the words *history, philosophy, literature* or *art,* only a crude understanding of the word song *(music?)* and *painting,* a bit of recognition of *dancing.* The only part of the quote he properly understood were the words: *heart, hand* and *on the skin.*

By skin he was referring to a dirty piece of animal skin. The skin was venerated by the young rebels. It was disintegrating. There was a plan to carve the words into stone, when the skin was no longer 'readable.'

Lloyd figured that Tom must have taught Iona the lines when she was a child. He was probably one of her few teachers; indeed, maybe he had been her *only* teacher. Regis, when alive, was known to have set up a few safe spots at remote and isolated places in the world, where they could `hide' certain important people. Perhaps he had done that for them. Maybe September had lived with them there, and then, when she left, made Tom a surrogate father for Iona. That, also, would have explained how Tom had escaped the general euthanasia of the elderly that occurred between YEAR GAIA ELEVEN and YEAR GAIA FOURTEEN.

Iona, in turn, decades later, must have passed on her knowledge, along with Tom's famous lines, to her new people, as if they were lines of poetry, as if they were lines of wisdom from the past...*prayers*...

There was no other plausible paradigm, no discernible theory to explain the rumors Lloyd had heard. There was no other credible explanation for the things that the captured members of the rebellion said, about Iona, about the legendary September, about the legendary Regis. Like it or not, the past, like a ghost, was coming back to haunt the Domes, the magisters, and Lloyd, too.

Three days after Tom's death, Lloyd took the contraband tome—*Expressions Without Illusions*—down from his secret, hidden library. He dusted it off. This time, he didn't skim it as he had done when he had first `rediscovered' Tom. He read it through from start to finish. What a devilish pleasure it was for Lloyd to read Tom's old writings. *Expressions Without Illusions* was published in the year 2036 A.D. Tom had been forty-two then. Lloyd realized that in the present, in YEAR GAIA FORTY-SIX, it was totally out of date, antiquated, completely irrelevant to the issues and problems of the contemporary world, but it was still a stimulating read.

Lloyd had never told another living soul that he read the forbidden book for the first time when he was sixteen years old. What an `eye-opener' it was (although, even then, the story was ridiculously out of date). He read it in complete secrecy. And now he was reading it again. Nobody knew that he had a copy of the rare `outlawed' book. Indeed, practically no one knew that the book, in any form, still existed.

Nine and one half days after Tom's death, (exactly as Tom had predicted) it was raining hard.

Off in the distance, Lloyd could see a startling bolt of lightning—a long finger-width—as it scratched a jagged vertical line splitting the night sky. The color of the lightning bolt was a deep yellow hue—bursting with ions. Eighteen seconds later came a long rumbling sound—the muffled sound of a crack of thunder, which arrived later, traveling the three and a half mile width of New York City.

The rain fell hard, harder, then even harder. Except for Tom, no one had anticipated this storm.

"Well! You can't blame it for everything," Lloyd said aloud listlessly, shrugging his shoulders and looking out at the rain as it drummed hard against the window. He couldn't stop himself from thinking about the brand-new wax job his servants had incorrectly put on his brand-new bubble car only twenty minutes earlier—and how the wax job would probably be spoiled by the sudden, unanticipated rain. A bubble car. Only special magisters could own a bubble car. No one knew how to apply a good wax job anymore; they were all too young to know how it was done in the old days.

Lightning struck again.

Lloyd was itching to get out of the Domes and have a look—see something—*see anything*—*with his sensory perception; see something that was real.* Maybe just a slice of nature, even if it were only a `hiccup of nature' (the grandmagisters talked about `hiccups of nature,' `coughs of nature,' nature being healthy, nature being sickly, nature needing a cure—as if nature were, *at last, their* patient).

Now more than ever, Lloyd wanted to view something up close, not just a computer-simulated model on Wallscreen, but something he could touch with his hands, hear with his ears, see with his eyes, smell with his nose, taste with his mouth. Something he knew *existed*.

A glare of blue light struck his face from a further flash of lightning, followed almost immediately by a loud clap of thunder. He turned abruptly to the window.

Lloyd pondered what Tom had said about the possibility of change in the conditions of the environment in the near future: changes not happening everywhere, but in places here and there. Maybe in a place like the Colorado plateau. Maybe in a place like the Western Quadrant.

Lloyd thought ruefully. He would visit the outdoors, some time soon.

Weather permitting, of course.

The End

the story continues...

September Snow is Book One of THE BLESSINGS OF GAIA series
Book Two: *Runes of Iona*
Book Three: *Embers of the Earth*
Book Four: *Auger's Touchstone*

RUNES OF IONA

Flinty scree, alluvial fans of gravel, biscuit pan, undulating ex-
pansions of seemingly endless sand dunes. Thirsty, dry-as-dust creek
beds, where thirty years earlier, water flowed freely, albeit sporadi-
cally, along deeply fissured river gulches: a desert made more desolate by man's attempt to control the weather.

Then steep craggy mountains and precipitous vertical drops,
leading to bottomless ravines of vine-choked (before the rains
stopped, semi-tropical) *barrancas,* surrounded by glistening mountains, capped with snow, affording huge vistas, and a puff of smoke
emitted every once in a while from the highest volcano-mountain of
them all.

But before arriving as far south as that, at Montezuma's door-
step so to speak, there was hell to be paid for first in the form of
passing through the Forbidden Zone. And even before exposure
to that horror, populated by grotesqueries, there were other oddi-
ties—trees, dead, suspended in a freeze-frame, like everything else,
all animal life-form and plant life-form in a Salvador Dali visage of
hell: withered grass, pitted wood, tailings of post-putrefied animal-
matter, all life radiated by extreme solar exposure due to ozone
depletion.

Then, the Forbidden Zone. Fifty miles south of the start of her
journey, Iona would have to enter the Forbidden Zone. And what
was *the Forbidden Zone?* It was an area picked clean, scoured-to-the-
bone, bleached of all life. It was the grimmest place on the surface of
the Earth.

By intervening in the process of nature, the zone was created by
a corps of Gaia-Dome engineers, who by experimentation in weather
alteration, created an impregnable fire-wall, separating climates on a
north-south axis. Upon the completion of this bold experiment, the
intermediate zone was transformed into a "no-go" swath of land.

Intense heat and the absence of water were its most important ingredients. Forming a critical link in what was envisioned to be a world-circling ring of fire, it stood as the principle dividing barrier separating the "sacred and privileged" climates of the north—from the "fend for yourself and good luck" climates of the south.

Iona was going to risk her life because passing through the Forbidden Zone meant that at midday the hills and flatlands would be fiery furnaces with temperatures of 140 degrees Fahrenheit.

One hundred miles beyond that point (perhaps less, perhaps more, nobody knew for sure), Iona would reach the other side of the wasteland of the Forbidden Zone, and perhaps find safety.

But nobody knew for sure what she'd find on the other side. More of the same? A little better climate? A little worse? Survival at a minimal level? Or no survival at all? No one knew for sure. Of course, later, the climate could only ameliorate, improve with time, but for that time— that was the most disturbing question.

In the year 2070, at the age of thirteen and a half, Iona left Tom at home, a home they had shared secretly as a sanctuary, clandestinely created by Iona's deceased father, the eminent world scientist Regis Snow, during the time he had been chief engineer of the global weather control system for the government. Only fifty miles south of their home, located on the edge of the Sonora Desert, and the great Western canyons and inviting caves of the Sierra Madre Occidental mountains of central-northern Mexico, the Forbidden Zone beckoned her. Alone, on foot, she headed south. She was going to have to travel twenty-five miles a day if she was going to have the slightest chance for survival.

Intuitively, she knew what her odds were. Analytically, she knew what she was up against.

Tom, the pessimist, had given her a chance of one in sixteen. Iona, the optimist, had given herself a change of one in four.

But what does one base the odds on, really? There wouldn't be any other performances. The quest would be spontaneous, unpredictable, unrepeatable. There would be only one roll of the dice.

With steps taken with neither daring pride nor bold experimentation, but with stillness, patience and nerves-of-steel composure, in the context of the next forty-five years, large doses of stillness, patience and nerves-of-steel composure were exactly what it was going to take to keep herself alive.

So Iona stepped into her future.